The Pride

Warwick Deeping

Alpha Editions

This edition published in 2024

ISBN 9789362098023

Design and Setting By

Alpha Editions
www.alphaedis.com

Email - info@alphaedis.com

As per information held with us this book is in Public Domain.
This book is a reproduction of an important historical work.
Alpha Editions uses the best technology to reproduce historical work
in the same manner it was first published to preserve its original nature.
Any marks or number seen are left intentionally to preserve.

Contents

PART I .... - 1 -

CHAPTER I .... - 2 -

CHAPTER II .... - 10 -

CHAPTER III .... - 23 -

CHAPTER IV .... - 29 -

CHAPTER V .... - 36 -

CHAPTER VI .... - 43 -

CHAPTER VII .... - 50 -

CHAPTER VIII .... - 59 -

CHAPTER IX .... - 65 -

CHAPTER X .... - 73 -

CHAPTER XI .... - 79 -

CHAPTER XII .... - 87 -

CHAPTER XIII .... - 96 -

CHAPTER XIV .... - 102 -

CHAPTER XV .... - 110 -

CHAPTER XVI .... - 117 -

CHAPTER XVII .... - 124 -

CHAPTER XVIII .... - 128 -

CHAPTER XIX .... - 133 -

CHAPTER XX .... - 136 -

CHAPTER XXI .... - 141 -

PART II .... - 145 -

CHAPTER XXII .... - 146 -

CHAPTER XXIII .... - 151 -

CHAPTER XXIV .... - 158 -

CHAPTER XXV .... - 164 -

CHAPTER XXVI .... - 173 -

CHAPTER XXVII .... - 178 -

CHAPTER XXVIII .... - 185 -

CHAPTER XXIX .... - 192 -

CHAPTER XXX .... - 200 -

CHAPTER XXXI .... - 205 -

CHAPTER XXXII .... - 210 -

CHAPTER XXXIII .... - 216 -

CHAPTER XXXIV .... - 221 -

CHAPTER XXXV .... - 229 -

CHAPTER XXXVI .... - 238 -

CHAPTER XXXVII .... - 248 -

CHAPTER XXXVIII .... - 256 -

CHAPTER XXXIX	- 266 -
CHAPTER XL	- 271 -
CHAPTER XLI	- 279 -
CHAPTER XLII	- 288 -
CHAPTER XLIII	- 294 -
CHAPTER XLIV	- 299 -
CHAPTER XLV	- 304 -
CHAPTER XLVI	- 308 -

PART I

CHAPTER I

THE COMING OF GUINEVERE

James Canterton was camping out in the rosery under the shade of a white tent umbrella.

It was a June day, and beyond the fir woods that broke the bluster of the south-west winds, a few white clouds floated in a deep blue sky. As for the rosery at Fernhill, no Persian poet could have found a more delectable spot in which to dream through the hours of a scented day, with a jar of purple wine beside him. An old yew hedge, clipped square, closed it in like a wall, with an opening cut at each corner where paths paved with rough stones disappeared into the world without. These four broad, grey paths, the crevices between the stones planted with purple aubretia and star-flowered rock plants, met in the centre of the rosery, where a sundial stood on a Gothic pillar. Next the yew hedge were rambling roses trained upon the trunks of dead fir trees. Numberless little grey paths branched off from the main ones, dividing up the great square court into some two score rose beds. And this June day this secret, yew-walled garden flamed with a thousand tongues of fire. Crimson, old rose, coral pink, blush white, damask, saffron, blood red, snow, cerise, salmon, white, orange, copper, gold, all the colours seemed alive with light, the rich green of the young foliage giving a setting of softness to the splendour of the flowers.

James Canterton was the big, placid, meditative creature needed for such a rose garden. He had a table beside him, and on it a litter of things—notebooks, a tobacco tin, an empty wine glass, a book on the flora of China, two briarwood pipes, and a lens set in a silver frame. He was sitting with his feet within a foot of a rose bush planted in a corner of one of the many beds, a mere slip of a tree that was about to unfold its first flower.

This rose, Canterton's latest creation, had four buds on it, three tightly closed, the fourth on the eve of opening. He had christened the new rose "Guinevere," and there was a subtle and virginal thrill about Guinevere's first flowering, the outer petals, shaded from coral to amber, beginning to disclose a faint inwardness of fiery gold. Canterton had sat there since eight in the morning, for he wanted to watch the whole unfolding of the flower, and his vigil might continue through most of the morrow. He would be down in the rosery when the dew glistened on the petals, nor would he leave it till the yellow rays of the horizontal sun poured over the yew hedge, and made every flower glow with a miraculous brilliance.

Canterton's catalogues were to be found in most well-to-do country houses, and his art had disclosed itself in many opulent gardens. A rich amateur in the beginning, he had chosen to assume the broader professional career, perhaps because his big, quiet, and creative brain loved the sending forth of rich merchandise, and the creation of beauty. As a searcher after new plants he had travelled half over the globe—explored China, the Himalayas, California, and South Africa. He was famous for his hybridisation of orchids, an authority on all trees and flowering shrubs, an expert whose opinions were valued at Kew. It was beauty that fired him, colour and perfumes, and at Fernhill, in this Surrey landscape, he had created a great nursery where beautiful things were born. As a trader, trading the gorgeous tints of azaleas and rhododendrons, or the glaucous stateliness of young cedars, he had succeeded as remarkably as he had succeeded as an artist. South, east, and west his work might be studied in many a garden; architects who conceived for the wealthy advised their patrons to persuade Canterton to create a setting.

His success was the more astonishing, seeing that those who set out to persuade their fellow men not only to see beauty, but to buy it, have to deal with a legion of gross fools. Nor would anyone have expected the world to have paid anything to a man who could sit through a whole day watching the opening bud of a new rose. Canterton was one of the family of the big, patient people, the men of the microscope and the laboratory, who discover great things quietly, and remain undiscovered by the apes who sit and gibber at a clown on a stage.

Canterton had picked up one of his pipes, when a maidservant appeared in one of the arches cut in the yew hedge. She sighted the man under the white umbrella and made her way towards him along one of the stone paths.

"The mistress sent me to find you, sir."

"Well, Mary?"

"She wants to speak to you, sir."

"I am busy for the moment."

The maid hid an amused sympathy behind a sedate manner.

"I'll tell Mrs. Canterton you are engaged, sir."

And she showed the practical good sense of her sympathy by leaving him alone.

Canterton stretched out his legs, and stared at Guinevere over the bowl of his empty pipe. His massive head, with its steady, deep-set, meditative eyes, looked the colour of bronze under the shade of the umbrella. It was a "peasant's" head, calm, sun-tanned, kind, with a simple profundity in its expression, and a quiet imaginativeness about the mouth. His brown hair, grizzled at the temples, had a slight curl to it; his teeth were perfect; his hands big, brown, yet finely formed. He was the very antithesis of the city worker, having much of the large purposefulness of Nature in him, never moving jerkily, or chattering, or letting his eyes snap restlessly at motes in the sunlight. A John Ridd of a man, yet much less of a simpleton, he had a dry, kind sparkle of humour in him that delighted children and made loud talkers feel uneasy. Sentimental people said that his eyes were sad, though they would have been nearer the truth if they had said that he was lonely.

Canterton filled his pipe, keeping a humorously expectant eye fixed on one particular opening in the yew hedge. There are people and things whose arrival may be counted on as inevitable, and Canterton was in the act of striking a match when he saw his wife enter the rosery. She came through the yew hedge with that characteristic scurry of hers suggesting the indefatigable woman of affairs in a hurry, her chin poking forward, the curve of her neck exaggerating the intrusive stoop of her shoulders.

Gertrude Canterton was dressed for some big function, and she had chosen primrose, the very colour that she should not have worn. Her large black hat with its sable feather sat just at the wrong angle; wisps of hair straggled at the back of her neck, and one of her gloves was split between the fingers. Her dress hinted at a certain fussy earnestness, an impatience of patience before mirrors, or perhaps an unconscious contempt for such reflectors of trifles. She was tall, narrow across the shoulders, and distinguished by a pallid strenuousness that was absolutely lacking in any spirit of repose. Her face was too big, and colourless, and the nose too broad and inquisitive about the nostrils. It was a face that seemed to grow larger and larger when she had talked anyone into a corner, looming up, white, and earnest and egotistical through a fog of words, the chin poking forward, the pale eyes set in a stare. She had a queer habit of wriggling her shoulders when she entered a room full of people, a trick that seemed strange in a woman of so much self-conceit.

"James! Oh, there you are! You must know how busy I am!"

Canterton lit his pipe.

"You are the busiest woman I know."

"It's a quarter to three, and I have to open the fête at three. And the men are not up at the house. I told Lavender——"

"Yes, no doubt. But we happen to be very busy here."

His wife elevated her eyebrows.

"James, do you mean to say——"

"The men are not going."

"But I told Lavender——"

He looked at her with an imperturbable good humour that knew perfectly well how to hold its own.

"Lavender comes to me for instructions. There are some things, Gertrude, that you don't quite understand. It is now just ten minutes to three."

The wife shrugged her shoulders over the hopelessness of this eccentric male. For the moment she was intensely irritated, being a woman with a craze for managing everybody and everything, and for striking the dominant note in the community in which she happened to live.

"Well, I think it is abominable——"

"What?"

"Making me look foolish, and keeping these men at work, when I had arranged for them to go to the fête. The whole neighbourhood will be represented. We have made a particular effort to get all the working people——"

Canterton remained genial and undisturbed.

"I think I told you that more than half the men are Radicals."

"All the more reason for getting into touch with them."

"Voluntarily, perhaps. The men were needed here."

"But I had seen Lavender——"

"I don't want to hurry you, but if you are to be there at three——"

She jerked her head, twitching her black hat farther off her forehead.

"Sometimes you are impossible. You won't interest yourself in life, and you won't let others be interested."

"I'm not quite so bad as that, Gertrude. I am no good at social affairs. You have the genius for all that."

"Exactly. But even in the matter of helping things on. Well, it is no use talking to you. I promised Lady Marchendale that I would be on the platform by three."

"You haven't much time."

"No, I haven't."

She let him see that she despaired of his personality, and walked off towards the house, a long, thin, yellow figure, like a vibrating wire that was always a blur of egotistical energy. She was angry, with the pinched and cold anger of a thin-natured woman. James was impossible, only fit to be left like a great bear among his trees and shrubs. Besides he had made her look a fool. These sixty men were to have followed her carriage, an impressive body of retainers tramping after her into Lady Marchendale's grounds.

Neither Guinevere the rose, nor the purpose of Canterton's day had been so much as noticed. He was always busy watching something, studying the life cycle of some pest, scanning the world of growth in the great nursery, and Gertrude Canterton was not interested in flowers, which meant that she was outside the world of her husband's life. These two people, though living in the same house, were absolute strangers to each other. The book of their companionship had been closed long ago, and had never been reopened. The great offence had arisen when James Canterton had chosen to become the professional artist and trader. His wife had never forgiven him that step. It had seemed so unnecessary, so vulgar, so exasperatingly irrational to a woman who was essentially a snob. From that time Gertrude Canterton had begun to excuse her husband to the world, to shrug her shoulders at him as an eccentric creature, to let her friends understand that Canterton was one of those abnormal people who are best left alone in their own peculiar corner. She never understood him, and never attempted to understand him, being too busy with her multifarious publicities to grasp the bigness and the beauty of this quiet man's mind.

Gertrude Canterton had a restless passion for managing things and people, and for filling her life with a conviction that she was indispensable. Her maternal instinct seemed to have become a perverted passion for administration. She was a Guardian of the Poor, Dame President of the local Primrose League Habitation, Secretary of the Basingford Coal and Clothing Club, Treasurer of the District Nurses Fund, an enthusiastic National Service Leaguer, on the committee of a convalescent home for London children that had been built within three miles of Basingford, a lecturer on Eugenics, a strenuous advocate of the Red Cross campaign, also a violent anti-Suffragist. She had caught a whole collection of the age's catch-cries, and used them perpetually with eager emphasis. "The woman's place is the home." "We must begin with the children." "Help, but not pauperisation." "The Ideal of the Empire." "The segregation of the unfit." She wanted to manage everybody, and was tacitly disliked by everybody, save by a select few, who considered her to be a remarkable and a very useful woman.

At three minutes past three Gertrude Canterton was on the platform in the marquee in Lady Marchendale's grounds, and making the short speech with which she was to open the Primrose League fête. Short speeches did not accord with Gertrude Canterton's methods of persuasion. She always had a very great deal to say, enjoyed saying it, and never paused to wonder whether people wanted to listen to her opinions. She spoke for twenty minutes in her thin and metallic voice, eagerly and earnestly, and keeping up that queer, sinuous wriggling of the trunk and shoulders that had made some wag christen her "The Earnest Eel."

The country crowd was bored after the first five minutes. Lord Parallax was to speak later, and the people had grown too accustomed to listening to Mrs. Canterton. There were a number of children sandwiched in among their elders, children who became either vacantly depressed or assertively restless. The real fun of the day was waiting, the roundabout, the races, the mugs of tea, and the buns.

Two men in flannel suits and Panama hats stood just outside the marquee doorway.

"Where's Parallax?"

"Up at the house, playing croquet with Grace Abercorn. I promised to fetch him, when the star turn was due. They'll think he has just rushed down from town by motor."

"Listen to the indefatigable woman."

"You know, she might be doing some sort of ultra-subtle Maud Allan business, if you put her in beads."

"My dear chap!"

"Fifteen minutes already, and we expected three. It is no use trying to stop her. She's like a soda water bottle with the cork out. You can't do anything till all the gas has escaped."

"I'll just go down and see how the Sports Committee are getting along. Oh, by the way, I've booked you and Ethel for our houseboat at Henley."

"Thanks. I'll remember."

On the lawn below Lady Marchendale's terrace garden Lord Parallax was flirting with a clever and audacious little woman in grey and silver. Ostensibly they were playing croquet, while old Percival Kex, Esq., sat in a

French cane chair under the lime tree, and quizzed Parallax when he came within range.

"Well, will you take my bet, or not?"

"Don't talk at the critical moment, sir. This game turns on the Suffrage question."

"Here, Gracie, do you hear him trying to shirk my challenge?"

Miss Abercorn trailed her mallet towards the lime tree. Percival Kex was a character, with his tin-plate face, bold head, and eyes like blackberries. His tongue fished in many waters, and his genial cynicism was infinitely refreshing.

"I have wagered Parallax six sevenpenny insurance stamps that he won't escape the Wriggling Lady."

"My dear sir, how can I, when——"

"Wait a moment. One handshake, six smiles, and three minutes' conversation will be allowed. After that you have got to keep clear, and I bet you you won't."

"Kex, I always lay myself out to be bored at these functions. That is why I am playing croquet, and attempting to get some compensation."

"Who's to snatch at that feather, Gracie, you or I? I suppose it is yours."

"Hallo, here's Meryon! I'm due on the boards."

"Miss Abercorn, I desire you to come and act as time-keeper, and to hold the stakes."

Percival Kex won his six insurance stamps without much difficulty. Parallax made his oration, and when the audience had dispersed, he became the immediate victim of Mrs. Canterton's enthusiasms. They paraded the grounds together, Parallax polite, stiff, and full of a disastrous disgust; Gertrude Canterton earnestly vivadous, poking her chin at him, and exerting all her public charm. Parallax was considered to be a great personality, and she insisted upon his being interesting and serious, giving him every opportunity to be brilliant upon such subjects as Welsh Disestablishment, the inadequacy of the Navy, and the importation of pork from China. She kept him for more than an hour, introduced him to numberless honest souls who were content with a shake of the hand, insinuated in every way that she knew that he was a very great man, but never suspected that he wanted to play croquet.

Parallax detached himself at last, and found Kex and Miss Abercorn having tea under the lime tree in that secluded corner where none of the Leaguers penetrated.

"By George, Kex, I've never been taken so seriously in my life! Let me see—where am I? I think I got bogged in Tariff Reform."

"We thought we would come and have tea, Parallax. We saw you were too occupied."

"Kex, you are an old scoundrel. Why didn't you rescue me when you had won your bet?"

"Sir, I am not a hero."

"Is there a whisky and soda to be had? Oh, here's a servant. Bring me a whisky and soda, will you?"

He sat down and looked reproachfully at Miss Abercorn.

"I suppose it would never occur to such a woman that a man might want to play croquet?"

"Croquet, Parallax! My dear fellow, think of the Empire, and——"

"Hang the Empire. Here's my whisky."

"Don't you think you had better make sure of it by going and drinking it in the shrubbery? She may follow you up to see what you've got to say on Eugenics."

"Miss Abercorn, will you protect me? Really, I have had too much Minerva."

"That apple! I always had a lot of sympathy with Paris. I think he was a particularly bright young man."

"One word, Kex: has the lady a husband?"

"She has."

"Thank God, and Heaven help him!"

CHAPTER II

LYNETTE FEEDS THE FAIRIES

About six o'clock James Canterton took leave of Guinevere, and passing out through the yew hedge, made his way down the rhododendron walk to the wicket gate that opened on the side of a hill. On this hill-side was the "heath garden" that tumbled when in full bloom like a cataract of purple and white wine till it broke against the shadowy edge of a larch wood. The spires of the larches descended in glimmering confusion towards the stream that ran among poplars and willows in the bottom of the valley.

Canterton followed a path that led into the larch wood where the thousands of grey black poles were packed so close together that the eye could not see for more than thirty yards. There was a faint and mysterious murmuring in the tree tops, a sound as of breathing that was only to be heard when one stood still. The ground was covered with thin, wiry grass of a peculiarly vivid green. The path curled this way and that among the larch trunks, with a ribbon of blue sky mimicking it overhead. The wood was called the wilderness, and even when a gale was blowing, it was calm and sheltered in the deeps among the trees.

Canterton paused now and again to examine some of the larches. He had been working at the spruce gall aphis disease, trying to discover a new method of combating it, or of lighting upon some other creature that by preying upon the pest might be encouraged to extirpate the disease. The winding path led him at last to the lip of a large dell or sunken clearing. It was a pool of yellow sunlight in the midst of the green glooms, palisaded round with larch trunks, its banks a tangle of broom, heather, bracken, whortleberry, and furze. There was a boggy spot in one corner where gorgeous mosses made a carpet of green and gold, and bog asphodel grew, and the sundew fed upon insects. All about the clearing the woods were a blue mist when the wild hyacinth bloomed in May.

Down below him in a grassy hollow a child with brilliant auburn hair was feeding a fire with dry sticks. She knelt intent and busy, serenely alone with herself, tending the fire that she had made. Beside her she had a tin full of water, an old saucepan, two or three potatoes, some tea and sugar twisted up together in the corner of a newspaper, and a medicine bottle half full of milk.

"Hallo—hallo!"

The auburn hair flashed in the sunlight, and the child turned the face of a beautiful and wayward elf.

"Daddy!"

She sprang up and raced towards him.

"Daddy, come along. I've got to cook the supper for the fairies."

Canterton had never evolved a more beautiful flower than this child of his, Lynette. She was his in every way, without a shred of her mother's nature, for even her glowing little head was as different from Gertrude Canterton's as fire from clay.

"Hallo, come along."

He caught her up with his big hands, and set her on his shoulder.

"Now then, what about Princess Puck? You don't mean to say the greedy little beggars have eaten up all that pudding we cooked them last night?"

"Every little bit."

"It must have been good. And it means that we shall have to put on our aprons."

On the short grass at the bottom of the clearing was a fairy ring, and to Lynette the whole wilderness was full of the little people. The dell was her playing ground, and she fled to it on those happy occasions when Miss Vance, her governess, had her hours of freedom. As for Canterton, he was just the child that she was, entering into all her fancies, applauding them, and taking a delight in her gay, elf-like enthusiasm.

"Have you seen Brer Rabbit to-night?"

"No."

"He just said 'How de do' to me as I came through the wood. And I saw old Sergeant Hedgehog taking a nap under a tuft of grass."

"I don't like old Hedgehog. I don't like prickly people, do you, daddy?"

"Not much."

"Like Miss Nickleton. She might be a pin-cushion. She's always taking out pins, and putting you all tidy."

"Now then, we've got to be very serious. What's the supper to be to-night?"

"Baked potatoes and tea."

"By Jove, they'll get fat."

Canterton set her down and threw himself into the business with an immense seriousness that made him the most convincing of playfellows. He took off his coat, rolled up his shirt sleeves, and looked critically at the fire.

"We want some more wood, daddy."

"Just so."

He went among the larches, gathered an armful of dead wood, and returned to the fire. Lynette was kneeling and poking it with a stick, her hair shining in the sunlight, her pale face with its hazel eyes full of a happy seriousness. Canterton knelt down beside her, and they began to feed the fire.

"Rather sulky."

"Blow, daddy."

He bent down and played Æolus, getting red in the face.

"I say, what a lot of work these fairies give us!"

"But won't they be pleased! I like to think of them coming out in the moonlight, and feasting, and then having their dance round the ring."

"And singing, 'Long live Lynette.'"

They heated up the water in the saucepan, and made tea—of a kind—and baked the potatoes in the embers of the fire. Lynette always spread the feast on the bottom of a bank near the fairy ring. Sergeant Hedgehog, black-eyed field mice, and an occasional rat, disposed of the food, but that did not matter so long as Lynette found that it had gone. Canterton himself would come down early, and empty the tea away to keep up the illusion.

"I think I'll be a fairy some night, Lynette."

Her eyes laughed up at him.

"Fancy you being a fairy, daddy! Why, you'd eat up all the food, and there wouldn't be room to dance."

"Come, now, I'm hurt."

She stroked his face.

"You're so much better than a fairy, daddy."

The sun slanted lower, and shadows began to cover the clearing. Canterton smothered the fire, picked up Lynette, and set her on his shoulders, one black leg hanging down on either side of his cerise tie, for Canterton always wore Irish tweeds, and ties that showed some colour.

"Off we go."

They romped through the larch wood, up the hill-side, and into the garden, Lynette's two hands clasped over her father's forehead. Fernhill House showed up against the evening sky, a warm, old, red-brick building with white window frames, roses and creepers covering it, and little dormer windows peeping out of the tiled roof. Stretches of fine turf were unfurled before it, set with beds of violas, and bounded by great herbaceous borders. A cedar of Lebanon grew to the east, a noble sequoia to the west, throwing sharp black shadows on the gold-green grass.

"Gallop, daddy."

Canterton galloped, and her brilliant hair danced, and her red mouth laughed. They came across the grass to the house in fine uproarious style, and were greeted by the sound of voices drifting through the open windows of the drawing-room.

Their irresponsible fun was at end. Canterton set the child down just as the thin primrose-coloured figure came to one of the open French windows.

"James, Mrs. Brocklebank has come back with me. Where is Miss Vance?"

Lynette replied for Miss Vance.

"She had a headache, mother."

"I might have inferred something of the kind. Look at the front of your dress, Lynette."

"Yes, mother."

"What have you been doing? And you have got a great hole in your left stocking, over the knee."

"Yes, mother, so I have."

"Lynette, how often have I told you——"

Mrs. Brocklebank or no Mrs. Brocklebank, Canterton interposed quietly in Lynette's defence.

"If it's anybody's fault it's mine, Gertrude. Let the child be a child sometimes."

She turned on him impatiently, being only too conscious of the fact that Lynette was his child, and not hers.

"How can you expect me to have any authority? And in the end the responsibility always rests with the woman."

"Perhaps—perhaps not. Run along, old lady. I'll come and say good night presently."

Lynette walked off to the south door, having no desire to be kissed by Mrs. Brocklebank in the drawing-room. She turned and looked back once at her father with a demure yet inimitable twinkle of the eyes. Canterton was very much part of Lynette's life. Her mother only dashed into it with spasmodic earnestness, and with eyes that were fussily critical. For though Gertrude Canterton always spoke of woman's place being the home, she was so much busied with reforming other people's homes, and setting all their social machinery in order, that she had very little leisure left for her own. A housekeeper managed the house by letting Mrs. Canterton think that she herself managed it. Miss Vance was almost wholly responsible for Lynette, and Gertrude Canterton's periodic plunges into the domestic routine at Fernhill were like the surprise visits of an inspector of schools.

"Mrs. Brocklebank is staying the night. We have some business to discuss with regard to the Children's Home."

Canterton detested Mrs. Brocklebank, but he went in and shook hands with her. She was a large woman, with the look of a very serious-minded white cow. Her great point was her gravity. It was a massive and imposing edifice which you could walk round and inspect, without being able to get inside it. This building was fitted with a big clock that boomed solemnly at regular intervals, always making the same sound, and making it as though it were uttering some new and striking note.

"I see you are one of those, Mr. Canterton, who like to let children run wild."

"I suppose I am. I'd rather my child had fine legs and a good appetite to begin with."

His wife joined in.

"Lynette could not read when she was six."

"That was a gross crime, Gertrude, to be sure."

"It might be called symptomatic."

"Mrs. Brocklebank, my wife is too conscientious for some of us."

"Can one be too conscientious, Mr. Canterton?"

"Well, I can never imagine Gertrude with holes in her stockings, or playing at honey-pots. I believe you wrote a prize essay when you were eleven, Gertrude, and the subject was, 'How to teach children to play in earnest.' If you'll excuse me, I have to see Lavender about one of the hothouses before I dress for dinner."

He left them together, sitting like two solemn china figures nodding their heads over his irresponsible love of *laissez-faire*. Mrs. Brocklebank had no children, but she was a great authority upon them, in a kind of pathological way.

"I think you ought to make a stand, Gertrude."

"The trouble is, my husband's ideas run the same way as the child's inclinations. I think I must get rid of Miss Vance. She is too easygoing."

"The child ought soon to be old enough to go to school. Let me see, how old is she?"

"Seven."

"Send her away next year. There is that very excellent school at Cheltenham managed by Miss Sandys. She was a wrangler, you know, and is an LL.D. Her ideas are absolutely sound. Psychological discipline is one of her great points."

"I must speak to James about it. He is such a difficult man to deal with. So immovable, and always turning things into a kind of quiet laughter."

"I know. Most difficult—most baffling."

Though three people sat down at the dinner table, it was a *diner à deux* so far as the conversation was concerned. The women discussed the Primrose League Fête, and Lord Parallax, whom Gertrude Canterton had found rather disappointing. From mere local topics they travelled into the wilderness of eugenics, Mrs. Brocklebank treating of Mendelism, and talking as though Canterton had never heard of Mendel. It amused him to listen to her, especially since the work of such master men as Mendel and De Vries formed part of the intimate inspiration of his own study of the strange beauty of growth. Mrs. Brocklebank appeared to have muddled up Mendelism with Galton's theory of averages. She talked sententiously of pure dominants and recessives, got her figures badly mixed, and uttered some really astonishing things that would have thrilled a scientific audience.

Yet it was dreary stuff when devitalised by Mrs. Brocklebank's pompous inexactitudes, especially when accompanied by an interminable cracking of nuts. She always ended lunch and dinner with nuts, munching them slowly and solemnly, exaggerating her own resemblance to a white cow chewing the cud.

Canterton escaped upstairs, passed Miss Vance on the landing, a motherly young woman with rich brown hair, and made his way to the nursery. The room was full of the twilight, and through the open window came the last notes of a thrush. Lynette was lying in a white bed with a green coverlet. Her mother had ordered a pink bedspread, but Miss Vance had thought of Lynette's hair.

Canterton sat on the edge of the bed.

"Well, Princess, are you a pure dominant?"

"I've said my prayers, daddy."

"Oh, that's good—very good! I wonder how the feast is getting on in the Wilderness?"

"They won't come out yet, not till the moon shines."

"Think of their little silver slippers twinkling like dewdrops on the grass."

"I wish I could see them, daddy. Have you ever seen a fairy?"

"I think I've caught a glimpse of one, now and again. But you have to be ever so good to see fairies."

"You ought to have seen lots, then, daddy."

He laughed, the quiet, meditative laugh of the man wise in his own humility.

"There are more wonderful things than fairies, Lynette. I'll tell you about them some day."

"Yes, do."

She sat up in bed, her hair a dark flowing mass about her slim face and throat, and Canterton was reminded of some exquisite white bud that promised to be an exquisite flower.

"Let's have some rhymes, daddy."

"What, more Bed Ballads?"

"Yes."

"What shall we start with?"

"Begin with cat."

"All right, let's see what turns up:

> "Outside the door there lay a cat,
> Aunt Emma thought it was a mat,
> And though poor Puss was rather fat,
> Aunt Emma left her, simply—flat."

"Oh, poor Pussy!"
"Rather too realistic for you, and too hard on the cat!"
"Make up something about Mister Bruin."
"Bruin. That's a stiff thing to rhyme to. Let's see:

> "Now, Mister Bruin
> Went a-wooin',
> The lady said 'What are you doin'!'

"I'm stumped. I can't get any farther."
"Oh, yes you can, daddy!"
"Very well."

> "Let's call him Mr. Bear instead,
> And say his mouth was very red.
> Miss Bruin had a Paris gown on,
> She was a sweet phenomenownon.
> The gloves she wore were just nineteens,
> Of course you know what that size means!
> Mr. Bear wore thirty-ones,
> But then he was so fond of buns.
> He asked Miss B. to be his wife,
> And said, 'I will lay down my life.'
> She answered him, 'Now, how much money
> Can you afford, and how much honey?'
> Poor B. looked rather brown at that,

For he was not a plutocrat.

'My dear,' he said, 'it makes me sore,

That I should be so very poor.

I'll start a bun shop, if you like,

And buy you a new motor-bike.'

She said, 'I know where all the buns would go,

And motor biking's much too low.'

Poor Teddy flew off in disgust,

Saying, 'Marry a Marquis if you must.'"

Lynette clapped her hands.

"What a horrid Miss Bruin! I hope she died an old maid!"

"No, she married Lord Grizzley. And he gave her twopence a week to dress on, and made her give him her fur to stuff his bath-chair cushions with."

"How splendid! That's just what ought to have happened, daddy."

When he had kissed her "good night," and seen her snuggle down with her hair spread out over the pillow, Canterton went down to the library and, in passing the door of the drawing-room, heard Mrs. Brocklebank's voice sending out its slow, complacent notes. This woman always had a curious psychical effect on him. She smeared all the fine outlines of life, and brought an unpleasant odour into the house that penetrated everywhere. What was more, she had the effect of making him look at his wife with that merciless candour that discovers every crudity, and every trifle that is unlovely. Gertrude was a most excellent woman. He saw her high forehead, her hat tilted at the wrong angle, her hair straggling in wisps, her finnicking vivacity, her thin, wriggling shoulders, the way she mouthed her words and poked her chin forward when she talked. The clarity of his vision often shocked him, especially when he tried to remember her as a slim and rather over-enthusiastic girl. Had they both changed so vastly, and why? He knew that his wife had become subtly repulsive to him, not in the mere gross physical sense alone, but in her mental odour. They ate together, but slept apart. He never entered her room. The idea of touching her provoked some fastidious instinct within him, and made him shrink from the imagined contact.

Sometimes he wondered whether Gertrude was aware of this strong and incipient repulsion. He imagined that she felt nothing. He had not lived with her for fifteen years without discovering how thick was the skin of her restless egotism. Canterton had never known anyone who was so completely and actively self-satisfied. He never remembered having seen her in tears. As for their estrangement, it had come about gradually when he had chosen to change the life of the amateur for the life of the trader. Then there was the child, another gulf between them. A tacit yet silent antagonism had grown up round Lynette.

On Canterton's desk in the library lay the manuscript of his "Book of the English Garden." He had been at work on it for two years, trying to get all the mystery and colour and beauty of growth into the words he used.

He sat down at the desk, and turned over the pages written in that strong, regular, and unhurried hand of his. The manuscript smelt of lavender, for he always kept a few sprigs between the leaves. But to-night something seemed lacking in the book. It was too much a thing of black and white. The words did not strike upon his brain and evoke a glow of living colour. Roses were not red enough, and the torch lily had not a sufficient flame.

"Colour, yes, colour!"

He sat back and lit his pipe.

"I must get someone to start the plates. I know just what I want, but I don't quite know the person to do it."

He talked to himself—within himself.

"Rogers? No, too flamboyant, not true. I want truth. There's Peterson. No, I don't like Peterson's style—too niggling. Loses the charm in trying to be too correct."

He was disturbed by the opening of a door, and a sudden swelling of voices towards him. He half turned in his chair with the momentary impatience of a thinker disturbed.

"Let us look it up under 'hygiene.'"

The library door opened, and the invasion displayed itself.

"We want to look at the encyclopædia, James."

"It's there!"

"I always feel so stimulated when I am in a library, Mr. Canterton. I hope you don't mind our——"

"Oh, not in the least!"

"I think we might make our notes here, Gertrude."

Gertrude Canterton was standing by a revolving book-stand looking out the volume they needed.

"Yes. James, you might get us the other light, and put it on the table."

He got up, fetched the portable red-shaded lamp from a book-stand, set it on the oak table in the centre of the room, and turned on the switch.

"Oh, and the ink, and a pen. Not one of your nibs. I can't bear J's."

"Something thinner?"

"Please. Oh, and some paper. Some of that manuscript paper will do."

They established themselves at the table, Mrs. Brocklebank with the volume, Gertrude with the pen and paper. Mrs. Brocklebank brought out her pince-nez, adjusted them half down her nose, and began to turn over the pages. Canterton took a book on moths from a shelf, and sat down in an easy chair.

"Hum—Hygiene. I find it here—public health, sanitary by-laws; hum—hum—sewage systems. I think we shall discover what we want. Ah, here it is!"

"The matron told me——"

"Yes, exactly. They had to burn pastilles. Hum—hum—septic tank. My dear, what is a septic tank?"

"Something not quite as it should be."

"Ah, exactly! I understand. Hum—let me see. Their tank must be very septic. That accounts for—hum—for the odour."

Canterton watched them over the top of his book. He could see his wife's face plainly. She was frowning and biting the end of the pen, and fidgeting with the paper. He noticed the yellow tinge of the skin, and the eager and almost hungry shadow lines that ran from her nose to the corners of her mouth. It was a passionless face, angular and restless, utterly lacking in any inward imaginative glow. Gertrude Canterton rushed at life, fiddled at the notes with her thin fingers, but had no subtle understanding of the meaning of the sounds that were produced.

Mrs. Brocklebank read like a grave cleric at a lectern, head tilted slightly back, her eyes looking down through her pince-nez.

"The bacterial action should produce an effluent that is perfectly clear and odourless. My dear, I think—hum—that there is a misconception somewhere."

Neither of them noticed that Canterton had left them, and had disappeared through the French window into the garden.

A full moon had risen, and in one of the shrubberies a nightingale was singing. The cedar of Lebanon and the great sequoia were black and mysterious and very still, the lawns a soft silver dusted ever so lightly with dew. Not a leaf was stirring, and the pale night stood like a sweet sad ghost looking down on the world with eyes of wisdom and of wonder.

Canterton strolled across the grass, and down through the Japanese garden where lilies floated in the still pools that reflected the moonlight. All the shadows were very sharp and black, the cypresses standing like obelisks, the yew hedge of the rosery a wall of obsidian. Canterton wandered up and down the stone paths of the rosery, and knocked his pipe out in order to smell the faint perfumes that lingered in the still air. He had lived so much among flowers that his sense of smell had become extraordinarily sensitive, and he could distinguish many a rose in the dark by means of its perfume. The full moon stared at him over the yew hedge, huge and yellow in a cloudless sky, and Canterton thought of Lynette's fairies down in the Wilderness tripping round the fairy ring on the dewy grass.

The sense of an increasing loneliness forced itself upon him as he walked up and down the paths of the rosery. For of late he had come to know that he was lonely, in spite of Lynette, in spite of all his fascinating problems, in spite of his love of life and of growth. That was just it. He loved the colours, the scents, and the miraculous complexities of life so strongly that he wanted someone to share this love, someone who understood, someone who possessed both awe and curiosity. Lynette was very dear to him, dearer than anything else on earth, but she was the child, and doubtless he would lose her when she became the woman.

He supposed that some day she would marry, and the thought of it almost shocked him. Good God, what a lottery it was! He might have to hand her over to some raw boy—and if life proved unkind to her! Well, after all, it was Nature. And how did marriages come about? How had his own come about? What on earth had made him marry Gertrude? What on earth made most men marry most women? He had been shy, rather diffident, a big fellow in earnest, and he remembered how Gertrude had made a little hero of him because of his travels. Yes, he supposed it had been suggestion. Every woman, the lure of the feminine thing, a dim notion that they would be fellow enthusiasts, and that the woman was what he had imagined woman to be.

Canterton smiled to himself, but the pathetic humour of life did not make him feel any less lonely. He wanted someone who would walk with him on such a night as this, someone to whom it was not necessary to say trite things, someone to whom a touch of the hand would be eloquent, someone who had his patient, watchful, wonder-obsessed soul. He was not spending half of himself, because he could not pour out one half of all that was in him. It seemed a monstrous thing that a man should have taught himself to see so much, and that he should have no one to see life with him as he saw it.

CHAPTER III

GUINEVERE HAS HER PORTRAIT PAINTED

The second day of Guinevere's dawning found Canterton in the rosery, under the white tent umbrella. It was just such a day as yesterday, with perhaps a few more white galleons sailing the sky and making the blue seem even bluer.

Guinevere's first bud was opening to the sun, the coral pink outer petals with their edging of saffron unfolding to show a heart of fire.

About eleven o'clock Lavender, the foreman, appeared in the rosery, an alert, wiry figure in sun hat, rich brown trousers, and a blue check shirt. Lavender was swarthy and reticent, with a pronounced chin, and a hooked nose that was like the inquiring beak of a bird. He had extraordinarily deep-set eyes, and these eyes of his were the man. He rarely missed seeing anything, from the first tinge of rust on a rose, to the beginnings of American blight on a fruit tree. As for his work, Lavender was something of a fanatic and a Frenchman. Go-as-you-please dullards did not like him. He was too ubiquitous, too shrewd, too enthusiastic, too quick in picking out a piece of scamped work, too sarcastic when he found a thing done badly. Lavender could label everything, and his technical knowledge was superb. Canterton paid him five hundred a year, knowing that the man was worth it.

Lavender came with a message, but he forgot it the moment he looked at the rose. His swarthy face lost all its reticence, and his eyes seemed to take fire under their overhanging eyebrows. He had a way of standing with his body bent slightly forward, his hands spread on the seat of his trousers, and when he was particularly interested or puzzled he rubbed his hands up and down with varying degrees of energy.

"She's out, sir!"

"What do you think of her, Lavender?"

The foreman bent over the rose, and seemed to inhale something that he found intoxicatingly pleasant.

"You've got it, sir. She's up above anything that has been brought out yet. Look at the way she's opening! You can almost see the fire pouring out. It's alive—the colour's alive."

Canterton smiled.

"Just like a little furnace all aglow."

"That flower ought to make the real people rave! It's almost too good for the blessed public. Any pinky thing does for the public."

"I am going to send the second flower to Mr. Woolridge."

"He'll go down on his knees and pray to it."

"So much the better for us. If anyone's praise is worth hearing his is."

"He's a wonder, sir, for a clergyman!"

Lavender rubbed his trousers, and then suddenly remembered what he had come for.

"There's a lady, sir, in the office. Wants to know whether she may come into the nursery and do some painting."

"Who is she?"

"Miss Carfax from Orchards Corner. I said I'd come and see you about it."

"Miss Carfax? I don't remember."

"They've been there about a year. The mother's an invalid. Quiet sort of woman."

"Oh, well, I'll see her, Lavender."

"Shall I bring her here?"

"Yes. I don't want to leave the rose till I have seen the whole cycle. And Mrs. Canterton said she was sending one of the maids down to cut some roses."

Lavender went off, and returned in about five minutes with a girl in a straw hat and a plain white linen dress. He stood in one of the openings through the yew hedge and pointed out Canterton to her with a practical forefinger.

"That's Mr. Canterton over there."

She thanked him and walked on.

Canterton was bending forward over the rose, and remained unaware of her presence till he heard footsteps close to him on the paved path.

"Mr. Canterton?"

"Yes."

He stood up, and lifted his hat. She was shy of him, and shy of asking for what she had come to ask. Her blue eyes, with their large pupils looked almost black—sensitive eyes that clouded quickly.

"I am afraid I am disturbing you."

He liked her from the first moment, because of her voice, a voice that spoke softly in a minor key, and did not seem in a hurry.

"No, not a bit."

"I'm Miss Carfax, and I paint a little. I wondered whether you would let me come and make some studies in your gardens."

"Won't you sit down?"

He turned the chair towards her, but she remained standing, her shyness lifting a little under the spell of his tranquil bigness. She became aware suddenly of the rosery. Her eyes swept it, glimmered, and something seemed to rise in her throat.

"Nothing but roses!"

Canterton found himself studying her profile, with its straight, low forehead, short nose, and sensitive mouth and chin. Her hair was a dense, lustrous black, waved back from the forehead, without hiding the shapeliness of her head. She wore a blouse that was cut low at the throat, so that the whole neck showed, slim but perfect, curving forward very slightly, so that her head was poised like the head of one who was listening. There was something flower-like in her figure, with its lithe fragility clothed in the simple white spathe of her dress.

Canterton saw her nostrils quivering. Her throat and bosom seemed to dilate.

"How perfect it is!"

"Almost at its best just now."

"They make one feel very humble, these flowers. A paint brush seems so superfluous."

For the moment her consciousness had become merged and lost in the colours around her. She spoke to Canterton as though he were some impersonal spirit, the genius of the place, a mind and not a man.

"There must be hundreds of roses here."

"Yes, some hundreds."

"And the dark wall of that yew hedge shows up the colours."

Canterton felt a curious piquing of his curiosity. The girl was a new creation to him, and she was strangely familiar, a plant brought from a new country—like and yet unlike something that he already knew.

He showed her Guinevere.

"How do you like this rose—here?"

Her consciousness returned from its voyage of wonder, and became aware of him as a man.

"Which one?"

"Here. It is the latest thing I have raised."

It was an imaginative whim on his part, but as she bent over the rose he fancied that the flower glowed with a more miraculous fire, and that its radiance spread to the girl's face.

"This is wonderful. The shading is so perfect. You know, it is a most extraordinary mixing and blending of colours."

"That was just the problem. Whether the flower would turn out a mere garish, gaudy thing."

"But it is exquisite."

"I have been sitting here for two whole days watching the bud open."

She turned to him with an impulsive flash of the eye.

"Have you? I like the idea of that. Just watching the dawn."

Her shyness had gone, and Canterton felt that an extraordinary thing had happened. She no longer seemed a stranger among his roses, although she had not been more than ten minutes in the rosery.

"Nature opens her secret doors only to those who are patient."

"And what a fascinating life! Like becoming very tiny, just a fairy, and letting oneself down into the heart of a rose."

He had it, the thing that had puzzled him. She was just such a child as Lynette, save that she was the woman. There was the same wonder, the same delightful half-earnest playfulness, the same seeing look in the eyes, the same sensitive quiver about the mouth.

She was gazing at Guinevere.

"Oh, that piques me, challenges me!"

"What, the flower?"

"It makes me think of the conquest of colours that I want to try."

He understood.

"Come and paint it."

"May I?"

"Certainly."

"If I might come and try."

"You had better come soon."

"This afternoon?"

"Why not?"

"It is very good of you, Mr. Canterton."

"Not a bit."

"Then I'll come."

She kept to her word, and reappeared about two o'clock with her paint box, a camp stool, and a drawing-block. Canterton had lunched in the rosery. He surrendered his place under the white umbrella, made her sit in the shade, and went to fetch a jug of water for her brushes. He rejoined her, bringing another garden chair with him, and so it happened that they spent the afternoon together.

Canterton smoked and read, while Eve Carfax was busy with her brushes. She seemed absorbed in her work, and Canterton, looking up from his book from time to time, watched her without being noticed. The intent poise of her head reminded him vaguely of some picture he had seen. Her mouth had a meditative tenderness, and her eyes were full of a quiet delight.

Presently she sat back in her chair, and held the sketch at arm's length. Her eyes became more critical, questioning, and there was a quiver of indecision about her mouth.

"Have you finished it?"

She glanced at him as though startled.

"In a way. But I can't quite make up my mind."

"May I see?"

She passed him the block and watched his face as he examined the work. Once or twice he glanced at Guinevere. Then he stood up, and putting the painting on the chair, looked at it from a little distance.

"Excellent."

She flushed.

"Do you think so?"

"I have never seen a better flower picture."

"It is such a subtle study in colours that I could not be sure."

"You must be very self-critical."

"Oh, I am!"

He turned and looked at her with a new expression, the respect of the expert for an expert's abilities.

"You have made a study of flowers?"

"Yes."

"Of course you must have done. I ought to know that."

Her colour grew richer.

"Mr. Canterton, I don't think I have ever had such praise. I mean, praise that I valued. I love flowers so much, and you know them so intimately."

"That we understand them together."

He almost added, "and each other."

CHAPTER IV

THE IMPORTUNATE BEGGAR

As Lavender had said, the Carfaxes lived at Orchards Corner.

Approaching the place you saw a line of scattered oaks and Scots firs, with straggling thorns and hollies between them along the line of a chestnut fence that had turned green with mould. Beyond the hollies and thorns rose the branches of an orchard, and beyond the orchard a plantation of yews, hollies, and black spruces. The house or cottage was hardly distinguishable till you turned down into the lane from the high road. It betrayed itself merely by the corner of a white window frame, the top of a red-brick chimney, and a patch of lichened tiling visible through the tangle of foliage.

The Carfaxes had been here a year, the mother having been ordered country air and a dry soil. They had sublet the orchard to a farmer who grazed sheep there, but had kept the vegetable garden with its old black loam, and the plot in front with its two squares of grass, filling nearly all the space between the house and the white palings. The grass was rather coarse and long, the Carfaxes paying a man to scythe it two or three times during the summer. There were flower-beds under the fence, and on every side of the two pieces of grass, and standard roses flanking the gravel path.

Eve met the man with the scythe in the lane as she walked home after her second day at Fernhill. She found her mother dozing in her basket-chair in the front garden where a holly tree threw a patch of shadow on the grass. Mrs. Carfax had her knitting-needles and a ball of white wool in her lap. She was wearing a lilac sun-bonnet, and a grey-coloured shawl.

The click of the gate-latch woke her.

"Have you had tea, mother?"

"No, dear; I thought I would wait for you."

Mrs. Carfax was a pretty old lady with blue eyes and a rather foolish face. She was remarkable for her sweetness, an obstinate sweetness that had the consistency of molasses, and refused to be troubled, let Fate stir ever so viciously. Her passivity could be utterly exasperating. She had accepted the whole order of the Victorian Age, as she had known it, declining to see any flaws in the structure, and ascribing any trifling vexations to the minute and multifarious fussiness of the Deity.

"You ought to have had tea, mother."

"My dear, I never mind waiting."

"Would you like it brought out here?"

"Just as you please, dear."

It was not daughterly, but Eve sometimes wished that her mother had a temper, and could use words that elderly gentlewomen are not expected to be acquainted with. There was something so explosively refreshing about the male creature's hearty "Oh, damn!"

That cooing, placid voice never lost its sweetness. It was the same when it rained, when the wind howled for days, when the money was shorter than usual, when Eve's drawings were returned by unsympathetic magazines. Mrs. Carfax underlined the adjectives in her letters, and had a little proverbial platitude for every catastrophe, were it a broken soap dish or a railway smash. "Patience is a virtue, my dear." "Rome was not built in a day." "The world is not helped by worry." Mrs. Carfax had an annuity of £100 a year, and Eve made occasional small sums by her paintings. They were poor, poor with that respectable poverty that admits of no margins and no adventures.

Mrs. Carfax was supremely contented. She prayed nightly that she might be spared to keep a home for Eve, never dreaming that the daughter suffered from fits of bitter restlessness when anything seemed better than this narrow and prospectless tranquillity. Mrs. Carfax had never been young. She had accepted everything, from her bottle onwards, with absolute passivity. She had been a passive child, a passive wife, a passive widow. Life had had no gradients, no gulfs and pinnacles. There were no injustices and no sorrows, save, of course, those arranged by an all-wise Providence. No ideals, save those in the Book of Common Prayer; no passionate strivings; no divine discontents. She just cooed, brought out a soft platitude, and went on with her knitting.

Eve entered the house to put her things away, and to tell Nellie, the infant maid, to take tea out into the garden.

"Take tea out, Nellie."

"Yes, miss. There ain't no cake."

"I thought I told you to bake one."

"Yes, miss. There ain't no baking powder."

"Oh, very well. I'll order some. Put a little jam out."

"There only be gooseberry, miss."

"Then we'll say gooseberry."

Eve returned to the garden in time to hear the purr of a motor-car in the main road. The car stopped at the end of the lane. A door banged, and a figure in black appeared beyond the gate.

It was the Cantertons' car that had stopped at the end of the lane, and it was Mrs. Canterton who opened the gate, smiling and nodding at Mrs. Carfax. Gertrude Canterton had paid a first formal call some months ago, leaving in Eve's mind the picture of a very expeditious woman who might whirl down on you in an aeroplane, make a few remarks on the weather, and then whirl off again.

"Please don't get up! Please don't get up! I mustn't stay three minutes. Isn't the weather exquisite. Ah, how do you do, Miss Carfax?"

She extended a hand with an affected flick of the wrist, smiling all the while, and wriggling her shoulders.

"Eve, fetch another chair, dear."

"Oh, please don't bother!"

"We are just going to have tea, Mrs. Canterton."

Eve gave her mother a warning look, but Mrs. Carfax never noticed other people's faces.

"Tell Nellie, dear."

Eve walked off to the house, chiefly conscious of the fact that there was no cake for tea. How utterly absurd it was that one should chafe over such trifles. But then, with women like Mrs. Canterton, it was necessary to have one's pride dressed to the very last button.

Two extra chairs and tea arrived. The conversation was never in danger of death when Gertrude Canterton was responsible for keeping up a babble of sound. If the other people were mute and reticent, she talked about herself and her multifarious activities. These filled all gaps.

"I must say I like having tea in the garden. You are, really, most sheltered here. Sugar? No, I don't take sugar in tea—only in coffee, thank you."

"It does rather spoil the flavour."

"We have a very exquisite tea sent straight to us from a friend of my husband's in Ceylon. It rather spoils me, and I have got out of the way of taking sugar. How particular we become, don't we? It is so easy to become selfish. That reminds me. I want to interest our neighbourhood in a society that has been started in London. What a problem London is."

Mrs. Carfax cooed sympathetically.

"And the terrible lives the people lead. We are very interested in the poor shop girls, and we have started an organisation which we call 'The Shop Girls' Rest Society.'"

"Eve, perhaps Mrs. Canterton will have some cake."

Eve was on edge, and full of vague feelings of defiance.

"I'm sorry, there isn't any cake."

"Eve, dear!"

"Oh, please, I so rarely take cake. Bread and butter is so much more hygienic and natural. I was going to tell you that this society we have started is going to provide shop girls with country holidays."

"How very nice!"

Mrs. Carfax felt that she had to coo more sweetly because of the absence of cake.

"I think it is quite an inspiration. We want to get people to take a girl for a week or a fortnight and give her good food, fresh air, and a sense of homeliness. How much the home means to women."

"Everything, Mrs. Canterton. Woman's place is the home."

"Exactly. And I was wondering, Mrs. Carfax, whether you would be prepared to help us. Of course, we shall see to it that the girls are really nice and proper persons."

The thought of the absence of cake still lingered, and Mrs. Carfax felt apologetic.

"I am sure, Mrs. Canterton, I shall be glad——"

Eve had grown stiffer and stiffer, watching the inevitable approach of the inevitable beggar. Gertrude Canterton had a genius for wriggling her way everywhere, even into other people's bedrooms, and would be putting them down for ten guineas before they were half awake.

"I am sorry, but I'm afraid it is out of the question."

She spoke rather brusquely, and Gertrude Canterton turned with an insinuating scoop of the chin.

"Miss Carfax, do let me——"

"Eve, dear, I'm sure——"

Eve was stonily practical.

"It is quite impossible."

"But, Eve——"

"You know, mother, we haven't a bed."

"My dear!"

"And no spare bedclothes. Mrs. Canterton may as well be told the truth."

There was a short silence. Mrs. Carfax looked as ruffled as it was possible for her to look, settled her shawl, and glanced inquiringly at Mrs. Canterton. But even to Gertrude Canterton the absence of bedclothes seemed final.

"I am sure, Mrs. Carfax, you would have helped us, if you had been able."

Eve persisted in being regarded as the responsible authority. She was quite shameless now that she had shown Mrs. Canterton the empty cupboard.

"You see, we have only one small maid, and everything is so adjusted, that we just manage to get along."

"Exactly so, Miss Carfax. I quite understand. But there is a little thing you could do for us. I always think that living in a neighbourhood makes one responsible for one's poorer neighbours. I am sure, Mrs. Carfax, that you will give a small subscription to the Coal and Clothing Club."

"With pleasure."

"It doesn't matter how small it is."

"Eve, dear, please go and fetch me some silver. I should like to subscribe five shillings. May I give it to you, Mrs. Canterton?"

"Thank you so very much. I will send you a receipt."

Eve had risen and walked off resignedly towards the cottage. It was she who was responsible for all the petty finance of the household, and five shillings were five shillings when one's income was one hundred pounds a year. It could not be spared from the housekeeping purse, for the money in it was partitioned out to the last penny. Eve went to her own room, and took a green leather purse from the rosewood box on her dressing-table. This purse held such sums as she could save from the sale of occasional small pictures and fashion plates. It contained seventeen shillings at this particular moment. Five shillings were to have gone on paints, ten on a new pair of shoes, and two on some cheap material for a blouse.

She was conscious of making instinctive calculations as she took out two half-crowns. What a number of necessities these two pieces of silver would buy, and the ironical part of it was that she could not paint without paints, or walk without shoes. It struck her as absurd that a fussy fool like this Canterton woman should be able to cause so much charitable inconvenience. Why had she not refused point blank, in spite of her mother's pleading eyes?

Eve returned to the garden and handed Mrs. Canterton the two half-crowns without a word. It was blackmail levied by a restless craze for incessant charitable activities. Eve would not have grudged it had it gone straight to a fellow-worker in distress, but to give it to this rich woman who went round wringing shillings out of cottagers!

"Thank you so much. Money is always so badly needed."

Eve agreed with laconic irony.

"It is, isn't it? Especially when you have to earn it!"

Gertrude Canterton chatted for another five minutes and then rose to go. She shook hands cordially with Mrs. Carfax, and was almost as cordial with Eve. And it was this blind, self-contentment of hers that made her so universally detested. She never knew when people's bristles were up, and having a hide like leather, she wriggled up and rubbed close, never suspecting that most people were possessed by a savage desire to say some particularly stinging thing that should bite through all the thickness of her egotism.

"Thank goodness!"

"Eve, you were quite rude! And you need not have said, dear———"

"Mother, I told the truth only in self-defence. I was expecting some other deserving charity to arrive at any moment."

"It is better to give, dear, than to receive."

"Is it? Of course, we needn't pay the tradesmen, and we can send the money to some missionary agency."

"Eve, dear, please don't be flippant. A word spoken in jest———"

"I'm not, mother. I'm most desperately serious."

Gertrude Canterton had a very successful afternoon. She motored about forty miles, trifled with three successive teas, and bored some seven householders into promising to consider the claims of the Shop Girls' Rest Society. She was very talkative at dinner, describing and criticising the various people from whom she had begged.

Canterton showed sudden annoyance.

"You went to the Carfaxes?"

"Yes."

"And got something from them?"

"Of course, James."

"You shouldn't go to such people."

Her face was all sallow surprise.

"Why, they are quite respectable, and——"

"Respectable! Do you think I meant that! You know, Gertrude, you charitable people are desperately hard sometimes on the real poor."

"What *do* you mean, James?"

"People like the Carfaxes ought not to be worried. You are so infernally energetic!"

"James, I protest!"

"Oh, well, let it pass."

"If you mean——Of course, I can send the money back."

He looked at her with a curious and wondering severity.

"I shouldn't do that, Gertrude. Some people are rather sensitive."

Canterton went into the library after dinner, before going up to say "good night" to Lynette. Within the last two days some knowledge of the Carfaxes and their life had come to him, fortuitously, and yet with a vividness that had roused his sympathy. For though James Canterton had never lacked for money, he had that intuitive vision that gives a man understanding and compassion.

His glance fell upon the manuscript of "The Book of the English Garden" lying open on his desk. An idea struck him. Why should not Eve Carfax give the colour to this book? To judge by her portrait of Guinevere, hers was the very art that he needed.

CHAPTER V

EVE ENTERS THE WILDERNESS

Eve Carfax read James Canterton's letter at breakfast, and her mother, who like many passive people, was vapidly inquisitive, wanted to know when the letter had come, why it had been written, what it said, and what it did not say.

Eve was a little flushed, and ready to fall into a reverie while looking along a vista of sudden possibilities. This frank and straightforward letter had brought a flutter of exultation into her life.

"Mr. Canterton wants me to do some flower pictures for him."

"How nice, dear! And shall you?"

"Of course—if I can."

"It must have been our subscription to——"

"Mother, is it likely?"

"I am sure Mrs. Canterton was most charming. Is he going to pay you for——"

"He doesn't say anything about it."

"He might not think it quite nice to say anything—just at first."

"I really don't know why it shouldn't be nice to mention a thing that we all must have. He wants me to go and see him."

Eve set off for Fernhill with a delightful sense of exhilaration. She was in a mood to laugh, especially at the incident of yesterday, and at the loss of those two half-crowns that had seemed so tragic and depressing. This might be her first big bit of luck, the beginning of a wider, finer life for which she yearned. She was amused at her mother's idea about Mrs. Canterton. Mrs. Canterton indeed! Why—the flow of her thoughts was sharply arrested, and held back by the uprising of a situation that suddenly appeared before her as something extraordinarily incongruous. These two people were married. This fussy, sallow-faced, fidgeting egotist, and this big, meditative, colour-loving man. What on earth were they doing living together in the same house. And what on earth was she herself doing letting her thoughts wander into affairs that did not concern her.

She suppressed the curious feeling of distaste the subject inspired in her, took a plunge into a cold bath of self-restraint, and came out close knit and vigorous. Eve Carfax had a very fastidious pride that detested anything that could be described as vulgarly curious. She wanted no one to finger her own intimate self, and she recoiled instinctively from any tendency on her own part towards taking back-door views of life. She was essentially clean, with an ideal whiteness that yet could flush humanly. But the idea of contemplating the soiled petals of other people's ideals repelled her.

Eve entered the Fernhill Nurseries by the great oak gates that opened through a high hedge of arbor vitæ. She found herself in a large gravelled space, a kind of quadrangle surrounded by offices, storerooms, stables, and packing sheds, all built in the old English style of oak, white plaster, and red tiles. The extraordinary neatness of the place struck her. It was like a big forecourt to the mysteries beyond.

She had her hand on the office bell when Canterton came out, having seen her through the window. He was in white flannels, and wearing a straw hat that deepened the colour of his eyes and skin.

"Good morning! We both appear to be punctual people."

He was smiling, and looking at her attentively.

"It was good of you to come up at once. I left it open. I think it would be a good idea if I took you over the whole place."

She answered his smile, losing a momentary shyness.

"I should like to see everything. Do you know, Mr. Canterton, you have set me up on the high horse, and——"

"Well?"

"I don't want to fall off. I have been having thrills of delightful dread."

"I know; just what a man feels before an exam., when he is pretty sure of himself."

"I don't know that I am sure of myself."

"If you can paint other things as you painted that rose, I don't think there is any need for you to worry."

The quiet assurance of his praise sent a shiver of exultation through her. What an encouraging and comforting person he was. He just intimated that he believed you could do a thing very well, and the thing itself seemed half done.

"Then I'll show you the whole place. I'm a bit of an egotist in my way."

"It's only showing someone what you have created."

He took her everywhere, beginning with what he called "the administrative department." She saw the great glass-houses, the stacks of bracken for packing, the piles of ash and chestnut stakes, the shed where three old men spent their time making big baskets and hampers, the rows and rows of frames, the packing and dispatch sheds, the seed room, the little laboratory, with its microscopes and microtome and shelves of bottles, the office where several clerks were constantly at work.

Canterton was apologetic.

"I have a craze for showing everything."

"It gives one insight. I like it."

"It won't tire you?"

"I think I am a very healthy young woman."

He looked at the fresh face, and at the lithe though fragile figure, and felt somehow that the June day had an indefinable perfume.

"I should like to show you some of the young conifers."

They were wonderful trees with wonderful names, quaint, solemn, and diminutive, yet with all the dignity of forests patriarchs. They grew in groves and companies, showing all manner of colours, dense metallic greens, soft blues, golds, silvers, greys, green blacks, ambers. Each tree had beauties and characteristics of its own. They were diminutive models of a future maturity, solemn children that would be cedars, cypresses, junipers, pines and yews.

They delighted Eve.

"Oh, the little people, ready to grow up! I never knew there were such trees—and such colours."

He saw the same look in her eyes as he had seen in the rosery, the same tenderness about the mouth.

"I walk about here sometimes and wonder where they will all go to."

"Yes, isn't it strange."

"Some day I want to do a book on trees."

"Do you? What's the name of that dear Japanese-looking infant there?"

"Retinospora Densa. You know, we nurserymen and some of the botanists quarrel about names."

"What does it matter? I tried to study botany, but the jargon———"

"Yes, it is pretty hopeless. I played a joke once on some of our botanical friends; sent them a queer thing I had had sent from China, and labelled it Cantertoniana Gloria in Excelsis. They took it quite seriously."

"The dears!"

Laughter passed between them, and an intimate flashing of the eyes that told how the joy of life welled up and met. They wandered on through acres of glowing maples, golden privets and elders, purple leaved plums, arbutus, rhododendrons, azaleas, and all manner of flowering shrubs. In one quiet corner an old gardener with a white beard was budding roses. Elsewhere men were hoeing the alleys between the straight rows of young forest trees, poplars, birches, elms, beeches, ilexes, mountain ashes, chestnuts, and limes. There were acres of fruit trees, acres of roses, acres of the commoner kind of evergreens, great waves of glooming green rolling with a glisten of sunlight over the long slopes of the earth. Eve grew more silent. She was all eyes—all wonder. It seemed futile to exclaim when there was so much beauty everywhere.

They came at last to a pleasaunce that was the glory of the hour, an herbaceous garden in full bloom, with brick-paved paths, box edging, and here and there an old tree stump or a rough arch smothered with clematis, or honeysuckle. Delphiniums in every shade of blue rose like the crowded and tapering *flèches* of a mediæval city. There were white lilies, gaudy gaillardias blazing like suns, campanulas, violas, foxgloves, snapdragons, mauve erigeron, monkshood, English iris, and scores of other plants. It was gorgeous, and yet full of subtle gradations of colour, like some splendid Persian carpet in which strange dyes merged and mingled. Bees hummed everywhere. Old red brick walls, half covered with various kinds of ivy, formed a mellow background. And away on the horizon floated the blue of the Surrey hills.

Eve stood motionless, lips slightly apart.

"Mr. Canterton!"

"You like it?"

"Am I to paint this?"

"I hope so."

"Let me pour out my humility."

He laughed gently.

"Oh, you can do it!"

"Can I? And the old walls! I should not have thought the place was so old."

"It isn't. I bought my bricks. Some old cottages were being pulled down."

"Thank God, sometimes, for money!"

She stood a moment, her chin raised, her eyes throwing long, level glances down the walks.

"Mr. Canterton, let me do two or three trial sketches before you decide anything."

"Just as you like."

"Please tell me exactly what you want."

"I want you to begin here, and in the rosery. You see this book of mine is going to be a big thing, a treasure house for the real people who want to know. I shall need portraits of individual flowers, and studies of colour effects during the different months. I shall also want illustrations of many fine gardens that have been put at my service. That is to say, I may have to ask you to travel about a little, to paint some of the special things, such as the Ryecroft Dutch garden, and the Italian gardens at Latimer."

As he spoke the horizon of her life seemed to broaden before her. It was like the breaking through of a winter dawn when the grey crevices of the east fill with sudden fire. Everything looked bigger, more wonderful, more alluring.

"I had no idea——"

He was watching her face.

"Well?"

"That it was to be such a big thing."

"It may take me two or three more years. I have allowed myself five years for the book."

She drew in her breath.

"Mr. Canterton, I don't know what to say. And I don't think you realise what you are offering me. Just—life, more life. But it almost frightens me that you should think——"

His eyes smiled at her understandingly.

"Paint me a few trial pieces. Begin with one of the borders here, and a rose bed in the rosery that I will show you. Also, give me a study of trees, and another of rocks and plants in the rock garden."

"I will begin at once."

He looked beyond her towards the blue hills.

"As to the terms between us, will you let me write you a letter embodying them?"

"Yes."

"You can have an agreement if you like."

She answered at once.

"No. I think, somehow, I would rather not. And please don't propose anything till you have seen more of what I can do."

Canterton led the way towards the rosery to show her the roses he wanted her to paint, and in passing through one of the tunnels in the yew hedge they were dashed into by a child who came flying like a blown leaf. It was Eve who received the rush of the impetuous figure. Her hands held Lynette to save her from falling.

"Hallo!"

Lynette's face lifted to hers with surprise and laughter, and a questioning shyness. Eve kept her hold for the moment. They looked at each other with an impulse towards friendliness.

"Lynette, old lady!"

"Daddy, Miss Vance has gone off——"

"Pop? Miss Carfax, let me introduce my daughter. Miss Lynette Canterton—Miss Carfax."

Eve slid her hands from Lynette's body, but the child's hands clung and held hers.

"I'm so sorry. I hope it didn't hurt? I don't think I've seen you before."

"Well, we rushed at each other when we did meet."

"Is daddy showing you the garden?"

"Yes."

"My name's Lynette—not like linnet, you know, but Lyn-net."

"And my name's Eve—just Eve."

"Who was made out of Adam's rib. Poor Mr. Adam! I wonder whether he missed it?"

They all laughed. Lynette kept hold of one of Eve's hands, and held out her other one to Canterton.

"Daddy, do come down to the Wilderness. I want to build a wagwim."

"Or wigwam?"

"I like wagwim better. Do come."

"Miss Canterton, I am most seriously occupied."

She tossed her hair, and turned on Eve.

"You'll come too, Miss Eve? Now I've invited you, daddy will have to come. Ask him."

Eve looked at Canterton, and there was something strange in the eyes of both.

"Mr. Canterton, I am requested to ask you———"

"I surrender. I may as well tell you, Miss Carfax, that very few people are invited into the Wilderness. It is fairyland."

"I appreciate it. Lynette, may I come and build a wagwim with you?"

"Yes, do. What a nice voice you've got."

"Have I?"

Eve blushed queerly, and was intimately conscious of Canterton's eyes looking at her with peculiar and half wondering intentness.

"I'm going to have dinner there. Mother is out, and Miss Vance is going to Guildford by train. And Sarah has given me two jam tarts, and some cheese straws, and two bananas———"

Canterton tweaked her hair.

"That's an idea. I'm on good terms with Sarah. We'll have some lunch and a bottle of red wine sent down to the Wilderness and picnic in a wagwim, if the wagwim wams by lunch time."

"Come along—come along, Miss Eve! I'll show you the way! I'm so glad you like wagwims!"

So these three went down to the Wilderness together, into the green light of the larch wood, and into a world of laughter, mystery and joy.

CHAPTER VI

WOMEN OF VIRTUE

The local committee of a society for the propagation of something or other had taken possession of Canterton's library, and Mrs. Brocklebank was the dominant lady. The amount of business done at these meetings was infinitesimal, for Mrs. Brocklebank and Gertrude Canterton were like battleships that kept up a perpetual booming of big guns, hardly troubling to notice the splutter of suggestions fired by the lesser vessels. The only person on the committee who had any idea of business was little Miss Whiffen, the curate's sister. She was one of those women who are all profile, a busy, short-sighted, argumentative creature who did her best to prevent Mrs. Brocklebank and Gertrude Canterton from claiming the high seas as their own. She fussed about like a torpedo boat, launching her torpedoes, and scoring hits that should have blown most battleships out of the water. But Mrs. Brocklebank was unsinkable, and Gertrude Canterton was protected by the net of her infinite self-satisfaction. Whatever Miss Whiffen said, they just kept on booming.

Sometimes they squabbled politely, while old Lady Marchendale, who was deaf, sat and dozed in her chair. They were squabbling this afternoon over a problem that, strange to say, had something to do with the matter in hand. Miss Whiffen had contradicted Mrs. Brocklebank, and so they proceeded to argue.

"Every thinking person ought to realise that there are a million more women than men in the country."

"I wasn't questioning that."

"Therefore the female birth rate must be higher than the male."

Miss Whiffen retorted with figures. She was always attacking Mrs. Brocklebank with statistics.

"If you look up the records you will find that there are about a hundred and five boys born to every hundred girls."

"That does not alter the situation."

"Oh, of course not."

"This scheme of helping marriageable young women to emigrate——"

Mrs. Brocklebank paused, and turned the big gun on Miss Whiffen.

"I said marriageable young women! Have you any objection to the term, Miss Whiffen?"

"Oh, not in the least! But does it follow that, because they marry when they get to the Colonies——"

"What follows?"

"Why, children."

"Marriages are more fruitful in a young country."

"But are they? When my married sister was home from Australia last time, she told me——"

Gertrude Canterton joined in.

"Yes, it's just the prevailing selfishness, the decadence of home life."

"Men are so much more selfish than they used to be."

"I think the women are as bad. And, of course, the question of population——"

Old Lady Marchendale, who had dozed off in her arm-chair by the window, woke up, caught a few fragmental words, and created a digression.

"They ought to be made to have them—by law!"

"But, my dear Lady Marchendale——"

"I see her ladyship's point."

"Every girl ought to have her own room."

"Of course, most certainly! But in the matter of emigration——"

"Emigration? What has emigration to do with the Shop Girls' Self Help Society?"

"My dear Lady Marchendale, we are discussing the scheme for sending young women to the Colonies."

"Bless me, I must have been asleep. I remember. Look at that lad of yours, Mrs. Canterton, out there in the garden. I'm sure he has cut his hand."

Lady Marchendale might be rather deaf, but she had unusually sharp eyes, and Gertrude Canterton, rising in her chair, saw one of the lads employed in the home garden running across the lawn, and wrapping a piece of sacking round his left hand and wrist.

She hurried to the window.

"What is the matter, Pennyweight?"

"Cut m' wrist, mum, swappin' the hedge."

"How careless! I will come and see what wants doing."

There had been First Aid classes in the village. In fact, Gertrude Canterton had started them. Miss Whiffen and several members of the committee followed her into the garden and surrounded the lad Pennyweight, who looked white and scared.

"Take that dirty sacking away, Pennyweight! Don't you know such things are full of microbes?"

"It's bleedin' so bad, mum."

"Let me see."

The lad obeyed her, uncovering his wrist gingerly, his face flinching. The inner swathings of sacking were being soaked with blood from the steady pumping of a half-severed artery.

Miss Whiffen made a little sibilant sound.

"Sssf, sssf—dear, dear!"

"A nasty cut."

Pennyweight hesitated between restive fright and awe of all these gentlewomen.

"Hadn't I better go t' Mr. Lavender, mum? It does bleed."

"Nonsense, Pennyweight! Miss Ronan, would you mind going in and ringing for the housekeeper? Tell her I want some clean linen, and some hot water and boracic acid."

Miss Whiffen was interested but alarmed.

"It's a cut artery. We ought to compress the brachial artery."

"Isn't it the femoral?"

"No, that's in the leg. You squeeze the arm just——"

"Exactly. Along the inside seam of the sleeve."

"But he has no coat on."

This was a poser. Gertrude Canterton looked annoyed.

"Where's your coat, Pennyweight?"

"Down by t' hedge, mum."

"If he had his coat on we should know just where to compress the artery."

No one noticed Canterton and Lynette till the man and the child were within five yards of the group.

"What's the matter?"

The lad faced round sharply, appeared to disentangle himself from the women, and to turn instinctively to Canterton.

"Cut m' wrist, sir, with the swap 'ook."

"We must stop that bleeding."

He pulled out a big bandanna handkerchief, passed it round the lad's arm, knotted it, and took a folding foot-rule from his pocket.

"Hold that just there, Bob."

He made another knot over the rule on the inside of the arm, and then twisted the extemporised tourniquet till the lad winced.

"Hurt?"

"No, sir."

"That's stopped it. Gertrude, send one of the maids down to the office and tell Griggs to ride down on his bicycle for Kearton. Feel funny, Bob?"

"Just a bit, sir."

"Lie down flat in the shade there. I'll get you a glass of grog."

Lynette, solemn and sympathetic, had stood watching her father, disassociating herself from her mother and Miss Whiffen, and the members of the committee.

"Wasn't it a good thing I found daddy, Bob?"

"It was, miss."

"The old ladies might have let you bleed to death, mightn't they?"

Bob looked sheepish, and Gertrude Canterton called Lynette away.

"Go to the nursery, Lynette. It is tea time."

Lynette chose to enter the house by the library window, and, finding old Lady Marchendale sitting there in the arm-chair, put up her face to be kissed. She liked Lady Marchendale because she had pretty white hair, and eyes that twinkled.

"Did you see Bob's bloody hand?"

"What, my dear?"

"Did you see Bob's bloody hand?"

"I can't quite hear, dear."

Lynette put her mouth close to Lady Marchendale's ear, and spoke with emphasis.

"Did—you—see—Bob's—bloody—hand?"

"Lynette, you must not use such words!"

Gertrude Canterton stood at the open window, and Lady Marchendale was laughing.

"What words, mother?"

"Such words as 'bloody.'"

"But it was bloody, mother."

"Bless the child, how fresh! Come and give me another kiss, dear."

Lynette gave it with enthusiasm.

"I do like your white hair."

"It is not so pretty as yours, my dear. Now, run along. We are very busy."

She watched Lynette go, nodding her head at her and smiling.

"I am so sorry, Lady Marchendale. The child is such a little savage."

"I think she's a pet. You don't want to make a little prig of her, do you?"

"She's so undisciplined."

"Oh, fudge! What you call being 'savage,' is being healthy and natural. You don't want to make the child a woman before she's been a child."

The gong rang for tea.

Eve was painting in the rosery when Mrs. Brocklebank persuaded the members of the committee that she—and therefore they—wanted to see Mr. Canterton's roses. It was a purely perfunctory pilgrimage, so far as Gertrude Canterton was concerned, and her voice struck a note of passive disapproval.

"I think there is much too much time and money wasted upon flowers."

"Oh, Mrs. Canterton! But isn't this just sweet!"

"I don't know very much about roses, but I believe my husband's are supposed to be wonderful."

She sighted Eve, stared, and diverged towards her down a side path, smiling with thin graciousness.

"Miss Carfax?"

Eve did not offer to explain her presence. She supposed that Gertrude Canterton knew all about her husband's book, and the illustrations that were needed.

"You are making a study of flowers?"

"Yes."

"That's right. I hope you will find plenty of material here."

"Mr. Canterton was kind enough to let me come in and see what I could do."

"Exactly. May I see?"

She minced round behind Eve, and looked over the girl's shoulder at the sketch she had on her lap.

"That's quite nice—quite nice! But what a lot of colour you have put into it."

"There is rather a lot of colour in the garden itself."

"Yes, but I'm afraid I can't see what you have put on paper——"

Miss Whiffen was clamouring to be told the name of a certain rose.

"Mrs. Canterton—Mrs. Canterton!"

"Yes, dear?"

"Do tell me the name of this rose!"

"I'll come and look. I can't burden my memory with the names of flowers. Perhaps it is labelled. Everything ought to be labelled. It is such a saving of time."

Eve smiled, and turning to glance at the rose bed she was painting, discovered a big woman in black hanging a large white face over the one particular rose in the garden. Mrs. Brocklebank had discovered Guinevere, and a cherished flower that was just opening to the sunlight.

Mrs. Brocklebank always carried a black vanity bag, though it did not contain such things as mirror, *papier poudre*, violet powder, hairpins, and scent. A notebook, two or three neat twists of string, a pair of scissors, a mother-of-pearl card-case, pince-nez, and a little bottle of corn solvent that she had just bought in Basingford—these were the occupants. Eve saw her open the bag, take out the scissors, and bend over Guinevere.

Eve dared to intervene.

"Excuse me, but that rose must not be touched."

Perhaps she put her protest crudely, but Mrs. Brocklebank showed hauteur.

"Indeed!"

"I believe Mr. Canterton wants that flower."

"What is it, Philippa?"

Mrs. Canterton had returned, and came wriggling and edging behind Eve.

"There is rather a nice bud here, and I was going to steal it, but this young lady——"

"Miss Carfax!"

Eve felt her face flushing.

"I believe Mr. Canterton wants that flower."

"Nonsense. Why, there are hundreds here. Take it, my dear, by all means, take it."

"I don't want to interfere with——"

"I insist. James is absolutely foolish about his flowers. He won't let me send a maid down with a basket. And we had such a quarrel once about the orchid house."

Eve turned and went back to her stool. Mrs. Brocklebank's eyes followed her with solemn disapproval.

"That's a rather forward young person."

"Do take the flower, Philippa."

"I will."

And the rose was tucked into Mrs. Brocklebank's belt.

CHAPTER VII

CANTERTON PURSUES MRS. BROCKLEBANK

Ten minutes later Eve saw Canterton enter the rosery.

He was walking slowly, his hands in his pockets, pausing from time to time to examine some particular rose bush for any signs of blight or rust. Eve's place was in the very centre of this little secret world of colour and perfume, and the grey paths led away from her on every side like the ground plan of a maze. There was some resemblance, too, to a silver web with strands spread and hung with iridescent dewdrops flashing like gems. In the midst of it all was the woman, watching, waiting, a mystery even to herself, while the man approached half circuitously, taking this path, and now that, drawing nearer and nearer to that central, feminine thing throned in the thick of June.

Canterton walked along the last path as though he had only just realised Eve's presence. She kept on with her work, looking down under lowered lashes at the sketching-block upon her knees.

"Still working?"

"Yes."

"Have you had any tea?"

"No."

"I'll have some sent out to you."

"Oh, please don't bother."

"You may as well make a habit of it when you are working here."

She lifted eyes that smiled.

"I am so very human, that sweet cakes and a cup of fine China tea——"

"Remain human. I have a very special blend. You shall have it sent out daily, and I will issue instructions as to the cakes. Hallo!"

He had discovered the spoiling of Guinevere.

"Someone has taken that rose."

His profile was turned to her, and she studied it with sympathetic curiosity.

"Mrs. Canterton and some friends have been here."

"Have they?"

"And a stout lady in black discovered Guinevere, and produced a pair of scissors. I put in a word for the rose."

He faced her, looking down with eyes that claimed her as a partisan.

"Thank you."

"I think the lady's name is Mrs. Brocklebank."

He was half angry, half amused.

"I might have suspected it. I suppose someone over-ruled your protest?"

"Yes."

She went on with her work, brushing in a soft background of grey stones and green foliage.

"Was Mrs. Canterton here?"

"Yes."

Her eyes remained fixed upon the rose in front of her, and the poise of her head and the aloofness of her eyes answered his question before he asked it.

"I want that rose most particularly. It has to go to one of the greatest rose experts in the country."

"Yes."

"Which way did they go?"

"Back to the house, I think."

"I'll go and have your tea sent out. And I want to catch Mrs. Brocklebank."

Canterton started in pursuit of the lady, found that she had only just left the house, and that he would catch her in the drive. He intended to be quite frank with her, knowing her to be the most inveterate snatcher up of trifles, one of those over-enthusiastic people who will sneak a cutting from some rare plant and take it home wrapped up in a handkerchief. Lavender had told him one or two tales about Mrs. Brocklebank, and how he had once surprised her in the rock garden busy with a trowel that she had brought in an innocent looking work-bag.

Canterton overtook her just before she reached the lodge gates, and found Guinevere being carried off as a victim in Mrs. Brocklebank's belt.

"I am afraid you have taken a rose that should not have been touched."

"Oh, Mr. Canterton, I'm sure I haven't!"

He looked whimsically at the rose perched on the top of a very ample curve.

"Well, there it is! My wife ought to have warned you——"

"She pressed me to take it. My dear Mr. Canterton, how was I to know?"

"Of course not."

He was amused by her emphatic innocence, especially when, by dragging in Eve Carfax's name, he could have suggested to her that he knew she was lying.

"You see, my wife knows nothing about flowers—what is valuable, and what isn't."

Mrs. Brocklebank began to boom.

"My dear Mr. Canterton, how can you expect it? I think it is very unreasonable of you. In fact, you ought to mark valuable flowers, so that other people should know."

He smiled at her quite charmingly.

"I suppose I ought. I suppose I am really the guilty party. Only, you see, my garden is really a shop, a big general store. And in a shop it is not supposed to be necessary to put notices on certain articles, 'This article is not to be appropriated.'"

"Mr. Canterton!"

She took the rose out of her belt, and in doing so purposely broke the stalk off close to the calyx.

"I think you are a very horrid man. Fancy suggesting——"

"I am a humorist, you know."

"I am afraid I have broken the stalk."

"It doesn't matter. I can have it wired."

He went and opened the lodge gates for her, and stood, hat in hand, as she passed out. He was smiling, but it was an uncomfortable sort of smile that sent Mrs. Brocklebank away wondering whether he was really quite a pleasant person or an ironical beast.

Canterton took the rose to Lavender, who was working through some of the stock lists in the office.

"Nearly lost, but not quite, Lavender."

The foreman looked cynical, but said nothing.

"Wire it up, and have it packed and sent off to Mr. Woolridge to-night. And, by the way, I have told Mrs. Brocklebank that if she wants any flowers in the future, she must apply to you."

"I shan't forget that little trowel of hers, sir, and our Alpines."

"Put up a notice, 'Trowels not admitted.' I am writing to Mr. Woolridge. Oh, and there are those American people coming to-morrow, who want to be shown roses, and flowering shrubs. Will you take them round? I fancy I shall be busy."

Canterton returned to the rosery, and, picking up a stray chair in one of the main paths, joined Eve Carfax, who had a little green Japanese tea-tray on her lap. She was pouring out tea from a tiny brown teapot, her wrist making a white arch, her lashes sweeping her cheek.

"They have brought your tea all right?"

"Yes."

"What about cakes?"

She bent down and picked up a plate from the path.

"Someone must fancy me a hungry schoolgirl."

"It looks rather like it. How is the painting going?"

"I am rather pleased with it."

"Good. On show soon?"

"I have only to put in a few touches."

He swung his chair round, and sat down as though it were the most natural thing in the world for him to come and talk to her. Her curious resemblance to Lynette may have tricked him into a mood that was partly that of the playmate, partly that of the father. Lynette, the child, had set him an impetuous example. "Miss Eve feels the fairies in the wood, daddy. She feels them there, just like me." That was it. Eve spoke and understood the same language as he and the child.

"I overtook Mrs. Brocklebank."

"And rescued Guinevere?"

"Yes, and the good dragon pretended to be very innocent. I did not drag your name in, though I was reproved for not labelling things properly, and so inviting innocent old ladies to purloin flowers."

"But you got the rose back?"

"Yes, and she managed to break the stalk off short in pulling it out of her belt. I wonder if you can tell me why the average woman is built on such mean lines?"

She gave him a sudden questioning glance which said, "Do you realise that you are going beneath the surface—that the real you in you is calling to the real me in me?"

He was looking at her intently, and there was something in his eyes that stirred a tremor of compassion in her.

"What I mean is, that the average woman seems a cad when she is compared to the average man. I mean, the women of the upper middle classes. I suppose it is because they don't know what work is, and because they have always led selfish and protected lives. They haven't the bigness of men—the love of fair-play."

Her eyes brightened to his.

"I know what you mean. If I described a girls' school to you——"

"I should have the feminine world in miniature."

"Yes. The snobbery, the cult of convention, the little sneaking jealousies, all the middle class nastiness. I hated school."

He was silent for some moments, his eyes looking into the distance. Then he began to speak in his quiet and deliberate way, like a man gazing at some landscape and trying to describe all that he saw.

"Life, in a neighbourhood like this, seems so shallow—so full of conventional fussiness. These women know nothing, and yet they must run about, like so many fashionable French clowns, doing a great deal, and nothing. I can't get the hang of it. I suppose I am always hanging my head over something that has been born, or is growing. One gets right up against the wonder and mystery of life, the marvellous complex of growth and colour. It makes one humble, deliberate, rather like a big child. Perhaps I lose my sense of social proportion, but I can't fit myself into these feminine back yards. And some women never forgive one for getting into the wrong back yard."

His eyes finished by smiling, half apologetically.

"It seems to me that most women would rather have their men respectable hypocrites than thinkers."

She put the tray aside, and brushed some crumbs from her skirt.

"The older sort of woman, perhaps."

"You mean——"

"Generations of women have never had a fair chance. They had to dance to the man's piping. And I think women are naturally conservative, sexually mistrustful of change—of new ideas."

"They carry their sex into social questions?"

"Or try to crush it. There is a sort of cry for equality—for the interplay of personality with personality—without all that——"

He bent forward, leaning his elbows on his knees.

"Have we men been guilty of making so many of our women fussy, conventional, pitiless fools? Have you ever run up against the crass prejudice, the merciless, blind, and arrogant self-assurance of the ordinary orthodox woman?"

She answered slowly, "Yes."

He seemed to wait for her.

"Well?"

"There is nothing to say."

"Absolute finality! Oh, I know! Everything outside the little rigid fence, unununderstandable, unmentionable! No vision, no real sympathy, no real knowledge. What can one do? I often wonder whether the child will grow up like that."

"Lynette?"

He nodded.

She looked at him with that peculiar brightening of the eyes and tender tremulousness of the mouth.

"Oh, no! You see, she's—she's sensitive, and not a little woman in miniature. I mean, she won't have the society shell hardened on her before her soul has done growing."

His face warmed and brightened.

"By George, how you put things! That's the whole truth in a nutshell. Keep growing. Keep the youngsters growing. Smash away the crust of convention!"

She began to gather up her belongings, and Canterton watched her cleaning her brushes and putting them back into their case. A subtle veil of shyness had fallen upon her. She had realised suddenly that he was no longer an impersonal figure sitting there and dispassionately discussing certain superficial aspects of life, but a big man who was lonely, a man who appealed to her with peculiar emphasis, and who talked to her as to one who could understand.

"I must be off home. I thought I should finish this to-day, but I will ask you not to look at it till to-morrow."

"Just as you please."

She strapped her things together, rose, and turned a sudden and frank face to his.

"Good-bye. I think Lynette will be ever so safe."

"I shall do my best to keep her away from the multitude of women."

Eve walked back through the pine woods to Orchards Corner, thinking of Canterton and Lynette, and of the woman who was too busy to know anything about flowers. How Gertrude Canterton had delivered an epigram upon herself by uttering those few words. She was just a restless shuttle in the social loom, flying to and fro, weaving conventional and unbeautiful patterns. And she was married to a man whose very life was part of the green sap of the earth, whose humility watched and wondered at the mystery of growth, whose heart was, in some ways, the heart of a child.

What a sacramental blunder!

She was a little troubled, yet conscious of a tremor of exultation. Was it nothing to her that she was able to talk to such a man as this. He was big, massive, yet full of an exquisite tenderness. She had realised that when she had seen him with the child. He had talked, and half betrayed himself, yet she, the woman to whom he had talked, could forgive him that. He was not a man who betrayed things easily. His mouth and eyes were not those of a lax and self-conscious egoist.

Eve found her mother sitting in the garden, knitting, and Eve's conscience smote her a little. Orchards Corner did not pulsate with excitements, and youth, with all its ardour, had left age to its knitting needles and wool.

"Have you been lonely, mother?"

"Lonely, my dear? Why, I really never thought about it."

Eve was always discovering herself wasting her sentiments upon this placid old lady. Mrs. Carfax did not react as the daughter reacted. She was vegetative and quite content to sit and contemplate nothing in particular, like a cat staring at the fire.

"Bring a chair and a book out, dear. These June evenings are so pleasant."

Eve followed her mother's suggestion, knowing very well that she would not be permitted to read. Mrs. Carfax did not understand being silent, her conversation resembling a slowly dripping tap that lets a drop fall every few seconds. She had never troubled to read any book that did not permit her to lose her place and to pick it up again without missing anything of importance. She kept a continuous sparrowish twittering, clicking her knitting needles and sitting stiffly in her chair.

"Have you had a nice day, dear?"

"Quite nice."

"Did you see Mr. Canterton?"

"Oh, yes, I saw him!"

"He must be a very interesting man."

"Yes."

"I should think his wife is such a help to him."

"Oh?"

"Looking after all the social duties, and improving his position. I don't suppose he would have held quite the same position in the neighbourhood without her. She was a Miss Jerningham, wasn't she? And, of course, that must have made a great deal of difference."

"I suppose it did, mother."

"Of course it did, my dear. Marriage makes or mars. Mrs. Canterton must be very popular—so energetic and public spirited, and, you see, one has to remember that Mr. Canterton is in trade. That has not kept them from being county people, and, of course, Mrs. Canterton is responsible for the social position. He must be very proud of his wife."

"Possibly. I haven't asked him, mother. I will, if you like."

Mrs. Carfax was deaf and blind to humour.

"My dear Eve, I sometimes think you are a little stupid."

"Am I?"

"You don't seem to grasp things."

"Perhaps I don't."

CHAPTER VIII

LYNETTE TAKES TO PAINTING

Eve Carfax was painting an easel picture of the walled garden when Lynette arrived with a camp-stool, a drawing book, a box of paints, and a little green watering-pot full of water.

"I want to make pictures. You'll teach me, won't you, Miss Eve?"

"I'll try to."

"I've got a lovely box of paints. What a nice music stand you've got."

"Some people call it an easel."

"I ought to have one, oughtn't I? I'll ask Mr. Beeby to make one. Mr. Beeby's the carpenter. He's such a funny man, with a round-the-corner eye."

Eve took the apprenticeship as seriously as it was offered, and started Lynette on a group of blue delphiniums, white lilies, and scarlet poppies. Lynette began with fine audacity, and red, white and blue splodges sprang up all over the sheet. But they refused to take on any suggestion of detail, and the more Lynette strove with them, the smudgier they became.

"Oh, Miss Eve!"

"How are you getting on?"

"I'm not getting on."

"The colours seem to have got on your fingers."

"They're all sticky. I oughtn't to lick them, ought I?"

"No. Try a rag."

"I'll go and wash in the gold-fish basin. The gold-fish won't mind."

She ran off into the Japanese garden, reappeared, borrowed one of Eve's clean rags, and stood watching the expert's brush laying on colours.

"You do do it beautifully."

"Well, you see, I have done it for years."

Lynette meditated.

"I shall be awful old, then, before I can paint daddy a picture. Can you draw fairies and animals?"

"Supposing I try?"

"Yes, do. Draw some in my book."

The easel picture was covered up and abandoned for the time being. The two stools were placed side by side, and the two heads, the auburn and the black, came very close together.

"I'll draw Mr. Puck."

"Yes, Mr. Puck."

"Mr. Puck is all round—round head, round eyes, round mouth."

"What a funny little round tummy you have given him!"

"You see, he's rather greedy. Now we'll draw Mr. Bruin."

"Daddy made such funny rhymes about Mr. Bruin. Give him a top-hat. Isn't that sweet? But what's he doing—sucking his fingers?"

"He has been stealing honey, and he's licking his paws."

"Now—now draw something out of the Bible."

"The Bible?"

"Yes. Draw God making Eve."

"That would take rather a long time."

"Well, draw the Serpent Devil, and God in the garden."

"I'll draw the serpent."

"What a lovely Snake Devil! Now, if I'd been God, I'd have got a big stick and hit the Snake Devil on the head. Wouldn't it have saved lots and lots of trouble?"

"It would."

"Then why didn't God do it?"

Eve was rescued by Canterton from justifying such theological incongruities. He found them with their heads together, auburn and black bent over Lynette's drawing-book. He stood for a moment or two watching them, and listening to their intimate prattle. This girl who loved the colour and the mystery of life as he loved them could be as a child with Lynette.

"You seem very busy."

Lynette jumped up.

"Daddy, come and look! Isn't Miss Eve clever?"

For some reason Eve blushed, and did not turn to look at Canterton.

"Here's Mr. Puck, and old Bruin, and Titania, and Orson, and the Devil Serpent. Miss Eve is just splendid at devils."

"Is she? That's rather a reflection."

He stood behind Eve and looked down over her shoulder.

"You have given the serpent a woman's head."

She turned her chin but not her eyes.

"Yes."

"Symbolism?"

"I may have been thinking of something you said the other day."

A full-throated and good-humoured voice was heard calling, "Lynette—Lynette!"

"Oh, there's Miss Vance! It's the music lesson. I'll show her the Serpent Devil. I'll come back, Miss Eve, presently."

"Yes, come back, little Beech Leaf."

They were silent for a few moments after she had gone.

"I like that name—'Little Beech Leaf.' Just the colour—in autumn, and racing about in the wind."

He came and stood in front of Eve.

"You seem to be getting on famously, you two."

Her eyes lifted to his.

"She's delightful! No self-consciousness, no showing off, and such vitality. And that hair and those elf's eyes of hers thrill one."

"And she likes you too, not a little."

Eve coloured.

"Well, if she does, it's like a bit of real life flying in through the narrow window of little worries, and calling one out to play."

"Little worries?"

"I don't want to talk about them—the importunities of the larder, and the holes in the house-linen, and the weekly bills. I am always trying to teach myself to laugh. And it is very good for one to be among flowers."

He glanced at the easel.

"You have covered up the picture. May I see it?"

"It is not quite finished. In twenty minutes——"

"May I come back in twenty minutes?"

"Oh, yes!"

"I like my own flowers to be just at their best when friends are to see them."

"Yes, you understand."

Canterton left her and spent half an hour walking the winding paths of the Japanese garden, crossing miniature waterways, and gazing into little pools. There were dwarf trees, dwarf hedges, and a little wooden temple half smothered with roses in which sat a solemn, black marble Buddha. This Buddha had caused a mystery and a scandal in the neighbourhood, for it had been whispered that Canterton was a Buddhist, and that he had been found on his knees in this little wooden temple. In the pools, crimson, white, and yellow lilies basked. The rocks were splashed with colour. Clumps of Japanese iris spread out their flat tops of purple and white and rose. Fish swam in the pools with a vague glimmer of silver and gold.

At the end of half an hour Canterton returned to the walled garden, and found Eve sitting before the picture, her hands lying in her lap. The poise of her head reminded him of "Beata Beatrix," but her face had far more colour, more passionate aliveness, and there was the sex mystery upon her mouth and in the blackness of her hair.

"Ready?"

She turned to him and smiled.

"Yes, you may look."

He stood gazing at her work in silence, yet with a profound delight welling up into his eyes. She watched his face, sensitively, hardly conscious of the fact that she wanted to please him more than anyone else in the world.

"Exquisite! By George, you have eyes!"

She laughed softly in a happy, exultant throat.

"I surprised myself. I think it must be Lynette's magic, and the fairies in the Wilderness."

"If you are going to paint like that, you ought to do big things."

"Oh, I don't know! There are not many people who really care."

"That's true."

He gazed again at the picture, and then his eyes suddenly sought hers.

"Yes, you can see things—you can feel the colour."

"Sometimes it is so vivid that it almost hurts."

They continued to look into each other's eyes, questioningly, wonderingly, with something akin to self-realisation. It was as though they had discovered each other, and were re-discovering each other every time they met and talked.

Lynette reappeared where the long walk ended in a little courtyard paved with red bricks, and surrounded by square-cut box hedges. She had finished her half-hour's music lesson with Miss Vance, and was out again like a bird on the wing. Canterton had insisted on limiting her lessons to three hours a day, though his ideas on a child's upbringing had clashed with those of his wife. There had been a vast deal of talking on Gertrude's part, and a few laconic answers on the part of her husband. Now and again, when the issue was serious, Canterton quietly persisted in having his own way. He never interfered with her multifarious schemes. Gertrude could fuss here, there, and everywhere, provided she did not tamper with Lynette's childhood, or thrust her activities into the serious life of the great gardens of Fernhill.

"Let's go and have tea in the Wilderness."

"Why not?"

"You'll come, Miss Eve?"

She snuggled up to Eve, and an arm went round her.

"I'm afraid I can't, dear, to-day."

"Why can't you?"

"I must go home and take care of my mother."

Lynette seemed to regard this as a very quaint excuse.

"How funny! Fancy anyone wanting to take care of my mother. Why, she's always wanting to take care of everybody else, 'cept me! I wonder if they like it? I shouldn't."

"Your mother is very kind to everybody, dear."

"Is she? Then why don't Sarah, and Ann, and Edith, and Johnson, like her? I know they don't, for I've heard them talking. They all love you, daddy."

Canterton looked at her gravely.

"You mustn't listen to what everybody says. And never tell tales of everybody. Come along, old lady, we'll go down to the Wilderness."

"I wish you'd come, Miss Eve."

"I wish I could, but I mustn't to-day."

"I do like you so much, really I do."

Eve drew Lynette close and kissed her with impulsive tenderness. And Canterton, who saw the love in the kiss, felt that he was standing at the gateway of mystery.

CHAPTER IX

LIFE AT FERNHILL

The Fernhill breakfast table was very characteristic of the Canterton *ménage*.

Gertrude Canterton came down ten minutes after the gong had sounded, bustling into the room with every sign of starting the day in a rush. Her hair looked messy, with untidy strands at the back of her neck. She wore any old dress that happened to come to hand, and as often as not she had a piece of tape hanging out, or a hook and eye unfastened. Breakfast time was not her hour. She looked yellow, and thin, and voracious, and her hands began fidgeting at once with the pile of letters and circulars beside her plate.

Canterton had half finished breakfast. He and his wife were as detached from each other at table as they were in all their other relationships. Gertrude was quite incapable of pouring out his tea, and never remembered whether the sugar was in or not. She always plunged straight into her chaotic correspondence, slitting the envelopes and wrappers with a table knife, and littering the whole of her end of the table with paper. She complained of the number of letters she received, but her restless egoism took offence if she was not pestered each morning.

Canterton had something to tell her, something that a curious sense of the fitness of things made him feel that she ought to know. It did not concern her in the least, but he always classed Gertrude and formalism together.

"I have arranged with Miss Carfax to paint the illustrations for my book."

Gertrude was reading a hospital report, her bacon half cold upon her plate.

"One moment, James."

He smiled tolerantly, and passed her his cup by way of protest.

"Anyhow, I should like some more tea."

"Tea?"

She took the cup, and proceeded to attempt two things at once.

"You might empty the dregs out."

She humoured his fussiness.

"I have something supremely interesting here."

"Meanwhile, the teapot is taking liberties. Inside the cup, my dear Gertrude!"

He had often seen her try to read a letter and fill a cup at the same moment. Sometimes she emptied the contents of the milk jug into the teapot, mistaking it for the hot water.

"Dear, dear!"

"It is rather difficult to concentrate on two things at once."

She passed him the cup standing in a sloppy saucer.

"I take sugar!"

"Do help yourself, James. I never can remember."

Gertrude finished glancing through the hospital report, and picked up a second letter.

"I wanted to tell you that I have engaged Miss Carfax to paint the pictures for my book."

"What book, James?"

"The book on English gardens."

"Oh, yes."

He saw her preparing to get lost in a long letter.

"Miss Carfax has quite extraordinary ability. I think I may find her useful in other ways. Each year we have more people coming to us, wanting us to plan their gardens. She could take some of that work and save me time."

"That will be very nice for you, James."

"I need a second brain here, a brain that has an instinct for colour and effect."

"Yes, I think you do."

He sat and gazed at her with grave and half cynical amusement. Such a piece of news might have seemed of some importance to the average married woman, touching as it did, the edge of her own empire, and Canterton, as he watched her wrinkling up her forehead over those sheets of paper, realised how utterly unessential he had become to this woman whom he had married. He was not visible on her horizon. She included him among the familiar fixtures of Fernhill, and was not sufficiently interested even to suspect that any other woman might come into his life.

From that time Eve Carfax came daily to Fernhill, and made pictures of roses and flowering shrubs, rock walls and lily pools, formal borders and wild corners where art had abetted Nature. Canterton had given her a list of the subjects he needed, a kind of floral calendar for her guidance. And from painting the mere portraits of plants and flowers she was lured on towards a desire to peer into the intricate inner life of all this world of growth and colour. Canterton lent her books. She began to read hard in the evenings, and to spend additional hours in the Fernhill nurseries, wandering about with a catalogue, learning the names and habits of plants and trees. She was absorbed into the life of the place. The spirit of thoroughness that dominated everything appealed to her very forcibly. She, too, wanted to be thorough, to know the life-stories of the flowers she painted, to be able to say, "Such and such flowers will give such and such combinations of colours at a certain particular time." The great gardens were full of individualities, moods, whims, aspirations. She began to understand Canterton's immense sympathy with everything that grew, for sympathy was essential in such a world as this. Plants had to be watched, studied, encouraged, humoured, protected, understood. And the more she learnt, the more fascinated she became, understanding how a man or a woman might love all these growing things as one loves children.

She was very happy. And though absorbed into the life of the place, she kept enough individuality to be able to stand apart and store personal impressions. Life moved before her as she sat in some corner painting. She began to know something of Lavender, something of the men, something of the skill and foresight needed in the production and marketing of such vital merchandise.

One of the first things that Eve discovered was the extent of Canterton's popularity. He was a big man with big views. He treated his men generously, but never overlooked either impertinence or slackness. "Mr. Canterton don't stand no nonsense," was a saying that rallied the men who uttered it. They were proud of him, proud of the great nurseries, proud of his work. The Fernhill men had their cricket field, their club house, their own gardens. Canterton financed these concerns, but left the management to the men's committee. He never interfered with them outside their working hours, never preached, never condescended. The respect they bore him was phenomenal. He was a big figure in all their lives—a figure that counted.

As for Gertrude Canterton, they detested her wholeheartedly. Her unpopularity was easily explained, for her whole idea of philanthropy was of an attitude of restless intrusion into the private lives of the people. She visited, harangued, scolded, and was mortally disliked for her multifarious interferences. The mothers were lectured on the feeding of infants, and the cooking of food. She entered cottages as though she were some sort of State inspector, and behaved as though she always remembered the fact that the cottages belonged to her husband.

The men called her "Mother Fussabout," and by the women she was referred to as "She." They had agreed to recognise the fact that Gertrude Canterton had a very busy bee in her bonnet, and, with all the mordant shrewdness of their class, suffered her importunities and never gave a second thought to any of her suggestions.

Visitors came almost daily to the Fernhill nurseries, and were taken round by Lavender, the foreman, or by Canterton himself. Sometimes they passed Eve while she was painting, and she could tell by the expression of Canterton's eyes whether he was dealing with rich dilettanti or with people who knew. Humour was to be got out of some of these tours of inspection, and Canterton would come back smiling over the "buy-the-whole-place" attitude of some rich and indiscriminate fool.

"I have just had a gentleman who thought the Japanese garden was for sale."

"Oh!"

"A Canadian who has made a fortune in land and wood-pulp and has bought a place over here. When I showed him the Japanese garden, he said, 'I'll take this in the lump, stones, and fish, and trees, and the summer-house, and the little joss house. See?'"

"Was he very disappointed when you told him?"

"Oh, no. He asked me to name a price for fixing him up with an identical garden, including a god. 'Seems sort of original to have a god in your garden.' I said we were too busy for the moment, and that gods are expensive, and are not to be caught every day of the week."

They laughed, looking into each other's eyes.

"What queer things humans are!"

"A madman turned up here once whose mania was water lilies. He had an idea he was a lotus eater, and he stripped and got into the big lily tank and made a terrible mess of the flowers. It took us an hour to catch him and get him out, and we had him on our hands for a week, till his people tracked him down and took him home. He seemed quite sane on most things, and was a fine botanist, but he had this one mad idea."

"Perhaps it was some enthusiasm gone wrong. One can sympathise with some kinds of madmen."

"When one looks at things dispassionately one might be tempted to swear that half our civilisation is absolutely mad."

He stood beside her for a while and watched her painting.

"You are getting quite a lot of technical knowledge."

"I want to be thorough. And Fernhill has aroused an extraordinary curiosity in me. I want to know the why and the wherefore."

He found that it gave him peculiar satisfaction to watch her fingers moving the brush. She was doing her own work and his at the same moment, and the suggestion of comradeship delighted him.

"It wouldn't do you any harm to go through a course of practical gardening. It all helps. Gives one the real grip on a subject."

"I should like it."

"I could arrange it for you with Lavender. It has struck me, too, that if you care to keep to this sort of work——"

She looked up at him with eyes that asked, "Why not?"

"You may want to do bigger things."

"But if the present work fills one's life?"

"I could find you plenty of chances for self-expression. Every year I have more people coming to me wanting plans for gardens, wild gardens, rose gardens, formal gardens. I could start a new profession in design alone. I am pretty sure you could paint people fine, prophetic pictures, and then turn your pictures into the reality."

"Could I?"

She flushed, and he noticed it, and the soft red tinge that spread to her throat.

"Of course you could, with your colour sense and your vision. You only want the technical knowledge."

"I am trying to get that."

"Do you know, it would interest me immensely, as an artist, to see what you would create."

"You seem to believe——"

"I believe you would have very fine visions which it would be delightful for me to plant into life."

She turned and looked at him with something in her eyes that he had never seen before.

"I believe I could do it, if you believe I can do it."

He had a sudden desire to stretch out his hand and to touch her hair, even as he touched Lynette's hair, with a certain playful tenderness.

Meanwhile Eve's friendship with Lynette became a thing of unforeseen responsibilities. Lynette would come running out into the gardens directly her lessons were over, search for Eve, and seat herself at her feet with all the devotedness of childhood that sets up idols. Sometimes Lynette brought a story-book or her paint-box, but these were mere superfluities. It was the companionship that mattered.

It appeared that Lynette was getting behind Miss Vance and her Scripture lessons, and she began to ask Eve a child's questions—questions that she found it impossible to answer. Miss Vance, who was a solid and orthodox young woman, had no difficulty at all in providing Lynette with a proper explanation of everything. But Lynette had inherited her father's intense and sensitive curiosity, and she was beginning to walk behind Miss Vance's machine-made figures of finality and to discover phenomena that Miss Vance's dogmas did not explain.

"Who made the Bible, Miss Eve?"

"A number of wise and good men, dear."

"Miss Vance says God made it."

"Well, He made everything, so I suppose Miss Vance is right."

"Has Miss Vance ever seen God?"

"I don't think so."

"But she seems to know all about Him, just as though she'd met Him at a party. Have you seen Him?"

"No."

"Has anyone?"

"No one whom I know."

"Then how do we know that God is God?"

"Because He must be God. Because everything He has made is so wonderful."

"But Miss Vance seems to know all about Him, and when I ask her how she knows she gets stiff and funny, and says there are things that little girls can't understand. Isn't God very fond of children, Miss Eve, dear?"

"Very."

"Doesn't it seem funny, then, that He shouldn't come and play with me as daddy does?"

"God's ever so busy."

"Is He busy like mother?"

"No; not quite like that."

All this was rather a breathless business, and Eve felt as though she were up before the Inquisition, and likely to be found out. Lynette's eyes were always watching her face.

"Oh, Miss Eve, where do all the little children come from?"

"God sends them, dear."

"Bogey, our cat, had kittens this morning. I found them all snuggling up in the cupboard under the back stairs. Isn't it funny! Yesterday there weren't any kittens, and this morning there are five."

"That's how lots of things happen, dear. Everything is wonderful. You see a piece of bare ground, and two or three weeks afterwards it is full of little green plants."

"Do kittens come like that?"

"In a way."

"Did they grow out of the cupboard floor? They couldn't have done, Miss Eve."

"They grew out of little eggs, dear, like chickens out of their eggs."

"But I've never seen kittens' eggs, have you?"

"No, little Beech Leaf, I haven't."

Eve felt troubled and perplexed, and she appealed to Canterton.

"What is one to tell her? It's so difficult. I wouldn't hurt her for worlds. I remember I had all the old solemn make-believes given me, and when I found them out it hurt, rather badly."

He smiled with his grave eyes—eyes that saw so much.

"Do you believe in anything?"

"You mean——"

"Do you think with the nineteenth-century materialists that life is a mere piece of mechanism?"

"Oh, no."

"Something or someone is responsible. We have just as much right to postulate God as we postulate ether."

"Yes."

"Could you conscientiously swear that you don't believe in some sort of prime cause?"

"Of course I couldn't."

"Well, there you are. We are not so very illogical when we use the word God."

She looked into the distance, thinking.

"After all, life's a marvellous fairy tale."

"Exactly."

"And sometimes we get glimmerings of the 'how,' if we do not know the 'why.'"

"Let a child go on believing in fairy tales—let us all keep our wonder and our humility. All that should happen is that our wonder and our humility should widen and deepen as we grow older, and fairy tales become more fascinating. I must ask Miss Vance to put all that Old Testament stuff of hers on the shelf. When you don't know, tell the child so. But tell her there is someone who does know."

Her eyes lifted to his.

"Thank you, so much."

"We can only use words, even when we feel that we could get beyond words. Music goes farther, and colour, and growth. I don't think you will ever hurt the child if you are the child with her."

"Yes, I understand."

CHAPTER X

TEA IN THE WILDERNESS

Canterton needed pictures of the Italian gardens at Latimer Abbey, and since he had received permission to show the Latimer gardens in his book, it devolved upon Eve Carfax to make a pilgrimage to the place. Latimer, a small country town, lay some seventy miles away, and Canterton, who knew the place, told Eve to write to the George Hotel and book a room there. The work might take her a week, or more, if the weather proved cloudy. Canterton wanted the gardens painted in full sunlight, with all the shadows sharp, and the colours at their brightest.

The day before Eve's journey to Latimer was a "Wilderness day." Lynette had made Eve promise to have a camp tea with her in the dell among the larches.

"Daddy says you like sweet cakes."

"Daddy's a tease."

"I asked Sarah, and she's made a lot of lovely little cakes, some with chocolate ice, and some with jam and cream inside."

"I shan't come just for the cakes, dear."

"No!"

"But because of you and your Wilderness."

"Yes, but you will like the cakes, won't you? Sarah and me's taken such a lot of trouble."

"You dear fairy godmother! I want to kiss you, hard!"

They started out together about four o'clock, Eve carrying the tea-basket, and Lynette a red cushion and an old green rug. The heath garden on the hill-side above the larch wood was one great wave of purple, rose, and white, deep colours into which vision seemed to sink with a sense of utter satisfaction. The bracken had grown three or four feet high along the edge of the larch wood, so that Lynette's glowing head disappeared into a narrow green lane. It was very still and solemn and mysterious in among the trees, with the scattered blue of the sky showing through and the sunlight stealing in here and there and making patterns upon the ground.

They were busy boiling the spirit kettle when Canterton appeared at the end of the path through the larch wood.

"Queen Mab, Queen Mab, may I come down into your grotto?"

Lynette waved to him solemnly with a hazel wand.

"Come along down, Daddy Bruin."

He climbed down into the dell laughing.

"That is a nice title to give a parent. I might eat you both up."

"I'm sure you'd find Miss Eve very nice to eat."

"Dear child!"

"How goes the kettle?"

"We are nearly ready. Here's the rug to sit on, daddy. Miss Eve's going to have the red cushion."

"The cushion of state. What about the cakes?"

"Sarah's made such lovely ones."

Eve's eyes met Canterton's.

"It was ungenerous of you to betray me."

"Not at all. It was sheer tact on my part."

Tea was a merry meal, with both Lynette and her father dilating on the particular excellences of the different cakes, and insisting that she would be pleasing Sarah by allowing herself to be greedy. In the fullness of time Canterton lit a pipe, and Lynette, sitting next him on the green rug with her arms about her knees, grew talkative and problematical.

"Isn't it funny how God sends people children?"

"Most strange."

"What did you say, daddy, when God sent you me?"

"'Here's another horrible responsibility!'"

"Daddy, you didn't! But wasn't it funny that I was sent to mother?"

"Lynette, old lady——"

"Now, why wasn't I sent to Miss Eve?"

Canterton reached out and lifted her into his lap.

"Bruin tickles little girls who ask too many questions."

In the midst of her struggles and her laughter his eyes met Eve's, and found them steady and unabashed, yet full of a vivid self-consciousness. They glimmered when they met his, sending a mesmeric thrill through him, and for the moment he could not look away. It was as though the child had flashed a mysterious light into the eyes of both, and uttered some deep nature cry that had startled them in the midst of their playfulness. Canterton's eyes seemed to become bluer, and more intent, and Eve's mouth had a tremulous tenderness.

Lynette was a young lady of dignity, and Canterton was reproved.

"Look how you've rumpled my dress, daddy."

"I apologise. Supposing we go for a ramble, and call for our baggage on the way back."

Both Eve and Canterton rose, and Lynette came between them, holding each by the hand. They wandered through the Wilderness and down by the pollard pool, where the swallows skimmed the still water. Lynette was mute, sharing the half dreamy solemnity of her elders. The playfulness was out of the day, and even the child felt serious.

It was past six when they returned to the garden, and Lynette, whose supper hour was due, hugged Eve hard as she said good-bye.

"You will write to me, Miss Eve, dear."

"Yes, I'll write."

She found that Canterton had not come to the point of saying good-bye. He walked on with her down one of the nursery roads between groups of rare conifers.

"I am going to walk to Orchards Corner. Do you mind?"

"No."

"I haven't met your mother yet. I don't know whether it is the proper time for a formal call."

"Mother will be delighted. She is always delighted."

"A happy temperament."

"Very."

They chose the way through the fir woods, and talked of the Latimer Abbey gardens, and of the particular atmosphere Canterton wanted her to produce for him.

"Oh, you'll get it! You'll get the very thing."

"What an optimist you are."

"Perhaps I am more of a mystic."

The mystery of the woods seemed to quicken that other mysterious self-consciousness that had been stirred by the child, Lynette. They were in tune, strung to vibrate to the same subtle, and plaintive notes. As they walked, their intimate selves kept touching involuntarily and starting apart, innocent of foreseeing how rich a thrill would come from the contact. Their eyes questioned each other behind a veil of incredulity and wonder.

"You will write to Lynette?"

"Oh, yes!"

There was a naive and half plaintive uplift of her voice towards the "yes."

"Little Beech Leaf is a warm-hearted fairy. Do you know, I am very glad of this comradeship, for her sake."

"You make me feel very humble."

"No. You are just the kind of elder sister that she needs."

He had almost said mother, and the word mother was in Eve's heart.

"Do you realise that I am learning from Lynette?"

"I don't doubt it. One ought to learn deep things from a child."

They reached the lane leading to Orchards Corner, and on coming to the white fence sighted Mrs. Carfax sitting in the garden, with the inevitable knitting in her lap. Canterton was taken in and introduced.

"Please don't get up."

Mrs. Carfax was coy and a little fluttered.

"Do sit down, Mr. Canterton. I feel that I must thank you for your great kindness to my daughter. I am sure that both she and I are very grateful."

"So am I, Mrs. Carfax."

"Indeed, Mr. Canterton?"

"For the very fine work your daughter is going to do for me. I was in doubt as to who to get, when suddenly she appeared."

Mrs. Carfax bowed in her chair like some elderly queen driving through London.

"I am so glad you like Eve's paintings. I think she paints quite nicely. Of course she studied a great deal at the art schools, and she would have exhibited, only we could not afford all that we should have liked to afford.

It is really most fortunate for Eve that you should be so pleased with her painting."

Her placid sing-song voice, with its underlining of the "sos" the "quites," and the "mosts," made Canterton think of certain maiden aunts who had tried to spoil him when he was a child. Mother and daughter were in strange contrast. The one all fire, sensitive aliveness, curiosity, colour; the other flat, sweetly foolish, toneless, apathetic.

Canterton stayed chatting with Mrs. Carfax for twenty minutes, while Eve sat by in silence, watching them with an air of dispassionate curiosity. Mrs. Carfax was just a child, and Canterton was at his best with children. Eve found herself thinking how much bigger, gentler, and more patient his nature was than hers. Things that irritated her, made him smile. He was one of the few masterful men who could bear with amiable stupidity.

When he had said good-bye to her mother, Eve went with him to the gate.

"Good-bye. Enjoy yourself. And when you write to Lynette, send me a word or two."

He held her hand for two or three seconds, and his eyes looked into hers.

"You will be delighted with Latimer."

"Yes. And I will try to bring you back what you want."

"I have no doubts as to that."

She stood for a moment at the gate, watching his broad figure disappear between the green hedgerows of the lane. A part of herself seemed to go with him, an outflowing of something that came from the deeps of her womanhood.

"Eve, dear, what a nice man Mr. Canterton is."

"Nice" was the principal adjective in Mrs. Carfax's vocabulary.

"Yes."

"So good looking, and such nice manners. You would never have thought that he——"

"Was in trade?"

"Not quite that, dear, but selling things for money."

"Of course, he might give them away. I suppose his social position would be greatly improved!"

"I don't think that would be quite feasible, dear. Really, sometimes, you are almost simple."

Canterton was walking through the woods, head bent, his eyes curiously solemn.

"What I want! She will bring me back what I want. What is it that I want?"

He came suddenly from the shadows of the woods into the full splendour of the evening light upon blue hills and dim green valleys. He stopped dead, eyes at gaze, a spasm of vague emotion rising in his throat. This sun-washed landscape appeared like a mysterious projection of something that lay deep down in his consciousness. What was it he wanted? A vital atmosphere such as this—comradeship, sympathy, passionate understanding.

CHAPTER XI

LATIMER

When Eve had left for Latimer, the routine of Canterton's working day ran with the same purposefulness, like a familiar path in a garden, yet though the scene was the same, the atmosphere seemed different, even as a well-known landscape may be glorified and rendered more mysterious by the light poured out from under the edge of a thunder cloud. A peculiar tenderness, a glamour of sensitiveness, covered everything. He was more alive to the beauty of the world about him, and the blue hills seemed to hang like an enchantment on the edge of the horizon. He felt both strangely boyish and richly mature. Something had been renewed in him. He was an Elizabethan, a man of a wonderful new youth, seeing strange lands rising out of the ocean, his head full of a new splendour of words and a new majesty of emotions. The old self in him seemed as young and fresh as the grass in spring. His vitality was up with the birds at dawn.

The first two days were days of dreams. The day's work was the same, yet it passed with a peculiar pleasureableness as though there were soft music somewhere keeping a slow rhythm. He was conscious of an added wonder, of the immanence of something that had not taken material shape. A richer light played upon the colours of the world about him. He was conscious of the light, but he did not realise its nature, nor whence it came.

On the third day the weather changed, and an absurd restlessness took possession of him. Rain came in rushes out of a hurrying grey sky, and the light and the warmth seemed to have gone out of the world. Mysterious outlines took on a sharp distinctness. Figures were no longer the glimmering shapes of an Arthurian dream. Canterton became more conscious of the physical part of himself, of appetites, needs, inclinations, tendencies. Something was hardening and taking shape.

He began to think more definitely of Eve at Latimer, and she was no longer a mere radiance spreading itself over the routine of the day's work. Was she comfortable at the old red-faced "George"? Was the weather interfering with her work? Would she write to Lynette, and would the letter have a word for him? What a wonderful colour sense she had, and what cunning in those fingers of hers. He liked to remember that peculiar radiant look, that tenderness in the eyes that came whenever she was stirred by something that was unusually beautiful. It was like the look in the eyes of a mother, or the light in the eyes of a woman who loved. He had seen it when she was looking at Lynette.

Then, quite suddenly, he became conscious of a sense of loss. He was unable to fix his attention on his work, and his thoughts went drifting. He felt lonely. It was as though he had been asleep and dreaming, and had wakened up suddenly, hungry and restless, and vaguely discontented.

Even Lynette's chatter was a spell cast about his thoughts. Having created a heroine, the child babbled of her and her fascinations, and Canterton discovered a secret delight in hearing Lynette talk of Eve Carfax. He could not utter the things that the child uttered, and yet they seemed so inevitable and so true, so charmingly and innocently intimate. It brought Eve nearer, showed her to him as a more radiant, gracious, laughing figure. Lynette was an enchantress, a siren, and knew it not, and Canterton's ears were open to her voice.

"I wonder if my letter will come to-day, daddy?"

"Perhaps!"

"It's over two—three days. It ought to be a big letter."

"A big letter for a little woman."

"I wonder if she writes as beautifully as she paints?"

"Very likely."

"And, oh, daddy, will she be back for our garden party?"

"I think so."

"Mother says I can't behave nicely at parties. I shall go about with Miss Eve, and I'll do just what she does. Then I ought to behave very nicely, oughtn't I?"

"Perfectly."

"I do love Miss Eve, daddy, don't you?"

"We always agree, Miss Pixie."

On the fourth day Lynette had her letter. It came by the morning's post, with a little devil in red and black ink dancing on the flap of the envelope. Lynette had not received more than three letters in her life, and the very address gave her a beautiful new thrill.

Miss Lynette Canterton,

Fernhill,

Basingford,

Surrey.

Lessons over, she went rushing out in search of her father, and, after canvassing various under-gardeners, discovered him in a corner of the rose nursery.

"Miss Eve's written, daddy! I knew she would. Would you like to read it? Here's a message for you."

He sat down on a wooden bench, and drawing Lynette into the hollow of one arm, took the letter in a big hand. It was written on plain cream paper of a roughish texture, with a little picture of the "George Hotel" penned in the right upper corner. Eve's writing was the writing of the younger generation, so different from the regular, sloping, characterless style of the feminine Victorians. It was rather upright, rather square, picturesque in its originality, and with a certain decorative distinctness that covered the sheet of paper with personal and intimate values.

> "Dear Lynette,—I am writing to you at a funny little table in a funny little window that looks out on Latimer Green. It has been raining all day—oh, such rain!—like thousands of silver wires falling down straight out of the sky. If you were here we would sit at the window and make pictures of the queer people—all legs and umbrellas—walking up and down the streets. Here is the portrait of an umbrella going out for a walk on a nice pair of legs in brown gaiters.
>
> "There is an old raven in the garden here. I tried to make friends with him, but he pecked my ankles. And they say he uses dreadful language. Wicked old bird! Here is a picture of him pretending to be asleep, with one eye open, waiting for some poor Puss Cat to come into the garden.
>
> "There is a nice old gardener who makes me tea in the afternoon, but I don't like it so much as tea in the Wilderness.
>
> "I want to be back to see you in your new party frock next Friday. I feel quite lonely without the Queen of the Fairies. If you were here I would buy you such cakes at the little shop across the road.
>
> "Please tell Mr. Canterton that the weather was very good to me the first two days, and that I hope he will like the pictures that I have painted.
>
> "Good-bye, Lynette, dear,

Much—much love to you, from

"Miss Eve."

Lynette was ecstatic.

"Isn't it a lovely letter, daddy? And doesn't she write beautifully? And it's all spelt just as if it were out of a book."

Canterton folded the letter with meditative leisureliness.

"Quite a lovely letter."

"I'm going to put it away in my jewel case."

"Jewel case? We are getting proud!"

"It's only a work-box, really, but I call it a jewel case."

"I see. Things are just what we choose to call them."

Canterton went about for the rest of the day with a picture of a dark-haired woman with a sensitive face sitting at a white framed Georgian window, and looking out upon Latimer Green where all the red-tiled roofs were dull and wet, and the rain rustled upon the foliage of the Latimer elms. He could imagine Eve drawing those pen-and-ink sketches for Lynette, with a glimmer of fun in her eyes, and her lips smiling. She was seventy miles away, and yet——He found himself wondering whether her thoughts had reached out to him while she was writing that letter to Lynette.

At Latimer the rain was the mere whim of a day, a silver veil let down on the impulse and tossed aside again with equal capriciousness. Eve was deep in the Latimer gardens, painting from nine in the morning till six at night, taking her lunch and tea with her, and playing the gipsy under a blue sky.

Save for that one wet day the weather was perfect for studies of vivid sunlight and dense shadow. Latimer Abbey set upon its hill-side, with the dense woods shutting out the north, seemed to float in the very blue of the summer sky. There was no one in residence, and, save for the gardeners, Eve had the place to herself, and was made to feel like a child in a fairy story, who discovers some enchanted palace all silent and deserted, yet kept beautiful by invisible hands. As she sat painting in the upper Italian garden with its flagged walks, statues, brilliant parterres, and fountains, she could not escape from a sense of enchantment. It was all so quiet, and still, and empty. The old clock with its gilded face in the turret kept smiting the hours with a quaint, muffled cry, and with each striking of the hour she had a feeling that all the doors and windows of the great house would open, and that gay ladies in flowered gowns, and gentlemen in rich brocades would come gliding out on to the terrace. Gay ghosts in panniers and coloured coats, powdered, patched, fluttering fans, and cocking swords, quaint in their stilted stateliness. The magic of the place seemed to flow into her work, and perhaps there was too much mystery in the classic things she painted. Some strange northern god had breathed upon the little sensuous pictures that should have suggested the gem-like gardens of Pompeii. Clipped yews and box trees, glowing masses of mesembryanthemum and pelargonium, orange trees in stone vases, busts, statues, masks, fountains and white basins, all the brilliancy thereof refused to be merely sensuous and delightful. There was something over it, a spirituality, a slight mistiness that softened the materialism. Eve knew what she desired to paint, and yet something bewitched her hands, puzzled her, made her dissatisified. The Gothic spirit refused to be conjured, refused to suffer this piece of brilliant formalism to remain untouched under the thinner blue of the northern sky.

Eve was puzzled. She made sketch after sketch, and yet was not satisfied. Was it mediævalism creeping in, the ghosts of old monks moving round her, and throwing the shadows of their frocks over a pagan mosaic? Or was the confusing magic in her own brain, or some underflow of feeling that welled up and disturbed her purpose?

Moreover, she discovered that another personality had followed her to Latimer. She felt as though Canterton were present, standing behind her, looking over her shoulder, and watching her work. She seemed to see things with his eyes, that the work was his work, and that it was not her personality alone that mattered.

The impression grew and became so vivid that it forced her from the mere contemplation of the colours and the outlines of the things before her to a subtle consciousness of the world within herself. Why should she feel that he was always there at her elbow? And yet the impression was so strong that she fancied that she had but to turn her head to see him, to talk to him, and to look into his eyes for sympathy and understanding. She tried to shake the feeling off, to shrug her shoulders at it, and failed. James Canterton was with her all the while she worked.

There was a second Italian garden at Latimer, a recreation, in the spirit, of the garden of the Villa d'Este at Tivoli, a hill garden, a world of terraces, stone stairways, shaded walks, box hedges, cypresses and cedars, fountains, cascades, great water cisterns. Here was more mystery, deeper shadows, a sadder note. Eve was painting in the lower garden on the day following the rain, when the lights were softer, the foliage fresher, the perfumes more pungent. There was the noise of water everywhere. The sunlight was more partial and more vague, splashing into the open spaces, hanging caught in the cypresses and cedars, touching some marble shape, or glittering upon the water in some pool. Try as she would, Eve felt less impersonal here than in the full sunlight of the upper garden. That other spirit that had sent her to Latimer seemed to follow her up and down the moss-grown stairways, to walk with her through the shadows under the trees. She was more conscious of Canterton than ever. He was the great, grave lord of the place, watching her work with steady eyes, compelling her to paint with a touch that was not all her own.

Sometimes the head gardener, who had tea made for her in his cottage, came and watched her painting and angled for a gossip. He was a superior sort of ancient, with a passion for unearthing the history of plants that had been introduced from distant countries. Canterton's name came up, and the old man found something to talk about.

"I don't say as I'm an envious chap, but that's the sort of life as would have suited me."

Eve paused at her work.

"Whose?"

"Why, Mr. Canterton's, Miss."

"You know Mr. Canterton by name?"

"Know him by name! I reckon I do! Didn't he raise Eileen Purcell and Jem Gaunt, and bring all those Chinese and Indian plants into the country, and hybridise Mephistopheles? Canterton! It's a name to conjure with."

Eve felt an indefinable pleasure in listening to the fame of the man whose work she was learning to share, for it was fame to be spoken of with delight by this old Latimer gardener.

"Mr. Canterton's writing a book, is he?"

"Yes, and I am painting some of the pictures for it."

"Are you now? I have a notion I should like that book. Aye, it should be a book!"

"The work of years."

"Sure! None of your cheap popular sixpenny amateur stuff. It'll be what you call 'de lucks,' won't it? Such things cost money."

Eve was silent a moment. The old man was genuine enough, and not touting.

"Perhaps Mr. Canterton would send you a copy. You would appreciate it. I'll give him your name."

"No, no, though I thank you, miss. A good tool is worth its money. I'm not a man to get a good thing for nothing. I reckon I'll buy that there book."

"It won't be published for two or three years."

"Oh, I'm in no hurry! I'm used to waiting for things to grow solid. Sapwood ain't no use to anybody."

Eve had a desire to see the hill garden by moonlight, and the head gardener was sympathetic.

"We lock the big gate at dusk when his lordship's away. But you come round at nine o'clock to the postern by the dovecot, and I'll let you in."

The hill garden's mood was suited to the full moon. Eve had dreamt of such enchantments, but had never seen them till that summer night. There was not a cloud in the sky, and the cypresses and cedars were like the black spires of a city. The alleys and walks were tunnels of gloom. Here and there a statue or a fountain glimmered, and the great water cisterns were pools of ink reflecting the huge white disc of the moon.

Eve wandered to and fro along the moonlit walks and up and down the dim stairways. The stillness was broken only by the splash of water, and by the turret clock striking the quarters.

It was the night of her last day at Latimer. She would be sorry to leave it, and yet, to-morrow she would be at Fernhill. Lynette's glowing head flashed into her thoughts, and a rush of tenderness overtook her. If life could be like the joyous eyes of the child, if passion went no further, if all problems remained at the age of seven!

How would Canterton like the pictures she had painted? A thrill went through her, and at the same time she felt that the garden was growing cold. A sense of unrest ruffled the calm of the moonlit night. She felt near to some big, indefinable force, on the edge of the sea, vaguely afraid of she knew not what.

She would see him to-morrow. It was to be the day of the Fernhill garden party, and she had promised Lynette that she would go.

She felt glad, yet troubled, half tempted to shirk the affair, and to stay with her mother at Orchards Corner.

A week had passed, and she could not escape from the knowledge that something had happened to her in that week.

Yet what an absurd drift of dreams was this that she was suffering. The moonlight and the mystery were making her morbid and hypersensitive.

To-morrow she would walk out into the sunlight and meet him face to face in the thick of a casual crowd. All the web of self-consciousness would fall away. She would find herself talking to a big, brown-faced man with steady eyes and a steady head. He was proof against such imaginings, far too strong to let such fancies cloud his consciousness.

Moreover they were becoming real good friends, and she imagined that she understood him. She had been too much alone this week. His magnificent and kindly sanity would make her laugh a little over the impressions that had haunted her in the gardens of Latimer.

CHAPTER XII

A WEEK'S DISCOVERY

Those who saw Lynette's swoop towards her heroine attached no esoteric meaning to its publicity. A sage green frock and a bronze gold head went darting between the figures on the Fernhill lawn.

Mrs. Brocklebank, who could stop most people in full career, as a policeman halts the traffic in the city, discovered that it was possible for her largeness to be ignored.

"Lynette, my dear, come and show me———"

Lynette whisked past her unheedingly. Mrs. Brocklebank tilted her glasses.

"Dear me, how much too impetuous that child is. I am always telling Gertrude that she is far too wild and emotional."

Mrs. Lankhurst, who was Mrs. Brocklebank's companion for the moment, threw back an echo.

"A little neurotic, I think."

Mrs. Lankhurst was a typical hard-faced, raddled, cut-mouthed Englishwoman, a woman who had ceased to trouble about her appearance simply because she had been married for fifteen years and felt herself comfortably and sexually secure. An unimaginative self-complacency seems to be the chief characteristic of this type of Englishwoman. She appears to regard marriage as a release from all attempts at subtilising the charm of dress, lets her complexion go, her figure slacken, her lips grow thin. "George" is serenely and lethargically constant, so why trouble about hats? So the good woman turns to leather, rides, gardens, plays golf, and perhaps reads questionable novels. The sex problem does not exist for her, yet Mrs. Lankhurst's "George" was notorious and mutable behind her back. She thought him cased up in domestic buckram, and never the lover of some delightful little *dame aux Camellias*, who kept her neck white, and her sense of humour unimpaired.

Lynette's white legs flashed across the grass.

"Oh, Miss Eve!"

Eve Carfax had stepped out through the open drawing-room window, a slim and sensitive figure that carried itself rather proudly in the face of a crowd.

"Lynette!"

"I knew you'd come! I knew you'd come!"

She held out hands that had to be taken and held, despite the formal crowd on the lawn.

"I'm so glad you're back."

A red mouth waited to be kissed.

"We have missed you—daddy and I."

"My dear——"

Mrs. Brocklebank was interested. So was her companion.

"Who is that girl?"

Mrs. Lankhurst had a way of screwing up her eyes, and wrinkling her forehead.

"A Miss Carfax. She lives with her mother near here. Retired tradespeople, I imagine. The girl paints. She is doing work for Mr. Canterton—illustrating catalogues, I suppose."

"The child seems very fond of her."

"Children have a habit of making extraordinary friendships. It is the dustman, or an engine-driver, or something equally primitive."

"I suppose one would call the girl pretty?"

"Too French!"

Mrs. Lankhurst nodded emphatically.

"Englishmen are so safe. Now, in any other country it would be impossible——"

"Oh, quite! I imagine such a man as James Canterton——"

"The very idea is indecent. Our men are so reliable. One never bothers one's head. Yet one has only to cross the Channel——"

"A decadent country. The women make the morals of the men. Any nation that thinks so much about dress uncovers its own nakedness."

The multi-coloured crowd had spread itself over the whole of the broad lawn in the front of the house, for Gertrude Canterton's garden parties were very complete affairs, claiming people from half the county. She had one of the best string bands that was to be obtained, ranged in the shade of the big sequoia. The great cedar was a kind of kiosk, and a fashionable London caterer had charge of the tea.

Lynette kept hold of Eve's hand.

"Where is your mother, dear?"

"Do you want to see mother?"

"Of course."

They wound in and out in quest of Gertrude Canterton, and found her at last in the very centre of the crowd, smiling and wriggling in the stimulating presence of a rear-admiral. She was wearing a yellow dress and a purple hat, a preposterous and pathetic combination of colours when the man she had married happened to be one of the greatest flower colourists in the kingdom. Eve shook hands and was smiled at.

"How do you do, Miss Garvice?"

"It isn't Garvice, mother."

Eve was discreet and passed on, but Lynette was called back.

"Lynette, come and say how do you do to Admiral Mirlees."

Lynette stretched out a formal hand.

"How do you do, Admiral Mirlees?"

The sailor gave her a big hand, and a sweep of the hat.

"How do you do, Miss Canterton? Charmed to meet you! Supposing you come and show me the garden?"

Lynette eyed him gravely.

"Most of it's locked up."

"Locked up?"

"Because people steal daddy's things."

"Lynette!"

"I'm very busy, Admiral, but I can give you ten minutes."

The sailor's eyes twinkled, but Gertrude Canterton was angry.

"Lynette, go and show Admiral Mirlees all the garden."

"My dear Mrs. Canterton, I am quite sure that your daughter is telling the truth. She must be in great demand, and I shall be grateful for ten minutes."

Lynette's eyes began to brighten to the big playful child in him.

"Lord Admiral, I think you must look so nice in a cocked hat. I've left Miss Eve, you see. She's been away, and she's my great friend."

"I won't stand in Miss Eve's way."

"But she's not a bit selfish, and I think I might spare half an hour."

"Miss Canterton, let me assure you that I most deeply appreciate this compliment."

Eve, left alone, wandered here and there, knowing hardly a soul, and feeling rather lost and superfluous. Happiness in such shows consists in being comfortably inconspicuous, a talker among talkers, though there are some who can hold aloof with an air of casual detachment, and outstare the crowd from some pillar of isolation. Eve had a self-conscious fit upon her. Gertrude Canterton's parties were huge and crowded failures. The subtle atmosphere that pervades such social assemblies was restless, critical, uneasy, at Fernhill. People talked more foolishly than usual, and were either more absurdly stiff or more absurdly genial than was their wont.

The string band had begun to play one of Brahms' Hungarian melodies. It was a superb band, and the music had an impetuous and barbaric sensuousness, a Bacchic rush of half-naked bodies whirling together through a shower of vine leaves and flowers. The talk on the lawn seemed so much gabble, and Eve wandered out, and round behind the great sequoia where she could listen to the music and be at peace. She wondered what the violinists thought of the crowd over yonder, these men who could make the strings utter wild, desirous cries. What a stiff, preposterous, and complacent crowd it seemed. Incongruous fancies piqued her sense of humour. If Pan could come leaping out of the woods, if ironical satyrs could seize and catch up those twentieth century women, and wild-eyed girls pluck the stiff men by the chins. The music suggested it, but who had come to listen to the music?

"I have been hunting you through the crowd."

She turned sharply, with all the self-knowledge that she had won at Latimer rushing to the surface. A few words spoken in the midst of the crying of the violins. She felt the surprised nakedness of her emotions, that she was stripped for judgment, and that sanity would be whipped into her by the scourge of a strong man's common sense.

"I have not been here very long."

She met his eyes and held her breath.

"I saw you with Lynette, but I could not make much headway."

Canterton had taken her hand and held it a moment, but his eyes never left her face. She was mute, full of a wonder that was half exultant, half afraid. All those subtle fancies that had haunted her at Latimer were becoming realities, instead of melting away into the reasonable sunlight. What had happened to both of them in a week? He was the same big, brown, quiet man of the world, magnanimous, reliable, a little reticent and proud, yet from the moment that he had spoken and she had turned to meet his eyes she had known that he had changed.

"I promised Lynette that I would come."

"Aren't you tired?"

"Tired? No. I left Latimer early, and after all, it is only seventy miles. I got home about twelve and found mother knitting just as though she had been knitting ever since I left her. Lynette looks lovely."

She felt the wild necessity of chattering, of covering things up with sound, of giving her thoughts time to steady themselves. His eyes overwhelmed her. It was not that they were too audacious or too intimate. On the contrary they looked at her with a new softness, a new awe, a kind of vigilant tenderness that missed nothing.

"I think you are looking very well."

"I am very well."

She caught quick flitting glances going over her, noticing her simple little black hat shaped like an almond, her virginal white dress and long black gloves. The black and white pleased him. Her feminine instinct told her that.

"I came round here to listen to the music."

"Music is expected at these shows, and not listened to. I always call this 'Padlock Day.'"

She laughed, glad of a chance to let emotions relax for a moment.

"Padlock Day! Do you mean——"

"There are too many Mrs. Brocklebanks about."

"But surely——"

"You would be surprised if I were to tell you how some of my choice things used to be pilfered on these party days. Now I shut up my business premises on these state occasions, for fear the Mrs. Brocklebanks should bring trowels in their sunshades."

"And instead, you give them good music?"

"Which they don't listen to, and they could not appreciate it if they did."

"You are severe!"

"Am I? Supposing these men gave us the Second Hungarian Rhapsody, how could you expect the people to understand it? In fact, it is not a thing to be understood, but to be felt. Our good friends would be shocked if they felt as Liszt probably meant people to feel it. Blood and wine and garlands and fire in the eyes. Well, how did you like Latimer?"

The blood rose again to her face, and she knew that the same light was in his eyes.

"Perfect. I was tempted to dream all my time away instead of painting. I hope you will like the pictures. There was something in the atmosphere of the place that bothered me."

"Oh?"

"Yes, just as though ghosts were trying to play tricks with my hands. The gardens are classic, renaissance, or what you please. It should have been all sunny, delightful formalism, but then——"

"Something Gothic crept in."

"How do you know that?"

"I have been to Latimer."

Her eyes met his with a flash of understanding.

"Of course. But I——Well, you must judge."

The music had stopped, and an eddy of the crowd came lapping round behind the sequoia. Canterton was captured by an impetuous amateur gardener in petticoats who had written a book about something or other, and who always cast her net broadly at an interesting man.

"Oh, Mr. Canterton, can you tell me about those Chinese primulas?"

To Eve Carfax it appeared part of the whimsical and senseless spirit of such a gathering that she should be carried up against Gertrude Canterton, whose great joy was to exercise the power of patronage.

"Miss Carfax, Mr. Canterton seems so pleased with your paintings. I am sure you are being of great use to him."

As a matter of fact, Canterton had hardly so much as mentioned Eve's art to his wife, and Eve herself felt that she had nothing to say to Gertrude Canterton. Her pride hardened in her and refused to be cajoled.

"I am glad Mr. Canterton likes my work."

"I am sure he does. Have you studied much in town?"

"For two or three years. And I spent a year in Paris."

"Indeed!"

Gertrude Canterton's air of surprise was unconsciously offensive.

"Do you ever paint portraits?"

"I have tried."

"I hear it is the most lucrative part of the profession. Now, miniatures, for instance—there has been quite a craze for miniatures. Have you tried them?"

"Oh, yes!"

"Really? We must see what you can do. You might show me a—a sample, and I can mention it to my friends."

Eve had become ice.

"Thank you, but I am afraid I shall not have the time."

"Indeed."

"I want to give all my energy to flower painting."

"I see—I see. Oh, Mrs. Dempster, how are you? How good of you to come. Have you had tea? No? Oh, do come and let me get you some!"

Eve was alone again, and conscious of a sense of strife within her. Gertrude Canterton's voice had raised an echo, an echo that brought back suggestions of antipathy and scorn. Those few minutes spent with her had covered the world of Eve's impressions with a cold, grey light. She felt herself a hard young woman, quite determined against patronage, and quite incapable of letting herself be made a fool of by any emotions whatever.

Glancing aside she saw Canterton talking to a parson. He was talking with his lips, but his eyes were on her. He had the hovering and impatient air of a man held back against his inclinations, and trying to cover with courtesy his desire to break away.

He was coming back to her, for there was something inevitable and magnetic about those eyes of his. A little spasm of shame and exultation glowed out from the midst of the half cynical mood that had fallen on her. She turned and moved away, wondering what had become of Lynette.

"I want to show you something."

She felt herself thrill. The hardness seemed to melt at the sound of his voice.

"Oh?"

"Let's get away from the crowd. It is really preposterous. What fools we all are in a crowd."

"Too much self-consciousness."

"Are you, too, self-conscious?"

"Sometimes."

"Not when you are interested."

"Perhaps not."

They passed several of Canterton's men parading the walks leading to the nurseries. Temporary wire fences and gates had been put up here and there. Canterton smiled.

"Doesn't it strike you as almost too pointed?"

"What, that barbed wire?"

"Yes. I believe I have made myself an offence to the neighbourhood. But the few people I care about understand. Besides, we give to our friends."

"I think you must have been a brave man."

"No, an obstinate one. I did not see why the Mrs. Brocklebanks should have pieces of my rare plants. I have even had my men bribed once or twice. You should hear Lavender on the subject. Look at that!"

He had brought her down to see the heath garden, and her verdict was an awed silence. They stood side by side, looking at the magnificent masses of colour glowing in the afternoon light.

"Oh, how exquisite!"

"It is rather like drinking when one is thirsty."

"Yes."

He half turned to her.

"I want to see the Latimer paintings. May I come down after dinner, and have a chat with your mother?"

She felt something rise in her throat, a faint spasm of resistance that lasted only for a moment.

"But—the artificial light?"

"I want to see them."

It was not so much a surrender on her part as a tacit acceptance of his enthusiasm.

"Yes, come."

"Thank you."

CHAPTER XIII

A MAN IN THE MOONLIGHT

It was no unusual thing for Canterton to spend hours in the gardens and nurseries after dark. He was something of a star-gazer and amateur astronomer, but it was the life of the earth by night that drew him out with lantern, collecting-box and hand lens. Often he went moth hunting, for the history of many a moth is also the history of some pestilence that cankers and blights the green growth of some tree or shrub. No one who has not gone out by night with a lantern to search and to observe has any idea of the strange, creeping life that wakes with the darkness. It is like the life of another world, thousand-legged, slimy, grotesque, repulsive, and yet full of significance to the Nature student who goes out to use his eyes.

Canterton had some of Darwin's thoroughness and patience. He had spent hours watching centipedes or the spore changes of myxomycetes on a piece of dead fir bough. He experimented with various compounds for the extinction of slugs, and studied the ways of wood-lice and earth worms. All very ridiculous, no doubt, in a man whose income ran into thousands a year. Sometimes he had been able to watch a shrew at work, or perhaps a queer snuffling sound warned him of the nearness of a hedgehog. This was the utilitarian side of his vigils. He was greatly interested, æsthetically and scientifically, in the sleep of plants and flowers, and in the ways of those particular plants whose loves are consummated at night, shy white virgins with perfumed bodies who leave the day to their bolder and gaudier fellows. Some moth played Eros. He studied plants in their sleep, the change of posture some of them adopted, the drooping of the leaves, the closing of the petals. All sorts of things happened of which the ordinary gardener had not the slightest knowledge. There were atmospheric changes to be recorded, frosts, dew falls and the like. Very often Canterton would be up before sunrise, watching which birds were stirring first, and who was the first singer to send a twitter of song through the grey gate of the dawn.

But as he walked through the fir woods towards Orchards Corner, his eyes were not upon the ground or turned to the things that were near him. Wisps of a red sunset still drifted about the west, and the trunks of the trees were barred in black against a yellow afterglow. Soon a full moon would be coming up. Heavy dew was distilling out of the quiet air and drawing moist perfumes out of the thirsty summer earth.

Blue dusk covered the heathlands beyond Orchards Corner, and the little tree-smothered house was invisible. A light shone out from a window as Canterton walked up the lane. Something white was moving in the dusk, drifting to and fro across the garden like a moth from flower to flower.

Canterton's hand was on the gate. Never before had night fallen for him with such a hush of listening enchantment. The scents seemed more subtle, the freshness of the falling dew indescribably delicious. He passed an empty chair standing on the lawn, and found a white figure waiting.

"I wondered whether you would come."

"I did not wonder. What a wash of dew, and what scents."

"And the stillness. I wanted to see the moon hanging in the fir woods."

"The rim will just be topping the horizon."

"You know the time by all the timepieces in Arcady."

"I suppose I was born to see and to remember."

They went into the little drawing-room that was Eve's despair when she felt depressed. This room was Mrs. Carfax's *lararium*, containing all the ugly trifles that she treasured, and some of the ugliest furniture that ever was manufactured. John Carfax had been something of an amateur artist, and a very crude one at that. He had specialised in genre work, and on the walls were studies of a butcher's shop, a fruit stall, a fish stall, a collection of brass instruments on a table covered with a red cloth, and a row of lean, stucco-fronted houses, each with a euonymus hedge and an iron gate in front of it. The carpet was a Kidderminster, red and yellow flowers on a black ground, and the chairs were upholstered in green plush. Every available shelf and ledge seemed to be crowded with knick-knacks, and a stuffed pug reclined under a glass case in the centre of a walnut chiffonier.

Eve understood her mother's affection for all this bric-à-brac, but tonight, when she came in out of the dew-washed dusk, the room made her shudder. She wondered what effect it would have on Canterton, though she knew he was far too big a man to sneer.

Mrs. Carfax, in black dress and white lace cap, sat in one of the green plush arm-chairs. She was always pleased to see people, and to chatter with amiable facility. And Canterton could be at his best on such occasions. The little old lady thought him "so very nice."

"It is so good of you to come down and see Eve's paintings. Eve, dear, fetch your portfolio. I am so sorry I could not come to Mrs. Canterton's garden party, but I have to be so very careful, because of my heart. I get all out of breath and in a flutter so easily. Do sit down. I think that is a comfortable chair."

Canterton sat down, and Eve went for her portfolio.

"My husband was quite an artist, Mr. Canterton, though an amateur. These are some of his pictures."

"So the gift is inherited!"

"I don't think Eve draws so well as her father did. You can see——"

Canterton got up and went round looking at John Carfax's pictures. They were rather extraordinary productions, and the red meat in the butcher's shop was the colour of red sealing wax.

"Mr. Carfax liked 'still life.'"

"Yes, he was a very quiet man. So fond of a littlelararium fishing—when he could get it. That is why he painted fish so wonderfully. Don't you think so, Mr. Canterton?"

"Very probably."

Eve returned and found Canterton studying the row of stucco houses with their iron gates and euonymus hedges. She coloured.

"Will the lamp be right, Eve, dear?"

"Yes, mother."

She opened her portfolio on a chair, and after arranging the lamp-shade, proceeded to turn over sketch after sketch. Canterton had drawn his chair to a spot where he could see the work at its best. He said nothing, but nodded his head from time to time, while Eve acted as show-woman.

Mrs. Carfax excelled herself.

"My dear, how queerly you must see things. I am sure I have never seen anything like that."

"Which, mother?"

"That queer, splodgy picture. I don't understand the drawing. Now, if you look at one of your father's pictures, the butcher's shop, for instance——"

Eve smiled, almost tenderly.

"That is not a picture, mother. I mean, mine. It is just a whim."

"My dear, how can you paint a whim?"

Eve glanced at Canterton and saw that he was absorbed in studying the last picture she had turned up from the portfolio. His eyes looked more deeply set and more intent, and he sat absolutely motionless, his head bowed slightly.

"That is the best classic thing I managed to do."

He looked at her, nodded, and turned his eyes again to the picture.

"But even there——"

"There is a film of mystery?"

"Yes."

"It was provoking. I'm afraid I have failed."

"No. That is Latimer. It was just what I saw and felt myself, though I could not have put it into colour. Show me the others again."

Mrs. Carfax knitted, and Eve put up sketch after sketch, watching Canterton's face.

"Now, I like that one, dear."

"Do you, mother?"

"Yes, but why have you made all the poplar trees black?"

"They are not poplars, mother, but cypresses."

"Oh, I see, cypresses, the trees they grow in cemeteries."

Canterton began to talk to Eve.

"It is very strange that you should have seen just what I saw."

"Is it? But you are not disappointed?"

His eyes met hers.

"I don't know anybody else who could have brought back Latimer like that. Quite wonderful."

"You mean it?"

"Of course."

He saw her colour deepen, and her eyes soften.

Mrs. Carfax was never long out of a conversation.

"Are they clever pictures, Mr. Canterton?"

"Very clever."

"I don't think I understand clever pictures. My husband could paint a row of houses, and there they were."

"Yes, that is a distinct gift. Some of us see more, others less."

"Do you think that if Eve perseveres she will paint as well as her father?"

Canterton remained perfectly grave.

"She sees things in a different way, and it is a very wonderful way."

"I am so glad you think so. Eve, dear, is it not nice to hear Mr. Canterton say that?"

Mrs. Carfax chattered on till Eve grew restless, and Canterton, who felt her restlessness, rose to go. He had come to be personal, so far as Eve's pictures were concerned, but he had been compelled to be impersonal for the sake of the old lady, whose happy vacuity emptied the room of all ideas.

"It was so good of you to come, Mr. Canterton."

"I assure you I have enjoyed it."

"I do wish we could persuade Mrs. Canterton to spend an evening with us. But then, of course, she is such a busy, clever woman, and we are such quiet, stay-at-home people. And I have to go to bed at ten. My doctor is such a tyrant."

"I hope I haven't tired you."

"Oh, dear, no! And please give my kind remembrance to Mrs. Canterton."

"Thank you. Good night!"

Canterton found himself in the garden with his hand on the gate leading into the lane. The moon had swung clear of the fir woods, and a pale, silvery horizon glimmered above the black tops of the trees. Canterton wandered on down the lane, paused where it joined the high road, and stood for a while under the dense canopy of a yew.

He felt himself in a different atmosphere, breathing a new air, and he let himself contemplate life as it might have appeared, had there been no obvious barriers and limitations. For the moment he had no desire to go back to Fernhill, to break the dream, and pick up the associations that Fernhill suggested. The house was overrun by his wife's friends who had come to stay for the garden party. Lynette would be asleep, and she alone, at Fernhill, entered into the drama of his dreams.

Mrs. Carfax and the little maid had gone to bed, and Eve, left to herself, was turning over her Latimer pictures and staring at them with peculiar intensity. They suggested much more to her than the Latimer gardens, being part of her own consciousness, and part of another's consciousness. Her face had a glowing pallor as she sat there, musing, wondering, staring into impossible distances with a mingling of exultation and unrest. Did he know what had happened to them both? Had he realised all that had overtaken them in the course of one short week?

The room felt close and hot, and turning down the lamp, Eve went into the narrow hall, opened the door noiselessly, and stepped out into the garden. Moonlight flooded it, and the dew glistened on the grass. She wandered down the path, looking at the moon and the mountainous black outlines of the fir woods. And suddenly she stopped.

A man was sitting in the chair that had been left out on the lawn. He started up, and stood bareheaded, looking at her half guiltily.

"Is it you?"

"I am sorry. I was just dreaming."

He hesitated, one hand on the back of the chair.

"I wanted to think——"

"Yes."

"Good night!"

"Good night!"

She watched him pass through the gate and down the lane. And everything seemed very strange and still.

CHAPTER XIV

MRS. CARFAX FINISHES HER KNITTING

It was a curious coincidence that Mrs. Carfax should have come to the end of her white wool that night, put her pins aside and left her work unfinished.

It was the last time that Eve heard the familiar clicking of the ivory pins, for Mrs. Carfax died quietly in her sleep, and was found with a placid smile on her face, her white hair neatly parted into two plaits, and her hands lying folded on the coverlet. She had died like a child, dreaming, and smiling in the midst of her dreams.

For the moment Eve was incredulous as she bent over the bed, for her mother's face looked so fresh and tranquil. Then the truth came to her, and she stood there, shocked and inarticulate, trying to realise what had happened. Sudden and poignant memories rose up and stung her. She remembered that she had almost despised the little old lady who lay there so quietly, and now, in death, she saw her as the child, a pathetic creature who had never escaped from a futile childishness, who had never known the greater anguish and the greater joys of those whose souls drink of the deep waters. A great pity swept Eve away, a choking compassion, an inarticulate remorse. She was conscious of sudden loneliness. All the memories of long ago, evoked by the dead face, rose up and wounded her. She knelt down, hid her face against the pillow, uttering in her heart that most human cry of "Mother."

Canterton was strangely restless that morning. Up at six, he wandered about the gardens and nurseries, and Lavender, who came to him about some special work that had to be done in one of the glasshouses, found him absent and vague. The life of the day seemed in abeyance, remaining poised at yesterday, when the moon hung over the black ridge of the fir woods by Orchards Corner. Daylight had come, but Canterton was still in the moonlight, sitting in that chair on the dew-wet grass, dreaming, to be startled again by Eve's sudden presence. He wondered what she had thought, whether she had suspected that he had been imagining her his wife, Orchards Corner their home, and he, the man, sitting there in the moonlight, while the woman he loved let down her dark hair before the mirror in their room.

If Lavender could not wake James Canterton, breakfast and Gertrude Canterton did. There were half a dozen of Gertrude's friends staying in the house, serious women who had travelled with batches of pamphlets and earnest-minded magazines, and who could talk sociology even at breakfast. Canterton came in early and found Gertrude scribbling letters at the bureau in the window. None of her friends were down yet, and a maid was lighting the spirit lamps under the egg-boiler and the chafing dishes.

"Oh, James!"

"Yes."

She was sitting in a glare of light, and Canterton was struck by the thinness of her neck, and the way her chin poked forward. She had done her hair in a hurry, and it looked streaky and meagre, and the colour of wet sand. And this sunny morning the physical repulsion she inspired in him came as a shock to his finer nature. It might be ungenerous, and even shameful, but he could not help considering her utter lack of feminine delicacy, and the hard, gaunt outlines of her face and figure.

"I want you to take Mrs. Grigg Batsby round the nurseries this morning. She is such an enthusiast."

"I'll see what time I have."

"Do try to find time to oblige me sometimes. I don't think you know how much work you make for me, especially when you find some eccentric way of insulting everybody at once."

"What do you mean, Gertrude?"

The maid had left the room, and Gertrude Canterton half turned in her chair. Her shoulders were wriggling, and she kept fidgeting with her pen, rolling it to and fro between her thumb and forefinger.

"Can't you imagine what people say when you put up wire fences, and have the gates locked on the day of our garden party?"

"Do you think that Whiteley would hold a party in his business premises?"

"Oh, don't be so absurd! I wonder why people come here."

"I really don't know. Certainly not to look at the flowers."

"Then why be so eccentrically offensive?"

"Because there are always a certain number of enthusiastic ladies who like to get something for nothing. I believe it is a feminine characteristic."

Mrs. Grigg Batsby came sailing into the room, gracious as a great galleon freighted with the riches of Peru. She was an extremely wealthy person, and her consciousness of wealth shone like a golden lustre, a holy effulgence that penetrated into every corner. Her money had made her important, and filled her with a sort of after-dinner self-satisfaction. She issued commands with playful regality, ordered the clergy hither and thither, and had a half humorous and half stately way of referring to any male thing as "It."

"My dear Mrs. Batsby, I have just asked James to take you round this morning."

The lady rustled and beamed.

"And is 'It' agreeable? I have always heard that 'Its' time is so precious."

"James will be delighted."

"Obliging thing."

Canterton was reserved and a little stiff.

"I shall be ready at eleven. I can give you an hour, Mrs. Batsby."

"'It' is really a humorist, Mrs. Canterton. That barbed wire! I don't think I ever came across anything so delightfully original."

Gertrude frowned and screwed her shoulders.

"I cannot see the humour."

"But I think Mrs. Batsby does. I have a good many original plants on my premises."

"Oh, you wicked, witty thing! And original sin?"

"Yes, it is still rather prevalent."

There was no queen's progress through the Fernhill grounds for Mrs. Grigg Batsby that morning, for by ten o'clock her very existence had been forgotten, and she was left reading the *Athenæum*, and wondering, with hauteur, what had become of the treacherous "It." Women like Mrs. Grigg Batsby have a way of exacting as a right what the average man would not presume to ask as a favour. That they should happen to notice anything is in itself a sufficient honour conferred upon the recipient, who becomes a debtor to them in service.

Canterton had drifted in search of Eve, had failed to find her, and was posing himself with various questions, when one of the under-gardeners brought him a letter. It had taken the man twenty minutes of hide and seek to trace Canterton's restless wanderings.

"Just come from Orchards Corner, sir. The young lady brought it."

"Miss Carfax?"

"No, sir, the young lady."

"I see. All right, Gibbs."

Canterton opened the letter, and stood reading it in the shade of a row of cypresses.

> "Dear Mr. Canterton,—Mother died in the night. She must have died in her sleep. I always knew it might happen, but I never suspected that it would happen so suddenly. It has numbed me, and yet made me think.
>
> "I wanted you to know why I did not come to-day.
>
> "Eve Carfax."

Canterton stood stock still, his eyes staring at Eve's letter. He was moved, strongly moved, as all big-hearted people must be by the sudden and capricious presence of Death. The little white-haired, chattering figure had seemed so much alive the night before, so far from the dark waters, with her child's face and busy hands. And Eve had written to tell him the news, to warn him why she had not come to Fernhill. This letter of hers—it asked nothing, and yet its very muteness craved more than any words could ask. To Canterton it was full of many subtle and intimate messages. She wanted him to know why she had stayed away, though she did not ask him to come to her. She had let him know that she was stricken, and that was all.

He put the letter in his pocket, forgot about Mrs. Grigg Batsby, and started for Orchards Corner.

All the blinds were down, and the little house had a blank and puzzled look. The chair that he had used the previous night still stood in the middle of one of the lawns. Canterton opened and closed the gate noiselessly, and walked up the gravel path.

Eve herself came to the door. He had had a feeling that she had expected him to come to her, and when he looked into her eyes he knew that he had not been wrong. She was pale, and quite calm, though her eyes looked darker and more mysterious.

"Will you come in?"

There was no hesitation, no formalism. Each seemed to be obeying an inevitable impulse.

Canterton remained silent. Eve opened the door of the drawing-room, and he followed her. She sat down on one of the green plush chairs, and the dim light seemed part of the silence.

"I thought you might come."

"Of course I came."

He put his hat on the round table. Eve glanced round the room at the pictures, the furniture and the ornaments.

"I have been sitting here in this room. I came in here because I realised what a ghastly prig I have been at times. I wanted to be hurt—and hurt badly. Isn't it wonderful how death strips off one's conceit?"

He leant forward with his elbows on his knees, a listener—one who understood.

"How I used to hate these things, and to sneer at them. I called them Victorian, and felt superior. Tell me, what right have we ever to feel superior?"

"We are all guilty of that."

"Guilty of despising other colour schemes that don't tone with ours. I suppose each generation is more or less colour-blind in its sympathies. Why, she was just a child—just a child that had never grown up, and these were her toys. Oh, I understand it now! I understood it when I looked at her child's face as she lay dead. The curse of being one of the clever little people!"

"You are not that."

She lay back and covered her eyes with her hands. It was a still grief, the grief of a pride that humbles itself and makes no mere empty outcry.

Canterton watched her, still as a statue. But his eyes and mouth were alive, and within him the warm blood seemed to mount and tremble in his throat.

"I think she was quite happy."

"Did I do very much?"

"She was very proud of you in her way. I could see that."

"Don't!"

"You are making things too deep, too difficult. You say, 'She was just a child.'"

Her hands dropped from her face.

"Yes."

"Your moods passed over her and were not noticed. Some people are not conscious of clouds."

She mused.

"Yes, but that does not make me feel less guilty."

"It might make you feel less bitter regret."

Canterton sat back in his chair, spreading his shoulders and drawing in a deep breath.

"Have you wired to your relatives?"

"They don't exist. Father was an only son, and mother had only one brother. He is a doctor in a colliery town, and one of the unlucky mortals. It would puzzle him to find the train fare. He married when he was fifty, and has about seven children."

"Very well, you will let me do everything."

He did not speak as a petitioner, but as a man who was calmly claiming a most natural right.

She glanced at him, and his eyes dominated hers.

"But—I can't bother you———"

"I can arrange everything. If you will tell me what you wish—what your mother would have wished."

"It will have to be very quiet. You see, we———"

"I understand all that. Would you like Lynette to come and see you?"

"Yes, oh, yes! I should like Lynette to come."

He pondered a moment, staring at the carpet with its crude patterning of colours, and when again he began to speak he did not raise his head to look at her.

"Of course, this will make no difference to the future?"

"I don't know."

"Tell me exactly."

"All mother's income dies with her. I have the furniture, and a little money in hand."

"Would you live on here, or take rooms?"

She hesitated.

"Perhaps."

His eyes rose to meet hers.

"I want you to stay. We can work together. I'm not inventing work for you. It's there. It has been there for the last two or three years."

He spoke very gently, and yet some raw surface within her was touched and hurt. Her mouth quivered with sensitive cynicism.

"A woman, when she is alone, must get money—somehow. It is bitter bread that many of us have to eat."

"I did not mean to make it taste bitter."

Her mouth and eyes softened instantly.

"You? No. You are different. And that——"

"Well?"

"And that makes it more difficult, in a way."

"Why should it?"

"It does."

She bent her head as though trying to hide her face from him. He did not seem to be conscious of what was happening, and of what might happen. His eyes were clear and far sighted, but they missed the foreground and its complex details.

He left his chair and came and stood by her.

"Eve."

"Yes?"

"Did I say one word about money? Well, let's have it out, and the dross done with. I ask you to be my illustrator, colour expert, garden artist—call it what you like. The work is there, more work than you can manage. I offer you five hundred a year."

She still hid her face from him.

"That is preposterous. But it is like you in its generosity. But I——"

"Think. You and I see things as no two other people see them. It is an age of gardens, and I am being more and more pestered by people who want to buy plants and ideas. Why, you and I could create some of the finest things in colour. Think of it. You only want a little more technical knowledge. The genius is there."

She appealed to him with a gesture of the hand.

"Stop, let me think!"

He walked to the window and waited.

Presently Eve spoke, and the strange softness of her voice made him wonder.

"Yes, it might be possible."

"Then you accept?"

"Yes, I accept."

CHAPTER XV

LYNETTE PUTS ON BLACK

Lynette had a little black velvet frock that had been put away in a drawer, because it was somewhat tarnished and out of fashion. Moreover, Lynette had grown three or four inches since the black frock had been made, and even a Queen of the Fairies' legs will lengthen. Over this dress rose a contest in which Lynette engaged both her mother and Miss Vance, and showed some of that tranquil and wise obstinacy that characterised her father.

Lynette appeared for lessons, clad in this same black frock, and Miss Vance, being a matter-of-fact and good-naturedly dictatorial adult, proceeded to raise objections.

"Lynette, what have you been doing?"

"What do you mean, Vancie?"

"Miss Vance, if you please. Who told you to put on that dress?"

"I told myself to do it."

"Then please tell yourself to go and change it. It is not at all suitable."

"But it is."

"My dear, don't argue! You are quite two years too old for that frock."

"Mary can let it out."

"Go and change it!"

Lynette had her moments of dignity, and this was an occasion for stateliness.

"Vancie, don't dare to speak to me like that! I'm in mourning."

"In mourning! For whom?"

"Miss Eve's mother, of course! Miss Eve is in mourning, and I know father puts on a black tie."

"My dear, don't be——"

"Vancie, I am going to wear this frock. You're not a great friend of Miss Eve's, like me. She's the dearest friend in the world."

The governess felt that the dress was eccentric, and yet that Lynette had a sentimental conviction that carried her cause through. Miss Vance happened to be in a tactless mood, and appealed to Gertrude Canterton, and to Gertrude the idea of Lynette going into mourning because a certain young woman had lost her mother was whimsical and absurd.

"Lynette, go and change that dress immediately!"

It was then that Canterton came out in his child. She was serenely and demurely determined.

"I must wear it, mother!"

"You will do nothing of the kind. The skirt is perfectly indecent."

"Why?"

"Your—your knees are showing."

"I am not ashamed of my knees."

"Lynette, don't argue! Understand that I will be obeyed. Go and change that dress!"

"I am very sorry, mother, but I can't. You don't know what great deep friends me and Miss Eve are."

Neither ridicule nor fussy attempts at intimidation had any effect. There was something in the child's eyes and manner that forbade physical coercion. She was sure in her sentiment, standing out for some ideal of sympathy that was fine and convincing to herself. Lynette appealed to her father, and to her father the case was carried.

He sided with Lynette, but not in Lynette's hearing.

"What on earth is there to object to, Gertrude?"

"It is quite absurd, the child wanting to go into mourning because old Mrs. Carfax is dead."

"Children have a way of being absurd, and very often the gods are absurd with them. The child shall have a black frock."

Gertrude twitched her shoulders, and refused to be responsible for Canterton's methods.

"You are spoiling that child. I know it is quite useless for me to suggest anything."

"You are not much of a child yourself, Gertrude. I am. That makes a difference."

Canterton had his car out that afternoon and drove twenty miles to Reading, with Lynette on the seat beside him. He knew, better than any woman, what suited the child, so Lynette had a black frock and a little Quaker bonnet to wear for that other child, Mrs. Carfax, who was dead.

Within a week Eve was back at Fernhill, painting masses of hollyhocks and sweet peas, with giant sunflowers and purple-spiked buddlea for a background. Perhaps nothing had touched her more than Lynette's black frock and the impulsive sympathy that had suggested it.

"I'm so sorry, Miss Eve, dear. I do love you ever so much more now."

And Eve had never been nearer tears, with Lynette snuggling up to her, one arm round her neck, and her warm breath on Eve's cheek.

It was holiday time, and Miss Vance's authority was reduced to the supervision of country walks, and the giving of a daily piano lesson. Punch, the terrier, accompanied them on their walks, and Miss Vance hated the dog, feeling herself responsible for Punch's improprieties. Her month's holiday began in a few days, and Lynette had her eyes on five weeks of unblemished liberty.

"Vancie goes on Friday. Isn't it grand!"

"But you ought not to be so glad, dear."

"But I am glad. Aren't you? I can paint all day like you, and we'll have picnics, and make daddy take us on the river."

"Of course, I'm glad you'll be with me."

"Vancie can't play. You see she's so very old and grown up."

"I don't think she is much older than I am."

"Oh, Miss Eve, years and years! Besides, you're so beautiful."

"You wicked flatterer."

"I'm not a flatterer. I'm sure daddy thinks so. I know he does."

Eve felt herself flushing, and her heart misgave her, for the lips of the child made her thrill and feel afraid. She had accepted the new life tentatively yet recklessly, trying to shut her eyes to the possible complexities, and to carry things forward with a candour that could not be questioned. She was painting the full opulence of one of the August borders, with Lynette beside her on a stool, Lynette who pretended to dabble in colours, but loved to make Eve talk. It was a day without wind; all sunlight, blue sky, and white clouds, with haze on the hills, and somnolence everywhere. Yet Eve was haunted by the sound of the splashing of the water in the Latimer gardens, a seductive but restless memory that penetrated all her thoughts.

"Wasn't it funny mother not wanting me to wear a black frock?"

"I don't know, dear."

"But why should she mind?"

Why, indeed? Eve found herself visualising Gertrude Canterton's sallow face and thin, jerky figure, and she felt chilled and discouraged. What manner of woman was this Gertrude Canterton, this champion of charities, this eager egoist, this smiler of empty smiles? Had she the eyes and ears, the jealous instincts of a woman? Did she so much as realise that the place she called her home hid the dust and dry bones of something that should have been sacred? Was she, in truth, so blindly self-sufficient, so smothered in the little vanities of little public affairs that she had forgotten she was a wife? If so, what an impossible woman, and what a menace to herself and others.

"Mother doesn't care for flowers, Miss Eve."

"Oh, how do you know?"

"I've never seen her pick any. And she can't arrange a vase. I've seen her try."

"But she may be fond of them, all the same."

"Then why doesn't she come out here with daddy?"

"Perhaps she has too much to do."

"But I never see her doing anything, like other people. I mean mending things, and all that. She's always going out, or writing letters, or having headaches."

Eve had a growing horror of letting Lynette discuss her mother. The child was innocent enough, but it seemed treacherous and unfair to listen, and made Eve despise herself, and shiver with a sense of nearness to those sexual problems that are covered with the merest crust of make-believe.

"Oh, here's Vancie!"

Eve glanced up and saw the governess approaching along the brick-paved path. Miss Vance was a matter-of-fact young person, but she was a woman, with some of the more feminine attributes a little exaggerated. She was suburban, orthodox as to her beliefs, absolutely without imagination, yet healthily inquisitive.

"Music, Lynette! What a nice bit of colour to paint, Miss Carfax."

"Quite Oriental, isn't it?"

These two women looked at each other, and Eve did not miss the apprizing and critical interest in Miss Vance's eyes. She was a little casual towards Eve, with a casualness that suggested tacit disapproval. The surface was hard, the poise unsympathetic.

"You ought to have good weather for your holiday. Where are you going?"

"Brighton!"

"Oh, Brighton!"

"We always go to Brighton!"

"A habit?"

"We are a family of habits."

She held out a large and rather red hand to Lynette, but Lynette was an individualist. She, too, understood that Miss Vance was a habit, a time-table, a schedule, anything but a playmate. They went off together, Miss Vance with a last apprizing glance at Eve.

One woman's attitude may have a very subtle influence on the mood of another. Most women understand each other instinctively, perhaps through some ancient sex-language that existed long before sounds became words. Eve knew quite well what had been exercising Miss Vance's mind, that she had been handling other people's intimacies, calculating their significance, and their possible developments. And Eve felt angry, rebellious, scornful, troubled. As a woman she resented the suggestiveness of this other woman's curiosity.

Ten minutes later, when Canterton strolled into the walled garden, he found Eve sitting idle, her hands lying in her lap. He saw her as a slim black figure posed in thought, with the border unfurled before her like some rich tapestry, with threads of purple and gold upon a ground of green.

She turned to him with a smile.

"Lynette has just gone."

He did not suspect that her smile was a defence and a screen.

"I hope the child does not interfere with your work."

"No. She lets me be quiet when something particularly delicate has to be done."

Canterton brought up a garden chair.

"Will it bother you if I take Lynette's place?"

"No."

"I think I am a little too big for her stool."

Eve resumed her painting, but she soon discovered that her attention flowed more strongly towards the man beside her than towards the flowers in the border. The tapestry kept blurring its outlines and shifting its colours, and she played with the work, becoming more and more absorbed in what Canterton was saying. And yet she was striving all the while to keep a space clear for her own individuality, so that her thoughts could move without merely following his.

Before very long she realised that she was listening to a thinker thinking aloud in the presence of the one woman who understood. He was so confident, so strong, so much above the hedgerows of circumstance, that she began to be more afraid for his sake than for her own. His words seemed ready to sweep her away into a rare and intimate future. It was ideal, innocent, almost boyish. He mapped out plans for her; talked of what they would create; declared for a yearly show of her pictures at Fernhill, and that her work must be made known in London. They could take the Goethe Gallery. Then he wanted pictures of the French and Italian gardens. She could make a tour, sketch the Riviera, paint rhododendrons and roses by the Italian lakes, and bring him back studies of Swiss meadows all blue and green and white in May or June. She had a future. He talked of it almost with passion, as though it were something that was very precious to his pride.

Eve's heart grew heavy. She began to feel a mute pity for Canterton and for herself. Her vision became so terribly clear and frank that she saw all that his idealist's eyes did not see, and felt all that he was too big and too magnanimous to feel. He did not trouble to understand the little world about him. Its perspective was not his perspective, and it had no knowledge of colour.

She became more and more silent, until this silence of hers was like a pool of water without a ripple, yet its passivity had a positive effect upon Canterton's consciousness. His eyes began to watch her face and to ask questions.

"Don't you see all this?"

"Oh, yes, I see it all!"

He was puzzled.

"Perhaps it does not strike you as real?"

She turned her face away.

"Don't you know that sometimes things may seem too real?"

He began to be absorbed into her silence of a minute ago. Eve made an effort, and picked up a brush. She guessed that something was happening in the heart of the man beside her, and she wondered whether the cold and conventional light of a more worldly wisdom would break in and enable him to understand.

"Eve!"

"Yes!"

She kept on with her work.

"Do you think that I have been talking like a fool?"

"Oh, no, not that."

"Then——"

She made herself meet his eyes.

"Sometimes the really fine things are so impossible. That's why life may be so sad."

CHAPTER XVI

JAMES CANTERTON AWAKES

Being an individualist, a man who had always depended upon himself, Canterton had very little of the social sensitiveness that looks cautiously to the right and to the left before taking a certain path. All his grown life, from his University days onwards, he had been dealing with big problems, birth, growth, decay, the eternal sacrament of sex, the beauty of earth's flowering. His vision went deep and far. His life had been so full of the fascination of his work that he had never been much of a social animal, as the social animal is understood in a country community. He observed trifles that were stupendously significant in the world of growth, but he had no mind for the social trifles round him. Had he had less brawn, less virility, less humour, it is possible that he would have been nothing more than an erudite fool, one of those pathetic figures, respected for its knowledge and pitied for its sappiness.

Canterton could convince men, and this was because he had long ago become a conviction to himself. It was not a self-conscious conviction, and that was why it had such mastery. It never occurred to him to think about the discretions and the formalities of life. If a thing seemed good to do, he did it; if it seemed bad, he never gave it a second thought. His men believed in him with an instinctive faith that would not suffer contradiction, and had Canterton touched tar, they would have sworn that the tar was the better for it, and Canterton's hands clean. He was so big, so direct, so just, so ready to smile and see the humour of everything. And he was as clean-minded as his child Lynette, and no more conscious than she was of the little meannesses and dishonourable curiosities that make most men and nearly all women hypocrites.

Canterton's eyes were open; but he saw only that which his long vision had taught him to see, and not the things that are focused by smaller people. That an idea seemed fine, and admirable, and good, was sufficient for him. He had not cultivated the habit of asking himself what other people might think. That was why such a man as Canterton may be so dangerous to himself and to others when he starts to do some big and unusual thing.

He knew now that he loved Eve Carfax. It was like the sudden rising of some enchanted island out of the sea, magical yet real, nor was he a gross beast to break down the boughs for the fruit and to crush the flowers for their perfumes. He had the atmosphere of a fine mind, and his scheme of values was different from the scheme of values recognised by more ordinary men. Perfumes, colours, beautiful outlines had spiritual and mystical meanings. He was not Pagan and not Christian, but a blend of all that was best in both.

To him this enchanted island had risen out of the sea, and floated, dew-drenched, in the pure light of the dawn. He saw no reason why he should bid so beautiful a thing sink back again and be lost under the waters. He had no desecrating impulses. Why should not two people look together at life with eyes that smiled and understood? They were harming no one, and they were transfiguring each other.

Canterton and his wife were dining alone, and for once he deliberately chose to talk to her of his work, and of his future plans. Gertrude would listen perfunctorily, but he was determined that she should listen. The intimate part of his life did not concern her, simply because she was no longer either in his personality or in his work. So little sympathy was there between them that they had never succeeded in rising to a serious quarrel.

"I am taking Miss Carfax into the business. I thought you might like to know."

So dead was her personal pride in all that was male in him, that she did not remember to be jealous.

"That ought to be a great opportunity for the girl."

"I shall benefit as much as she will. She has a very remarkable gift, just something I felt the need of and could not find."

"Then she is quite a discovery?"

Canterton watched his wife's face and saw no clouding of its complacency.

"She will be a very great help in many ways."

"I see. You will make her a kind of fashion-plate artist to produce new designs."

"Yes."

"I had thought of doing something for the girl. I had suggested to her that she might paint miniatures."

"I think I shall keep her pretty busy."

"I have only spoken to her once or twice, and she struck me as rather reserved, and stiff. I suppose she and Lynette———"

"She and Lynette get on wonderfully."

"So Miss Vance told me. And, of course, that black frock——I hope she doesn't spoil the child."

"Not a bit. She does her good."

"Lynette wants someone with plenty of common sense to discipline her. I think Miss Vance is really excellent."

"A very reliable young woman."

"She's not too sentimental and emotional."

They had finished dessert, and Gertrude Canterton went straight to her desk to write some of those innumerable letters that took up such a large part of her life. Letter-writing was one of her methods of self-expression, and her busy audacity was never to be repelled. She wrote to an infinite number of charitable institutions for their literature; to authors for autograph copies of their books to sell at bazaars; to actors for their signatures and photographs; to cartoonists for some sketch or other on which money might be raised for some charitable purpose; to tradesmen for free goods, offering them her patronage and a fine advertisement on some stall.

Canterton did not wait for coffee, but lit a pipe and strolled out into the garden, and walking up and down in a state of wonder, tried to make himself realise that he and Gertrude were man and wife.

Had the conversation really taken place? Had they exchanged those cold commonplaces, those absurd phrases that should have meant so much? Had he known Gertrude less well, he might have been touched by the appearance of the limitless faith she had in him, by her blind and serene confidence that was not capable of being disturbed. But he knew her better than that. He was hardly so much as a shadow in her life, and when a second shadow appeared beside hers she did not notice it. She seemed to have no sense of possession, no sexual pride. Her mental poise was like some people's idea of heaven, a place of beautiful and boundless indifference misnamed "sacred love," a state that was guilty of no preferences, no passions, no anguish, no divine despair.

And then there leapt in him a sudden and subtle exultation. This splendid comradeship that life was offering to him, what could be cried against it, what was there that could be condemned? It touched no one but their two selves, could hurt no one. The one woman who might have complained was being robbed of nothing that she desired. As for marriage, he had tried it, and saw that it served a certain need. For five years he had lived the life of a celibate, and the god in him was master of the beast. He thought no such thoughts of Eve. She was sunlight, perfumes, the green gloom of the woods, water shining in the moonlight, all the music that was and would be, all the fairy tales that had been told, all the ardour of words spoken in faith. She was one whose eyes could quench all the thirsts of his manhood. To be with her, to be hers, was sufficient.

Canterton was hardly conscious of the physical part of himself, as he took a path along one of the cypress walks, passed out by a wicket gate, and crossed the road into the fir woods. Dusk had fallen, but there was still a faint grey light under the trees, and there was no undergrowth, so that one would walk along the woodland aisles as along the aisles of a church. A feeling of exultation possessed him. The very stillness of the woods, the darkness that began to drown all distances, were personal and all-enveloping.

A light was shining in one of the lower windows of the little house at Orchards Corner when Canterton came to the gate at the end of the lane. He paused there, leaning his arms on the gate. The blind was up and the curtain undrawn, and he could see Eve sitting at a table, and bending over a book or writing a letter.

Canterton crossed the lawn and stood looking in at the lighted window. Eve was sitting at the table with her back towards him, and he saw the outline of her head, and the glow of the light upon her hair. She was wearing a blouse cut low at the throat, and he could see the white curve of her neck as she bent over the table. There were books and papers before her. She appeared to be reading and making notes.

He spoke her name.

"Eve!"

Her profile came sharply against the lamplight. Then she pushed the chair back, rose, and walked to the window. The lower sash was up. She rested her hands on the sill.

"Is it you?"

The light was behind her, and her face vague and shadowy, but he had a feeling that she was afraid. Her bare white forearms, with the hands resting on the window-sill, looked hard and rigid.

"Have I frightened you?"

"Perhaps—a little."

"I wanted to talk to you."

She did not answer him for the moment.

"I am all alone to-night."

"I thought you had the girl with you."

"I let her go down to the village."

He had come to her in a fog of mystical love, and through the haze of his vision her set and human face became the one real thing in the world. Her voice had a wounded sound, and she spoke as from a little distance. There was resistance here, a bleak dread of something, and yet a desire that what was inevitable should be understood.

"You'll forgive me?"

"Perhaps."

"I felt I must talk to you."

"As you talked yesterday morning?"

"Why not?"

"I—I thought perhaps that you had understood."

His full consciousness of all that was in his heart would not suffer him to feel such a thing as shame. But a great tenderness reached out to her, because he had heard her utter a cry of pain.

"Have I hurt you by coming here?"

She stared beyond him, trying to think.

"We were to live like good comrades, like fellow artists, were we not?"

"I told you how the future offers us beautiful friendship."

She made a little impatient movement.

"I knew it would be difficult while you were talking. And now you are making it impossible."

"I cannot see it."

"You are blind—with a man's blindness."

She leant her weight on her arms, and bending slightly towards him, spoke with peculiar gentleness.

"You look at the horizon, you miss the little things. Perhaps I am more selfish and near-sighted, for your sake, if not for my own. Jim, don't make me say what is hateful even to be thought."

It was the first time that she had called him by the familiar name, the name sacred to his lad's days, and to the lips of his men friends. He stood looking up at her, for she was a little above him.

"I like that word—Jim. But am I blind?"

"Hopelessly."

"Can it hurt either of us, this comradeship? Why, Eve, child, how can I talk all the boyish stuff to you? It's bigger, finer, less selfish than all that. I believe I could think of you as I think of Lynette—married some day to a good fellow——"

She broke in with sudden passion.

"No, you are wrong there—utterly wrong."

"Am I wrong—everywhere?"

"Can't you guess that it hurts terribly, all this? It's so impossible, and you won't see it. Let's get back—back to yesterday."

"Eve, is there ever a yesterday?"

She shivered and drew back a little.

"Jim, don't try to come too near me. You make me say it. You make me say the mean things."

"It's not physical nearness."

"Ah, you may think that! But you are forgetting all the little people."

"The little people! Are we to be little because they are shorter than we are? The neighbourhood knows me well enough."

She came forward again to the window with a kind of tender and stooping pity.

"Jim, how very innocent you are. Yes, I know—I know it is precious, and perilous. Listen! Supposing you were to lose Lynette—oh, why will you make me say the mean, hideous things?"

"Lose Lynette! Do you mean——"

"Jim, I am going to shut the window."

He raised an arm.

"Wait! Good God!"

"No, no! Good night!"

She closed the window, and dragged the curtains across it.

Canterton stood at gaze a moment, before walking away across the grass.

Eve was listening, stricken, yet trying not to feel afraid.

---

*

CHAPTER XVII

LYNETTE INTERPOSES

At such a parting of the ways, Canterton's elemental grimness showed itself. He was the peasant, sturdy, obstinate, steady-eyed, ready to push out into some untamed country, and to take and hold a new domain. For under all his opulent culture and his rare knowledge lay the patient yet fanatical soul of the peasant. He was both a mystic and a child of the soil, not a city dweller, mercurial and flippant, a dog at the heels of profit and loss.

Eve had talked of the impossible, but when he took Lynette by the hand and went down with her into the Wilderness, Canterton could not bring himself to play the cynic. Sitting in the bracken, and watching Lynette making one of her fairy fires, he felt that it was Eve's scepticism that was impossible, and not his belief in a magnanimous future. He was so very sure of himself that he felt too sure of other people. His name was not a thing to be made the sport of rumour. Men and women had worked together before now; and did the world quarrel with a business man because he kept a secretary or a typist? Moreover, he believed himself to be different from the average business man, and what might have meant lust for one spoke of a sacrament to the other.

"Daddy, why didn't Miss Eve come yesterday?"

"She had work at home, Princess."

"And to-day too?"

"It seems so."

"Why don't we go and see her, then?"

"Why not?"

The mouth of the child had offered an inspiration. Was it possible to look into Lynette's eyes and be scared by sinister suggestions? Why, it was a comradeship of three, not of two. They were three children together, and perhaps the youngest was the wisest of the three.

"Lynette, come here, old lady! Miss Eve thinks of going away."

"Miss Eve going away?"

"Yes."

"Oh, no, daddy, how can she?"

"Well, one has only to get into a train, even if it be a train of thought."

Lynette was kneeling between her father's knees.

"I'll ask her not to go."

"You might try it."

"Oh, yes, let's! Let's go down to Orchards Corner now—at once!"

Eve had been suffering, suffering for Canterton, Lynette and herself. She saw life so clearly now—the lights and shadows, the sunlit spaces, the sinister glooms, the sharp, conventional horizons. Canterton did not know how much of the woman there was in her, how very primitive and strong were the emotions that had risen to the surface of her consciousness. The compact would be too perilous. She knew in her heart of hearts that the youth in her desired more than a spiritual dream, and she was trying to harden herself, to build up barriers, to smother this splendid thing, this fire of the gods.

She had taken her work out into the garden, and was striving against a sense of perfunctoriness and the conviction that the life at Fernhill could not last. She had more than hinted at this to Canterton, bracing herself against his arguments, and against all the generous steadfastness of his homage that made the renunciation harder for her to bear.

And now an impetuous tenderness attacked her at white heat, a thing that came with glowing hair and glowing mouth, and arms that clung.

Lynette had run up the lane in front of Canterton, and Lynette was to make Eve Carfax suffer.

"Oh, Miss Eve, it isn't true, is it?"

"What isn't true, dear heart?"

"That you are going right away."

Eve felt a thickness at the throat. All that was best in life seemed conspiring to tempt and to betray her.

"I may have to go, dear."

"But why—why, when we love you so much? Aren't you happy?"

"When I am with you, yes. But there are all sorts of things that you wouldn't understand."

"Oh, but I could!"

"Perhaps some day you will."

"But, Miss Eve, you won't really go, will you?"

Canterton came in at the white gate, and Eve's eyes reproached him over the glowing head of the child. "It is ungenerous of you," they said, "to let the child try and persuade me."

She hugged Lynette with sudden passion.

"I don't want to go, dear, but some big devil fairy is telling me I shall have to."

She was shy of Canterton, and ready to hide behind the child, for there was a grim purposefulness about his idealism that made her afraid. His eyes hardly left her, and, though they held her sacred, they would have betrayed everything to the most disinterested of observers.

"I thought I would work at home on some of these sketches."

"And Lynette and I have been making a fire in the Wilderness. We missed you."

Eve felt stifled. Lynette was looking up into her face, and she was fingering the white lace collar round the child's neck. She knew that she must face Canterton. It was useless to try to shirk the challenge of such a man.

"Isn't it close to-day? Lynette, dear, what about some raspberries? I'm so thirsty."

"Where are they, Miss Eve? Aren't they over?"

"No, they are a late kind. You know, round behind the house. Ask Anne for a dish."

"I'll get a rhubarb leaf, and pick the biggest for you."

"Dear heart, we'll share them."

Lynette ran off, and they were left alone together. Canterton had brought up a deck chair, and was looking over some of Eve's sketches that lay in a portfolio on the grass. His silence tantalised her. It was a force that had to be met and challenged.

"I sent Lynette away because I wanted to speak to you."

He laid the sketch aside and sat waiting.

"Why did you let her come to tempt me?"

"Because I can see no real reason why you should go."

Her eyes became appealing.

"Oh, how blind! And you let the child rush at me, let me feel her warm arms round my neck. It was not fair to me, or to any of us."

"To me it did not seem unfair, because I do not think that I am such a criminal."

"I know; you are so sure of yourself. But if you thought that the child would persuade me, you were very much deceived. It has made me realise more than anything else that I cannot go on with the life at Fernhill."

He bent forward in his chair.

"Eve, I tell you from my heart that you are wrong. I want you to be something of a mother to Lynette. I can give the man's touches, but my fingers are not delicate enough to bring out all the charm. Think, now."

She sat rigid, staring straight before her.

"I have made up my mind."

"It is the privilege of wise minds to change, Eve. I want you as well as Lynette."

"Don't make me suffer. Do you think it is easy?"

"Let me show you——"

"No, no! If you try to persuade me, I shall refuse to listen."

And then silence fell on both of them, for Lynette returned with a large rhubarb leaf holding a little mountain of red fruit.

CHAPTER XVIII

EVE SPEAKS OUT

Eve felt very restless that evening, and with seeming illogicality went up to her room at the old-time hour of nine.

The day had been close and sultry, and the bedroom still felt hot after the hours of scorching sunlight on the tiles. Eve drew the curtains back, and opened the casement to its widest, for the upper windows were still fitted with the old lead-lights. The sill was deep, nearly a foot and a half broad, and Eve half lay and half leant upon it while the night air streamed in.

And what a night! All jet and silver; for the moon was up over the fir woods, just as on the night when her mother died. The stillness was the stillness of a dawn where no birds sing. The nightingale had long been mute, and the nightjar preferred the oak woods in the clayland valleys. Eve's ears could not snatch a single sound out of that vast motionless landscape, with its black woods and mysterious horizons.

The silence made her feel lonely, eerily lonely, like a sensitive child lost in a wood. She remembered how she had started awake at night sometimes, terrified by this horror of loneliness, and crying out "Mother, mother!" It was absurd that the grown woman should feel like the child, and yet she found herself hungering for that little placid figure with its boring commonplaces and amiable soft face. What a prig she had been! She had let that spirit of superiority grow in her, forgetting that the hands that were always knitting those foolish woollen superfluities had held and comforted her as a child. Now, in the white heat of an emotional ordeal, she missed the nearness of that commonplace affection. What a mistake it was to be too clever; for when the heart ached, one's cleverness stood by like a dreary pedagogue, helpless and dumb.

The stillness! She wished those dim stars would send down astral rain, and patter on this roof of silence. The sound of dripping water would be welcome. Yes, and those Latimer fountains, were they still murmuring under the cypresses, or did not the spirit of sage economy turn off the water-cocks and shut down the sluices? Life! It, too, was so often a shutting down of sluices. The deep waters had to be tamed, dammed back, kept from pouring forth as they desired. Modern conventional life was like a canal with its system of locks. There were no rapids, no freshets, no impetuous cataracts. You went up, steadily, respectably, lock by lock; you came down steadily, and perhaps just as respectably. In between was the gliding monotony of the long stretches between artificial banks, with either a religious tow-rope or a puffing philosopher to draw you.

She suffered on account of the stillness and this atmosphere of isolation, and yet the nearness of some very human incident was as a stabbing pain compared to a dull ache. Leaning there over the window-sill, with the moonlight glimmering on the lozenged glass in the lattices, she knew that she was looking towards Fernhill and all that it represented. Lynette, the child; the great gardens, that wide, free spacious, colour-filled life; Canterton's comradeship, and even more than that. The whole future quivered on one sensitive thread. A breeze could shake it away as a wind shakes a dewdrop from the web of a spider.

She told herself that Canterton must have realised by now the impossible nature of the position he was asking her to assume. If he only would go back to the yesterday of a month ago, and let that happy, workaday life return! But then, would she herself be content with that? She had sipped the wine of Tristan and Isoult, and the magic of it was in her blood.

Her thoughts had come to this point, when something startled her. She had heard the latch of the gate click. There was a man's figure standing in the shade of a holly that grew close to the fence.

Eve was not conscious of any fear, only of an intense curiosity—a desire to know whether she was on the brink of some half foreseen crisis. It might be a tramp, it might be the man who came courting her girl Anne; but Anne had gone to bed with a headache an hour before Eve had come to her own room.

In spite of these other possibilities, she felt prophetically convinced that it was Canterton. She did not move away from the window, knowing that the man, whoever he was, must have seen the outline of her head and shoulders against the light within. Her heart was beating faster. She could feel it as she leant with her bosom pressing upon the window-sill.

She knew Canterton the moment he moved out into the moonlight, and, crossing the grass, came and stood under her window. He was bareheaded, and his face, as he looked up at her, gave her an impression of pallid and passionate obstinacy.

"I had to come!"

She felt a flutter of exultation, but it was the exultation of tragedy.

"Madman!"

"No, I am not mad. It is the sanest moment of my life."

"Then all the rest of the world is mad. Supposing—supposing the girl is still awake. Supposing——Oh, there are a hundred such suppositions! You risk them, and make me risk them."

"Because I am so sure of myself. I take the risk to promise you a homage that shall be inviolate. Am I a fool? Do you think that I have no self-control—that I shall ever cause this most spiritual thing to be betrayed? I tell you I can live this life. I can make it possible for you to live it."

Eve raised herself on her elbows, and seemed to be listening. There was the same stillness everywhere, the stillness that had been broken by Canterton's voice.

She leant out and spoke to him in an undertone.

"I will come down. I suppose I must let you say all that you have to say."

She put out the light and felt her way out of the room and down the stairs into the hall. Her brain felt as clear as the sky out yonder, though the turmoil in her heart might have been part of the darkness through which she passed. Unlocking and unbolting the door, she found Canterton waiting.

"You are making me do this mad thing."

She had not troubled to put on a hat, and her face was white and clear and unhidden. Its air of desperate and purposeful frankness struck him. Her eyes looked straight at his, steadily and unflinchingly, with no subtle glances, no cunning of the lids.

"Let's go down to the woods. Come!"

She spoke as though she had taken command of the crisis, snatched it out of his strong hands. And Canterton obeyed her. They went down the lane in the high shadow of the hedgerows and across the main road into the fir woods, neither of them uttering a word.

Eve paused when they had gone some two hundred yards into the woods. The canopy of boughs was a black vaulting, with here and there a crevice where the moonlight entered to fall in streaks and splashes upon the tree trunks and the ground. On every side were the crowding fir boles that blotted out the distance and obscured each other. The woodland floor was covered deep with pine needles, and from somewhere came the smell of bracken.

"Now, let me hear everything."

He appeared a little in awe of her, and for the moment she was the stronger.

"I have told you all that there is to tell. I want you to be the bigger part of my life—the inward life that not another soul knows."

"Not even Lynette?"

"She is but a child."

Eve began to walk to and fro, and Canterton kept pace with her.

"Let's be practical. Let's be cold, and sure of things. You want me to be a spiritual wife to you, and a spiritual mother to Lynette?"

"Yes."

"And you think you can live such a life?"

"I know I can."

She was smiling, the strange, ironical, half-exultant smile of a love that is not blind.

"You are sure of yourself. Let me ask you a question. Are you sure of me?"

He looked at her searchingly in the dim light.

"Eve, I am not vain enough to ask you whether——"

"Whether I care?"

"You have said it."

She paused, gazing at the ground.

"Is a man so much slower than a woman?"

"Sometimes one does not dare to think——"

"But the woman knows without daring."

He stood silently before her, full of that devout wonder that had made him such a watcher in Nature's world.

"Then, surely, child——"

Her face and eyes flashed up to him, and her hands quivered.

"Don't call me child! Haven't you realised that I am a woman?"

"The one woman."

"There, it is all so impossible! And you don't understand."

He spoke gently, almost humbly.

"Why is it impossible? What is it that I don't understand?"

"Oh, dear man, must I show you everything? This is why it is impossible."

Her arms went out and were round his neck. Her mouth was close to his. In the taking of a breath she had kissed him, and he had returned the kiss, and his arms were round her.

"Jim, don't you understand now? I care too much. That is why it is impossible."

CHAPTER XIX

AN HOUR IN THE FIR WOODS

The warm scent of the fir woods was about them, and a darkness that made their very thoughts seem secret and secure. They were the lovers of some ancient tale wandering in an old forest of enchantments, seeing each other's faces pale and yearning in the dim light under the trees.

Eve rested against Canterton's outspread arm, her head upon his shoulder, as they wandered to and fro between the tall trunks of the firs. They were like ghosts gliding side by side, for the carpet of pine needles deadened the sound of their footsteps, and they spoke but little, in voices that were but murmurs.

For a brief hour they were forgetting life and its problems, letting self sink into self, surrendering everything to an intimate exultation in their nearness to each other. Sometimes they would pause, swayed by some common impulse, and stand close together, looking into each other's eyes.

They spoke to each other as a man and woman speak but once or twice in the course of a lifetime.

"Dear heart, is it possible that this is you?"

"Am I not flesh and blood?"

"That you should care!"

"Put your hand here. Can you not feel my heart beating?"

He would slip his hand under her head, draw her face to his, and kiss her forehead, mouth and eyes. And she would sigh with each kiss, closing her eyes in a kind of ecstasy.

"Did you ever dream of me?"

"Often."

"It sounds like a child's question. Strange—I wonder if our dreams crossed. Did you ever dream while I was at Latimer?"

"Nearly every night."

"And I of you. And all through the day you were with me. I felt you standing beside me. That's why I painted Latimer as I did."

Canterton had moments of incredulity and of awe. He would stand motionless, holding Eve's hands, and looking down into her face.

"It is very wonderful—very wonderful!"

His man's awe made her smile.

"What a boy you are!"

"Am I?"

"I love you like that. And yet, really, you are so strong and masterful. And I could trust you utterly, only——"

"Only?"

"You, and not myself. Oh, if we could never wake again!"

A plaintive note came into her voice. She was beginning to think and to remember.

"Eve!"

"Ah, that name!"

"Is it so impossible now?"

She reached up and gripped his wrist.

"Don't spoil this! Oh, don't spoil it! It will have to last us both for a lifetime. Take me back, dear; it is time."

He felt a relaxing of her muscles as though she had suddenly grown faint and hesitating.

"Not yet."

"Yes, now. I ask it of you, Jim."

They began to wander back towards the road, and sometimes a shaft of moonlight struck across their faces. Their exultation weakened, the wings of their flight together were fluttering back towards the ground.

"Eve, to-morrow——"

She turned her face to his and spoke with a whispering vehemence.

"There can be no to-morrow."

"But, dear heart!"

"I could not bear it. Have pity on me, Jim. And remember——"

They saw the white road glimmering beyond the black fir trunks. Eve paused. They stood for some moments in silence.

"Say good-bye to me here."

"I will say good night."

"Oh, my dearest—my dear!"

He held her very close, and she felt the strength of his great arms. The breath seemed to go out of her body, her eyes were closed.

"Now, let me go."

He released her, and she stepped back just a little unsteadily, but trying to smile.

"Good-bye! Go back now."

She turned, went out of the wood, and crossed the moonlit road. It lay between them like some dim river of the underworld. And Canterton was left standing in the gloom of the fir woods.

CHAPTER XX

NIGHT AND A CHILD

Eve relocked the door of the cottage, and stood in the darkness of the hall, trying to realise all that had happened.

It was like coming back out of a dream, save that the dream remained as a compelling and fateful reality, a power, a parting of the ways, a voice that cried "Explicit!" Her clarity of vision returned as she stood there in the darkness. There was only one thing to be done, whatever anguish the doing of it might cause her.

Yet for the moment she shrank from this renunciation, this surrender of the things that made life desirable, this going forth into a world of little poverties, little struggles, little sordid anxieties. It was hard, very hard to leave this spacious existence, this corner of the earth where beauty counted, and where she had been so happy in her work. Why had he made it so hard for her? And yet, though she was in pain, her heart could not utter any accusation against him. He had misunderstood her, and she had had to ruin everything by showing him the truth.

This part of her life was ended, done with; and Eve repeated the words to herself as she felt her way up the stairs and into her room. She lit the candle and stood looking about her. How cold and small and matter-of-fact the place seemed. The whole atmosphere had changed, and the room no longer felt like hers. The bedclothes were neatly turned back, but she knew that she would never sleep in that bed again. It was absurd—the very idea of sleep, when to-morrow——

She sat on the bed awhile, thinking, forcing herself to make those plans that shape themselves like hot metal poured into a mould. A hunger for physical activity seized her. She might falter or break down if she did too much thinking. Feeling under the bed, she dragged out a light leather valise, and opening it began to tumble out a collection of tissue paper, odd pieces of dress material, ribbons and scraps of lace. The very first thing she saw when she went to open the hanging cupboard was the big straw sun-hat she had worn at Latimer and Fernhill. That inanimate thing, hanging there, sent a shock of pain through her. She felt things as a sensitive child feels them, and sorrow was more than a mere vague regret.

Presently the valise was packed, and her more personal trifles collected into a handbag. She began to open all the drawers and cupboards, to sort her clothes and lay them on the bed. Once or twice she went downstairs to fetch books or something she specially needed, pausing outside the maid's door to listen, but the girl was fast asleep. Eve sorted out all her Fernhill and Latimer studies, tied them up in brown paper, and addressed them to Canterton. Her portfolios, paint boxes, and a few odd canvases she packed into a stout parcel, labelled them, and carried them up to her room.

Then, as to money. Eve kept it locked in a little drawer in a cabinet that stood in a corner of her bedroom, and though she went to count it, she knew what was there, almost to the last penny. Seventeen pounds, thirteen shillings and ninepence. There were a pass and cheque-book also, for she had a hundred pounds in a bank at Reading, Canterton having paid her the first instalment of her salary. Eve felt loath to consent to thinking of the money as her own. Perhaps she would return it to him, or keep it untouched, a sentimental legacy left her by this memorable summer.

It was one in the morning when she lit a fresh candle and went down into the dining-room to write letters. The first was to a local house-agent and auctioneer, stating that she was leaving Basingford unexpectedly, and that the maid would deposit the keys of Orchards Corner at his office, and desiring him to arrange for a sale of all her furniture. The next letter was to Anne, the maid. Eve enclosed a month's wages and an odd sum for current expenses, and asked her to pack two trunks and have them taken to the station and sent to the luggage office at Waterloo. Eve drew out a list of the things that were to be packed. Everything else was to be disposed of at the sale.

Then came the letter to James Canterton.

> "I am taking the only course that seems open to me, and believe me when I say that it is best for us both.
>
> "I am leaving you the Latimer pictures, and all the studies I made at Fernhill. You will find them here, on the table, wrapped up and addressed to you.
>
> "I am giving Mr. Hanstead orders to sell all the furniture.
>
> "It is probable that I shall try to make some sort of career for myself in London.
>
> "Perhaps I will write to you, when my new life is settled. Don't try to see me. I ask you, from my heart, not to do that.
>
> "Kiss Lynette, and make her think the best you can.
>
> "I am sealing this and leaving it here for you with the pictures.

"EVE."

A great restlessness came upon her when she had completed all these preparations, and she felt a desire to rush out and end the last decisive phase of her life at Fernhill. She hunted up a local time-table, and found that the first train left Basingford at half-past six in the morning. The earliness of the hour pleased her. The valise and bag were not very heavy, and she could walk the two miles to the station before the Basingford people were stirring.

Then a new fear came upon her, the fear that Canterton might still be near, or that he would return. A book that she picked up could not hold her attention, and the old bent cane rocking-chair that she had used so often when she was feeling like a grown child, made her still more restless. She went over the house, reconsidering everything, the clothes laid out on the bed, the furniture she was to leave, and whether it would be worth her while to warehouse the rather ancient walnut-cased piano, with its fretwork and magenta-coloured satin front. She wrote labels, even started an inventory, but abandoned it as soon as she entered her mother's room.

The watch on her dressing-table told her that it was five-and-twenty minutes to four. Dawn would be with her before long, and the thought of the dawn made the little house seem dead and oppressive. She put on a pair of stout shoes, and, letting herself out into the garden, made her way to the orchard at the back of the house.

It had grown very dark before the dawn, and the crooked apple trees were black outlines against an obscure sky. They made her think of bent, decrepit, sad old men. The grass had been scythed a month ago, and the young growth was wet with dew. Everything was deathly still. Not a leaf moved on the trees. It was like a world of the dead.

She walked up and down for a long while before a vague greyness began to spread along the eastern horizon. A bird twittered. The foliage of the trees changed from black to an intense greyish blue. The fruit became visible—touches of gold, and maroon, and green. Eve could see the dew on the grass, the rust colour of the tiles on the roof, the white frames of the windows. A rabbit bolted across the orchard, and disappeared through the farther hedge.

She stood watching, wondering, and her wonder went out to the man who had caused her to suffer this pain. How had the night gone with him? What was he doing? Had he slept? Was he suffering? And then the first flush of rose came into the pearl grey east. Great rays of light followed, diverging, making the clouds a chaos of purple and white. Presently Eve saw the sun appear, a glare of gold above the fir woods.

She returned to the house, put on her hat and coat, made sure that she had her watch and purse, and carried her bag and her valise downstairs. She would leave Orchards Corner at half-past five, and there was time for a meal before she went. The girl had left dry wood ready on the kitchen stove. Eve boiled the kettle, made tea, and ate her breakfast at the kitchen table, listening all the while for any sound of the girl moving overhead. But the silence of the night still held. No one was to see her leave Orchards Corner.

Eve had wondered whether James Canterton was suffering. It is not given to many of us to feel acutely, or to travel beyond the shallows of an emotional self-pity, but Canterton had much of the spirit of the Elizabethans—men built for a big, adventurous, passionate play. He had slept no more than Eve had done, and had spent most of the night walking in the woods and lanes and over the wastes of heather and furze. He, too, was trying to realise that this experience was at an end, that a burning truth had been shown him—that they had flown too near the sun, and the heat had scorched their wings.

Yet his mood was one of rebellion. He was asking why and wherefore, thrusting that masterful creativeness of his against the conventional barriers that the woman had refused to challenge. For the first time his vitality was running in complete and tumultuous opposition to the conventional currents that had hardly been noticed by him till his will was defied. The scorn of theory was upon him, and he felt the strong man's desire to brush the seeming artificiality aside. Had he not made self-restraint his own law, and was he to herd with men who put their signatures openly to the sexual compact, and broke their vows in secret?

Eve was afraid, not only for herself, but for him and for Lynette. But, good God! had he ever intended to force her to sacrifice herself, to defy society, or to enter into a conspiracy of passion? Was it everything or nothing with such a woman? If so, she had shown a touching magnanimity and wisdom, and uttered a cry that was heroic. But he could not believe it; her pleading that this love of theirs was mad and impossible. It was too pathetic, her confessing that she could not trust herself. He was strong enough to be trusted for them both. The night had made everything more sacred. He would refuse to let her sacrifice their comradeship.

Canterton, too, saw the dawn come up, and the sun appear as a great splash of gold. He was standing on the south-east edge of the Wilderness, with the gloom of the larch wood behind him, and as the sun rose, its level rays struck on the stream in the valley, and the deep pool among the willows where the water lay as black and as still as glass.

A clear head and a clean body. The whim that seized him had logic and symbolism. He walked down over the wet grass to the pool among the willows, where a punt lay moored to a landing stage, and a diving board projected over the water. Canterton stripped and plunged, and went lashing round and round the pool, feeling a clean vigour in his body, as his heart and blood answered the cold sting of the water.

It was half-past six when he made his way back up the hill to the gardens. A glorious day had come, and the dew still sparkled on the flowers. Wandering across the lawns he saw an auburn head at an open window, and a small hand waving a towel.

"Daddy, I'm coming—I'm coming!"

He looked up at her like a man who had been praying, and whose eyes saw a sign in the heavens.

"Hallo! Up with the lark!"

"Let's go down to the Wilderness."

"Come along, Queen Mab."

"I've only got to put my frock on."

"You're just the very thing I want."

CHAPTER XXI

THE WOMAN'S EYES IN THE EYES OF A CHILD

Lynette asked her father to tell her a story. They were walking through the wet bracken on the edge of the larch wood, Canterton holding the child's hand.

"Presently, little Beech Leaf. A good fairy is talking to me, and I must listen."

"Then I'll keep ever so quiet till she's done."

Canterton had looked into the eyes of the child, and had seen the woman's eyes, Eve's eyes, in the child's. For Eve's eyes had been like the eyes of Lynette, till he, the man, had awakened a more primitive knowledge in them. He remembered how it had been said that the child is a finer, purer creation than either the man or the woman, and that the sex spirit is a sullying influence, blurring the more delicate colours; and Eve had had much of the child in her till he, in all innocence, had taught her to suffer.

A great pity overtook him as he looked down at Lynette, and wondered how he would feel if some blind idealist were ever to make her suffer. His pity showed him what love had failed to discover. He understood of a sudden how blind, how obstinate, and over-confident he must have seemed to Eve. He had killed all the child in her, and aroused the woman, and then refused to see that she had changed.

"I have been torturing her."

His compassion was touched with shame.

"You are making it so impossible."

That cry of hers had a new pathos. It was she who had suffered, because she had seen things clearly, while he had been too masterful, too sure of himself, too oblivious of her youth. One could not put the language of Summer into the mouth of Spring. It was but part of the miracle of growth that he had been studying all these years. Certain and inevitable changes had to occur when the sun climbed higher and the sap rose.

Canterton paused while they were in the thick of the larch wood.

"Lynette, old lady!"

"Yes, daddy?"

"The fairy has just said that we ought to go and see Miss Eve."

"What a sensible fairy. Yes, do let's go. She may let me see her do her hair."

Canterton smiled. He meant to carry Lynette on his shoulders into the garden of Orchards Corner, to hold her up as a symbol and a sign, to betray in the child his surrender. Assuredly it was possible for them to be healed. He would say, "Let's go back into yesterday. Try and forgive me for being blind. We will be big children together, you and I, with Lynette."

Some warning voice seemed to speak to him as they entered the lane, questioning this plan of his, throwing out a vague hint of unexpected happenings. He heard Eve saying good-bye over yonder among the fir trees. She had refused to say good night.

He set Lynette down under the hedge, and spoke in a whisper.

"We'll play at hide and seek. I'll go on and see if I can find her."

"Yes. I'll hide, and jump out when you bring her into the lane, daddy."

"That's it."

He wondered what sort of night Eve had spent, and his eyes were instinctively towards her window as he walked up the path to the house. His ring was answered almost immediately. The little, bunchy-figured maid stood there, looking sulky and bewildered.

"Is Miss Carfax in?"

The girl's eyes stared.

"No, she ain't. She's gone to London, and ain't coming back."

"When did she go?"

"Must have been this morning before I was up. She'd 'ad 'er breakfast, and written me a letter. She's left everything to me, and I don't know which way to turn. There's luggage to be packed and sent off to London, and the house to be cleaned, and the keys to be taken to Mr. Hanstead's. I'm fair bothered, sir. I ain't going to sleep 'ere alone, and my 'ome's at Croydon. Maybe my young man's mother will take me in."

"If not some of my people can."

"Miss Carfax left a letter for you, sir."

"Let me have it."

The girl went into the dining-room, and Canterton followed her. The letter was lying on the parcel that contained the Latimer and Fernhill pictures. He went to the window, broke the seal, and read Eve's letter.

The girl watched him, and he was conscious of her inquisitive eyes. But his face betrayed nothing, and he acted as though there were nothing wonderful about this sudden flight.

"Miss Carfax did not tell you that she was expecting the offer of work in London?"

"No, sir."

"I see. She has been sent for rather hurriedly. A very fine situation I believe. You had better follow out her orders. This parcel is for me."

He took it under his arm, went to the front door, and called Lynette.

"No hide and seek this morning."

He wanted the girl to see Lynette, but he did not want Lynette to hear the news.

"Isn't she in?"

Canterton met her as she came up the path.

"Not at home, Princess, and Anne's as busy as can be, and I've got this parcel to carry back."

"What's in it, daddy?"

"Pictures."

And he felt that he carried all the past in those pictures.

Lynette wondered why he walked so fast, and why his face looked so quiet and funny. She had to bustle her slim legs to keep up with him, and he had nothing whatever to say.

"What a hurry you're in, daddy."

"I have just remembered I've got to go down to the village before breakfast. And, by George! here's something I have forgotten to give to Lavender. Will you take it, old lady, while I go down to the village?"

"Yes, daddy."

He gave her an envelope he had in his pocket. It contained nothing but some seeds he had taken from a plant a few days ago, but the ruse served.

Canterton left the parcel of pictures at one of the lodges. It took him just twenty minutes to reach Basingford station, for he had to walk through the village after taking some of the field paths at a run. A solitary milk cart stood in the station yard, and a clattering of cans came from the up platform. Canterton entered the booking office, glanced into the waiting-room, and strolled through to the up platform. There was no Eve. The place was deserted, save for a porter and the driver of the milk cart, who were loading empty cans on to a truck.

Canterton remembered that he had a freight bill in his pocket, and that he owed the railway company three pounds and some odd silver. He called the porter.

"Gates!"

The man came at once, touching his cap.

"Is the goods office open?"

"Yes, sir."

"I have a bill I owe them. Anyone there to take the money?"

"They'll be ready for that, Mr. Canterton."

"Oh, by the way, Gates, did Miss Carfax catch her train all right? I mean the early one?"

"The lady from Orchards Corner, sir?"

"Yes. You know Miss Carfax."

"To be sure. She was earlier than me, sir, and down here before I got the booking office swept out."

"That's good. I'm glad she caught it. Good morning, Gates."

"Good morning, sir."

As Canterton walked across to the goods office, he found himself confessing to a bitter and helpless sense of defeat. He had made this woman suffer, and it seemed out of his power now even to humble himself before her. She had fled out of his life, and appealed to him not to follow her—not to try and see her. It was better for them both, she had said, to try and forget, but he knew in his heart of hearts that it would never be forgotten.

PART II

CHAPTER XXII

BOSNIA ROAD

It is a suggestive thought that the characteristic effects of our execrable climate have nowhere shown themselves more forcibly than in the atmosphere of the London suburbs. That these suburbs are in some subtle respects the results of our melancholy grey skies no one can doubt. Even the raw red terraces scattered among the dingier and more chastened rows of depressed houses, betray a futile and rather boisterous attempt to introduce a butcher-boy cheerfulness into a world of smuts and rain. The older, sadder houses have taken the tint of their surroundings. They have been poised all these years between the moil and fog of the city, and a countryside that was never theirs, a countryside that is often pictured as wrapped in eternal June, but which for nine months out of the twelve knows grey gloom, mud, and rain.

Their activities alone must have given the modern English such cheerfulness as they possess, while the climate has made them a nation of grumblers. Perhaps the Industrial Revolution saved us from our weather.

Coal and power came and gave us something to do. For what has been the history of England, but the watering of the blood of those who came to dwell in her. It is not necessary to thank the Roman rule for the decadence of the Britons, when their Saxon conquerors in turn sank into sodden, boorish ignorance. The Normans brought red blood and wine to the grey island, but by the fifteenth century the blend had become coarse, cruel, and poor. With the Elizabethans, half the world rushed into new adventure and romance, and England revived. But once again the grey island damped down the ardour, the enthusiasms and the energies of the people. During the first half of the eighteenth century, the population was stagnant, the country poor, coarse and apathetic. Then King Coal arose, and lit a fire for us, and a few great men were born. We found big things to do, and were renewed, in spite of our climate. Yet the question suggests itself, will these subtle atmospheric influences reassert themselves and damp us down once more in the centuries that are to come?

Eve Carfax had elected to live in a London suburb, and had chosen Highbury, perhaps because of childish recollections of pleasant half holidays spent there with a friend of her mother's, afternoons when muffins and fancy cakes had made bread and butter superfluous, and a jolly old lady had discovered occasional half-crowns in her purse. Eve had taken two rooms in a little red house in Bosnia Road. Why it should have been called Bosnia Road she could not imagine. Each house had a front door with stained glass and a brass letter box, a tiny strip of front garden faced with a low brick wall topped by an iron railing, an iron gate, and a red tiled path. All the houses looked exactly alike. Most of them had a big china bowl or fern pot on a table or pedestal in the window of the ground floor room. There was no originality either in the texture or the draping of the curtains. None of the houses in Bosnia Road had any of that sense of humour possessed by the houses in a village street. There were no jocular leerings, no rollicking leanings up against a neighbour, no expressive and whimsical faces. They were all decently alike, respectably uniform, staring at each other across the road, and never moved to laughter by the absurd discovery that the architect had unconsciously perpetrated a cynical lampoon upon the suburban middle classes.

When one is fighting for the bare necessities of life, one is not conscious of monotony. For Eve, as an adventuress, it had been a question of gaining a foothold and a grip on a ledge with her fingers, and her energies had been concentrated on hanging to the vantage she had gained. She had had good luck, and the good luck had been due to Kate Duveen.

Kate Duveen was an old friend, and Eve had hunted her out in her Bloomsbury lodgings on the third day of her coming to London. They had been at school together before the Carfaxes had taken a cottage in Surrey. Kate Duveen was a brown, lean, straight-backed young woman, with rather marked eyebrows, firm lips, and shrewd eyes. She was a worker, had always been a worker, and though more than one man had wanted to marry her, she had no desire either for marriage or for children. She was a comrade rather than a woman. There was no colour either in her face or in her dress, and her one beauty was her hair. She had a decisive, unsentimental way with her, read a great deal, attended, when possible, every lecture given by Bernard Shaw, and managed to earn about two hundred pounds a year.

It was Kate Duveen who had introduced Eve into Miss Champion's establishment.

Miss Champion's profession was somewhat peculiar, though not unique. Her offices were in a turning off Oxford Street, and were situated on the first floor. She was a kind of universal provider, in the sense that she supplied by means of her female staff, the various needs of a cultured and busy public. She equipped men of affairs and politicians with secretaries and expert typists. There were young women who could undertake mechanical drawing or architects' plans, illustrate books, copy old maps and drawings, undertake research work in the British Museum, design fashion plates, supervise entertainments, act as mistress of the revels at hydros and hotels. Miss Champion had made a success of the venture, partly because she was an excellent business woman, and partly because of her personality.

Snow-white hair, a fresh face, a fine figure. These points had helped. She was very debonair, yet very British, and mingled an aristocratic scent of lavender with a suggestion of lawn sleeves. Her offices had no commercial smell. Her patrons were mostly dilettanti people with good incomes, and a particular hobby, authorship, public affairs, china, charities. Miss Champion had some imagination, and the wisdom of a "Foresight." Good form was held sacred. She was very particular as to that old-fashioned word "deportment." Her gentlewomen had to be gentlewomen, calm, discreet, unemotional, neat looking lay figures, with good brains and clever hands.

Kate Duveen had introduced Eve to Miss Champion, and Miss Champion happened to have a vacancy that Eve could fill. A patron was writing a book on mediæval hunting, and wanted old pictures and woodcuts copied. Another patron was busy with a colour-book called "Ideal Gardens," and was asking for fancy plates with plenty of atmosphere. There was some hack research work going begging, and designs for magazine covers to be submitted to one or two art editors, and Eve was lucky enough to find herself earning her living before she had been two weeks in town.

The day's routine did not vary greatly. She breakfasted at a quarter to eight, and if the weather was fine she walked a part or even the whole of the way to Miss Champion's, following Upper Street and Pentonville Road, and so through Bloomsbury, where she picked up Kate Duveen. If it was wet she trammed, but she detested the crush for a seat, being a sensitive individualist with a hatred of crowds, however small. Some days she spent most of her time in the Museum reading-room, making notes and drawings which she elaborated afterwards at her desk at Miss Champion's. If she had nothing but illustrating to do or plates to paint she spent all the day at the office. They were given an hour for lunch, and Eve and Kate Duveen lunched together, getting some variety by patronising Lyons, the Aerated Bread Company, and the Express Dairy in turn. After these very light lunches, and much more solid conversations, came four or five hours more work, with half an hour's interval for tea. Eve reached Bosnia Road about half past six, often glad to walk the whole way back after the long sedentary hours. At seven she had meat tea, the meat being represented by an egg, or three sardines, or two slices of the very smallest tongue that was sold. Her landlady was genteel, florid, and affable, with that honeyed affability that is one of the surest signs of the humbug. She was a widow, and the possessor of a small pension. Her one child, a gawk of a youth, who was an under-clerk somewhere in the City, had nothing to recommend him. He was a ripening "nut," and advertised the fact by wearing an enormous collar, a green plush Homburg hat, a grey suit, and brown boots on the Sabbath. Some time ago he had bought a banjo, but when Eve came to Bosnia Road, his vamping was as discordant and stuttering as it could be. He had a voice, and a conviction that he was a comedian, and he could be heard exclaiming, "Put me among the Girls," a song that always moved Eve to an angry disgust. Now and again he met her on the stairs, but any egregious oglings on his part were blighted before they were born.

"She's a suffragette! I know 'em."

That was what he said to his mother. Had he been put among such girls, his little, vain Georgy Porgy of a soul would have been mute and awed.

Eve's evenings were very lonely. Sometimes Kate Duveen came up from Bloomsbury, but she was a busy woman, and worked and read most nights. If it was fine, Eve went out and walked, wandering round outside Highbury Fields, or down the quiet Canonbury streets, or along Upper Street or Holloway Road. It was very dismal, and these walks made her feel even more lonely than the evenings spent in her room. It seemed such a drifting, solitary existence. Who cared? To whom did it matter whether she went out or stayed at home? As for her sitting-room, she could not get used to the cheap red plush suite, the sentimental pictures, the green and yellow carpet, the disastrous ornaments, the pink and green tiles in the grate. Her own workaday belongings made it a little more habitable, but she felt like Iolanthe in a retired licensed victualler's parlour.

The nights when Kate Duveen came up from Bloomsbury were full of intelligent relief. They talked, argued, compared ambitions and ideals, and trusted each other with intimate confessions. Several weeks passed before Eve gave Kate Duveen some account of that summer at Fernhill, and Kate Duveen looked stiff and hard over it, and showed Canterton no mercy.

"It always seems to be a married man!"

Eve was up in arms on the other side.

"He was different."

"Oh, yes, I know!"

"Kate, I hate you when you talk like this."

"Hate me as much as you like, my dear, you will see with my eyes some day. I have no patience with men."

Eve softened her passionate partisanship, and tried to make her friend understand.

"Till one has gone through it one does not know what it means. After all, we can't stamp out Nature, and all that is beautiful in Nature. I, for one, don't want to. It may have made me suffer. It was worth it, just to be loved by that child."

"Children are not much better than little savages. Don't dream sentimental dreams about children. I remember what a little beast I was."

"There will always be some part of me that you won't understand, Kate."

"Perhaps. I've no patience with men—selfish, sexual fools. Let's talk about work."

CHAPTER XXIII

LIFE AND LETTERS

Saturday afternoons and Sundays gave the pause in Eve's week of scribbling and reading, and drawing at desk and table. She was infinitely glad of the leisure when it came, only to discover that it often brought a retrospective sadness that could not be conjured away.

Sometimes she went to a matinée or a concert on Saturday afternoon, alternating these breaks with afternoons of hard work. For the Fernhill days, with their subsequent pain and restlessness had left her with a definite ambition. She regarded her present life as a means to an end. She did not intend to be always a scribbler of extracts and a copier of old woodcuts, but had visions of her own art spreading its wings and lifting her out of the crowd. She tried to paint on Sundays, struggling with the atmosphere of Bosnia Road, and attempting to make use of the north light in her back bedroom, while she enlarged and elaborated some of the rough sketches in her sketch book. Her surroundings were trite and dreary enough, but youth and ardour are marvellous torch-bearers, and many a fine thing has been conceived and carried through in a London lodging-house. She had plans for hiring a little studio somewhere, or even of persuading Mrs. Buss, her landlady, to let her have a makeshift shed put up in the useless patch of back garden.

When she looked back on the Fernhill days, they seemed to her very strange and wonderful, covered with a bloom of mystery, touched with miraculous sunlight. She hoped that they would help her to do big work. The memories were in her blood, she was the richer for them, even though she had suffered and still suffered. Now that she was in London the summer seemed more beautiful than it had been, nor did she remind herself that it had happened to be one of those rare fine summers that appear occasionally just to make the average summer seem more paltry. When she had received a cheque for some eighty pounds, representing the sum her furniture had brought her after the payment of all expenses, she had written to Canterton and returned him the hundred pounds he had paid her, pleading that it irked her memories of their comradeship. She had given Kate Duveen's address, after asking her friend's consent, and in her letter she had written cheerfully and bravely, desiring Canterton to remember their days together, but not to attempt to see her.

"You will be kind, and not come into this new life of mine. I am not ashamed to say that I have suffered, but that I have nothing to regret. Since I am alone, it is best that I should be alone. You will understand. When the pain has died down, one does not want old wounds reopened.

"I think daily of Lynette. Kiss her for me. Some day it may be possible for me to see her again."

Three weeks passed before Kate Duveen handed Eve a letter as they crossed Russell Square in the direction of Tottenham Court Road. It was a raw, misty morning, and the plane trees, with their black boles and boughs, looked sombre and melancholy.

"This came for you."

She saw the colour rise in Eve's face, and the light that kindled deep down in her eyes.

"Not cured yet!"

"Have I asked to be cured?"

Eve read Canterton's letter at her desk at Miss Champion's. It was a longish letter, and as she read it she seemed to hear him talking in the fir woods below Orchards Corner.

"DEAR EVE,—I write to you as a man who has been humbled, and who has had to bear the bitterness of not being able to make amends.

"I came to see things with your eyes, quite suddenly, the very morning that you went away. I took Lynette with me to Orchards Corner, to show her as a symbol of my surrender. But you had gone.

"I was humbled. And the silence that shut me in humbled me still more.

"I did not try to discover things, though that might have been easy.

"As to your leaving Fernhill so suddenly, I managed to smother all comment upon that.

"You had been offered, unexpectedly, a very good post in London, and your mother's death had made you feel restless at Orchards Corner. That was what I said.

"Lynette talks of you very often. It is, 'When will Miss Eve come down to see us?' 'Won't she spend her holidays here?' 'Won't you take me to London, daddy, to see Miss Eve?'

"As for this money that you have returned to me, I have put it aside and added a sum to it for a certain purpose that has taken my fancy. I let you return it to me, because I have some understanding of your pride.

"I am glad, deeply glad, that good luck has come to you. If I can serve you at any time and in any way, you can count on me to the last breath.

"I am a different man, in some respects, from the man I was three months ago. Try to realise that. Try to realise what it suggests.

"If you realise it, will you let me see you now and again, just as a comrade and a friend?

"Say yes or no.

"JAMES CANTERTON."

Eve was bemused all day, her eyes looking through her work into infinite distances. She avoided Kate Duveen, whose unsentimental directness would have hurt her, lunched by herself, and walked home alone to Bosnia Road. She sat staring at the fire most of the evening before she wrote to Canterton.

"Your letter has made me both sad and happy, Jim. Don't feel humbled on my account. The humiliation should be mine, because neither the world nor I could match your magnanimity.

"Sometimes my heart is very hungry for sight of Lynette.

"Yes, I am working hard. It is better that I should say 'No.'

"EVE."

Four days passed before Kate handed her another letter.

"Perhaps you are right, and I am wrong. If it is your wish that I should not see you, I bow to it with all reverence.

"Do not think that I do not understand.

"Some day, perhaps, you will come to see Lynette. Or I could bring her up to town and leave her at your friend's for you to find her. I promise to lay no ambuscades. When you have gone I can call for her again.

"I should love her better because she had been near you."

Kate Duveen was hard at work one evening, struggling, with the help of a dictionary, through a tough book on German philosophy, when the maid knocked at her door.

"What is it, Polly?"

The girl's name was Ermentrude, but Kate persisted in calling her Polly.

"There's a gentleman downstairs, miss. 'E's sent up 'is card. 'E wondered whether you'd see 'im."

Kate glanced at the card and read, "James Canterton."

She hesitated a moment.

"Yes, I will see him. Ask him up."

Her hard, workaday self had risen as to a challenge. She felt an almost fierce eagerness to meet this man, to give him battle, and rout him with her truth-telling and sarcastic tongue. Canterton, as she imagined him, stood for all the old man-made sexual conveniences, and the social makeshift that she hated. He was the big, prejudiced male, grudging a corner of the working world to women, but ready enough to make use of them when his passions or his sentiments were stirred.

When he came into the room she did not rise from the table, but remained sitting there with her books before her.

"Miss Duveen?"

"Yes. Will you shut the door and sit down?"

She spoke with a rigid asperity, and he obeyed her, but without any sign of embarrassment or nervousness. There was just a subtle something that made her look at him more intently, more interestedly, as though he was not the sort of man she had expected to see.

"It is Mr. Canterton of Fernhill, is it not?"

"Yes."

She was merciless enough to sit there in silence, with her rigid, watchful face, waiting for him to break the frost. Her mood had passed suddenly beyond mere prejudice. She felt the fighting spirit in her piqued by a suspicion that she was dealing with no ordinary man.

He sat in one of her arm-chairs, facing her, and meeting her eyes with perfect candour.

"I am wondering whether I must explain——"

"Your call, and its object?"

"Yes."

"I don't think it is necessary. I think I know why you have come."

"So much the better."

She caught him up as though he were assuming her to be a possible accomplice.

"I may as well tell you that you will get nothing out of me. She does not live here."

"Perhaps you will tell me what you imagine my object to be."

"You want Eve Carfax's address."

For the first time she saw that she had stung him.

"Then I can assure you you are wrong. I have no intention of asking for it. It is a point of honour."

She repeated the words slowly, and in a quiet and ironical voice.

"A point of honour!"

She became conscious of his smile, a smile that began deep down in his eyes. It angered her a little, because it suggested that his man's knowledge was deeper, wiser, and kinder than hers.

"I take it, Miss Duveen, that you are Eve's very good friend."

"I hope so."

"That is exactly why I have come to you. Understand me, Eve is not to know that I have been here."

"Thank you. Please dictate what you please."

"I will. I want you to tell me just how she is—if she is in really bearable surroundings?"

Kate's eyes studied him over her books. Here was something more vital than German philosophy.

"Mr. Canterton, I ought to tell you that I know a little of what has happened this summer. Not that Eve is a babbler——"

"I am glad that you know."

"Really. I should not have thought that you would be glad."

"I am. Will you answer my question?"

"And may I ask what claim you have to be told anything about Eve?"

He answered her quietly, "I have no right at all."

A smile, very like a glimmer of approval, flickered in her eyes.

"You recognise that. Wasn't it rather a pity———"

"Miss Duveen, I have not come here to justify anything. I wanted a fine, working comradeship, and Eve showed me, that for a particular reason, it was impossible. Till I met her there was nothing on earth so dear to me as my child, Lynette. When Eve came into my life she shared it with the child. Is it monstrous or impertinent that I should desire to know whether she is in the way of being happy?"

Kate saw in him a man different from the common crowd of men, and Eve's defence of him recurred to her. His frankness was the frankness of strength. His bronzed head, with its blue eyes and generous mouth began to take on a new dignity.

"Mr. Canterton, I am not an admirer of men."

"You should have studied flowers."

"Thank you. I will answer your question. Eve is earning a living. It is not luxury, but it is better than most women workers can boast of. She works hard. And she has ambitions."

He answered at once.

"I am glad of that. Ambition—the drive of life, is everything. You have given me good news."

Kate Duveen sat in thought a moment, staring at the pages of German philosophy.

"Mr. Canterton, I'm interested. I am going to be intrusive. Is it possible for a man to be impersonal?"

"Yes, and no. It depends upon the plane to which one has climbed."

"You could be impersonally kind to Eve."

"I think that I told you that I am very fond of my youngster, Lynette. That is personal and yet impersonal. It is not of the flesh."

She nodded her head, and he rose.

"I will ask you to promise me two things."

"What are they?"

"That if Eve should wish to see Lynette, I may leave the child here, and call for her again after Eve has gone?"

Kate considered the point.

"Yes, that's sensible enough. I can see no harm in it. And the other thing?"

"That if Eve should be in trouble at any time, you will promise to let me know?"

She looked at him sharply.

"Wait! It flashed across your mind that I am waiting for my opportunity? You are descending to the level of the ordinary man whom you despise. I asked this, because I should want to help her without her knowing."

Kate Duveen stood up.

"You scored a hit there. Yes, I'll promise that. Of course, Eve will never know you have been here."

"I rely on you there. Men are apt to forget that women have pride."

She held out a hand to him.

"There's my pledge. I can assure you that I had some bitter things under my tongue when you came in. I have not said them."

"They could not have hurt more than some of my own thoughts have hurt me. That's the mistake people make. The whip does not wound so much as compassion."

"Yes, that's true. A blow puts our egotism in a temper. I'll remember that!"

"I am glad that you are Eve's friend."

Kate Duveen stood looking down into the fire after Canterton had gone.

"One must not indulge in absolute generalities," she thought. "Men can be big—sometimes. Now for this stodgy old German."

CHAPTER XXIV

EVE'S SENSE OF THE LIMITATIONS OF LIFE

Eve's London moods began to be more complex, and tinged with discontent.

The homelessness of the great city depressed her. She felt its chaotic vastness, knowing all the while that there was ordered purpose behind all its seeming chaos, and that all its clamour and hurry and crowded interplay of energies had meaning and significance. There were some few men who ruled, and who perhaps understood, but the crowd! She knew herself to be one of the crowd driven forward by necessity that barked like a brisk sheepdog round and about a drove of sheep. Sometimes her mood was one of passionate resentment. London was so abominably ugly, and the eternal and seemingly senseless hurry tired her brain and her eyes. She had no cockney instincts, and the characteristic smells of the great city aroused no feeling of affectionate satisfaction. The odours connected with burnt oil and petrol, pickle and jam factories, the laying of asphalt, breweries, Covent Garden, the Meat Market, had no familiar suggestiveness. Nor did the shops interest her for the moment. She had left the more feminine part of herself at Fernhill, and was content to wear black.

London gave her to the full the "damned anonymous" feeling, making her realise that she had no corner of her very own. The best of us have some measure of sensitive egoism, an individuality that longs to leave its personal impress upon something, even on the sand by the seashore, and London is nothing but a great, trampled cattle-pen, where thousands of hoofs leave nothing but a churn of mud. People build pigeon houses in their back yards, or train nasturtiums up strings, when they live down by Stepney. Farther westwards it is the sensitive individualism that makes many a Londoner country mad. The self-conscious self resents the sameness, the crowding mediocrity, the thousands of little tables that carry the same food for thousands of people, the thousands of seats in indistinguishable buses and cars, the thousands of little people who rush on the same little errands along the pavements. For there is a bitter uniformity even in the midst of a luxurious variety, when the purse limits the outlook, and a week at Southend-on-Sea may be the wildest of life's adventures.

Eve began to have the country hunger very badly. Autumn had gone, and the winter rains and fogs had set in, and her thoughts went back to Fernhill as she remembered it in summer, and as she imagined it in autumn. What a green and spacious world she had left. The hush of the pine woods on a windless day, when nothing moved save an occasional squirrel. The blaze of roses in June. The blue horizons, the great white clouds sailing, the purple heathland, the lush valleys with their glimmerings of water! What autumn pictures rose before her, tantalising her sense of beauty. She saw the bracken turning bronze and gold, the larch woods changing to amber, the maples and beeches flaming pyres of saffron, scarlet and gold. Those soft October mornings with the grass grey with dew, and the sunlight struggling with white mists. She began to thirst for beauty, and it was a thirst that picture galleries could not satisfy.

Even that last letter of hers to Canterton toned with her feeling of cramped finality. She had written "No," but often her heart cried "Yes," with an impetuous yearning towards sympathy and understanding. What a masterful and creative figure was his when she compared him with these thousands of black-coated men who scuttled hither and thither on business that was someone else's. She felt that she could be content with more spiritual things, with a subtle perfume of life that made this City existence seem gross and material and petty.

Her daily walks from Highbury to Miss Champion's helped to accentuate the tendencies of these moods of hers. Sometimes Kate Duveen would walk a great part of the way back with her, and Eve, who was the more impressionable of the two, led her friend into many suggestive discussions. Upper Street, Islington, saddened her. It seemed so typical of the social scheme from which she was trying to escape.

"Doesn't all this make you feel that it is a city of slaves?"

"That depends, perhaps, on one's digestion."

"But does it? These people are slaves, without knowing it. Things are thrust on them, and they think they choose."

"Nothing but suggestion, after all."

"Look, I will show you."

Eve stopped in front of a picture shop.

"What's your opinion of all that is in there?"

"Hopeless, sentimental tosh, of course. But it suits the people."

"It is what is given them, and they take it. There is not one thing in that window that has any glimmer of genius, or even of distinction."

"What do you expect in Islington?"

"I call it catering for slaves, and that worst sort of slavery that does not realise its own condition."

They walked on and passed a bookshop. Eve turned back.

"Look again!"

Kate Duveen laughed.

"I suppose, for instance, that annoys you?"

She pointed to a row of a dozen copies of a very popular novel written by a woman, and called "The Renunciation."

"It does annoy me."

"That toshy people rave over tosh! A friend of mine knows the authoress. She is a dowdy little bourgeoise who lives in a country town, and they tell me that book has made her ten thousand pounds. She thinks she has a mission, and that she is a second George Eliot."

"Doesn't it annoy you?"

"Why should it? Fools' money for a fool's tale. What do you expect? I suppose donkeys think that there is nothing on earth like a donkey's braying!"

"All the same, it helps my argument, that these people are slaves, only capable of swallowing just what is given them."

"I dare say you are right. We ought to change a lot of this in the next fifty years!"

"I wonder. You see, he taught me a good deal, in the country, about growth and evolution, and all that has come from the work of Mendel, De Vries and Bates. He doesn't believe in London. He called it an orchid house, and said he preferred a few wholesome and indigenous weeds."

"All the more reason for believing that this sort of London won't last. We shall get something better."

"We may do, if we can get rid of some of the politicians."

It was about this time that Eve began to realise the limitations of her present life, and to look towards a very problematical future. It seemed more than probable that "means to the end" would absorb all her energies, and that the end itself would never arrive. She found that her hack work was growing more and more supreme, and that she had no leisure for her own art. She felt tired at night, and on Saturdays she was more tempted to go to a theatre than to sit at home in Bosnia Road and try to produce pictures. Sundays, too, became sterile. She stayed in bed till ten, and when she had had breakfast she found the suburban atmosphere weighing upon her spirits. Church bells rang; decorous people in Sunday clothes passed her window on their way to church or chapel. If she went for a walk she everywhere met a suggestion of respectable relaxation that dominated her energies and sent her home depressed and cynical. As for the afternoons, they were spoilt for her by Mr. Albert Buss's banjo, though how his genteel mother reconciled herself to banjo-playing on a Sunday Eve could not imagine. Three or four friends joined him. Eve saw them saunter in at the gate, with dandy canes, soft hats, and an air of raw doggishness. They usually stared hard at her window. The walls and floors were thin, and Eve could hear much that they said, especially when Mrs. Buss went out for her afternoon walk, and left the "nuts" together. They talked about horse-racing and girls.

"She's a little bit of all right!"

"You bet!"

"Ain't afraid to go home in the dark!"

"What sort of young lady's the lodger, Bert? Anything on?"

"Not my style. Ain't taking any!"

"Go on, you don't know how to play up to a girl. I'd get round anything in London."

Just about dusk Mr. Buss and his friends sauntered out on love adventures, and Mrs. Buss sat down at her piano and sung hymns with a sort of rolling, throaty gusto. Eve found it almost unendurable, so much so that she abandoned the idea of trying to use her Sundays at Bosnia Road, and asked Kate Duveen to let her spend the day with her in Bloomsbury.

On weekdays, when it happened to be fine and not too cold, she and Kate would spend the twenty minutes after lunch in St. James's Park, sitting on a seat and watching the irrepressible sparrows or the machinations of a predatory cat. The bare trees stood out against the misty blue of the London horizon, and even when the sun shone, the sunlight seemed very thin and feeble. Other people sat on the seats, and read, or ate food out of paper bags. Very rarely were these people conversational. They appeared to have many thoughts to brood over, and nothing to say.

Kate Duveen had noticed a change in Eve. There was a different look in her eyes. She, too, was less talkative, and sometimes a cynical note came into her voice.

"What are you thinking about?"

"Was I thinking?"

"You haven't said anything for five minutes."

"One can be conscious of an inner atmosphere, without calling it thought."

"Much fog about?"

Some of the sensitive fire came back into Eve's eyes.

"Kate, I am horribly afraid of being crushed—of becoming one of the crowd. It seems to me that one may never have time to be oneself."

"You mean that the effort to live leaves no margin?"

"That's it. I suppose most of us find in the end that we are the slaves of our hack work, and that our ambitions die of slow starvation. Think of it. Think of the thousands of people who had something to do or say, and were smothered by getting a living."

"It's the usual thing. I felt it myself. I nearly gave up; but I set my teeth and scratched. I've determined to fight through—to refuse to be smothered. I'll get my independence, somehow."

"Sometimes I feel that I must throw up all this bread and butter stuff, and stake everything on one adventure."

"Then don't do it. I have seen people try it. Ninety-nine out of the hundred come back broken, far worse off than they were before. They're humble, docile things for the rest of their lives. Carry the harness without a murmur. Not a kick left, I know."

"I have been thinking of a secretaryship. It might give me more leisure—breathing space——"

"Try it!"

"Are you being ironical?"

"Not a bit. I'll speak to Miss Champion. She's not a bad sort, so long as you are tweety-tweety and never cause any complications."

"I wish you would speak to her."

"I will."

Kate Duveen had peculiar influence with Miss Champion, perhaps because she was not afraid of her. Miss Champion thought her a very sound and reliable young woman, a young woman whose health and strength seemed phenomenal, and who never caused any friction by going down with influenza, and so falling into arrears with her work. Kate Duveen had made herself a very passable linguist. She could draw, type, scribble shorthand, do book-keeping, write a good magazine article or edit the ladies' page of a paper. Every year she spent her three weeks' holiday abroad, and had seen a good deal of Germany, Italy and France. Miss Champion always said that Kate Duveen had succeeded in doing a very difficult thing—combining versatility with efficiency.

"So Miss Carfax would like a secretaryship? I suppose you think her suitable?"

"There is not a safer girl in London."

"I understand you. Because she has looks."

"I think you can ignore them. She is very keen to get on."

"Very well. I will look out for something to suit her."

"I'm much obliged to you, Miss Champion. I believe in Eve Carfax."

CHAPTER XXV

HUGH MASSINGER, ESQ.

Hugh Massinger, Esq., was a person of some distinction as a novelist, and an æsthetic dabbler in Gothic mysteries. His novel "The Torch Lily" had had a great sale, especially in the United States, where an enthusiastic reviewer had compared it to Flaubert's "Salambo." Hugh Massinger had edited "Marie de France" and the "Romance of the Rose," issued an abridged "Froissart," and published books on "The Mediæval Colour-sense," and "The Higher Love of Provence." His poems, sensuous, Swinburnian fragments, full of purple sunsets and precious stones, roses, red mouths and white bosoms had fascinated some of those erotic and over-civilised youngsters who turn from Kipling as from raw meat.

When Miss Champion offered Eve the post of secretary to Hugh Massinger, she accepted it as a piece of unexpected good fortune, for it seemed to be the very berth that she had hoped for, but feared to get.

Miss Champion said some characteristic things.

"Of course, you know who Mr. Massinger is? Yes. You have read 'The Torch Lily'? A little bold, but so full of colour. I must warn you that he is just a trifle eccentric. You are to call and see him at ten o'clock to-morrow at his flat in Purbeck Street. The terms are two pounds a week, which, of course, includes my commission."

"I am very grateful to you, Miss Champion. I hope I shall satisfy Mr. Massinger."

Miss Champion looked at her meaningly.

"The great thing, Miss Carfax, is to be impersonal. Always the work, and nothing but the work. That is how my protegées have always succeeded."

Eve concluded that Hugh Massinger was rather young.

Miss Champion had stated that he was eccentric, but it was not the kind of eccentricity that Eve had expected to find in Purbeck Street. A youngish manservant with a bleached and dissolute face showed her into a long room that was hung from floor to ceiling with black velvet. The carpet was a pure white pile, and with the ceiling made the room look like a black box fitted with a white bottom and lid. There was only one window, and no furniture beyond a lounge covered with blood-red velvet, two bronze bowls on hammered iron pedestals, an antique oak table, two joint-stools, and a very finely carved oak court-cupboard in one corner. The fire burnt in an iron brazier standing in an open fireplace. There were no mirrors in the room, and on each square of the black velvet hangings a sunflower was embroidered in gold silk. Heraldic glass had been inserted into the centre panels of the window, and in the recess a little silver tripod lamp burnt with a bluish flame, and gave out a faint perfume.

Eve had walked from Kate Duveen's. It was the usual wet day, and the streets were muddy, and as she sat on the joint-stool the valet had offered her she saw that she had left footprints on the white pile carpet. It seemed rather an unpropitious beginning, bringing London mud into this eccentric gentleman's immaculate room.

She was still looking at the footprints, when the black hangings were pushed aside, and a long, thin, yellow-faced young man appeared. He was wrapped in a black velvet dressing-gown, and wore sandals.

"Miss Carfax, I presume?"

Eve had risen.

"Yes."

"Please sit down. I'm afraid I am rather late this morning."

Any suggestion of subtle and decadent wickedness that the room possessed was diluted by Hugh Massinger's appearance. There was a droopingness about him, and his face was one of those long yellow faces that fall away in flaccid curves from the forehead to the chin. His nose drooped at the tip, his eyes were melancholy under drooping lids; his chin receded, and lost itself rather fatuously in a length of thin neck. His hair was of the same tint as his smooth, sand-coloured face, where a brownish moustache rolled over a wet mouth. He stooped badly, and his shoulders were narrow.

"I called on Miss Champion some days ago. My work requires special ability. Shall I explain?"

"Please."

He smiled like an Oriental, and, curling himself on the lounge, brought a black metal cigarette case out of the pocket of his dressing-gown.

"Do you mind if I smoke?"

"Not in the least."

"Perhaps you will join me?"

"I'm afraid I don't."

She was surprised when he laughed a rather foolish laugh.

"That's quite a phrase, 'The Women who Don't!' I keep a toyshop for phrases."

He puffed his cigarette and began to explain the work to her in a soft and sacramental voice that somehow made her want to laugh. He talked as though he were reading blank-verse or some prose poem that was full of mysterious precocity. But she forgot his sing-song voice in becoming conscious of his eyes. They were moonish and rather muddy, and seemed to be apprizing her, looking her up and down and in and out with peculiar interest. She did not like Hugh Massinger's eyes. They made her feel that she was being touched.

"I am writing a book on mediæval life, especially in regard to its æsthetic values. There is a good deal of research to be done, and old illustrations, illuminations and tapestries to be reproduced. It is to be a big book, quite comprehensive."

Eve soon discovered that Hugh Massinger could not be impersonal in anything that he undertook. The "I" "I" "I" oozed out everywhere.

"Miss Champion assured me that you are a fine colourist. Colour is the blood of life. That is why people who are colour mystics can wear black. The true colour, like the blood, is underneath. I noticed, directly I came into the room, that you were wearing black. It convinced me at once that you would be a sympathetic worker. My art requires sympathy."

She smiled disarmingly.

"I'm afraid my black is conventional."

"I should say that it is not. I suppose you have worked in the Museum?"

"For two or three months."

"Deathly place! How life goes to dust and to museums! I'll not ask you to go there more than I can help."

His melancholy eyes drooped over her, and filled her with a determination to be nothing but practical. She thought of Kate Duveen.

"It's my work, and I'm used to it."

"The place kills me."

"I don't mind it at all. I think most of us need a certain amount of work to do that we don't like doing, because, if we can always do what we like, we end by doing nothing."

He blinked at her.

"Now, I never expected to hear you say that. It is so very British."

"I make a living in England!" and she laughed. "Will you tell me exactly what you want me to do?"

Massinger gathered himself up from the lounge, went to the oak cupboard, and brought out a manuscript book covered with black velvet, and with the inevitable sunflower embroidered on it.

"I had better give you a list of the books I want you to dip into."

Eve took a notebook and a pencil from her bag, and for the next ten minutes she was kept busy scribbling down ancient and unfamiliar titles. Many of them smelt of Caxton, and Wynkyn de Worde, and of the Elizabethans. There were books on hunting, armour, dress, domestic architecture, painted glass, ivories and enamels; also herbals, chap-books, monastic chronicles, Exchequer rolls and copies of charters. Hugh Massinger might be an æsthetic ass, but he seemed to be a somewhat learned one.

"I think you will map out the days as follows: In the morning I will ask you to go to the Museum and make notes and drawings. In the afternoon you can submit them to me here, and I will select what I require, and advise you as to what to hunt up next day. I suppose you won't mind answering some of my letters?"

"Miss Champion said that I was to act as your secretary."

"Blessed word! I am pestered with letters. They tried to get me to manage several of those silly pageants. They don't understand the Middle Ages, these moderns."

She wanted to keep to practical things.

"What time shall I go to the Museum?"

He stared.

"I never worry about time—when you like."

"And how long will you want me here?"

"I never work after five o'clock, except, of course, when I feel creative."

She stood up, putting her notebook back into her bag.

"Then, shall I start to-morrow?"

"If it pleases you."

"Of course."

He accompanied her to the door, and opened it for her, looking with half furtive intentness into her face.

"I think we shall get on very well together, Miss Carfax."

"I hope so."

She went out with a vague feeling of contempt and distaste.

Within a week Eve discovered that she was growing interested in her new work, and also interested, in a negative fashion, in Hugh Massinger. He was a rather baffling person, impressing her as a possible genius and as a palpable fool. She usually found him curled up on the lounge, smoking a hookah, and looking like an Oriental, sinister and sleepy. For some reason or other, his smile made her think of a brass plate that had not been properly cleaned, and was smeary. Once or twice the suspicion occurred to her that he took drugs.

But directly he began to use his brain towards some definite end, she felt in the presence of a different creature. His eyes lost their sentimental moonishness; his thin and shallow hands seemed to take a virile grip; his voice changed, and his mouth tightened. The extraordinary mixture of matter that she brought back from the Museum jumbled in her notes was seized on and sorted, and spread out with wonderful lucidity. His knowledge astonished her, and his familiarity with monkish Latin and Norman French and early English. The complex, richly coloured life of the Middle Ages seemed to hang before him like a splendid tapestry. He appeared to know every fragment of it, every shade, every faded incident, and he would take the tangle of threads she brought him and knot them into their places with instant precision. His favourite place was on the lounge, his manuscript books spread round him while he jotted down a fact here and there, or sometimes recorded a whole passage.

But directly his intellectual interest relaxed he became flabby, sentimental, and rather fulsome in his personalities. The manservant would bring in tea, and Massinger would insist on Eve sharing it with him. He always drank China tea, and it reminded her of Fernhill, and the teas in the gardens, only the two men were so very different. Massinger had a certain playfulness, but it was the playfulness of a cat. His pale, intent eyes made her uncomfortable. She did not mind listening while he talked about himself, but when he tried to lure her into giving him intimate matter in return, she felt mute, and on her guard.

This new life certainly allowed her more leisure, for there were afternoons when Hugh Massinger did not work at all, and Eve went home early to Bosnia Road. On these afternoons she managed to snatch an hour's daylight, but the stuff she produced did not please her. She had all the craftsman's discontent in her favour, but the glow seemed to have gone out of her colours.

Kate Duveen wanted to know all about Hugh Massinger. She had read some of his poetry, and thought it "erotic tosh."

Eve was quite frank.

"He interests me, but I don't like him."

"Why not?"

"Instinct! Some people don't strike one as being clean."

She described the black velvet room, and the way Massinger dressed. Kate's nostrils dilated.

"Faugh, that sort of fool! Do you mean to say he receives you in a dressing-gown and sandals?"

"It is part of the pose."

"I wonder why it is that when a man is clever in the artistic way, he so often behaves like an ass? I thought the art pose was dying out. Can you imagine Bergson, or Ross, or Treves, or Nansen, dressing up and scenting themselves and sitting on a divan? People who play with words seem to get tainted, and too beastly self-conscious."

"He rather amuses me."

"Do his lips drop honey? If there is one kind of man I hate it's the man who talks clever, sentimental slosh."

"I don't encourage the honey."

Kate came in flushed one day to the little corner table they frequented in one of Lyons's shops. It was an unusual thing for Kate to be flushed, or to show excitement. Something had happened.

"Great news?"

Her eyes shone.

"I've got it at last."

"Your travelling berth?"

"Yes. A serious-minded young widow wants a travelling companion, secretary, etc. Rage for cosmopolitan colour, pictures and peoples. We begin with Egypt, go on to the Holy Land, Damascus, Constantinople.

Then back to the South of France, do Provence and the towns and châteaux, wander down to Italy and Sicily, and just deign to remember the Tyrol and Germany on the way home. It's gorgeous!"

Eve flushed too.

"Kate, I am glad."

"My languages did it! She can speak French, but no German or Italian. And the pay's first-class. I always wanted to specialise in this sort of vagabondage."

"You'll write books!"

"Who knows! We must celebrate. We'll dine at the Hotel d'Italie, and go and see Pavlova at the Palace. It's my day."

Despite her delight in Kate's good fortune, Eve had a personal regret haunting the background of her consciousness. Kate Duveen was her one friend in London. She would miss her bracing, cynical strength.

They dined at the Hotel d'Italie in one of the little upper rooms, and Kate talked Italian to the waiters, and made Eve drink her health in very excellent Barolo. She had been lucky in getting seats at the Palace, two reserved tickets having been sent back only ten minutes before she had called.

Eve had never seen Pavlova before, and the black-coated and conventional world melted out of her consciousness as she sat and watched the Russian dancer. That fragile, magical, childlike figure seemed to have been conceived in the heart of a white flame. It was life, and all the strange and manifold suggestions of life vibrating and glowing in one slight body. Eve began to see visions, as she sat in the darkness and watched Pavlova moving to Chopin's music. Pictures flashed and vanished, moods expressed in colour. The sun went down behind black pine woods, and a wind wailed. A half-naked girl dressed in skins and vine leaves fled from the brown arms of a young barbarian. A white butterfly flitted among Syrian roses. She heard bees at work, birds singing in the dawn. And then, it was the pale ghost of Francesca drifting through the moonlight with death in her eyes and hair.

Then the woman's figure was joined by a man's figure, and Liszt's Second Hungarian Rhapsody was in the air. The motive changed. Something bacchic, primitive, passionate leapt in the blood. Eve sat thrilled, with half-closed eyes. Those two figures, the woman's and the man's, seemed to rouse some wild, elemental spirit in her, to touch an undreamt-of subconsciousness that lay concealed under the workaday life. Desire, the exultation of desire, and the beauty of it were very real to her She felt breathless and ready to weep.

When it was over, and she and Kate were passing out with the crowd, a kind of languor descended on her, like the languor that comes after the senses have been satisfied. It was not a sensual feeling, although it was of the body. Kate too was silent. Pavlova's dancing had reacted on her strangely.

"Let's walk!"

"Would you rather?"

"Yes."

"As far as my rooms. Then I shall put you in a taxi."

They had to wait awhile before crossing the road, as motors were swarming up.

"That woman's a genius. She made me feel like a rusty bit of clockwork!"

"She had a most extraordinary effect on me!"

Kate took Eve's arm.

"The thing's pure, absolutely pure, and yet, she seems to show you what you never believed was in you. It's the soul of the world coming out to dance, and making you understand all that is in us women. Heavens, I found myself feeling like a Greek girl, a little drunk with wine, and still more drunk with love."

"Kate—you!"

"Yes, and it was not beastly, as those things usually are. I'm not an emotional person. I suppose it is the big subconscious creature in one answering a language that our clever little heads don't understand."

Eve was thinking.

"I envy that woman!"

"Why?"

"Because she has a genius, and because she has been able to express her genius, and because she has succeeded in conquering the crowd. They don't know how clever she is, but they go and see her dance. Think what it means being a supreme artist, and yet popular. For once the swine seem to appreciate the pearl."

They were making their way through a crowd of loiterers at the corner of Tottenham Court Road, when a tall man brushed against them and stepped aside. He wore a black wideawake hat, a low collar with a bunchy black silk tie, and a loose black coat with a tuberose in the buttonhole. He stared first at Kate, and then at Eve with a queer, comprehensive, apprizing stare. Suddenly he took off his hat.

The women passed on.

"Beast!"

Kate's mouth was iron.

"That was Hugh Massinger."

"Hugh Massinger!"

"Yes."

"Eve, I said 'beast,' and I still mean it."

"Your impression?"

"Yes. I don't think old Champion ought to have sent you to that sort of man."

CHAPTER XXVI

KATE DUVEEN GOES ABROAD

Although Hugh Massinger had reached the cynical age of thirty-seven, he had been so well treated by the Press and the public, that he had no cause to develop a sneer. His essential self-satisfaction saved him from being bored, for to be very pleased with oneself is to be pleased with life in general. His appetites were still ready to be piqued, and he had the same exotic delight in colour that he had had when he was an undergraduate of twenty, and this reaction to colour is one of the subtlest tests of a man's vitality. When the sex stimulus weakens, when a man becomes even a little disillusioned and a little bored, he no longer thrills to colours. It is a sign that the youth in him is growing grey.

Hugh Massinger's senses were abnormally excitable. He was city bred, and a sitter in chairs, and a lounger upon lounges, and his ideas upon flowers, woods, fields and the country in general were utterly false, hectic and artificial. He was the sort of sentimentalist who was always talking of the "beautiful intrigues of the plants," of "the red lust of June," and the "swelling bosom of August." His art was a sexual art. His thoughts lay about on cushions, and he never played any kind of game.

About this time Eve discovered that his sentimentality was growing more demonstrative. It was like a yellow dog that fawned round and round her chair, but seemed a little afraid of coming too near. He took a great deal of trouble in trying to make her talk about herself, and in thrusting a syrupy sympathy upon her.

"You are looking tired to-day," he would say, "I shan't let you work."

She would protest that she was not tired.

"Really, I am nothing of the kind."

"And I have quick eyes. It is that horrible reading-room full of fustiness and indigence. I am ashamed to to send you there."

She would laugh and study to be more conventional.

"Mr. Massinger, I am a very healthy young woman, and the work interests me."

"My work?"

"Yes."

"That is really sweet of you. I like to think your woman's hands have dabbled in it. Tell me, haven't you any ambitions of your own—any romantic schemes?"

"Oh, I paint a little in my spare time!"

"The mysteries of colour. You are a vestal, and your colour dreams must be very pure. Supposing we talk this afternoon, and let work alone? And Adolf shall make us coffee."

Adolf made excellent coffee, and in the oak court-cupboard Massinger kept liqueur glasses and bottles of choice liqueur. It was a harmless sort of æsthetic wickedness, a little accentuated by occasional doses of opium or cannabis indica. Eve would take the coffee, but she could never be persuaded to touch the Benedictine. It reminded her of Massinger's moonish and intriguing eyes.

At that time she thought of him as a sentimental ass, a man with a fine brain and no common sense. She posed more and more as a very conventional young woman, pretending to be a little shocked by his views of life, and meeting his suggestive friendliness with British obtuseness. She gave him back Ruskin, the Bensons and Carlyle when he talked of Wilde. And yet this pose of hers piqued Massinger all the more sharply, though she did not suspect it. He talked to himself of "educating her," of "reforming her taste," and of "teaching her to be a little more sympathetic towards the sweet white frailties of life."

Early in December Kate's last evening came, and Eve spent it with her in the Bloomsbury rooms. There were the last odds and ends of packing to be done, the innumerable little feminine necessaries to be stowed away in the corners of the "steamer" trunks. Eve helped, and her more feminine mind offered a dozen suggestions to her more practical friend. Kate Duveen was not a *papier poudre* woman. She did not travel with a bagful of sacred little silver topped boxes and bottles, and her stockings were never anything else but black.

"Have you got any hazeline and methylated spirit?"

"No."

"You must get some on the way to the station. Or I'll get them in the morning. And have you plenty of thick veiling?"

"My complexion is the last thing I ever think of."

"You have not forgotten the dictionaries, though."

"No, nor my notebooks and stylo."

They had supper together, and then sat over the fire with their feet on the steel fender. Kate Duveen had become silent. She was thinking of James Canterton, and the way he had walked into her room that evening.

"Eve!"

"Yes!"

"I am going to break a promise in order to keep a promise. I think I am justified."

"What is it?"

"He came here to see me one evening about two months ago."

"Whom do you mean?"

"James Canterton."

"And you didn't tell me!"

"He asked me to promise not to tell, and I liked him for it. I was rather astonished, and I snapped at him. He took it like a big dog. But he asked me to promise something else."

"What was it?"

"That if ever things were to go badly with you, I would let him know."

She glanced momentarily at Eve and found that she was staring at the fire, her lips parted slightly, as though she were about to smile, and her eyes were full of a light that was not the mere reflection of the fire. Her whole face had softened, and become mysteriously radiant.

"That was like him."

"Then I may keep my promise?"

"Yes."

"I think I can trust you both."

Eve said nothing.

She saw Kate off in her cab next morning before going to her work at the Museum. They held hands, but did not kiss.

"I'm so glad that you've had this good luck. You deserve it."

"Nonsense. Write; and remember that promise."

"I hope there will be no need for you to keep it. Good-bye, dear! You've been so very good to me."

She was very sad when Kate had gone, and in the great reading-room such a rush of loneliness came over her that she had but little heart for work. She fell to thinking of Canterton, and of the work they had done together, and the thought of Hugh Massinger and that flat of his in Purbeck Street made her feel that life had cheapened and deteriorated. There was something unwholesome about the man and his art. It humiliated her to think that sincerity had thrust this meaner career upon her.

Punctually at two o'clock she rang the bell of the flat in Purbeck Street. Adolf admitted her. She disliked Adolf's smile. It was a recent development, and it struck her as being latently offensive.

Hugh Massinger was curled up on the lounge, reading one of Shaw's plays. He loathed Shaw, but read him as a dog worries something that it particularly detests. He sat up, his moonish eyes smiling, and Eve realised for the first time that his eyes and Adolf's were somewhat alike.

She sat down at the table, and began to arrange her notebooks.

"You look *triste* to-day."

"Do I?"

"I am growing very understanding towards your moods."

She caught the challenge on the shield of a casual composure.

"I lost a friend this morning."

"Not by death?"

"Oh, no! She has gone abroad. One does not like losing the only friend one has in London."

He leaned forward with a gesture of protest.

"Now you have hurt me."

"Hurt you, Mr. Massinger!"

"I thought that I was becoming something of a friend."

She made herself look at him with frank, calm eyes.

"It had not occurred to me. I really am very much obliged to you. Shall I begin to read out my notes?"

He did not answer for a moment, but remained looking at her with sentimental solemnity.

"My dear lady, you will not put me off like that. I am much too sympathetic to be repulsed so easily. I don't like to see you sad. Adolf shall make coffee, and we will give up work this afternoon and chatter. You shall discover a friend——"

She said, very quietly:

"I would rather work, Mr. Massinger. Work is very soothing."

CHAPTER XXVII

THE BOURGEOIS OF CLARENDON ROAD

Mrs. Buss had surrendered at last to Eve's persuasions, and a jobbing carpenter had erected a section-built shed in the back garden at Bosnia Road. The shed had a corrugated iron roof, and Mrs. Buss had stipulated that the roof should be painted a dull red, so that it might "tone" with the red brick houses. The studio was lined with matchboarding, had a skylight in the roof, and was fitted with an anthracite stove. The whole affair cost Eve about twenty-five pounds, with an additional two shillings added to the weekly rent of her rooms. She paid for the studio out of the money she had received from the sale of the furniture at Orchards Corner, and her capital had now dwindled to about forty-five pounds.

Every morning on her way towards Highbury Corner, Eve passed the end of Clarendon Grove, a road lined with sombre, semi-detached houses, whose front gardens were full of plane trees, ragged lilacs and privets, and scraggy laburnums. Eve, who was fairly punctual, passed the end of Clarendon Grove about a quarter to nine each morning, and there was another person who was just as punctual in quite a detached and unpremeditated way. Sometimes she saw him coming out of a gate about a hundred yards down Clarendon Grove, sometimes he was already turning the corner, or she saw his broad fat back just ahead of her, always on the same side of the street.

She christened him "the Highbury Clock," or "the British Bourgeois." He was a shortish, square-built man of about five-and-forty, with clumsy shoulders, a round head, and big feet. He turned his toes out like a German when he walked, and he always went at the same pace, and always carried a black handbag. His face was round, phlegmatic, good tempered, and wholly commonplace, the eyes blue and rather protuberant, the nose approximating to what is vulgarly called the "shoe-horn type," the mouth hidden by a brownish walrus moustache. He looked the most regular, reliable, and solid person imaginable in his top-hat, black coat, and neatly pressed grey trousers. Eve never caught him hurrying, and she imagined that in hot weather he ought to wear an alpaca coat.

They sighted each other pretty regularly for some three months before chance caused them to strike up a casual acquaintanceship. One wet day the Bourgeois gave up his seat to Eve in a crowded tram. After that he took off his hat to her whenever she happened to pass across the end of Clarendon

Grove in front of him. One morning they arrived at the corner at the same moment, and the Bourgeois wished her "good morning."

They walked as far as Upper Street together. It seemed absurd for two humans whose paths touched so often not to smile and exchange a few words about the weather, and so it came about that they joined forces whenever the Bourgeois was near enough to the corner for Eve not to have to indulge in any conscious loitering.

He was a very decent sort of man, and his name was Mr. Parfit. He was something in the neighbourhood of Broad Street, but what it was he did not state, and Eve did not inquire. In due course she discovered that he was a bachelor, that he had lived for fifteen years in the same rooms, that he had a passion for romantic novels, and that he went regularly to Queen's Hall. He spent Sunday in his slippers, reading *The Referee*. A three weeks' holiday once a year satisfied any vagrant impulses he might feel, and he spent these three weeks at Ramsgate, Hastings or Brighton.

"I like to be in a crowd," he told Eve, "with plenty of youngsters about. There's nothing I like better than sitting on the sands with a pipe and a paper, watching the kids making castles and pies, and listening to Punch and Judy. Seems to make one feel young."

She liked Mr. Parfit, and often wondered why he had not married. Perhaps he was one of those men who preferred being a very excellent uncle rather than a bored father, for she gathered that he was fond of other people's children, and was always ready with his pennies. He had a sly, laborious, porcine humour, and a chuckle that made his cheeks wrinkle and his eyes grow smaller. He was exceedingly polite to Eve, and though at times he seemed inclined to be good-naturedly personal, she knew that it was part of his nature and not a studied attempt at familiarity.

Eve was glad to have this very human person to talk to, for she found life increasingly lonely, now that Kate Duveen had gone. Mr. Parfit had a fatherly way with him, and though his culture was crude and raw, he had a shrewd outlook upon things in general that was not unamusing. London, too, was in the thick of the mud and muck of a wet winter, and Eve found that she was growing more susceptible to the depressing influence of bad weather. It spoilt her morning's walk, and caused a quite unnecessary expenditure on trams and 'buses, and roused her to a kind of rage when she pulled up her blind in the morning and saw the usual drizzle making the slate roofs glisten. She associated her new studio with rain, for there always seemed to be a pattering sound upon the corrugated iron roof when she shut herself in to work.

She grew more moody, and her moodiness drove her into desperate little dissipations, such as a seat in the upper circle at His Majesty's or the Haymarket, a dinner at an Italian restaurant, or a tea at Fuller's. She found London less depressing after dark, and learnt to understand how the exotic city, with its night jewels glittering, appealed to people who were weary of greyness. Her sun-hunger and her country-hunger had become so importunate that she had spent one Sunday in the country, taking train to Guildford, and walking up to the Hog's Back. The Surrey hills had seemed dim and sad, and away yonder she had imagined Fernhill, with its fir woods and its great pleasaunce. She had felt rather like an outcast, and the day had provoked such sadness in her that she went no more into the country.

The extraordinary loneliness of such a life as hers filled her at times with cynical amusement. How absurd it was, this crowded solitude of London; this selfish, suspicious, careless materialism. No one bothered. More than once she felt whimsically tempted to catch some passing woman by the arm, and to say "Stop and talk to me. I am human, and I have a tongue." After tea she would often loiter along Regent Street or Oxford Street, looking rather aimlessly into the shops, and studying the faces of the people who passed; but she found that she had to abandon this habit of loitering, for more than once men spoke to her, looking in her face with a look that made her grow cold with a white anger.

It was inevitable that she should contrast this London life with the life at Fernhill, and compare all other men with James Canterton. She could not help making the comparison, nor did the comparison, when made, help her to forget. The summer had given her her first great experience, and all this subsequent loneliness intensified the vividness of her memories. She yearned to see Lynette, to feel the child's warm hands touching her. She longed, too, for Canterton, to be able to look into his steady eyes, to feel his clean strength near her, to realise that she was not alone. Yes, he was clean, while these men who passed her in the streets seemed horrible, greedy and pitiless. They reminded her of the people in Aubrey Beardsley's drawings, people with grotesque and leering faces, out of whose eyes nameless sins escaped.

The flat in Purbeck Street offered her other contrasts after the rain and the wet streets and the spattering mud from the wheels of motor-buses. It was eccentric but unwholesome, luxurious, and effeminate, with suggestions of an extreme culture and an individual idea of beauty. Coming straight from a cheap lunch eaten off a marble-topped table to this muffled, scented room, was like passing from a colliery slum to a warm and scented bath in a Roman villa. Eve noticed that her shoes always seemed muddy, and she laughed over it, and apologised.

"I always leave marks on your white carpet."

"You should read Baudelaire in order to realise that a thing that is white is of no value without a few symbolical stains. Supposing I have a glass case put over one of your footprints, so that Adolf shall not wash them all away?"

That was just what she disliked about Hugh Massinger. He was for ever twisting what she said into an excuse for insinuating that he found her charming and provocative. He did not play at gallantry like a gentleman. A circuitous cleverness and a natural cowardliness kept him from being audaciously frank. He fawned like a badly bred dog, and she liked his fawnings so little that she began to wonder at last whether this fool was in any way serious.

One morning it snowed hard before breakfast for about an hour, and by one o'clock London was a city of slush. Eve felt depressed, and her shoes and stockings and the bottom of her skirt were sodden when she reached the flat in Purbeck Street. Adolf smiled his usual smile, and confessed that Mr. Massinger had not expected her.

"Ma Donna! I never thought you would brave this horrible weather."

He threw a book aside and was up, solicitous, and not a little pleased at the chance of being tender.

"I suppose English weather is part of the irony of life!"

"Good heavens! Your shoes and skirt are wet!"

"A little."

He piled two or three cushions in front of the fire.

"Do sit down and take your shoes and stockings off, and dry your skirt."

She sat down and took off her shoes.

"Stockings too! I can be very fatherly and severe. Do you think it immodest to show your bare feet? You must have a liqueur; it will warm you."

"I would rather not."

"Oh, come! You are a pale Iseult to-day."

"Thank you, I would rather not."

"Then Adolf shall make us coffee."

He rang the bell.

"Adolf, coffee and some biscuits! And bring that purple scarf of mine."

The scarf arrived first, and Massinger held it spread over his hands like a shop-assistant showing off a length of silk.

"Two little white empresses shall wear the purple. No work this afternoon. I am going to try to make you forget the weather."

Adolf came in noiselessly with the coffee, set it on a stool beside Eve, and departed just as noiselessly, and with an absolutely expressionless face. The way he had of effacing himself made Eve more conscious of his existence.

The fire was comforting, so was the coffee. She could have slipped into a mood of soothed indolence if Massinger had not been present. But his leering obsequiousness had disturbed her, and she found herself facing that eternal problem as to how a woman should behave to a man who employed her and paid for her time. Was it necessary to quarrel with all this sentimental by-play? She still held to her impression that he was a very great ass.

"This detestable climate! It brutalises us. It makes one understand why the English drink beer, and love to see the red corpses of animals hung up in shops. A gross climate, and a gross people."

Eve had wrapped the purple scarf round her feet.

"If we could be sure of a little sunshine every other day!"

She was staring at the fire, and Massinger was studying her with an interested intentness. Thought and desire were mingled at the back of his pale eyes.

"Sunshine—clear, yellow light! Don't you yearn for it?"

"Who does not? With the exception of the people who have been baked in the tropics."

"And it is so near. The people who are free can always find it."

He lay back against the cushions on the lounge, his eyes still on her, and shining with an incipient smile.

"You leave the grey country at dusk, and travel through the night, and then the dawn comes up, all orange and gold, and the cypresses hold up their beckoning fingers. There the sea is blue, and there are flowers, roses, carnations, wallflowers, stocks, and mimosa; oranges and lemons hang on the trees, and the white villas shine among palms and olives."

His voice became insinuating, and took on its sing-song blank-verse cadence.

"Have you ever seen Monte Carlo?"

"No."

"It is a vulgar world to the vulgar. But that delectable little world has an esoteric meaning. The sun shines, and it is easier to make love under a blue sky. And then, all those little towns on the edge of the blue sea, and the grey rock villages, and the adventures up mule-paths. Think of a mule-path, and pine woods, and sunlight, and a bottle of red wine."

She laughed, but with a tremor of self-consciousness.

"It is useful to think of such things, just to realise how very far away they are."

"Nothing is far away, when one has the magic carpet of gold. Have the courage to dream, and there you are."

He got up, wandered round the room with a wavering glance at her, and then came across to the fire.

"Just think of 'Monte' and the sunlight, and the gay pagan life. It is worth experiencing. Dream of it for a week in London. Are you getting dry?"

He went down suddenly on one knee and felt her skirt, and in another moment he had touched one of her feet.

"The little white empress is warm. How would she like to walk the terraces at Monte Carlo?"

Eve kept very still. She had an abrupt glimpse of the meaning of his suggestions, and of all that was moving towards her in this man's mind. Intuition told her that she would rebuff him more thoroughly by treating him as a sentimental idiot than by flattening him with anger, as if he were a man.

"Please don't do that. It's foolish, and makes me want to laugh. I think it's time we were serious. I am ready for work."

For an instant his eyes looked sulky and dangerous.

"What a practical person it is."

"And what a long time you have taken to find that out. I'm afraid I'm not in the least sentimental."

Hugh Massinger went back to the lounge like a cat that has been laughed at.

CHAPTER XXVIII

CANTERTON'S COTTAGE AND MISS CHAMPION'S MORALITY

Three days before Christmas, Eve spent a quarter of an hour in a big toyshop in quest of something that she could send Lynette, and her choice came to rest upon a miniature cooking-stove fitted with a three-trayed oven, pots and pans, and a delightful little copper kettle. The stove cost her a guinea, but it was a piece of extravagance that warmed her heart.

She wrote on a card:

"For cooking Fairy Food in the Wilderness. Miss Eve sends ever so much love."

Eve had kept back one Latimer sketch, a little "post card" picture of a stone Psyche standing in thought on the edge of a marble pool, with a mass of cypresses for a background, and a circle of white water lilies at her feet. She sent the picture to Canterton with a short letter, but she did not give him her address.

> "I feel that I must send you Christmas wishes. This is a little fragment I had kept by me, and I should like you to have it. Plenty of hard work keeps me from emulating the pose of Psyche in the picture. I am spending Christmas alone, but I shall paint, and think of Lynette entertaining Father Christmas.
>
> "My friend, Kate Duveen, has gone abroad for six months. I think when the spring comes I shall be driven to escape into the country as an artistic tramp.
>
> "I have just built a studio. It measures fourteen feet by ten, and lives in a back garden. So one is not distracted by having beautiful things to look at.
>
> "I send you all the wishes that I can wish.
>
> "EVE."

When she posted the letter and sent off Lynette's parcel, she felt that they were passing across a vacant space into another world that never touched her own. It was like a dream behind her consciousness. She wondered, as she wandered away from the post office, whether she would ever see Fernhill again.

If the incident saddened her and accentuated her sense of loneliness, that letter of hers, and the picture of the Latimer Psyche, saddened Canterton still more poignantly. It was possible that he had secretly hoped that Eve would relent a little, and that she would suffer him to approach her again and let his honour spend itself in some comradely service. He did not want to open up old wounds, but he desired to know all that was happening to her, to feel that she was within sight, that he did not love a mere memory.

Lynette's delight baffled him.

"Now, that's just what I wanted. Isn't it like Miss Eve to think of it? I must write to her, daddy. Where's she say she's living now?"

"In London."

"Why doesn't she come for Christmas?"

"Because she's so very busy. You write and thank her, old lady, and I'll send your letter with mine."

Lynette produced a longish letter, and Canterton wrote one of his own. He enclosed a five pound note, addressed the envelope to Miss Eve Carfax, c/o Miss Kate Duveen, and sent it into the unknown to take its chance.

He had written:

"It still hurts me not a little that you will not trust me with your address. I give you my promise never to come to you unless you send for me.

"Buy yourself something for the studio from me and Lynette. Even if you spend the money on flowers I shall be quite happy."

And since Kate Duveen's landlady did not know Eve's address, and happened to be a conscientious soul, Canterton's letter was put into another envelope and sent to hunt Kate down in the land of the lotus and the flamingo.

Christmas Day was bright and frosty, and Canterton wandered out alone after breakfast with Eve's letter in his pocket. The great nurseries were deserted, and Canterton had this world of his to himself, even the ubiquitous Lavender not troubling to go beyond the region of the hot-houses. Canterton left the home gardens behind, cut across a plantation of young pines, cypresses and cedars towards some of the wilder ground that had been largely left to Nature. Here, under the northerly shelter of a towering fir wood there happened to be an out-cropping of rock, brown black hummocks of sandstone piled in natural disorder, and looking like miniature mountains.

Building had been going on here, and it was the building itself that held Canterton's thoughts. A cottage stood with its back to the fir wood, a Tudor cottage built of oak and white plaster, and deep thatched with blackened heather. The lattices were in, and blinked back the December sunlight. A terrace of flat stones had been laid in front of the cottage, and a freshly planted yew hedge shut in the future garden that was still littered with builders' debris, mortar-boards, planks, messes of plaster and cement. The windows of the cottage looked southwards towards the blue hills, and just beyond the yew hedge lay the masses of sandstone that were being made into a rock garden. Earth had been carted and piled about. Dwarf trees, saxifrages, aubrietias, anemones, alyssum, arabis, thrift, sedums, irises, hundreds of tulips, squills, crocuses, and narcissi had been planted. By next spring the black brown rocks would be splashed with colour—purple and white, blue and gold, rose, green and scarlet.

On the cross-beam of the timber porch the date of the year had been cut. Canterton stood and looked at it, thinking how strange a significance those figures had for him.

He took a key out of his pocket, unlocked the door, and climbed the half finished staircase to one of the upper rooms. And for a while he stood at the window, gazing towards the December sun hanging low in the southern sky.

Would she ever come to live in this cottage?

He wondered.

Canterton rarely discussed his affairs with anybody, and the cottage had been half built before Gertrude had heard of its existence. And when she had discovered it, Canterton had told her quite calmly what it was for.

"I shall have to have help here. Eve Carfax may come back. She is trying this berth in London for a year. She understands colour-gardening better than anybody I have come across. If she fails me, I shall have to get someone else. I think Drinkwater is making a very good job of the cottage. I wanted something that is not conventional."

Gertrude had suggested that if the cottage were likely to remain unoccupied for a while she might use it temporarily as a country rest-house for some of a London friend's rescued "Magdalens." She had been surprised at the almost fierce way Canterton had stamped on the suggestion.

"Thank you. You will do nothing of the kind."

It was not part of his dream that this speculative cottage that he had built for Eve should be so used.

Besides, every detail had been thought out to please eyes that sought and found the beauty in everything. The little dining-room was to be panelled oak, the window-seats were deep enough to make cushioned lounges where one could lie and read. All the timber used was oak, from the beams that were left showing in the ceiling to the panel-work of the cupboards and the treads and newel-posts of the stairs. The door-fittings were of hammered steel, the hearths laid with dark green tiles. A little electric light plant was to be fitted, with a tiny gas engine and dynamo in an outhouse behind the cottage.

Canterton spent the greater part of Christmas morning wandering from room to room, studying the views from the different windows, and examining the work the men had put in during the previous week. He also drew a trial plan of the garden, sitting on one of the window-seats, and using a pencil and the back of a letter. Both cottage and garden were parts of a piece of speculative devotion, and in them his strength found self-expression.

Meanwhile "the Bourgeois" of Clarendon Grove became very much more talkative just about Christmas time. Eve met him at the corner of the road on three successive mornings, and his person suggested holly berries, roast beef, and a pudding properly alight. He seemed festive and unable to help being confidential.

"Suppose you'll be going away to friends?"

She told Mr. Parfit that she would be spending Christmas quite alone.

"I say, that's not good for you! What, no kids, and no party?"

"No."

"Christmas isn't Christmas without kids. I always go to my sister Jane's at Croydon. Good sort, Jane. Two boys and two girls. All healthy, too. Makes you feel young to see them eat. I always go down on Christmas Eve with a Tate's sugar box full of presents. That's the sort of Christmas that suits me A1!"

He looked at her benignantly.

"Should you like to know Jane? She's a good sort."

"I should like to know her."

"Look here! I'll tell her to come and call on you. Do the social thing. Pity you can't join us all for Christmas. We'd soon make you feel at home."

His eyes were a trifle apologetic, but very kind, and his kindness touched her. He was quite sincere in what he said, and she discovered a new sensitiveness in him.

"It's good of you to think of such a thing. One finds life rather lonely at times. Croydon is a long way off, but perhaps your sister will come and see me some day."

He began to talk very fast of a sudden.

"Oh, you'd like Jane, and she'd like you, and the youngsters are jolly kids, and not a bit spoilt. We must fix up the social business. I'm a fool of a bachelor. I was made to be married, but somehow I haven't. Funny thing, life! One gets in a groove, and it takes something big to get one out again."

He laughed, and wished her good morning rather abruptly, explaining that he was going down to the City by train.

Eve had felt touched, amused, and a little puzzled. She thought what an excellent uncle he must make with the round, Christmas face, and the Tate's sugar-box full of presents. And on Christmas morning she found a parcel from him lying on the breakfast table.

He had sent her a big box of chocolates and two new novels, and had written a note. It was a rather clumsy and apologetic note, but it pleased her.

> "DEAR MISS CARFAX,—Please accept these trifles. I don't know whether you will think me an impertinent old fogey, but there you are. I couldn't send you a turkey, you know. Too large an order for one.
>
> "I wish you were spending Christmas with us. Better luck next year.
>
> "Very sincerely yours,
>
> "JOHN PARFIT."

Eve found it rather a struggle to pull through Christmas, and then, as though for a contrast, came her disagreement with Hugh Massinger. It was a serious disagreement, so serious that she took a taxi back to Bosnia Road at three in the afternoon, angry, shocked, and still flushed with scorn.

She went down to Miss Champion's next morning, and was immediately shown into Miss Champion's private room. The lady of the white hair and the fresh face had put on the episcopal sleeves. She met Eve with an air of detached and judicial stateliness, seated herself behind her roll-top desk, and pointed Eve to a chair.

"I have come to tell you that I have given up my secretaryship."

She had a feeling that Hugh Massinger had put in an early pleader, and she was not surprised when Miss Champion picked up a letter that was lying open on the desk.

"This is a most deplorable incident, Miss Carfax."

Her tone challenged Eve.

"It is more contemptible than deplorable!"

"Mr. Massinger has written me a letter, a letter of apology and explanation. Of course, I have nothing to say in defence of such misunderstandings. But you actually struck him."

Eve's face flamed.

"Yes, you must understand——"

"But I fail to understand."

"The man is a cad."

"Miss Carfax, these things don't happen unless a woman is indiscreet. I think I insisted on your remembering that a woman must be impersonal."

Eve was amazed. She had come to Miss Champion, counting on a woman's sympathy, and some show of decent scorn of a man who misused a situation as Hugh Massinger had done.

"Miss Champion, you suggest it was my fault."

"Mr. Massinger is a man of culture. He has written, giving me an explanation. I do not say that I accept it in its entirety. But without some provocation, thoughtless provocation, perhaps——"

"May I see the letter?"

"Certainly not. It is confidential."

"Of course, he accuses me? It was a cowardly thing—a mean thing."

"He offers explanations."

"Which you accept?"

"With certain reservations, yes."

Eve held her breath. She felt humiliated, angry, and astonished.

"I never thought it possible that you would take such a view as this."

"Let me explain, Miss Carfax, that I cannot help taking this view. I have to insist on an absolutely impersonal attitude. My profession cannot be carried on satisfactorily without it. I regret it, but I am afraid you are not quite suited to delicate positions of responsibility."

Eve said quietly, "Please don't go into explanations. You would rather not have me on your staff."

"I am a stickler for etiquette, rather old-fashioned. One has to be."

"Yes, I understand. So long as everything looks nice on the surface. I think we had better say nothing more. I only came to tell you the truth, and sometimes the truth is awkward."

She rose, biting her lip, and keeping her hands clenched. It was monstrous, incredible, that this woman should be on the man's side, and that she should throw insinuations in her face. If she had surrendered to Hugh Massinger and kept quiet, nothing would have been said, and nothing might have happened. She felt nauseated, inflamed.

"I am sorry, Miss Carfax——"

"Oh, please don't say that! It makes me feel more cynical."

CHAPTER XXIX

EARNING A LIVING

The affair of Hugh Massinger, and Miss Champion's attitude towards it, provided Eve with an experience that threw a glare of new light upon the life of a woman who sets out to earn her own living. She had no need to go to the dramatists to be instructed, for she had touched the problem with her own hands, and discovered the sexual hypocrisy that Kate Duveen had always railed at. Here was she, lonely and struggling on the edge of life, and a man of Hugh Massinger's reputation and intelligence could do nothing more honourable to help her than to suggest the advantages of a sentimental seduction. Miss Champion, the woman, had failed to take the woman's part. Her middle-class cowardice was all for hushing things up, for accusing the insulted girl of indiscretions, for reproaching her with not failing to be a temptation to men. No smoke without some fire. It was safer to discharge such a young woman than to defend her. And Miss Champion's nostrils were very shy and sensitive. She was an automatic machine that reacted to any copper coin that could be called a convention. Certain things never ought to happen, and if they happened they never ought to be mentioned.

This affair inaugurated hard times for Eve, nor did the bitterness that it aroused in her help her to bear the new life with philosophy. It had had something of the effect on her that the first discovery of sex has upon a sensitive child. She felt disgusted, shocked, saddened. Life would never be quite the same, at least, so she told herself, for this double treachery had shaken her trust, and she wondered whether all men were like Hugh Massinger, and all women careful hypocrites like Miss Champion.

She longed for Kate Duveen's sharp and acrid sincerity. Hers was a personality that might take the raw taste out of her mouth, but Eve did not write to Kate to tell her what had happened. Her pride was still able to keep its own flag flying, and it seemed contemptible to cry out and complain over the first wound.

One thing was certain, her income had stopped abruptly. She had about thirty-five pounds left to her credit at the bank. The rent of her rooms was a pound a week, and she found that her food cost her about twelve shillings, this sum including the sixpenny lunches and fourpenny teas that she had in the City. Putting her expenditure at thirty-five shillings a week, she had enough money to last her for twenty weeks, granted, of course, that nothing unexpected happened, and that she had not to face a doctor's bill.

It behoved her to bustle round, to cast her net here, there, and everywhere for work. She entered her name at several "Agencies," but found that the agents were none too sanguine when she had to confess that she could neither write shorthand nor use a typewriter. Her abilities were of that higher order whose opportunities are more limited. People did not want artistic cleverness. The need was all for drudges.

During her first workless week at Bosnia Road, she designed a number of fashion plates, and painted half a dozen little pictures. She called at one of the despised picture shops, and suggested to the proprietor that he might be willing to sell these pictures on commission. The proprietor, a depressed and flabby dyspeptic, was not encouraging.

"I could fill my window with that sort of stuff if I wanted to. People don't want flowers and country cottages. Can't you paint pink babies and young mothers, and all that?"

Eve went elsewhere, and after many wanderings, discovered a gentleman in the West Central district who was ready to show her pictures in his window. He was a little more appreciative, and had a better digestion than the man who had talked of babies.

"Yes, that's quite a nice patch of colour. I don't mind showing them. People sometimes like to get the real thing—cheap."

"What would one ask for a thing of this kind?"

"Oh, half a crown to five shillings. One can't expect much more."

"Not so much as for a joint of meat!"

He was laconic.

"Well, you see, miss, we've all got digestions, but not many of us have taste."

Her next attempt was to dispose of some of her dress designs, and since she had become familiar at Miss Champion's with the names of certain firms who were willing to buy such creations, she knew where to find a possible market. It seemed wiser to call in person than to send the designs by post, and she spent a whole day trying to interview responsible persons in West End establishments. One firm rebuffed her with the frank statement that they were over-supplied with such creations. At two other places she was told to leave her designs to be looked at. At her last attempt she succeeded in obtaining an interview with a hungry-looking and ill-tempered elderly woman who was writing letters in a little glass-panelled office at the back of a big shop.

Eve disliked the woman from the first glance, but she was grateful to her for having taken the trouble to give her an interview.

"I wondered whether Messrs. Smith might have any use for designs for new spring and summer frocks?"

The woman looked at her from under cunning eyelids.

"Sit down. Let me see."

Eve unwrapped the drawings and handed them to the person in authority, who glanced through them as though she were shuffling a pack of cards.

"Had any technical training? Not much, I think."

"I have lived in Paris."

"That's an excuse, I suppose. There are one or two possible ideas here. Leave the designs. I'll consider them."

She laid them down on her desk and looked at Eve in a way that told her that she was expected to go.

"I had better leave my address."

"Isn't it on the cards?"

"No!"

"Then write it."

She pushed a pen and ink towards Eve, and turned to resume the work that had been interrupted.

When Eve had gone, the good lady picked up the designs, looked them carefully through, and then pushed the button of a bell in the wall behind her. A flurried young woman with a snub nose, and untidy yellow hair, came in.

"Here, Miss Rush, copy those two. Then pack them all up and send them back to the address written on that one. Say we've looked at them, and that none are suitable."

The snub-nosed young woman understood, and two of Eve's designs were appropriated, at a cost to Messrs. Smith of twopence for postage. That was good business. The whole batch was returned to Eve in the course of three days, with a laconic type-written statement that the designs had received careful consideration, but had been found to be unsuitable.

She had not seen Mr. Parfit since the loss of her secretaryship, in fact, not since Christmas, the morning walks to Highbury Corner having become unnecessary. On the afternoon of the second Saturday in January, Eve happened to be standing at her window, dressed to go out, when she saw him strolling along the path on the other side of the road. He glanced at her window as he passed, and, turning when he had gone some thirty yards, came slowly back again.

A sudden hunger for companionship seized her, a desire to listen to a friendly voice, and to feel that she was not utterly alone. She hurried out, drawing on her gloves, and found "the Bourgeois of Clarendon Grove" on the point of repassing her doorway.

He raised his hat, beamed, and came across.

"Why, here you are! I hope you haven't been ill?"

"No."

"I began to get quite worried."

It gave her pleasure to find that someone had troubled to wonder what had happened.

"I have given up my post, and so I have no reason for starting out early."

His round eyes studied her attentively.

"Oh, that's it!"

He had sense enough not to begin by asking questions.

"I was just going to take a breather round by the Fields. Suppose you're booked for something?"

"No."

"Well, why shouldn't I tell you all about Christmas! Jane's coming to look you up."

"That's very good of her."

They started off together with a tacit acceptance of the situation, Mr. Parfit showing an elaborate politeness in taking the outside of the pavement. His whole air was that of a cheery and paternal bachelor on his very best and most benignant behaviour. And Eve, without knowing quite why, trusted him.

"We had a gorgeous time down at Croydon."

"I'm so glad. I enjoyed the chocolates and the books. I suppose the sugar-box was a great success?"

"Rather! I had a joke with the kids. I had two lots of presents, one lot on top, the other down below. Up above there were two pairs of socks for Percy, a prayer-book for Fred, a box of needles and cottons for Beatie, and a goody-goody book for Mab. You should have seen their faces, and the way the little beggars tried to gush and do the polite. 'Oh, uncle, it's just what I wanted!' But it was all right down below. They found the right sort of loot down there."

Eve laughed, and was surprised at the spontaneity of her own laughter. She had not laughed like that for many weeks.

"I think you must be a delightful uncle."

"Now, do you, really? It really makes it seem worth doing, you know. You'd like the kids."

"I'm sure I should."

"They're little sports, the lot of them."

She found presently that he was trying to turn the conversation towards herself, and he manœuvred with more delicacy than she had imagined him to possess. She met the attempt by making a show of frankness.

"I did not like my berth, so I threw it up. Meanwhile I am trying to do a little business in paintings and fashion plates, while I look out for something else."

"Suppose you are rather particular?"

"I don't want to take just anything that comes, if I can help it."

"Of course not. You've got brains."

"I can't do the ordinary things that women are supposed to do—type and write shorthand and keep books."

She noticed that his expression had grown more serious.

"We're all for utility in these days, you know. Beastly unromantic world. We can only get our adventures by reading novels. I'm sorry for the girls who have to work. They don't get fair opportunities, or a fair starting chance, except the few who can afford to spend a little money on special education. It's no fun supplying cheap labour."

"I suppose not."

He drew a very deep and mind-deciding breath.

"No offence meant, but if I can be of use at any time, just give me the word."

"It's very kind of you to say that."

"Nonsense, not a bit of it. We are both workers, aren't we?"

Some days Eve got panic. A great cloud shadow seemed to be drifting towards her, and already she felt it chilling her, and shutting out the sunlight. She asked herself what was going to happen if she spent all her capital before she found a means of earning money regularly, and she lay awake at night, plotting all manner of schemes. Her sense of loneliness and isolation became a black cupboard into which Fate shut her ever and again as a harsh nurse shuts up a disobedient child. She thought of leaving Bosnia Road and of moving into cheaper quarters, and she cut her economies to the lowest point. Even Mrs. Buss's face reflected her penuriousness, for the florid woman was less succulently urbane, and showed a tendency to be curt and off-hand.

Eve had begun to realise what a great city meant, with its agonies and its struggles. It was like a huge black pool in which one went drifting round and round with thousands of other creatures, clutching at straws, and even at other struggling things in the effort to keep afloat. There was always the thought of the ooze below, and the horror of submergence. Sometimes this troubled mind-picture reminded her of the wreck of the Titanic, with hundreds of little black figures swarming like beetles in the water, drowning each other in the lust to live. It was when the panic moods seized her that she was troubled by these morbid visions, for one loses one's poise at such times, and one's fears loom big and sinister as through a fog.

She had sold one picture in a fortnight, and it had brought her exactly three and sixpence. Her fashion-plates were returned. The various agencies were able to offer her situations as a domestic servant, the reality being indecently disguised under the description of "lady help." She rebelled at the suggestion, and even a panic mood could not reduce her to considering that particular form of slavery, her pride turning desperate and aggressive, and crying out that it would be better for her to indulge in any sort of adventure, to turn suffragette and break windows, rather than go into some middle-class household as an anomaly, and be the victim of some other woman's moods and prejudices.

Certain assertions that Canterton had made to her developed a sharp and vital significance. It ought not to be necessary for sensitive women to have to go down and work in the shambles. Money is a protective covering; art a mere piece of beautiful flimsiness that cannot protect the wearer from cold winds and contempt. The love of money is nothing more than the love of life and the harmony of full self-expression. Only amazing luck or a curious concatenation of coincidences can bring ability to the forefront when that ability starts with an empty pocket. People do not want art, but only to escape from being bored. Most of those who patronise any form of art do so for the sake of ostentation, that their money and their success may advertise themselves.

She realised now what she had lost in abandoning that life at Fernhill, and she looked back on it as something very near the ideal, green, spacious, sympathetic, free from all the mean and petty anxieties, a life wherein she could express all that was finest in her, without having to dissipate her enthusiasm on the butter-dish or the coal-box. It had meant protection and comradeship. She was sufficiently human in a feminine sense to feel the need of them, and there was a sufficiency of the clinging spirit in her to make her regret that she had gained a so-called independence. She was nearer now to discovering why some women are loved and others ignored. Evolution has taught the male to feel protective, and the expressing of this protective tenderness provides man with one of the most beautifying experiences that life can give. The aggressive and independent woman may satisfy a new steel-bright pride, but she has set herself against one of the tendencies of Nature. Argue as one may about evolving a new atmosphere, of redistributing the factors of life, this old fact remains. The aggressive and independent woman will never be loved in the same way. No doubt she will protest that her aim is to escape from this conception of love—sexual domination, that is what it has been dubbed, and rightly so in the multitude of cases. But a cloud of contentions cannot damp out the under-truth. The newmade woman will never challenge all that is best in man. She will continue to remain in ignorance of what man is.

Even in her panic moments Eve could not bring herself to write to Canterton. She felt that she could not reopen the past, when it was she who had closed it. She recoiled from putting herself in a position that might make it possible for him to offer her money.

One of the hardest parts of it all was that she had to live the whole time with her anxious economies. She could not afford to escape from them, to pay to forget. A shilling was a big consideration, a penny every bit a penny. Once or twice, when she was feeling particularly miserable, she let herself go to the desperate extent of a half-crown seat in the pit. And the next day she would regret the extravagance, and lunch on a scone and a glass of milk.

Then Mr. Parfit appeared in the light of a provider of amusements. One Thursday evening she had a note from him, written in his regular, commercial hand.

> "Dear Miss Carfax,—I have three dress-circles for a matinée of 'The Lost Daughter' on Saturday afternoon. Jane is coming up from Croydon. Will you honour me by joining us? We might have a little lunch at Frascati's before the theatre. I shall be proud if you accept, and I want you to meet Jane.
>
> "Very sincerely yours,
>
> "John Parfit."

She did accept, glad to escape from herself for an afternoon, and refusing to ask herself any serious questions. Mr. Parfit was in great spirits. Eve discovered "Sister Jane" to be a stout, blonde, good-humoured woman with an infinite capacity for feeling domestic affection. She studied Eve with feminine interest, and meeting her brother's eyes, smiled at him from time to time with motherly approval.

The play was a British Public play, sentimentally sexual, yet guardedly inoffensive. Eve enjoyed it. She found that John Parfit had to use his handkerchief, and that he became thick in the throat. She did not like him any the less for being capable of emotion. It seemed to be part of his personality.

Afterwards they had tea together, and Mr. Parfit's benevolence became tinged with affectionate playfulness. He made jokes, teased his sister, and tried to make Eve enter into a guessing competition as to which fancy cakes each would choose.

She appreciated his discretion when he put her in a taxi, gave the driver four shillings, and packed her off to Bosnia Road. He himself was going to see Jane off at Charing Cross. Also, he and Jane had something to discuss.

"Well, old thing, how does she strike you?"

"I'm a cautious soul, John, but I'm a woman, and we're quick about other women. She's the right stuff, even if she's clever, and a little proud. It doesn't do a girl any harm to have a little pride. Fine eyes, too, and good style."

"I knew you'd think that."

"Did you now? What do you know about women, you great big baby?"

CHAPTER XXX

MORE EXPERIENCES

January and February passed, and Eve's capital dwindled steadily, with no very obvious prospect of her being able to replenish it. She sold three more small pictures, and had one or two dress designs accepted by a woman's journal, but these fragments of good fortune were more than counterbalanced by a piece of knavish luck. One wet day, just as it was getting dusk, she had her vanity-bag snatched from her. It contained five pounds that she had drawn from the bank about half an hour before. She never had another glimpse of the bag or of the thief. Her balance had been reduced now to sixteen pounds, and all that she had foreseen in her panic moods seemed likely to be fulfilled.

Her diet became a diet of milk and buns, tea, stale eggs, and bread and butter. She spent nothing on dress, and wore her shoes long after they should have gone to the cobbler. She planned to do most of her own washing at home, drying it in front of her sitting-room fire, and putting up with the moist, steamy smell and her landlady's contemptuous face. Mrs. Buss's affability was beginning to wear very thin, for it was a surface virtue at its best. Poverty does not always inspire that human pity that we read of in sentimental stories. Primitive peoples have a horror of sickness and death, and civilisation has developed in many of us a similar horror of tragic poverty. It is to be found both in people who have struggled, and in those who have never had to struggle, and Mrs. Buss belonged to the former class. To her, poverty was a sour smell that associated itself with early and bitter memories. It brought back old qualms of mean dread and envy. She had learnt to look on poverty as a pest, and anyone who was contaminated with it became a source of offence. She recognised all the symptoms in Eve's pathetic little economies, and straightway she began to wish her out of the house.

Eve noticed that Mrs. Buss's voice became a grumbling murmur when she heard her talking to her son. Intuition attached a personal meaning to these discontented reverberations, and intuition was not at fault.

"I haven't slaved all my life to let rooms to people who can't pay! I know how the wind blows! She's getting that mean, meat once a week, and a scuttle of coal made to last two days! Next thing'll be that she'll be getting ill."

Albert was not interested, and his mother's grumblings bored him.

"Why don't you turn her out?"

"I shall have to wait till she's short with her week's money. And then, you may have to wait a month or two before you can get another let. It's a noosance and a shame."

Eve began to answer the advertisements in one or two daily papers, and to spend a few shillings in advertising on her own account. The results were not encouraging. It seemed to be a meaner world than she had imagined it to be, for people wanted to buy her body and soul for less than was paid to an ordinary cook. In fact, a servant girl was an autocrat, a gentlewoman a slave. She rebelled. She refused to be sweated—refused it with passion.

She advertised herself as willing to give painting lessons, but nothing came of it, save that one of her advertisements happened to catch Mr. Parfit's eyes. Sister Jane had called, and her brother had taken Eve twice to a theatre, and once to a concert. He dared to question her solicitously about the ways and means of life.

"How are you getting along, you know? Don't mind me, I'm only everybody's uncle."

She did not tell him the worst.

"I can't quite get the thing I want."

"How many people are doing what they want to?"

"Not many."

"One in a hundred. I wanted to be a farmer, and I'm stuck on a stool. We grumble and grouse, but we have to put on the harness. Life's like that!"

She was looking thin and ill, and he had noticed it.

"Wait a bit. Seems to me I shall have to play the inquiring father. You're not playing the milk and bun game, are you?"

"Sometimes."

He looked indignant, yet sympathetic.

"That's just what you women do, mess up your digestions with jam and tea and cake. A doctor told me once that he had seen dozens of girls on the edge of scurvy. You must feed properly."

"I get all I want."

His kindly, emotional nature burst into flame.

"Now, Miss Carfax, you've just got to tell me if you're wanting any sympathy, sympathy of the solid sort, I mean. Don't stand on ceremony. I'm a man before I'm a ceremony."

She found herself flushing.

"Thank you so much. I understand. I will tell you if I ever want to be helped."

"Promise."

"Yes."

"That's a dear, good girl."

Mrs. Buss's prophetic pessimism was justified by the event. Raw weather, leaky shoes and poor food may have helped in the overthrow, but early in March Eve caught influenzal pneumonia. The whole house was overturned. A trained nurse followed the doctor, and the nurse had to be provided with a bed, Mr. Albert Buss being reduced to sleeping on a sitting-room sofa. His mother's grumbling now found a more ready echo in him. What was the use of making oneself uncomfortable for the benefit of a nurse who was plain and past thirty, and not worth meeting on the stairs?

Mrs. Buss grumbled at the extra housework and the additional cooking.

"Just my luck. Didn't I say she'd get ill? She'll have to pay me more a week for doing for the nurse and having my house turned upside down."

But for the time being Eve was beyond the world of worries, lost in the phantasies of fever, dazed by day, and delirious at night. She was bad, very bad, and even the bored and harassed middle-class doctor allowed that she was in danger, and might need a second nurse. But at the end of the second week the disease died out of her, and she became sane and cool once more, content to lie there in a state of infinite languor, to think of nothing, and do nothing but breathe and eat and sleep.

She found flowers on the table beside her bed. John Parfit had sent them. He had discovered that she was seriously ill, and he had been calling twice a day to inquire. Every evening a bunch of flowers, roses, violets, or carnations, was brought up to her, John Parfit leaving them at Bosnia Road on his way home from the City.

Eve would lie and look at the flowers without realising all that they implied. Illness is often very merciful to those who have cares and worries. It dulls the consciousness, and brooking no rival, absorbs the sufferer into a daze of drowsiness and dreams. The body, in its feverish reaction to neutralise the poison of disease, is busy within itself, and the mind is drugged and left to sleep.

As her normal self returned to her, Eve began to cast her eyes upon the life that had been broken off so abruptly, and she discovered, to her surprise, that the things that had worried her no longer seemed to matter. She felt numb, lethargic, too tired to react to worries. She knew now that she had not been far from death, and the great shadow still lay near to her, blotting out all the lesser shadows, so that they were lost in it.

All the additional expense that she was incurring, the presence of the nurse, John Parfit's flowers, Mrs. Buss's grumbling voice, all these phenomena seemed outside the circle of reality. She recognised them, without reacting to them. So benumbed was she that the idea of spending so much money did not frighten her.

She managed to write a cheque, and the nurse cashed it for her when she went for her daily walk.

Mrs. Buss's accounts were asked for and sent up, and Eve did not feel one qualm of distress when she glanced at the figures and understood that her landlady was penalising her mercilessly for being ill. She paid Mrs. Buss, and turned her attention to the doctor.

"You won't mind my mentioning it, but I shall be very grateful if you will let me know what I owe you."

He was a thin man, with a head like an ostrich's, and a jerky, harassed manner. Struggle was written deep all over his face and person. His wife inked out the shiny places on his black coat, and he walked everywhere, and did not keep a carriage.

"That's all right, that's all right!"

"But I am serious. You see, with a limited income, one likes to meet things as they come."

"Oh, well, if it will please you. But I haven't quite finished with you yet."

"I know. But you won't forget?"

Poor devil! He was not in a position to forget anyone who owed him money.

The nurse went, having swallowed up six guineas. The doctor's bill came in soon after Eve had moved downstairs to her sitting-room. It amounted to about three pounds, and Eve paid it by cheque. Another weekly bill from Mrs. Buss confronted her, running the doctor's account to a close finish. Eve realised, after scribbling a few figures, that she was left with about four pounds to her credit.

She was astonished at her own apathy. This horror that would have sent a chill through her a month ago, now filled her with a kind of languid and cynical amusement. The inertia of her illness was still upon her, dulling the more sensitive edge of her consciousness.

A week after she had come downstairs she went out for her first walk. It was not altogether a wise proceeding, especially when its psychological effects showed themselves. She walked as far as Highbury Corner, felt the outermost ripples of the London mill-pond, and promptly awoke.

That night she had a relapse and was feverish, but it was no longer a restful, drowsy fever, but a burning and anxious torment. Life, the struggling, fitful, mean, contriving life was back in her blood, with all its dreads intensified and exaggerated. She felt the need of desperate endeavour, and was unable to stir in her own cause. It was like a dream in which some horror approaches, and one is unable to run away.

She was another week in bed, but she did not send for the doctor. And at the end of the week she met Mrs. Buss's last bill. It left her with three shillings and fourpence in cash.

In seven days she would be in debt to her landlady, to the red-faced, grumbling woman whose insolent dissatisfaction was already showing itself.

Well, how was she to get the money? What was she to do?

There was the sign of the Three Balls. She had a few rings and trinkets and her mother's jewellery, such as it was. Also, she could dispose of the studio.

Lastly, there was John Parfit—John Parfit, who was still sending her flowers. She had had a note from him. He wanted to be allowed to come and see her.

CHAPTER XXXI

THE BOURGEOIS PLAYS THE GENTLEMAN

The Saturday on which John Parfit came to see Eve was one of those premature spring days that makes one listen for the singing of birds. The little front garden was full of sunlight, and a few crocuses streaked the brown earth under the window. The Bourgeois arrived with a great bunch of daffodils, their succulent stems wrapped in blue tissue paper.

"Well, how are you now? How are you? Brought you a few flowers!"

He was shy with the shyness of a big, good-natured creature who was slow to adapt himself to strange surroundings. A feminine atmosphere had always rendered John Parfit nervous and inarticulate. He could talk like a politician in an office or a railway carriage, but thrust him into a drawing-room with a few women, and he became voiceless and futile.

"Well, how are we?"

He put his top-hat on the table, and stood the flowers in it as though it were a vase.

"But your poor hat!"

"Why, what's the matter?"

"They are such sappy things. I must thank you for all the flowers. They helped me to get well."

He removed the daffodils, and wandered round the room till he found an empty pot that agreed to rid him of them.

"Don't you bother—don't you get up! I'll settle them all right."

He came back to the fire, rubbing his hands and smiling. The smile died a sudden death when he dared to take his first good look at Eve, and with it much of his self-consciousness seemed to vanish. He sat down rather abruptly, staring.

"I say, you have had a bad time!"

"I'm afraid I have."

She looked thin, and ill, and shadowy, and plain, and her eyes were the eyes of one who was worried. A tremulous something about her mouth, the droop of her neck, the light on her hair, stirred in John Parfit an inarticulate compassion. The man in him was challenged, appealed to, touched.

"I say, you've been bad, you know!"

"But I'm getting better."

"You're—you're so white and thin!"

He spoke in an awed voice, his glance fixed on one of her hands that rested on the arm of her chair.

"I wanted to have a talk, you know. But I shall tire you."

"No."

She heard him draw a big breath.

"Look here, I'm a fool at expressing myself, but you've been having a bad time. I mean, as to the money. Beastly thing money. I've guessed that. Seems impertinent of me, but, by George! well, I can't help it. It's upset me, seeing you like this. It's made me start saying something I didn't mean to mention."

He was out of breath, and sat watching her for one dumb, inarticulate moment, his hands clenched between his knees.

"Look here, you may think me a fool, but I tell you one thing, I can't stand the thought of a girl like you having to scrape and scramble. I can't stand it. And I shouldn't have had the cheek, but for feeling like this. I'll just blurt it out. I've been thinking of it for weeks. Look here, let me take care of you—for life, I mean. I'm not a bad sort, and I don't think I shall be a selfish beast of a husband. There's nothing I won't do to make you happy."

He sat on the edge of the chair, his hands still clenched between his knees. As for Eve, she was distressed, touched, and perhaps humbled. She told herself suddenly that she had not faced this man fairly, that she had not foreseen what she ought to have foreseen. The room felt close and hot.

"I say, I haven't offended you? It mayn't seem quite sporting, talking like this, when you've been ill, but, by George! I couldn't help it."

She said very gently:

"How could I be offended? Don't you know that you are doing me a very great honour?"

"Oh, I say, do you mean it?"

"Of course."

Eve saw a hand come out tentatively and then recede, and in a flash she understood what the possible nearness of this man meant to her. She shivered, and knew that in the intimate physical sense he would be hopelessly repellent. She could not help it, even though he had touched her spiritually, and made her feel that there were elements of fineness in him that were worthy of any woman's trust.

He had been silent for some seconds, and his emotions could not be stopped now that they were discovering expression.

"Look here, I'm forty-six, and I'm going bald, but I'm a bit of a boy still. I was made to be married, but somehow I didn't. I've done pretty well in business. I've saved about seven thousand pounds, and I'm making nine hundred a year. You ought to know. I'm ready to do anything. We could take a jolly little house out somewhere—Richmond, or Hampstead, say, the new garden place. And I don't know why we shouldn't keep a little motor, or a trap. Of course, I'm telling you this, because you ought to know. I'm running on ahead rather, but it's of no consequence. I only want you to know what's what."

He was out of breath again, and she sat and stared at the fire. His rush of words had confused her. It was like being overwhelmed with food and water after one had been dying of hunger and thirst and fear in a desert. His essential and half pathetic sincerity went to her heart, nor could she help her gratitude going out to him. Not for a moment did she think of him as a fat, commonplace sentimentalist, a middle-aged fool who fell over his own feet when he tried to make love. He was more than a good creature. He was a man who had a right to self-expression.

She rallied her will-power.

"I don't know what to say to you. I suppose I am feeling very weak."

He rushed into self-accusation.

"There, I've been a selfish beast. I oughtn't to have come and upset you like this. But I couldn't help telling you."

"I know. It hasn't hurt me. But you have offered me such a big thing, that I am trying to realise it all. I don't think I'm made for marriage."

"Oh, don't say that! I know I'm a blundering idiot!"

"No, no, it is not you! It is marriage."

"You don't believe in marriage?"

"Not that. I mean, for myself. I don't think I could make you understand why."

He looked puzzled and distressed.

"It's my fault. I couldn't do the thing delicately. I'm clumsy."

"No, no. I have told you that it is not that."

"Well, you think it over. Supposing we leave it till you get stronger?"

"But you are offering everything and I nothing."

"Nonsense! Besides, I don't believe in marrying a woman with money. I'd rather have the business on my own back. Of course, I should settle two or three thousand on you, you know, so that you would have a little income for pin-money. I think that's only fair to a woman."

She coloured and felt guilty.

"I think you are more generous than fair. Don't say any more. I'll—I'll think it over."

He got up and seized his hat.

"That's it—that's it. You think it over! I'm not one of those fellows who thinks that a woman is going to rush at him directly he says come. It means a lot to a woman, a dickens of a lot. And you're not quite yourself yet, are you? It's awfully good of you to have listened."

He reached for her hand, bent over it with cumbrous courtesy, and covered up a sudden silence by getting out of the room as quickly as he could.

When John Parfit had gone, Eve lay back in her chair with a feeling of intense languor. All the strength and independence seemed to melt out of her, and she lay like a tired child on the knees of circumstance.

And then it was that she was tempted—tempted in this moment of weariness, by the knowledge that a way of escape lay so very near. She had been offered a protected life, food, shelter, a generous allowance, love, leisure, all that the orthodox woman is supposed to desire. He was kind, understanding in his way, reliable, a man whose common sense was to be trusted, and he would take her away from this paltry scramble, pilot her out of the crowd, and give her an affection that would last. Her intuition recognised the admirable husband in him. This middle-class man had a rich vein of sentiment running through his nature, and he was not too clever or too critical to tire.

Dusk began to fall, and the fire was burning low. It was the hour for memories, and into the dusk of that little suburban room, glided a subtle sense of other presences, and she found herself thinking of Canterton and the child. If she were to have a child like Lynette. But it could not be Lynette—it could not be his child, the child of that one man. She sat up, shocked and challenged. What was she about to do? Sell herself. Promise to give something that it was not in her power to give. Deceive a man who most honestly loved her. It would be prostitution. There was only one man living to whom she could have granted complete physical comradeship. She was not made to be touched by other hands.

She rose and lit the gas, and sat down at the table to write a letter. She would tell John Parfit the truth; put the shame of temptation out of her way.

It was not a long letter, but it came straight from her heart. No man could be offended by it—hurt by it. It was human, honourable, a tribute to the man to whom it was written.

When she had addressed and stamped it, she rang the bell for Mrs. Buss.

"I should be very much obliged if you could have this posted for me."

Mrs. Buss was affable, having smelt matrimony and safe money.

"Certainly, miss. I'll send Albert down to the pillar-box. Excuse me saying it; but you do look pounds better. You've got quite a colour."

And she went out, simpering.

CHAPTER XXXII

EVE DETERMINES TO LEAVE BOSNIA ROAD

After she had written to John Parfit, Eve kept the promise she had made to Kate Duveen, but qualified her confession by an optimism that took the sting out of the truths that she had to tell. She made light of the Massinger affair, even though she had some bitter things to say about Miss Champion. "One learns to expect certain savageries from the ordinary sort of man, but it shocks one when a woman makes you bear all the responsibility, so that she may not offend a patron. That was the really sordid part of the experience." She hinted vaguely that someone wanted to marry her, but that she had no intention of marrying. She made light of her illness, and wrote of her financial experiences with cynical gaiety. "My landlady's face is a barometer that registers the state of my weather. Of late, the mercury has been low. Another woman whom I can manage to pity! Do not think that I am in a parlous and desperate state. I want to go through these experiences. They give one a sense of proportion, and teach one the value of occasional recklessness. We are not half reckless enough, we moderns. We are educated to be too careful. In future, I may contemplate adventures."

It is probable that John Parfit's proposal and its psychological effects on her rallied her pride, for she threw off the lethargy of convalescence, and turned anew to meet necessity. John Parfit had answered her letter by return, and he had succeeded in fully living up to his ideal of what was "sport." "Playing the game,"—that is the phrase that embodies the religion of many such a man as John Parfit.

> "Nothing could have made me admire you more than the straight way you have written. Nothing like the truth. It may be bitter, but it's good physic. Well, I shall be here. Think it over. It's the afterwards in marriage that counts, not the courting, and I'd do my best to make the afterwards what it should be.
>
> "You'll let me see you sometimes, won't you? I shan't bother you. I'm not a conceited ass, and I'll wait and take my chance."

March winds and more sunshine were in evidence, and the weather had a drier and more energetic temper. Eve started out on expeditions. She took two rings, a gold watch, and a coral necklace to a pawnshop in

Holloway, and raised three pounds on the transaction. It amused her, tucking the pawn-ticket away in her purse. These last refuges are supposed to have a touch of the melodramatic, but she discovered that expectation had been harder to bear than the reality, and that just as one is disappointed by some eagerly longed for event, so the disaster that one dreads turns out to be a very quiet experience, relieved perhaps by elements of humour.

She paid Mrs. Buss's weekly bill, and studied the woman's recovered affability with cynical tolerance. Mrs. Buss still believed her to be on the way towards matrimony, and somehow a woman who is about to be married gains importance, possibly because other women wonder what she will make of that best and most problematical of states.

It is easy to raise money on some article of value, but it is a much harder matter to persuade people to offer money in return for the activities that we call work. Eve went the round of the agencies without discovering anything that could be classed above the level of cheap labour. There seemed to be no demand for artistic ability. At least, she did not chance upon the demand if it happened to exist. Her possibilities seemed to be limited to such posts as lady help or companion, posts that she had banned as the uttermost deeps of slavery. A factory worker was far more free. She could still contemplate sinking some of her pride, and starting life as a shop-girl, a servant, or a waitress.

At one agency the manageress, whose lack of patience made her tell the brusque truth on occasions, went so far as to suggest that Eve might take a place as parlourmaid in a big house. She had a smart figure and a good appearance. Some people were dispensing with menservants, and were putting their maids into uniform and making them take the place of butler and footman. The position of such a servant was preferable to the lot of a lady-help. Wouldn't Eve think it over?

Eve said she would. She agreed with the manageress in thinking that there were gleams of independence in such a life, especially when one had gained a character and experience, learnt to look after silver and to know about wines.

None the less, she was discouraged and rebellious, and on her way home after one of these expeditions, she fell in with John Parfit. It was the man of six-and-forty who blushed, not Eve. She had to help him over the stile of his self-consciousness.

"Yes, I am ever so much better. Won't you walk a little way with me? I've had tea, and I thought of having a stroll round the Fields."

He put himself at her side with laborious politeness, and because of his shyness he could do nothing more graceful than blurt out questions.

"Got what you want yet?"

"No, not yet."

He frowned to himself.

"Not worrying, are you?"

"I'm learning not to worry. Nothing is as bad as it seems."

He looked at her curiously, puzzled, and troubled on her account.

"It's a matter of temperament. Perhaps you are not one of the worrying sort."

"But I am. One finds that one can learn not to worry about the things that just concern self. The thing that does worry us is the thought that we may make other people suffer any loss."

He said bluntly, "Bills?"

Eve laughed.

"In brief, bills. But I am perfectly solvent, and I could get work tomorrow if I chose to take it."

"But you don't. It's pride."

"Yes, pride."

He walked on beside her in his solid, broad-footed way, staring straight ahead, and keeping silent for fully half a minute.

Then he said abruptly:

"It hasn't made any difference, you know."

It was her turn to feel embarrassed.

"But you understood——"

"Yes, I understood all right. But I want to say just this, I respect you all the more for having been straight with me, and if you'll let me have a waiting chance, I'll make the best of it. I won't bother you. I've got a sense of proportion. I'm not the sort of man a woman would get sentimental over in a hurry."

Her eyes glimmered.

"You are one of the best men I have ever met. In a city of cads, it is good to find a man who has a sense of honour."

He went very red, and seemed to choke something back.

"I shan't forget that in a hurry. But look here, put the other thing aside, and let's just think of ourselves as jolly good friends. Now, I want you to let me do some of the rough and tumble for you. I'm used to it. One gets a business skin."

"I am not going to bother you."

"Bosh! And if you happen to want—well, you know what, any of the beastly stuff we pay our bills with——"

She began to show her distress.

"Don't, please. I know how generously you mean it all, but I'm so made that I can't bear to be helped, even by you. Just now my pride is raw, and I want to go alone through some of these experiences. You may think it eccentric."

He stared hard at nothing in particular.

"I don't know. I suppose it's in the air. Women are changing."

"No, don't believe that. It's only some of the circumstances of life that are changing, and we are altering some of our methods. That's what life is teaching me. That's why I want to go on alone. I shall learn so much more."

"I should have thought that most people would fight shy of learning in such a school."

"Yes, and that is why most of us remain so narrow and selfish and prejudiced. We refuse to touch realities, and we won't understand. I want to understand."

He walked on, expanding his chest, and looking as though he were smothering a stout impulse to protest.

"All right; I see. Anyway, I shall be round the corner. You won't forget that, will you?"

"No, for you have helped me already."

"Have I?"

"Of course. It always helps to be able to believe in someone."

Three days later Eve rang for Mrs. Buss and had an interview with the woman. She was amused to find that she herself had hardened perceptibly, and that she could lock her sentiments away when the question was a question of cash.

Her frankness astonished Mrs. Buss.

"I want to explain something to you. I mean to stay here for another three weeks, but I have no more money."

The landlady gaped, not knowing whether this was humour or mere barefaced self-confidence.

"You're going to be married, then?"

"No."

"You say you haven't any money, and you expect me——"

"There is the studio."

"A shed like that's no use to me."

"It cost me about twenty-five pounds, with the stove and fittings, and it is only a few months old. It is made to take to pieces. Shall I sell it, or will you? I was thinking that it might be worth your while."

Mrs. Buss discovered glimmerings of reason. An incipient, sly smile glided round her mouth.

"Oh, I see! You think I could drive a better bargain?"

"I do."

The middle-class nature was flattered.

"You'll be owing me about four pounds ten. And we might get twelve or thirteen pounds for the studio."

It was studio now, not shed.

"Yes. I shall pay your bill, and give you a fifteen per cent. commission on the sale. Do you know anyone who might buy it?"

"I'm not so sure, miss, that I don't."

Mrs. Buss's eyes were so well opened that she put on her bonnet, went round to a local builder's, and, telling him a few harmless fibs, persuaded him to buy the studio and its stove for thirteen pounds ten. The builder confessed, directly they had completed the bargain, that the studio was the very thing a customer of his wanted. He said he would look round next day and see the building, and that if he found it all right, he would hand over the money. He came, saw, and found nothing to grumble at, and before the day was out he had resold the studio for twenty pounds, stating blandly that it had originally cost thirty-five pounds, and that it was almost new, and that the gentleman had got a bargain.

Mrs. Buss brought the money to Eve, one five pound note, eight sovereigns, and ten shillings in silver, and Eve handed over four pounds, and the commission.

"We can settle for any odds and ends when I go."

"Thank you, miss. I may say you have treated me very fairly, miss. And would you mind if I put up a card in the window?"

"No."

"You see, it's part of my living. If one loses a week or two, it's serious."

"Of course."

So a card with "Apartments" printed on it went up in Eve's window, helping her to realise that the term of her sojourn in Bosnia Road was drawing to a close.

CHAPTER XXXIII

WOMAN'S WAR

It was during these last weeks at Bosnia Road that Eve became fully conscious of that spirit of revolt that is one of the dominating features of contemporary life, for she was experiencing in her own person the thoughts and tendencies of a great movement, suffering its discontents, feeling its hopes and passions.

When she tried to analyse these tendencies in herself, she was confronted with the disharmonies of her life, disharmonies that reacted all the more keenly on a generous and impulsive nature. She was necessary to nobody, not even to the man who had thought that it would be pleasant to marry her, for she knew that in a month he would be as contented as ever with his old bachelor life. She had no personal corner, no sacred place full of the subtle and pleasant presence of the individual "I." She had none of the simple and primitive responsibilities that provide many women with a natural and organic satisfaction.

A new class had arisen, the class of the unattached working women, and she was sharing the experiences of thousands. It was a sense of defencelessness that angered her. She had no weapon. She could only retaliate upon society by shutting her mouth and holding her head a little higher. Her individuality was threatened. She was denied the chance of living a life of self-expression, and was told with casual cynicism that she must do such work as society chose to offer her, or starve.

Of course, there were the chances of escape, the little, secret, fatal doorways that men were willing to leave open. Some women availed themselves of these opportunities, nor was Eve so prejudiced as to imagine that all women were martyrs and less hot blooded than the men. She had had the same doors opened to her. She might have become a mistress, or have married a man who was physically distasteful to her, and she understood now why many women were so bitter against anything that was male. It was not man, but the sex spirit, and all its meaner predilections.

Ninety-nine men out of a hundred concerned themselves with nothing but a woman's face and figure. They reacted to physical impressions, and Eve realised the utter naturalness of it all. The working woman had got outside the old conventions. She was trying to do unsexual things, and to talk an unsexual language to men who had not changed. It was like muddling up business and sentiment, and created an impossible position, so long as the male nature continued to react in the way it did. Sexual solicitation or plain indifference, these were the two extreme fates that bounded the life of the working woman.

Eve told herself that there were exceptions, but that society, in the mass, moved along these lines. She had listened to Kate Duveen—Kate Duveen, who was a fanatic, and who had made it her business to look into the conditions under which working women lived. The shop-girl, the servant, the waitress, the clerk, the typist, the chorus-girl, the street-walker; always they held in their hands the bribe that men desired, that bribe so fatal to the woman when once it had been given. Eve began to understand the spirit of revolt by the disgust that was stirred in her own heart. This huge sexual machine. This terrible, primitive groundwork upon which all the shades of civilisation were tagged like threads of coloured silk. There was some resemblance here between the reaction of certain women against sex, and the reaction of the early Christians against the utter physical smell of the Roman civilisation. To live, one must be born again. One must triumph over the senses. One must refuse to treat with men on the old physical understanding. They are the cries of extremists, and yet of an extremity that hopes to triumph by urging a passionate and protesting celibacy. A million odd women in the United Kingdom, over-setting the sex balance, and clamouring, many of them, that they will not be weighed in the old sexual scale.

Eve caught the spirit of rebellion, divorced as she was from any comradeship with men. It is so much easier to quarrel with the hypothetical antagonists whom one meets in the world of one's own brain. Bring two prejudiced humans together, get them to talk like reasonable beings, and each may have some chance of discovering that the other is not the beast that he or she had imagined. It is when masses of people segregate and refuse to mix that war becomes more than probable.

Insensibly, yet very surely, Eve began to imbibe this feeling of antagonism. It made her take sides, even when she happened to read the account of some law case in the paper. And this tacit antagonism abetted her in her refusal to accept the cheap labour that society, "male society," she called it, chose to offer her. It behoved women to stand out against male exploitation, even if they had to suffer for the moment. Yet her revolt was still an individual revolt. She had not joined herself to the crowd. She wanted to complete her personal experiences before associating herself with the great mass of discontent, and she meant to go through to the end—to touch all the realities. Perhaps she was a little feverish in her sincerity. She had been ill. She had been badly fed. She had been worried, and she was in a mood that demanded that specious sort of realism that is to the truth what a statue is to the living body.

Her last morning at Bosnia Road turned out to be warm and sunny. She was ready to smile at contrasts, and to draw them with a positive and perverse wilfulness. Breakfast was just like other breakfasts, only different. The brown teapot with the chip out of its lid stood there, familiar yet ironical. The marmalade dish, with its pinky roses and silver-plated handle that was wearing green, reminded her that it would meet her eyes no more. The patchwork tea-cosy was like a fat and sentimental old lady who was always exclaiming, "Oh, dear, what a wicked world it is!" Even the egg-cup, with its smudgy blue pattern, had a ridiculous individuality of its own. Eve felt a little emotional and more than a little morbid, and ready to laugh at herself because a teapot and an egg-cup made her moralise.

She had packed all her belongings, paid Mrs. Buss, and ordered a "growler" to call at half-past ten. The cabman was punctual. He came into the narrow hall, rubbing his boots on the doormat, a cheerful ancient, a bolster of clothes, and looking to be in perpetual proximity to breathlessness and perspiration. He laid his old top-hat on the floor beside the staircase, and went up to struggle with Eve's boxes.

Mrs. Buss had let Eve's rooms, and had nothing to complain of. For the time being her attention was concentrated on seeing that the cabman did not knock the paint off the banisters.

"Do be careful now!"

A red-faced man was descending under the shadow of a big black trunk.

"All right, mum. Don't you worry, mum!"

He breathed hard and diffused a scent of the stable.

"Them chaps as builds 'ouses don't think of the luggidge and foornitoore. 'Old up, there!"

A corner of the trunk jarred against the wall and left a gash in the paper. Mrs. Buss made a clucking sound with her tongue.

"There, didn't I say!"

"Did I touch anythink?"

"Now, mind the hat-stand! And the front door was painted three months ago."

"Don't you worry, mum. It ain't the first time luggidge and me 'as gone out walkin' together!"

Mrs. Buss turned to Eve who was standing in the sitting-room doorway.

"That's just the British working-man to a T. He earns his living by doing one thing all his life, and he does it badly. My poor husband found that out before he died. I do hope I've made you feel comfortable and homely? I always try to do my best."

"I'm sure you do."

She was glad when the loading up business was over, and she was driving away between the dull little houses.

Eve had written to book a room at a cheap hotel in Bloomsbury, an hotel that had been brought into being by the knocking together of three straight-faced, dark-bricked old houses. She drove first to the hotel, left a light trunk and a handbag there, and then ordered the cabman to go on to Charing Cross where she left the rest of her luggage in the keeping of the railway company.

A sudden sense of freedom came over her when she walked out of the station enclosure, after paying and tipping the driver of the growler, who was surprised at the amount of the tip. She had been delivered from suburbia, and her escape from Bosnia Road made her the more conscious of the largeness and the stimulating complexity of life. She felt a new exhilaration, and a sense of adventure that glimpsed more spacious happenings. It was more like the mood that is ascribed to the young man who rides out alone, tossing an audacious sword.

Eve decided to treat herself to a good lunch for once, and she walked to Kate Duveen's Italian restaurant in Soho, and amplified and capped the meal with a half bottle of claret, coffee, and a liqueur. She guessed that she had plenty of Aerated Bread shop meals before her. After lunch she took a motor-bus to the Marble Arch, wandered into the park, and down to the Serpentine, and discovering an empty seat, took the opportunity of reviewing her finances. She found that she had five pounds sixteen shillings and fivepence left. The Bloomsbury hotel charged four and sixpence for bed and breakfast, and she would be able to stay there for some three weeks, if she had the rest of her meals at tea-shops and cheap restaurants.

Eve sat there for an hour, watching the glimmer of the water and the moving figures, growing more and more conscious of the vast, subdued murmur that drifted to her from beyond the bare trees. Neither the pitch nor the volume of the sound varied, though it was pierced now and again by the near note of a motor horn. The murmur went on and on, grinding out its under-chant that was made up of the rumbling of wheels, the plodding of hoofs, the hooting of horns, the rattle and pant of machinery, the voices of men and women. This green space seemed a spot of silence in the thick of a whirl of throbbing, quivering movement. She had always hated London traffic, but to-day it had something to say to her.

The sun shone, the spring was in, and it was warm there, sitting on the seat. The water blinked, sparrows chirped, waterfowl uttered their cries, children played, daffodils were in bloom. Eve felt herself moving suddenly to a fuller consciousness of modern life. Her brain seemed to pulsate with it, to glow with a new understanding.

Conquest! She could understand the feverish and half savage passion for conquest that seized many men. To climb above the crowd, to get money, to assert one's individuality, brutally perhaps, but at all costs and against all comers. People got trampled on, trodden under. It was a stampede, and the stronger and the more selfish animals survived. Yet society had some sort of legal conscience. It had to make some show of clearing up its rubbish and its wreckage. The pity of it was that there was so much "afterthought," when "forethought" might have saved so much disease and disaster.

She pictured to herself all those women and girls working over yonder, the seamstresses and milliners, the clerks, typists, shop-girls, waitresses, factory hands, *filles de joie*—what a voiceless, helpless crowd it seemed. Was the clamour for the vote a mere catch cry, one of those specious demagogic phrases that pretended to offer so much and would effect so little? Was it not the blind, passionate cry of a mass of humanity that desired utterance and yearned for self-expression? Could anything be altered, or was life just a huge, fateful phenomenon that went its inevitable way, despite all the talk and the fussy little human figures? She wondered. How were things going to be bettered? How were the sex spirit and the commercial spirit going to be chastened and subdued?

CHAPTER XXXIV

EVE PURSUES EXPERIENCE

During the next two weeks Eve's moods fluctuated between compassionate altruism and bitter and half laughing scorn. Life was so tremendous, so pathetic, so strenuous, so absurd. For the time being she was a watcher of other people's activities, and she spent much of her time tramping here, there and everywhere, interested in everything because of her new prejudices. She was glad to get out of the hotel, since it was full of a certain type of American tourists—tall, sallow women who talked in loud, harsh voices, chiefly about food and the digestion of food, where they had been, and what they had paid for things. The American man was a new type to Eve—a mongrel still in the making. The type puzzled and repelled her with its broad features, and curious brown eyes generally seen behind rimless glasses. Sometimes she sat and watched them and listened, and fancied she caught a note of hysterical egoism. Their laughter was not like an Englishman's laughter. It burst out suddenly and rather fatuously, betraying, despite all the jaw setting and grim hunching of shoulders, a lack of the deeper restraints. They were always talking, always squaring themselves up against the rest of the world, with a neurotic self-consciousness that realised that it was still only half civilised. They suggested to Eve people who had set out to absorb culture in a single generation, and had failed most grotesquely. She kept an open mind as to the men, but she disliked the women wholeheartedly. They were studies in black and white, and crude, harsh studies, with no softness of outline.

One Sunday she walked to Hyde Park and saw some of the suffragist speakers pelted with turf by a rowdily hostile crowd. The occasion proved to be critical, so far as some of her tendencies were concerned. Militancy had not appealed to her. There was too much of the "drunk and disorderly" about it, too much spiteful screaming. It suggested a reversion to savage, back-street methods, and Eve's pride had refused to indulge in futile and wholly undignified exhibitions of violence. There were better ways of protesting than by kicking policemen's shins, breaking windows, and sneaking about at midnight setting fire to houses. Yet when she saw these women pelted, hooted at, and threatened, the spirit of partisanship fired up at the challenge.

She was on the outskirts of the crowd, and perhaps her pale and intent face attracted attention. At all events, she found a lout, who looked like a young shop-assistant, standing close beside her, and staring in her face.

"Votes for women!"

His ironical shout was an accusation, and his eyes were the eyes of a bully. And of a sudden Eve understood what it meant for a woman to have to stand up and face the coarse male element in the crowd, all the young cads who were out for horseplay. She was conscious of physical fear; a shrinking from the bestial thoughtlessness of a mob that did things that any single man would have been ashamed to do.

The fellow was still staring at her.

"Now, then, 'Votes for Women!' Own up!"

He jogged her with his elbow, and she kept a scornful profile towards him, though trembling inwardly.

Someone interposed.

"You there, leave the young lady alone! She's only listening like you and me."

The aggressor turned with a snarl, but found himself up against a particularly big workman dressed in his Sunday clothes.

"You're an old woman yourself."

"Go home and sell stockings over the counter, and leave decent people alone."

Eve thanked the man with a look, and turned out of the crowd. The workman followed her.

"'Scuse me, miss, I'll walk to the gates with you. There are too many of these young blackguard fools about."

"Thank you very much."

"I've got a lot of sympathy with the women, but seems to me some of 'em are on the wrong road."

She looked at him interestedly. He was big and fresh coloured and quiet, and reminded her in his coarser way of James Canterton.

"You think so?"

"It don't do to lose your temper, even in a game, and that's what some of the women are doing. We're reasonable sort of creatures, and it's no use going back to the old boot and claw business."

"What they say is that they have tried reasoning, and that men would not listen."

He laughed.

"That's rot! Excuse me, miss. You've got to give reason a chance, and a pretty long chance. Do you think we working men won what we've got in three months? You have to go on shoving and shoving, and in the end, if you've got common sense on your side, you push the public through. You can't expect things turned all topsy-turvy in ten minutes, because a few women get up on carts and scream. They ought to know better."

"They say it is the only thing that's left."

His blue eyes twinkled.

"Not a bit of it, miss. The men were coming round. We're better chaps, better husbands and fathers than we were a hundred years ago. You know, miss, a man ain't averse to a decent amount of pleasant persuasion. It don't do to nag him, or he may tell you to go to blazes. Well, I wish you good afternoon."

They had reached the gates, and he touched the brim of his hard hat, smiling down at her with shrewd kindness.

"I'm very grateful to you."

He coloured up, and his smile broadened, and Eve walked away down Oxford Street, doing some pregnant thinking.

The man had reminded her of Canterton. What was Canterton's attitude towards this movement, and what was her attitude to Canterton now that she had touched more of the realities of life? When she came to analyse her feelings she found that Canterton did not appear to exist for her in the present. Fernhill and its atmosphere had become prehistoric. It had removed into the Golden Age, above and beyond criticism, and she did not include it in this world of struggling prejudices and aspirations. And yet, when she let herself think of Canterton and Lynette, she felt less sure of the sex antagonism that she was encouraging with scourge and prayer. Canterton seemed to stand in the pathway of her advance, looking down at her with eyes that smiled, eyes that were without mockery. Moreover, something that he had once said to her kept opposing itself to her arbitrary and enthusiastic pessimism. She could remember him stating his views, and she could remember disagreeing with him.

He had said, "People are very much happier than you imagine. Sentimentalists have always made too much of the woe of the world. There is a sort of thing I call organic happiness, the active physical happiness of the animal that is reasonably healthy. Of course we grumble, but don't make the mistake of taking grumbling for the cries of discontented misery. I believe that most of the miserable people are over-sensed, under-bodied neurotics. They lack animal vitality. I think I can speak from experience, since I have mixed a good deal with working people. In the mass they are happy, much happier, perhaps, than we are. Perhaps because they don't eat too much, and so think dyspeptically."

That saying of Canterton's, "People are much happier than you imagine" haunted Eve's consciousness, walked at her side, and would not suffer itself to be forgotten. She had moments when she suspected that he had spoken a great truth. He had told her once to read Walt Whitman, but of what use was that great, barbaric, joyous person to her in her wilful viewing of sociological problems? It was a statement that she could test by her own observations, this assertion that the majority of people are happy. The clerks and shopmen who lunched in the tea-shops talked hard, laughed, and made a cheerful noise. If she went to the docks or Covent Garden Market, or watched labourers at work in the streets, she seemed to strike a stolid yet jocose cheerfulness that massed itself against her rather pessimistic view of life. The evening crowds in the streets were cheerful, and these, she supposed, were the people who slaved in shops. The factory girls out for the dinner hour were merry souls. If she went into one of the parks on Sunday, she could not exactly convince herself that she was watching a miserable people released for one day from the sordid and hopeless slavery of toil.

The mass of people did appear to be happy. And Eve was absurdly angry, with some of the prophet's anger, who would rather have seen a city perish than that God should make him appear a fool. Her convictions rallied themselves to meet the challenge of this apparent fact. She contended that this happiness was a specious, surface happiness. One had but to get below the surface, to penetrate behind the mere scenic effects of civilisation to discover the real sorrows. What of the slums? She had seen them with her own eyes. What of the hospitals, the asylums, the prisons, the workhouses, the sweating dens, even the sordid little suburbs! She was in a temper to pile Pelion on Ossa in her desire to storm and overturn this serene Olympian assumption that mankind in the mass was happy.

In walking along Southampton Row into Kingsway, she passed on most days a cheerful, ruddy-faced young woman who sold copies of *Votes for Women*. This young woman was prettily plain, but good to look at in a clean and comely and sturdy way. Eve glanced at her each day with the eyes of a friend. The figure became personal, familiar, prophetic. She had marked down this young woman who sold papers as a Providence to whom she might ultimately appeal.

It seemed to her a curious necessity that she should be driven to try and prove that people were unhappy, and that most men acted basely in their sexual relationships towards women. This last conviction did not need much proving.

Being in a mood that demanded fanatical thoroughness, Eve played with the ultimate baseness of man, and made herself a candle to the night-flying moths. She repeated the experience twice—once in Regent Street, and once in Leicester Square. Nothing but fanaticism could have made such an experiment possible, and have enabled her to outface her scorn and her disgust. Several men spoke to her, and she dallied with each one for a few seconds before letting him feel her scorn.

She spent the last night of her stay in the Bloomsbury hotel sitting in the lounge and listening to three raucous American women who were talking over their travels. They had been to Algiers, Egypt, Italy, the South of France, and of course to Paris. The dominant talker, who had gorgeous yellow hair, not according to Nature, and whose hands were always moving restlessly and showing off their rings, seemed to remember and to identify the various places she had visited by some particular sort of food that she had eaten! "Siena, Siena. Wasn't that the place, Mina, where we had ravioli?"

"Did you go to Ré's at Monte Carlo? It's an experience to have eaten at Ré's." "I shan't forget the Nile. The Arab boy made some bad coffee, and I was sick in the stomach." They went on to describe their various hagglings with hotel-keepers, cabmen, and shop-people, and the yellow-haired lady who wore "nippers" on a very thin-bridged, sharp-pointed nose, had an exhilarating tale to tell of how she had stood out against a Paris taxi-driver over a matter of ten cents. Eve had always heard such lavish tales of American extravagance, that she was surprised to discover in these women the worst sort of meanness, the meanness that contrives to be generous on a few ostentatious occasions by beating all the lesser people's profits down to vanishing point. She wondered whether these American women with their hard eyes, selfish mouths, and short-fingered, ill-formed, grasping hands were typical of this new hybrid race.

It amused her to contrast her own situation with theirs. When to-morrow's bill was paid, and her box taken to Charing Cross station, she calculated that she would have about twelve pence left in her purse. And she was going to test another aspect of life on those twelve pennies. It would not be ravioli, or luncheon at Ré's.

Eve packed up her box next morning, paid her bill, and drove off to Charing Cross, where she left her box in the cloak-room. She had exactly elevenpence left in her purse, and it was her most serious intention to make these eleven pennies last her for the best part of two days. One thing that she had lost, without noticing it, was her sense of humour. Fanaticism cannot laugh. Had Simeon Stylites glimpsed but for a moment the comic side of his existence, he would have come down off that pillar like a cat off a burning roof.

The day turned out to be a very tiring one for her, and Eve found out how abominably uncomfortable London can be when one has no room of one's own to go to, and no particular business to do. She just drifted about till she was tired, and then the problem was to find something upon which to sit. She spent the latter part of the morning in the gardens below Charing Cross Station, and then it began to rain. Lunch cost her threepence—half a scone and butter, and a glass of milk. She dawdled over it, but rain was still falling when she came out again into the street. A station waiting-room appeared to be her only refuge, for it was a sixpenny day at the National Gallery, and as she sat for two hours on a bench, wondering whether the weather was going to make the experiment she contemplated a highly realistic and unpleasant test of what a wet night was like when spent on one of the Embankment seats.

The weather cleared about four o'clock, and Eve went across to a tea-shop, and spent another threepence on a cup of tea and a slice of cake. She had made a point of making the most of her last breakfast at the hotel, but she began to feel abominably hungry, with a hunger that revolted against cake. After tea she walked to Hyde Park, sat there till within half an hour of dusk, and then wandered back down Oxford Street, growing hungrier and hungrier. It was a very provoking sign of health, but if one part of her clamoured for food, her body, as a whole, protested that it was tired. The sight of a restaurant made her loiter, and she paused once or twice in front of some confectionery shop, and looked at the cakes in the window. But sweet stuffs did not tempt her. They are the mere playthings of people who are well fed. She found that she had a most primitive desire for good roast meat, beef for preference, swimming in brown gravy, and she accepted her appetite quite solemnly as a phenomenon that threw an illuminating light upon the problems of existence.

Exploring a shabbier neighbourhood she discovered a cheap cook-shop with a steaming window and a good advertising smell. There was a bill of fare stuck up in the window, and she calculated that she could spend another three pennies. Sausages and mashed potatoes were to be had for that sum, and in five minutes she was sitting at a wooden table covered with a dirty cloth, and helping herself to mustard out of a cracked glass pot.

It was quite a carnal experience, and she came out refreshed and much more cheerful, telling herself with naive seriousness that she was splitting life up into its elements. Food appeared to be a very important problem, and hunger a lust whose strength is unknown save to the very few, yet she was so near to her real self that she was on the edge of laughter. Then it occurred to her that she was not doing the thing thoroughly, that she had lapsed, that she ought to have started the night hungry.

There was more time to be wasted, and she strolled down Shaftesbury Avenue and round Piccadilly Circus into Regent Street. The pavements were fairly crowded, and the multitude of lights made her feel less lonely. She loitered along, looking into shop windows, and she had amused herself in this way for about ten minutes before she became aware of another face that kept appearing near to hers. She saw it reflected in four successive windows, the face of an old man, spruce yet senile, the little moustache carefully trimmed, a faint red patch on either cheek. The eyes were turned to one side, and seemed to be watching something. She did not realise at first that that something was herself.

"How are you to-night, dear?"

Eve stared straight through the window for some seconds, and then turned and faced him. He was like Death valeted to perfection, and turned out with all his senility polished to the last finger nail. His lower eyelids were baggy, and innumerable little veins showed in the skin that looked tightly stretched over his nose and cheekbones. He smiled at her, the fingers of one hand picking at the lapel of his coat.

"I am glad to see you looking so nice, dear. Supposing we have a little dinner?"

"I beg your pardon. I think you must be rather short-sighted!"

She thought as she walked away, "Supposing I had been a different sort of woman, and supposing I had been hungry!"

She made direct for the river after this experience, and, turning down Charing Cross and under the railway bridge, saw the long sweep of the darkness between the fringes of yellow lights. There were very few people about, and a raw draught seemed to come up the river. She crossed to the Embankment and walked along, glancing over the parapet at the vaguely agitated and glimmering surface below. The huge shadow of the bridge seemed to take the river at one leap. The lapping of the water was cold, and suggestively restless.

Then she turned her attention to the seats. They seemed to be full, packed from rail to rail with indistinct figures that were huddled close together. All these figures were mute and motionless. Once she saw a flutter of white where someone was picking broken food out of a piece of newspaper. And once she heard a figure speaking in a monotonous grumbling voice that kept the same level.

Was she too late even for such a refuge? She walked on and at last discovered a seat where a gap showed between a man's felt hat and a woman's bonnet. Eve paused rather dubiously, shrinking from thrusting herself into that vacant space. She shrank from touching these sodden greasy things that had drifted like refuse into some sluggish backwater.

Then a quiver of pity and of shame overcame her. She went and thrust herself into the vacant place. The whole seat seemed to wriggle and squirm. The man next to her heaved and woke up with a gulp. Eve discovered at once that his breath was not ambrosial.

She felt a hand tugging at something. It belonged to the old woman next to her.

"'Ere, you're sitting on it!"

"I beg your pardon."

She felt something flat withdrawn. It was a bloater wrapped up in a bit of paper, but the woman did not explain. She tucked the thing away behind her and relapsed. The whole seat resettled itself. No one said anything. Eve heard nothing but the sound of breathing, and the noise made by the passing of an occasional motor, cab, or train.

CHAPTER XXXV

THE SUFFRAGETTE

The night spent on the Embankment seat was less tragic than squalidly uncomfortable. Wedged in there between those hopeless other figures, Eve had to resist a nauseating sense of their physical uncleanness, and to overcome instincts that were in wholesome revolt. Her ears and nostrils did not spare her. There was a smell of stale alcohol, a smell of fish, a smell of sour and dirty clothes. Moreover, the man who sat on her right kept rolling his head on to her shoulder, his dirty felt hat rubbing her ear and cheek. She edged him off rather roughly, and he woke up and swore.

"What the ——— are you shovin' for?"

After that she did not attempt to wake him again, turning her face as far away as possible when his slobbery, stertorous mouth puffed against her shoulders.

As for the seat—well, it was her first experience of sitting all night in one position, on a sort of unpadded reality. Her back ached, her neck ached, her legs ached. She was afraid of waking the man beside her, and the very fact that she dared not move was a horror in itself. She felt intolerably stiff, and her feet and hands were cold. She found herself wondering what would happen if she were to develop a desire to sneeze. Etiquette forbade one to sneeze in such crowded quarters. She would wake her neighbour and get sworn at.

Then the tragic absurdity of the whole thing struck her. It was absurd, but it was horrible. She felt an utter loathing of the creatures on each side of her, and her loathing raised in her an accusing anger. Who was responsible? She asked the question irritably, only to discover that in answering it she was attacked by a disturbing suspicion that she herself, every thinking creature, was responsible for such an absurdity as this. Physical disgust proved stronger than pity. She reminded herself that animals were better cared for. There were stables, cowsheds, clean fields, where beasts could shelter under trees and hedges. Worn-out horses and diseased cattle were put out of the way. Why were not debauched human cattle got rid of cleanly upon the same scientific plan, for they were lower and far more horrible than the beasts of the field.

She was surprised that this should be what one such night seemed destined to teach her. These people were better dead. She could feel no pity at all for the beast who snored on her shoulder. She could not consent to justify his becoming what he was. Ill luck, fate, a bad heritage, these were mere empty phrases. She only knew that she felt contaminated, that she loathed these wretched, greasy creatures with an almost vindictive loathing. Her skin felt all of a creep, shrinking from their uncleanness.

As to her visions of a regenerated civilisation, her theoretical compassions, what had become of them? Was she not discovering that even her ideals were personal, selective, prejudiced? These people were beyond pity. That was her impression. She found herself driven to utter the cry, "For God's sake let us clean up the world before we begin to build up fresh ideas. This rubbish ought to be put out of the way, burnt, or buried. What is the use of being sentimental about it?" Pity held aloof. She had a new understanding of Death, and saw him as the great Cleanser, the Furnaceman who threw all the unclean things into his destructor. What fools men were to try and cheat Death of his wholesome due. The children ought to be saved, the really valuable lives fought for; but this gutter stuff ought to be cleaned up and got rid of in grim and decent silence.

Eve never expected to sleep, but she slept for two hours, and woke up just before dawn.

It was not a comfortable awakening. She felt cold and stiff, and her body ached, and with the return of consciousness came that wholesome horror of her neighbours, a horror that had taught her more than all the sociological essays she could have read in a lifetime. The man's head was on her shoulder. He still spluttered and blew in his sleep.

Eve decided to sit it out; to go through to the bitter end. Moreover, she was curious to see the faces of these people by daylight. A strange stillness prevailed; there was no wind, and the river was running noiselessly. Once or twice the sound of regular footsteps approached, and the figure of a policeman loomed up and passed.

A thin light began to spread, and the whole scene about her became a study in grey. The sky was overcast, canopied with ashen clouds that were ribbed here and there with lines of amethyst and white. The city seemed to rise out of a gloomy and mysterious haze, dim, sad, and unreal. The massive buildings looked like vague grey cliffs. The spires were blurred lines, leaden coloured and unglittering. There had been a sprinkling of rain while she had slept, for the pavements were wet and her clothes damp to the touch. She shivered. It was so cold, and still, and dreary.

The stillness had been only a relative stillness, for there were plenty of sounds to be distinguished. A line of vans rumbled over one of the bridges, a train steamed into Charing Cross. She heard motor horns hooting in the scattered distance, and she was struck by the conceit that this was the dawn song of the birds of the city.

The light became hard and cold, and she wondered when her neighbours would wake. A passing policeman looked at her curiously, seemed inclined to stop, but walked on.

Turning her head she found she could see the face of the man next to her. His old black bowler hat had fallen off and lay on the pavement. Eve studied him, fascinated by her own disgust, and by his sottish ugliness. His skin was red, blotched, and pitted like an orange, black hair a quarter of an inch long bristled over his jowl and upper lip. His eyelids and nose were unmentionable. He wore no collar, and as he lounged there she could see a great red flabby lower lip jutting out like the lip of a jug. His black hair was greasy. He was wearing an old frock coat, whose lapels were all frayed and smeary, as though he were in the habit of holding himself up by them.

Eve turned away with qualms of disgust, and glanced at the old woman. Her face, as she slept, had an expression of absurd astonishment, the eyebrows raised, the mouth open. Her face looked like tallow in a dirty, wrinkled bladder. She had two moles on one cheek, out of which grey hairs grew. Her bonnet had fallen back, and her open mouth showed a few rotten black teeth.

A man at the end of the seat was the first to wake. He sat up, yawned, and blew his nose on his fingers. Then the sot next to Eve stirred. He stretched his legs, rolled his head to one side, and, being still half asleep, began to swear filthily in a thick, grumbling voice. Suddenly he sat up, turned, and stared into Eve's face. His red brown eyes were angry and injected, the sullen, lascivious eyes of a sot.

"Good mornin'!"

She caught the twinge of insolent raillery in his voice. Even his brutishness was surprised by the appearance of his neighbour, and he had a reputation for humour. Eve looked away.

He made facetious remarks, half directed to her, half to the world at large.

"Didn't know I was in such —— genteel company. Never had no luck. Suppose I've had m' head on your shoulder all night and didn't know it. Didn't kiss me, did you, while I was sleeping like an innocent babe?"

Another face peered round at her, grinning. Then the old woman woke up, snuffled, and wiped her mouth on the back of her hand.

"Bin rainin', of course?"

Eve said that she thought it had. The old woman's eyes seemed to be purblind, and without curiosity. A sudden anxiety stole over her face. She felt behind her, drew out the bit of newspaper, opened it, and disclosed the fish.

She smelt it, and then began to eat, picking it to pieces with her fingers.

The red-faced man reached for his hat and put it on with a sullen rakishness. He was looking at Eve out of the corners of his eyes. Being a drunkard, he was ugly-tempered in the morning, and the young woman had given him the cold shoulder.

"Stuck up bit of goods. Looks like the lady. Been up to it, have yer? I know all about that. Governess, eh? Some old josser of a husband and a screechin' wife, and out yer go into the street!"

She was more struck by the vindictive, threatening way he spoke than by the vile things he said. Her impressions of the night grew more vivid and more pitiless. Something hardened in her. She felt cold and contemptuous, and quite capable of facing this human animal.

"Be quiet, please!"

She turned and looked at him steadily, and his dirty eyelids flickered.

"Mayn't I speak, blast yer?"

"If you speak to me as you are speaking, I will stop the next constable and give you in charge."

"Goo' lord! What the hell are you doin' here, may I ask?"

She kept her eyes on him.

"I came here just for an experience, because I felt sorry for people, and wanted to see what a night here was like. I have learnt a good deal."

"Ah!"

Something fell out of his face. It relaxed, his lower lip drooping.

"You've learnt somethin'."

She felt pitiless, nauseated.

"I have. I hope before long that we shall have the sense to put people like you in a lethal chamber. You would be better dead, you know."

Eve got up and walked away, knowing that in the future there would be certain creatures whom she could not pity—creatures whom she would look at with the eyes of Nature, eyes that condemn without pity. She wondered whether the amateurs who indulged in sentimental eugenics had ever spent a night sitting on a seat next to a degenerate sot. She doubted it. The reality would upset the digestion of the strongest sentimentalist.

She felt so stiff and cold that she started to walk briskly in the direction of Westminster. A light, drizzling rain began to fall, making the city and the river look even dirtier and uglier, though there is a fascination about London's courtesan ugliness that makes soft Arcadian prettiness seem inane and unprovocative. Nor does bad weather matter so much in a city, which is a consideration in this wet little island.

Eve had not walked far before she discovered that she was hungry. No shops would be open yet, but in allowing some whim to take her across Westminster Bridge she happened on an itinerant coffee-stall at the corner of a side street. Her last two pennies went in a cup of coffee and two massive slabs of bread and butter. The keeper of the stall, a man with a very shiny and freshly shaved chin and cynical blue eyes, studied her rather doubtfully, as did a tram-driver and two workmen who came up for breakfast. Eve noticed that the men were watching her, behind their silence. Her presence there at such an hour was an abnormal phenomenon that caused them furiously to think.

She heard them recover their voices directly she had moved away.

"Bet you she's been up to something. 'Eard of any fires down your way, Jack?"

"No. Think she's one of them dirty militant sneaks?"

"I wouldn't mind bettin' you that's what she is. Dirty, low-down game they're playing. I've a good mind to follow her up, and tip a copper the wink."

But the speaker remained to talk and to drink another cup of mahogany-coloured tea.

"That's just it. These suffragette women ain't got no notion of sport. Suppose they belong to the sort as scratches and throws lamps."

The coffee-stall keeper interjected a question.

"What about the chaps who burnt ricks and haystacks before the Reform Bill, and the chaps who smashed machines when they first put 'em into factories?"

"Well, they burnt and broke, but they did it like men."

"Women ain't in the same situation."

"Ain't they? They can make 'emselves 'eard. Do yer think my ol' woman goes about the 'ouse like a bleatin' lamb? Garn, these militants are made all wrong inside. Fine sort of cause you've got when yer go sneakin' about at three in the mornin', settin' empty 'ouses alight. That's 'eroic, ain't it?"

These men had set Eve down as a militant, and they had come precious near the truth.

She was on the edge of militancy, impelled towards strenuous rebellion by an exasperated sense of the injustice meted out to women, and by brooding upon the things she herself had experienced. It was a generous impulse in the main, mingling some bitterness with much enthusiasm, and moving with such impetuosity that it smothered any sound thinking. For the moment she was abnormal. She had half starved herself, and during weeks of loneliness she had encouraged herself to quarrel with society. She did not see the pathetic absurdity of all this spiritual kicking and screaming, being more than inclined to regard it as splendid protest than as an outburst of hysteria, a fit of tantrums more suited to an ill-balanced and uneducated servant girl.

A shrill voice carries. The frenzied few have delayed so often the very reforms that they have advocated. And there is a sort of hysterical enthusiasm that tricks the younger and more generous spirits, and acting like crude alcoholic drink, stirs up a so-called religious revival or some such orgy of purblind egoism as this phenomenon of militancy. The emotions make the brain drunk, and the power of sound reasoning is lost. The fools, the fanatics, the self-advertisers, the notoriety hunters, and the genuine idealists get huddled into one exclamatory, pitiable mob. And it is one of the tragic facts of life that the soul of a mob is the soul of its lowest and basest members. All the finer, subtler sensitive restraints are lost. A man of mind may find himself shouting demagogic cries next to some half drunken coal-heaver.

Now Eve Carfax was on the edge of militancy, and it was a debatable point with her whether she should begin her campaign that day. Necessity advised something of the kind, seeing that her purse was empty. Yet she could not quite convince a sensitive and individualistic pride that the breaking of a shop window or a scuffle with the police would be an adequate and suitable protest.

She walked about for an hour in the neighbourhood of Trafalgar Square, trying to escape from a treacherous self-consciousness that refused to suffer the adventure to be treated as an impersonal affair. The few people whom she passed stared rather hard, and so persistently, that she stopped to examine herself in a shop window. A dark green blind and the plate glass made an admirable mirror. It showed her her hair straggling most disgracefully, and the feminine part of her was shocked.

Her appearance mattered. She did not realise the significance of the little thrill of shame that had flashed through her when she had looked at herself in the shop window; and even when she made her way to St. James's Park and found an empty seat she deceived herself into believing that she had come there to think things out, and not to tidy her hair, with the help of the little mirror and the comb she carried in her vanity bag. Moreover she felt that she had been chilled on that Embankment seat, and a cold in the head is not heroic. She had her protest to make. The whole day loomed over her, big with possibilities. It made her feel very small and lonely, and cold and insecure.

Hazily, and with a vague audacity that had now deserted her, she had assured herself that she would strike her blow when the hour came; but now that she was face to face with the necessity she found that she was afraid. Even her scorn of her own fear could not whip her into action. Her more sensitive and spiritual self shrank from the crude publicity of the ordeal. If she did the thing she had contemplated doing, she knew that she would be hustled and roughly handled. She saw herself with torn clothes and tumbled hair. The police would rescue and arrest her. She would be charged, convicted, and sent to prison.

She did not fear pain, but she did fear the inevitable and vulgar scuffle, the rough male hands, the humiliation of being at the mercy of a crowd. Something prouder than her pride of purpose rose up and refused to prostitute itself in such a scrimmage. She knew how some of these women had been handled, and as she sat there in the hush of the early morning she puzzled over the psychological state of those who had dared to outrage public opinion. Either they were supreme enthusiasts or women with the souls of fishwives, or drunk with zeal, like those most offensive of zealots, the early Christians, who scolded, spat, and raved until they had exasperated some Roman magistrate into presenting them with martyrdom. She discovered that she had not that sort of courage or effrontery. The hot, physical smell of the ordeal disgusted her.

Yet Nature was to decide the question for her, and the first interposition of that beneficent tyrant began to manifest itself as soon as the stimulating effect of the hot coffee had worn off. Eve felt chilly, an indefinable restlessness and a feeling of malaise stole over her. She left the seat in the park, and walking briskly to warm herself, came into Pall Mall by way of Buckingham Gate. The rush of the day was beginning. She had been conscious of the deepening roar of the traffic while she had been sitting over yonder, and now it perplexed her, pressed upon her with a savage challenge.

She had thought to throw the straw of herself into this torrent of strenuous materialism. For the moment she was very near to laughter, near twitting herself with an accusation of egregious egoism. Yet it was the ego—the intimate, inward I—that was in the ascendant. The hurrying figures that passed her on the pavement made her recoil into her impressionable individualism. She felt like a hyper-sensitive child, shy of being stared at or of being spoken to. The hurry and the noise bothered her. Her head began to ache. Her will power flagged. She was feverish.

Eve walked and walked. There seemed nothing for her to do in this feverish city, but to walk and to go on walking. A significant languor took possession of her. She was conscious of feeling very tired, not merely with physical tiredness, but with an utter weariness of spirit. Her mind refused to go on working. It refused to face any responsibility, to consider any enterprise.

It surprised her that she did not grow hungry. On the contrary, the sight of food in a window nauseated her. Her head ached more, and her lips felt dry. Flushes of heat went over her, alternating with tremors of cold. Her body felt limp. Her legs did not seem to be there, even though she went on walking aimlessly along the pavements. The faces of the people whom she passed began to appear grotesque and sinister. Nothing seemed very real. Even the sound of the traffic came from a long way off. By twelve o'clock she was just an underfed young woman with a temperature, a young woman who should have been in bed.

Eve never quite knew how the idea came to her. She just found it there quite suddenly, filling the whole lumen of her consciousness. She would go and speak to the rosy-faced suffragette who sold papers at the corner of Southampton Row. She did not realise that she had surrendered, or that Nature might be playing with her as a wise mother plays with a child.

Eve was quite innocently confident that the young woman would be there. The neatly dressed, compact figure seemed to enlarge itself, and to dominate the very city. Eve went up Shaftesbury Avenue, and along New Oxford Street. She was nearly run over at one crossing. A taxi driver had to jam on his brakes. She did not notice his angry, expostulatory glare.

"Now then, miss, wake up!"

It was the male voice, the voice of organised society. "Wake up; move along in the proper groove, or stand and be run over!" The words passed over and beyond her. It was a feverish dream walk to the corner of Southampton Row. Then she found herself talking to the young woman who sold papers.

"I meant to do something. I'm not strong enough. I have been out all night on the Embankment."

She was conscious of a strong presence near her; of a pleasant practical voice speaking.

"Why, you're ill! Have you had anything to eat?"

"Some coffee and bread and butter at half-past five. I have been walking about."

"Good gracious! You're feverish! Let me feel."

She gripped a hot hand.

"Thought so. Have you any money?"

To Eve money presented itself as something that was yellow and detestable. It was part of the heat in her brain.

"No. I spent the last of it this morning. I want to explain——"

The paper-seller put a hand under Eve's arm.

"Look here, you'll faint if you stay out here much longer. I'll take you to friends. Of course, you are one of us?"

"I have been trying to earn a living, and to keep my pride."

"A thing that men generally manage to make impossible!"

They had to wait for some traffic to pass, and to Eve the street seemed full of vague glare and confusion. She was aware of a firm grip on her arm, and of the nearness of something that was comforting and protective. She wanted to sink down into some soft, soothing substance, to drink unlimited cold water, and not to be bothered.

The body had decided it. There was to be no spasm of physical protest. Nature had determined that Eve should go to bed.

CHAPTER XXXVI

PALLAS

Not even her intimates knew the nature of the humiliations and the sufferings that had created Mrs. Falconer's attitude towards man.

She was a tall and rather silent woman, fair-haired, grey-eyed, with a face that was young in outline and old in its white reserve. There was nothing slipshod or casual about her. She dressed with discrimination, yet even in the wearing of her clothes she suggested the putting on of armour, the linking up of chain mail. Someone had nicknamed her "Pallas." She moved finely, stood still finely, and spoke in a level, full-toned voice that had a peculiar knack of dominating the conversation without effort and without self-consciousness. People turned and looked at her directly she entered a room.

Yet Mrs. Falconer did not play to her public. It was not the case of a superlatively clever woman conducting an ambitious campaign. There was something behind her cold serenity, a silent forcefulness, a superior vitality that made people turn to her, watch her, listen to what she said. She suggested the instinctive thought, "This woman has suffered; this woman knows; she is implacable; can keep a secret." And all of us are a little afraid of the silent people who can keep secrets, who watch us, who listen while we babble, and who, with one swift sentence, send an arrow straight to the heart of things while we have been shooting all over the target.

Sentimentalists might have said that Mrs. Falconer was a splendid white rose without any perfume. Whether the emotions had been killed in her, whether she had ever possessed them, or whether she concealed them jealously, was a matter of conjecture. She was well off, had a house near Hyde Park and a cottage in Sussex. She was more than a mere clever, highly cultured woman of the world. Weininger would have said that she was male. The name of Pallas suited her.

Eve Carfax had lain in bed for a week in a little room on the third floor of Mrs. Falconer's house, and during that week she had been content to lie there without asking herself any questions. The woman doctor who attended her was a lanky good fellow, who wore pince-nez and had freckles all over her face. Eve did not do much talking. She smiled, took what she was given, slept a great deal, being aware of an emptiness within her that had to be filled up. She had fallen among friends, and that was sufficient.

The window of her room faced south, and since the weather was sunny, and the walls were papered a soft pink, she felt herself in a pleasant and delicate atmosphere. She took a liking to Dr. Alice Keck. The freckled woman had been a cheeky, snub-nosed flapper on long stilts of legs, and her essential impudence had lingered on, and mellowed into a breezy optimism. She had the figure of a boy, and talked like a pseudo-cynical man of forty.

"You want turning out to grass for a month, then all the kick will come back. You have done enough experimenting on your own. I tried it once, and I didn't like it!"

"When can I see Mrs. Falconer?"

Mrs. Falconer's name seemed to instil sudden seriousness into Dr. Alice Keck.

"Oh, in a day or two!"

"I haven't seen her yet, and I want to thank her."

"Take my advice, and don't."

"Why not?"

"Oh, it is not in her line—the emotions! You'd feel foolish, as though you had taken a box of matches to set light to the North Pole."

"That sounds rather discouraging."

"Rot! Wait and see. They call her Pallas, you know. If you begin hanging emotions on Kate Falconer you'll end up by thinking you are shoving tinsel and beads on a fine statue. I'll tell her you want to see her. I think she wants to see you."

Eve's vitality was returning, and one of the first evidences of its return showed itself in a curiosity concerning this woman who had befriended her. All the little delicate refinements of life had been given her—flowers, books, early tea served in dainty china, a bottle of scent had even been placed on the table beside her bed. These things had seemed feminine and suggestive. The room had a warmth of atmosphere that did not seem to belong to the house of a woman who would not care to be thanked.

But from the very first moment that Eve saw Kate Falconer in the flesh, she understood the aptness of Alice Keck's similes. Eve was unusually intuitive. She felt an abnormal presence near her, something that piqued her interest.

"I am glad that you are so much better."

She came and sat down beside the bed, and Eve could see her profile against the window. A warm, evening light was pouring in, but Pallas's white face and grey dress were not warmed by it. There was nothing diaphanous or flamboyant about her; neither was she reactive or absorbent. The poise was complete; the whole world on one side, this woman on the other.

She made Eve feel self-conscious.

"I am much better, thanks to all your kindness."

"It was the obvious thing to do."

"I cannot quite look at it like that."

It struck her as absurd that this woman should speak of doing what was obvious. Eve's intuition did not hail her as an obvious person, though it was possible that Mrs. Falconer's cold brilliancy made what seemed complex to most people, obvious to her. There was a moment's constraint, Eve feeling herself at a disadvantage.

"I thought you might like to talk."

"I ought to explain things a little."

"You are under no obligation to explain anything. We women must help one another. It is part of the new compact."

"Against men?"

"Against male dominance."

"I should like to tell you some of my experiences!"

"I should like to hear them!"

Eve found it difficult to begin. She doubted whether this woman could distinguish the subtle emotional colour shades, but in this she was mistaken. She soon discovered that Mrs. Falconer was as experienced as a sympathetic Romish priest, yet the older woman seemed to look at life objectively, and to read all its permutations and combinations as a mathematician may be able to read music at sight.

"You have just worked out all the old conclusions, but there is nothing like working out a thing for oneself. It is like touching, seeing, tasting. I suppose it has made you one of the so-called fanatics?"

"I want things altered!"

"To what extent?"

"I want the divorce law made equal, and I want divorce made easier. I want commercial equality. I want it understood that an unmarried woman who has a child shall not be made to carry all the supposed disgrace!"

Mrs. Falconer turned in her chair. Her face was in the shadow, and Eve could not see her eyes very plainly, but she felt that she was being looked at by a woman who regarded her views as rather crude.

"I should like you to try and think in the future, not only in the present."

"I have tried that, but it all seems so chaotic."

"I suppose you know that there are certain life groups where the feminine element is dominant?"

"You mean spiders and bees?"

"Exactly! It is my particular belief that woman had her period of dominance and lost it. It has been a male world, so far as humanity is concerned, for a good many thousand years. And what has European man given us? Factories, mechanics, and the commercial age. I think we can do better than that."

"You mean that we must make woman the dominant force?"

"Isn't that obvious?"

It was obvious, splendidly obvious, when one had the thorough audacity to regard it in that light.

"But how——"

"By segregating the sexes, massing ourselves against the men, by refusing them everything that they desire as men. We shall use the political machinery as well. Man is the active principle, woman more passive, but passivity must win if it remains obdurate. Why have women always surrendered or sold themselves? Haven't we that in us which gives us the right to rule?"

"Motherhood?"

"Yes, motherhood! We are the true creators."

"But men——"

"The best of them shall serve."

"And how can you be sure of persuading all women to mass themselves into one sisterhood?"

"That is just the problem we have to deal with. It will be solved so soon as the ordinary woman is taught to think woman's thought."

Eve lay mute, thinking. It was very easy to theorise on these lines, but what about human nature? Could one count, even in the distant future, on the ordered solidarity of a whole sex? Would every woman be above her own impulses, above the lure of the emotions? It seemed to Eve that Mrs. Falconer who talked of developments as being obvious, was overlooking the most obvious of opponents—Nature.

"But do you think that men will ever accept such a state of things?"

"Of course they would resist."

"It would mean a sex war. They are stronger than we are!"

"No, not stronger! Besides, methods of violence, if we come to them, can be used now by women as well as by men. The trigger and the fuse are different from the club. I don't count on such crude methods. We are in the majority. We shall just wear men out. We can bear more pain than they can."

"But what an immense revolution!"

"Yet it has happened. We see it in insect life, don't we? How did it come about?"

"I don't know."

"But it is there, a fact."

"Yes. All the same, when I had finished reading a book on the ways of bees, I thought that they were detestable little beasts."

"Because they killed off the useless males, and let the queen assassinate her rivals. We are not bees. We shall do better than that."

Her level, full-toned voice had never varied, and she talked with perfect and assured serenity of turning society upside down. She was a fanatic with ideas and a subnormal temperature. She believed what she foresaw. It was like one of the Fates deigning to be conversational in a drawing-room.

She rose, and, walking to the window, looked down into the street.

"Do you think that women would have perpetrated London? It took man to do that. I must not tire you. Have you everything you want?"

"Thank you, everything."

"I will come up and see you again to-morrow."

Eve had plenty of leisure for meditation, and Mrs. Falconer's theories gave her abundant material for thought. Rest in bed, with good food, and pleasant refinements round her had restored her normal poise, and she found that there was far less edge to her enthusiasm. She was a little shocked by the discovery. The disharmonies of the life that she had been studying had not changed, and she was troubled by this discovery that she did not react as she had reacted two weeks ago. When we are young we are distressed by the subtle transfigurations that overtake our ideals. We hatch so many eggs that persist in giving us ducklings instead of chickens. We imagine that we shall always admire the same things, believe the same beliefs, follow out the strenuous beginnings. When changes come, subtle, physical changes, perhaps, we are astonished at ourselves. So it was with Eve when she discovered that her enthusiasm had passed from a white heat to a dull and more comfortable glow. Accusing herself of inconstancy, lack of sustained purpose, did not explain the change in the least. She tried to convince herself that it was mere sloth, the result of a comfortable bed and good food.

In a day or two she found herself driven to explain a second surprising fact, a growing hostility towards Mrs. Falconer. It was not a dislike that could be reasoned with and suppressed, but a good, vigorous, temperamental hatred as natural and as self-assertive as hunger, thirst, or passion. It seemed to Eve abominable that she should be developing such an attitude towards this woman, who had shown her nothing but kindness, but this irresponsible antipathy of hers seemed to have leapt up out of some elemental underworld where intellect counted as nothing.

Mrs. Falconer came up daily to talk to her as to a fellow fanatic, and her temperament roused in Eve an instinctive sense of resistance. She found herself accusing her hostess to herself of intolerance and vindictiveness. It was like listening to a hell-fire sermon preached against the male sex, a denunciation that was subtilised with all the cleverness of a mind that had played with all the scientific theories of the day. Mrs. Falconer was a vitalist. She hated the mechanical school with fine consistency, and clasped hands with Bergson and Hans Driesch. Yet she disagreed with some of her fellow mystics in believing that women possessed more of the "*élan vital*" than man. Therefore, woman was the dominant force of the future, and it behoved her to assert her power.

Eve found herself on tip-toe to contradict Mrs. Falconer, just as one is tempted to jump up and contradict the dogmatist who talks down at us from the pulpit. She tried to argue one or two things out, but soon realised that this woman was far too clever for her, far too well armed. Mrs. Falconer had masked batteries everywhere. She had reserves of knowledge that Eve had no chance of meeting. And yet, though she could not meet her arguments, Eve had an intense conviction that Mrs. Falconer's ideals were hopelessly wrong. There was la revanche behind it all. Her head could not confute the theorist, but her heart did. Human nature would not be cajoled.

She had an idea that Mrs. Falconer was a very busy woman. The house seemed full of voices, and of the sound of coming and going, but Eve did not discover how busy her hostess was till Dr. Alice Keck let her go downstairs. There were two big rooms on the second floor fitted up like offices, with a dozen women at work in them. Letters were being written, directories consulted, lists of names made out, statistics compiled, money received and disbursed. People came and went, brought and received information. There was no laughter. Everyone was in grim earnest.

Eve saw Mrs. Falconer's personality translated into action. This rich woman's house was a nerve centre of the new movement, and Mrs. Falconer's presence suggested one of those subtle ferments that are supposed to stimulate the complex processes of life. She did nothing herself. She was a presence. People came to her when they needed the flick of her advice. She co-ordinated everything.

Eve was introduced to all these girls and women, and was given a table to herself with several sheets of foolscap and a file of papers. Mrs. Falconer came and stood by her, and explained the work she wanted her to do.

"There is nothing like attacking people with facts. They penetrate the British skull! We are collecting all these cases, and making a register of them. We shall publish them in a cheap form, and have them sent all over the country."

"You want all these papers fair copied?"

"Yes. They are in the rough, just as they were sent in to us. You will find that they are numbered."

Eve discovered that she had before her a series of reports dealing with well-authenticated cases of women who had been basely treated by men. Some of them were written on ordinary letter paper, others on foolscap, and not a few on the backs of circulars and bills. Nor was the batch that had been given her the first that had been handled. Each case was numbered, and Eve's batch began at 293.

There was a sordid and pathetic similarity about them all.

"M—— W——, typist, 31, orphan. Engaged to be married to a clerk. The man borrowed her savings, got her into trouble, and then refused to marry her. Girl went into Queen Charlotte's hospital. Baby born dead. The mother developed puerperal fever, but recovered. She was unable to get work for some time, and went into domestic service. Her health broke down. She is now in a workhouse infirmary."

"V—— L——. A particularly cruel case that ended in suicide. She had spent a little sum of money that had been left her, on educating herself. Obtained a very good post as secretary. Her employer took her with him to Paris, pretending that as she could speak French she would be very useful to him in certain business transactions. Drugs were used. Five months later the girl committed suicide in London by throwing herself under a Tube train."

All day, and for several days, Eve worked at these pathetic records, till she felt nauseated and depressed. It was a ghastly indictment drawn up against man, and yet it did not have the effect on her that Mrs. Falconer had expected. It did not drive her farther towards fanaticism. On the contrary, she was overcome by a feeling of helplessness and of questioning compassion. It was all so pitiable and yet so inevitable as things were, and through all the misery and the suffering she was brought to see that the whole blame could not be credited to the man. It was the system more than the individual.

A function that is natural and clean enough in itself has been fouled by the pruderies of priests and pedants. Sex has been disguised with all manner of hypocrisies and make-believes. Society pretends that certain things do not happen, and when Nature insists upon their happening, Society retaliates upon the woman by calling her foul names and making her an outcast. The men themselves are driven by the system to all those wretched meannesses, treacheries, deceptions. And the worst of it all is that Society tries to keep the truth boxed up in a cellar. English good form prides itself with a smirk on not talking about such things, and on playing the ostrich with its head under a pew cushion. Nature is not treated fairly and squarely. We are immorally moral in our conventions. Until we decide to look at sex cleanly and wholesomely, stripping ourselves of all mediæval nastiness and cowardly smuggery, we shall remain what we are, furtive polygamists, ashamed of our own bodies, and absurdly calling our own children the creatures of sin.

The work depressed Eve. Her fellow workers were hardly more enlivening. They belonged to a distinct type, the neutral type that cannot be appealed to either as man or woman. Meals were served at a long table in one of the lower rooms, and Eve noticed that her neighbours did not in the least care what they ate. They got through a meal as quickly as possible, talking hard all the time. Now Eve did care about what she ate, and whether it was delicately served. She had the palate of a healthy young woman, and it mattered to her whether she had ragged mutton and rice pudding every day, or was piqued by something with a flavour.

She was carnal. She told herself so flatly one afternoon as she went up to her bedroom, and the charge produced a thrill of natural laughter. She had a sudden wild desire to run out and play, to be greedy as a healthy child is greedy, to tumble hay in a hay field, to take off her clothes and bathe in the sea. The natural vitality in her turned suddenly from all this sour, quarrelsome, pessimistical campaigning and demanded life—the life of feeling and seeing.

The house oppressed her, so she put on her hat and escaped, and made her way into the park. May was in, green May, with lush grass and opening leaves. The sun shone. There was sparkle in the air. One thought of wood nymphs dancing on forest lawns while fauns piped and jigged, and the great god Pan delighted himself with wine and honey. It was only a London park, but it was the nearest thing to Nature that Eve could find. Her heart expanded suddenly. An irrational, tremulous joyousness came over her. She wanted to sing, to weep, to throw herself down and bury her face in the cool green grass. The country in May! She had a swift and passionate desire for the country, for green glooms and quiet waters and meadows dusted with gold. To get out of this loathsome complication of tragedies, to breathe smokeless air, to think of things other than suicides, prostitutions, treacheries, the buying and selling of souls.

She felt like a child before a holiday, and then she thought of Lynette. What a vision of wholesomeness and of joy! It was like cool water bubbling out of the earth, like a swallow gliding, a thrush singing at dawn. She could not bear to think of wasting all the spring in London. She must escape somehow, escape to a healthier outlook, to cooler thinking.

When she went back Mrs. Falconer sent for her. Eve wondered afterwards whether it was a coincidence or not that Mrs. Falconer should have said what she did that day.

"You have not been looking well. You want a change!"

"I almost think I do."

"You don't like me. It is a pity."

Eve was taken by surprise.

"Don't like you?"

"It is quite obvious to me, but it does not make any difference. I knew it, almost from the first. A matter of temperament. I understand some things better than you suspect. You want action, more warmth of movement. This statistical work disgusts you. I can give you your opportunity."

Eve remained mute. It was useless to protest in the presence of such a woman.

"Two of our missionaries are going to tour in Sussex and Surrey. I think you might join them. I wonder if you are strong enough."

"Oh, yes!"

"You see, they tramp most of the way, and speak in the villages, and small towns. Sometimes they are treated rather roughly."

Eve beheld the green country within the clasp of her arms, and was ready to accept anything.

"Yes, I'll go. I should love to go. I'm strong, and I'm not afraid. I think I want action."

"Yes, you are not made for dealing with harsh facts. They disgust you too much, and weaken you. It is all temperament. You are one of those who must spend themselves, obtain self-expression."

"I wonder how you know that?"

"My dear, I was a woman before I became a thinker."

CHAPTER XXXVII

ADVENTURES

Three women with dusty shoes and brown faces came along under the Downs to Bignor village. They wore rough brown skirts, white blouses, and straw hats, and each carried a knapsack strapped over her shoulder.

Now Bignor is particularly and remotely beautiful, especially when you have left the flat country behind you and climbed up to the church by the winding lanes. It is pure country, almost uninvaded by modernity, and so old in the midst of its perennial youth that you might hardly wonder at meeting a Roman cohort on the march, or a bevy of bronze-haired British girls laughing and singing between the hedgerows. The village shop with its timber and thatch might be a wood-cut from a romance. The Downs rise up against the blue, and their solemn green slopes, over which the Roman highway climbs, seem to accentuate the sense of silence and of mystery. Great beech woods shut in steep, secret meadows. There are lush valleys where the grass grows tall, and flowers dream in the sunlight.

The three women came to Bignor church, and camped out in the churchyard to make their midday meal. Eve Carfax was one of them, brown, bright-eyed, with a red mouth that smiled mysteriously at beauty. Next to her sat Joan Gaunt, lean, strenuous, with Roman nose, and abrupt sharp-edged mouth. Her wrists and hands were big-boned and thin. The line of her blouse and skirt showed hardly a curve. She wore square-toed Oxford shoes, and very thick brown stockings. Lizzie Straker sat a little apart, restless even in repose, a pinched frown set permanently between her eyebrows, her assertive chin uptilted. She was the eloquent splutterer, a slim, mercurial woman with prominent blue eyes and a lax mouth, who protruded her lips when she spoke, and whose voice was a challenge.

Eve had wanted to turn aside to see the remains of the Roman villa, but her companions had dropped scorn on the suggestion.

"Wasting time on a few old bits of tesselated pavement! What have we got to do with the Romans? It's the present that matters!"

Eve had suggested that one might learn something, even from the Romans, and the glitter of fun in her eyes had set Lizzie Straker declaiming.

"What tosh! And you call yourself an artist, and yet admire the Romans. Don't you know that artists were slaves at Rome? Don't ask me to consider any society that subsisted on slavery. It's dead; doesn't come into one's line of vision. I call archæology the most abominable dilettante rot that was ever invented to make some old gentlemen bigger bores than their neighbours."

And so she had spluttered on all the way to Bignor church, working her voluble mouth, and punching the air with a small brown fist. The eloquence was still in her when she opened her packet of sandwiches, and her energy divided itself between declamation and disposing of mouthfuls of bread and ham.

Eve sat looking countrywards, thinking, "Oh, do be quiet!" She wanted to lose herself in the beauty of the landscape, and she was in a mood to be delighted by a fern growing in a wall, or by the way the fresh green of a tree caught the sunlight. For the moment her spirit escaped and climbed up among the branches of an old yew, and fluttered there in the sparkling gloom, while Lizzie Straker kept up her caterwauling below.

They had been on the open road for a fortnight, and Lizzie Straker still had the autumn tints of a black eye that an apple thrown in a Sussex village had given her. They had been hustled and chased on two occasions, Joan Gaunt coming in for most of the eggs and flour, perhaps because of her fierce leathery face and her defiant manner. Eve had recollections of cleaning herself in a station waiting-room, while a sergeant and two constables guarded the door. And, strange to say, some of her sympathies had been with the crowd.

These three women had tramped and suffered together, yet each day only emphasised Eve's discovery that she was failing to tone with her companions. They had begun by boring her, and they were beginning to exasperate her, rousing a spirit of antagonism that was ready to criticise them without mercy. Never in her life had Eve been in the presence of two such masses of ferocious prejudice. Their attitude towards the country was in complete contrast to hers. They were two blind fanatics on a pilgrimage, while Eve was a wayfarer whose eyes and ears and nostrils were open to Nature. Joan Gaunt and Lizzie Straker lived for words, bundles of phrases, arguments, assertions, accusations. They were two polemical pamphlets on legs sent out walking over God's green earth.

Eve noticed that their senses were less alive than hers, and that they were absurdly unobservant. Perhaps they had passed a cottage garden full of wallflowers, blood red and gold, and Eve had asked, "Did you smell them?"

"Smell what?"

"The flowers."

"What flowers?"

"The wallflowers in that garden."

They had neither seen nor smelt anything, and they had looked at her as though she were a sentimental trifler.

On another occasion, an orchard in bloom, filling a green hollow between two woods, had made Eve stand gazing.

"Isn't that perfect?"

Lizzie Straker saw nothing but what her mad prejudices were allowing her to see.

"I should like to come along with an axe and chop down all those trees. It would make quite a good protest."

Eve had felt satirical.

"Why shouldn't we blow up Chanctonbury Ring?"

And they had taken her seriously.

"We should want such a lot of dynamite."

"But it's an idea, quite an idea."

At the small town of Battle they had thirsted to blow up the great abbey gateway, while Eve was letting her eyes take in all the grey beauty of the stonework warmed by the evening sunlight. These two women had "a mad" against property. Protest by violence was becoming an obsession with them. They were like hostile troops marching through a rich and hated land.

Now, from the very first day in the country, a change had come over Eve. A crust of hardness seemed to have fallen from her, and once more she had felt herself to be the possessor of an impressionable and glowing body, whose skin and senses responded to the sunlight, the winds, the colours and the scent of the earth. She no longer felt like a little pricking thorn in the big body of life. She belonged to the earth. She was in the apple blossom and in the red flare of a bed of tulips. Self was no longer dissevered from the all-consciousness of the life round her. The tenderness came back to her, all those mysterious, elusive and exultant moods that came she knew not whence and went she knew not whither. She had ceased to be a pathological specimen corked up in a bottle, and had become part of the colour and the smell, the joy and the pathos of things vital.

In the fields Eve saw lambs at play, skipping absurdly, butting each other. Birds were singing and making love, and the bees were busy in the furze. A sense of the immensity, of the exultant rush of life, possessed her. And this pilgrimage of theirs, all this spouting and declaiming, this lean-necked heroism, seemed futile and rather ridiculous. Was one to tell Nature that she must stand aside, and order youth not to look into the eyes of youth? It might serve for the few. They were like children making castles and dykes and rivulets on the sands, within the reach of the sea. Eve imagined that Nature must be amused, but that she would wipe out these eccentricities so soon as they began to bore her. She felt herself in the midst of elemental things; whereas Joan Gaunt had studied botany in a museum.

That afternoon they marched on to Pulborough, and, entering an inn, announced to the landlord that they intended staying for the night. Joan Gaunt managed the practical side of the pilgrimage. She entered the inn with the air of an officer commanding food and beds in time of war.

"Three bedrooms, and a cold supper at nine!"

The landlord was a Sussex man, short, stolid, and laconic. He looked at Joan Gaunt out of staring blue eyes, and asked whether their luggage had been left at the station.

"We have not got any luggage. We are on a walking tour. You can give us our tea in the garden."

Joan Gaunt did not hear what the landlord said to his wife, who was cleaning table-silver in a pantry at the end of a long passage. It was terse and unflattering, and included such phrases as, "Three tooth brushes and a change of stockings." "A scrag of mutton without so much as a frill to the bone end."

The three comrades had tea in the garden, and were studied suspiciously by the landlord's wife, a comely little woman with bright, brown eyes. The few words that she uttered were addressed to Eve.

"A nice May we're having!"

"Splendid."

And then Joan Gaunt proceeded to make an implacable enemy of her by telling her to see that the beds were properly aired.

About seven o'clock Pulborough discovered that it had been invaded by suffragettes. Three women had stationed themselves with their backs to a wall at a place where three roads met, and one of the women—it was Lizzie Straker—brandished a small flag. Pulborough gathered. The news spread somehow even to the outlying cottages. Stale eggs are to be found even in the country, and a certain number of stale eggs rushed to attend the meeting.

Lizzie Straker was the speaker, and the people of Pulborough appeared to discover something intensely funny in Lizzie Straker. Her enthusiastic and earnest spluttering tickled them. The more she frowned and punched the air with that brown fist of hers, the more amusing they found her. The Executive had not been wise in its choice of an itinerant orator, for Lizzie Straker lost her temper very quickly on such occasions, and growing venomous, began to say scathing things, things that even a Sussex brain can understand.

Some of the younger spirits began to jeer.

"Do you wonder she be'unt married!"

"Can't she talk! Like a kettle a-boiling over!"

"What's she wanting a vote for?"

"I'll tell you for why; to have laws made so as all the pretty girls shall be sent off to Canada."

Their humour was hardly less crude than Lizzie Straker's sneering superiority. And then an egg flew, and broke against the wall behind Joan Gaunt's head. The crowd closed in threateningly. The flag was snatched from Lizzie Straker, and someone threw a dead mouse in Joan Gaunt's face.

The retreat to the inn was not dignified. The rest of the eggs followed them, but for some reason or other Eve was spared. Her two comrades came in for all the honour. The crowd accompanied them to the inn, and found the blue-eyed landlord standing in the doorway.

"Chuck 'em out, Mister Crowhurst!"

"We don't want the likes of them in Pulborough!"

Joan Gaunt was for pushing her way in, and the landlord gave way. He said a few words to the crowd, shut the door, and followed the suffragettes into the long passage.

"Sorry, ladies, but you'll have to turn out. I can't keep you. It isn't safe."

Lizzie Straker's claws were still out.

"But you have got to. You keep a public house. It's the law!"

A voice chimed in from the end of the passage:

"John, I won't have those women in my house! No, I won't; that's a fact. They've got neither sense nor manners."

"All right, my dear."

"If I had my way, I'd have them all put in asylums. Disgusting fools. I don't care; let them summon us. I won't have them in my house."

Joan Gaunt tried her Roman manner.

"I shall insist on staying. Where are the police?"

"That's right, call for the men."

"Where are the police?"

The landlord grinned.

"Can't say. I'll take you out the back way, and through the orchard into the fields. It's getting dark."

"But we are not going."

"I shall let the crowd in, ladies, in three minutes. That's all I have got to say."

Eve ran upstairs and brought down the three knapsacks.

"Let's go," she said, "we're causing a lot of bother."

"That's the only sensible one of the lot," said the voice, "and what's more, she's worth looking at."

The crowd was growing restive and noisy. There was the sound of breaking glass. The landlord jerked a thumb in the direction of the front door.

"There you are—they're getting nasty. You come along with me!"

They went under protest, with the exception of Eve, who paused at the end of the passage and spoke to the little woman with the brown eyes.

"I'm sorry. I'll send some money for the glass. And what do we owe for the tea?"

"Three shillings, miss. Thank you. And what do you do it for?"

Eve laughed.

"Oh, well, you see——"

"I wouldn't go along with those scrags, if I were you. It's silly!"

The little woman had pluck, for she went out to cajole the crowd, and kept it in play while her husband smuggled the suffragettes through the garden and orchard and away across the fields. They escaped unmolested, and the dusk covered their retreat.

After the landlord had left them they walked about three miles and lost themselves completely and thoroughly in a net-work of by-roads. Shelter for the night became a consideration, and it was Eve who sighted a haystack in the corner of a field, and who suggested it as a refuge. They scrambled over a gate and found that the haystack had been cut into, and that there was a deep fragrant walled recess sheltered from the road.

Lizzie Straker began to pull down some loose hay and spread it to make a cushion.

"We must teach those savages a lesson. We ought to set fire to this in the early morning."

Eve was tired of Lizzie Straker.

"I don't think that would be sport, burning the thing that has sheltered you."

The hay was fragrant, but it could not mask the odour that had attached itself to her companions' clothes. Eve had been spared the rotten eggs, but she was made to suffer indirectly, and persuaded to edge away into the corner of the recess. They had had to fly without their supper, and a few dry rock-cakes and some biscuits were all that they had in their knapsacks.

Lizzie Straker produced a candle-end and a box of matches. It was a windless night, and by the light of the candle the two women examined each other's scars.

"We might get some of it off with the hay."

"Isn't it disgusting! And no water to wash in."

They proceeded to rub each other down, taking turns in holding the candle.

Eve had a suggestion to make.

"You will have to get some new blouses at the next town. I shall have to go in and shop for you."

They glanced at her critically, realising for the first time that she had escaped without any of the marks of martyrdom.

"Didn't you get any?"

"No; you seem to have been the favourites."

"Disgusting savages!"

"The Sussex people always were the worst boors in England."

When they had made some sort of job of their mutual grooming, and had eaten a few rock-cakes and biscuits, Joan Gaunt unbuttoned her blouse and drew from the inner depths a long white envelope. Lizzie Straker sidled nearer, still holding the candle. Eve had not seen this envelope before.

She stood up and looked down over their shoulders as they sat. Joan Gaunt had drawn out a sheet of foolscap that was covered with cipher.

Lizzie Straker pointed an eager finger.

"That's the place. It's between Horsham and Guildford."

"And there's no proper caretaker, only a man at the lodge."

"We can make a blaze of it. We shall hear from Galahad at Horsham."

They were human enough to feel a retaliating vindictiveness, after the way they had been pelted at Pulborough, and Eve, looking down at the paper that Joan Gaunt held, realised at last that they were incendiaries as well as preachers. She could not read the precious document, but she guessed what it contained.

"Is that our Black List?"

"Yes."

They did not offer to explain the cipher to her, for she was still something of a probationer. Moreover the candle was guttering out, and Lizzie Straker had to smother it in the grass beside the stack. Eve returned to her corner, made a nest, took off her hat, and, turning her knapsack into a pillow, lay down to look at the stars. A long day in the open had made her sleepy, but Joan Gaunt and Lizzie Straker were still talking. Eve fell asleep, with the vindictive and conspiring murmur of their voices in her ears.

CHAPTER XXXVIII

THE MAN WITH THE MOTOR

Eve woke with the scent of hay in her nostrils, and her hair was damp with dew.

She sat up, and from that brown nook on the hill-side looked out upon a world that was all white mist, with a great silver sun struggling out of the east. Each blade of grass had its droplet of dew. The air was still as deep water. From a wood in the valley came the sound of the singing of birds.

Her two companions were still asleep, Joan Gaunt lying with her mouth wide open, her face looking grey and old. Eve picked up an armful of hay, went a few paces forward, and sat down so that she could see everything without having to look over the bodies of the sleeping women.

It was like watching the birth of a world. The veil of white mist hid miraculous happenings, and the singing of the birds down yonder was like the exultation of souls that beheld and marvelled. Mystery! The stillness seemed to wait. In a little while the white veil would be withdrawn.

Then the vapour became full of sudden motion. It rolled in great drifts, rose, broke into little wisps of smoke, and half lost itself in yellow light. The interplay was wonderful to watch. Sometimes the mist closed in again, hiding what it had half revealed, only to drift away once more like torn masses of gossamer. A great yellow ray of sunlight struck abruptly across the valley, fell upon the wood where the birds were singing, and splashed it with gold. Then the mist seemed to be drawn up like a curtain. Colour came into the landscape, the bronze and yellow of the budding oaks, the delicate green of young beech leaves, the sables of yews and firs, the blue of the sky, the green of the fields. It was all wet, fragrant, glittering, like an elf world lifted suddenly out of the waters of an enchanted sea.

Someone sneezed. Eve turned sharply, and found Joan Gaunt was awake, and sitting up. Wisps of hay had got tangled in her hair, her blouse looked like an impressionist sunset, and one side of her face was red and mottled from lying on the canvas knapsack. She had been awake for ten minutes, and had pulled out a notebook and was scribbling in it with a pencil.

Eve thought that she was turning the May morning into a word picture, but she soon noticed that Joan Gaunt's eyes did not rise above the level of her notebook.

"Busy already?"

"Yes."

"Isn't it wonderful?"

"What?"

"Why, all that."

Eve swept a hand towards the valley where the smoking squadrons of the mist were in full flight before the gold spears of the sun.

"It looks as though it has been abominably damp. I'm quite stiff and I've caught cold."

She blew her nose hard, and, like the impervious enthusiast that she was, resumed her scribbling. Eve left her undisturbed, and returning to her corner of the recess let her hair down, and spent ten minutes brushing it. She had very fine hair, it reached well below her waist, and Lizzie Straker, who had just woke up, found something to say on the subject.

"It must be a nuisance, having a fleece like that."

"Why?"

"So beastly hot. I should like to have mine cut quite short."

The obvious answer, though Eve did not give it, was that some people's hair did not matter.

She went exploring in quest of somebody who would provide them with towels and water, and also with breakfast. And when they did get breakfast at a little farmhouse over the hill, her companions had to thank Eve for it, for the farmer's wife was not a persuadable person, and would certainly have refused anything to Joan Gaunt or Lizzie Straker. Their white blouses were splashed and streaked with yellow, but luckily the sitting-room was rather dark, and the farmer's wife was not observant.

But Eve had seen these blouses in the full sunlight, and was candid in her criticism.

"You must stop at the next village, and buy a couple of new blouses!"

"Why, what does it matter?"

Lizzie Straker was in a touchy and argumentative mood.

"They really look too terrible!"

"I don't care. It is a reflection on those savages."

"I suppose you don't want to be too conspicuous when you are out to burn houses!"

This was sound sense, and they halted that day within a mile or two of Horsham and let Eve go on alone to buy two new blouses. The transfiguration was contrived in the corner of a wood, and the egg-stained relics were rolled up and stowed away in their knapsacks.

Apparently they were expected at Horsham, not by the public or the police, but by the elderly gentlewoman at whose front door Joan Gaunt knocked. They were received with enthusiasm by an excitable lady with a high, narrow forehead and prominent teeth. She could talk nearly as fast as Lizzie Straker, and she gave them a most excellent tea.

"I think it is splendid, perfectly splendid, this heroic uprising of the women of England. The Government can't stop us. How can they stop us? We have got the men stalemated."

Eve did not take to her hostess, and their hostess did not take to Eve. She looked at her with the veiled prejudices of a very plain woman for a girl who had more than good looks. Moreover, Eve had recovered her sense of humour, and these enthusiasts were rendered suspicious and uneasy by a glimmer of fun in the eyes. People who could laugh were not vindictively and properly in earnest.

"They can't stop us. They can't crush women who are not afraid of dying! Isn't it glorious the way those noble girls have fought and refused to eat in prison? I know one woman who kept four wardresses at bay for half an hour. She kicked and struggled, and they had to give up trying to feed her. What fools we are making the men look! I feel I want to laugh in the faces of all the men I meet!"

Eve asked mildly: "And do you?"

"Do what?"

"Laugh when you meet them?"

"Well, no, not quite. It wouldn't be dignified, would it? But I think they see the triumph in my eyes."

Their hostess had forgotten that a letter had come for Joan Gaunt, and she only remembered it when Joan asked if it had arrived.

"Of course—how silly of me! I locked it up in my bureau. I was so fascinated listening to all your adventures."

She fetched the letter, and Joan Gaunt read it. She smiled her leathery smile, and passed the letter over to Lizzie Straker.

"To-morrow night, where the road to Godalming branches off from the Horsham-Guildford road."

The hostess thrilled and upset her cup.

"How exciting—how splendid! I can guess, yes, what you are going to do. And you will be able to stay the night here? How nice. The people here are such barbarians; so narrow. I try to spread the great ideal, but they don't seem to care."

At all events she treated them nobly, and Eve was able to enjoy the sensuous delight of a good hot bath. She went to bed early, leaving her hostess and the two pioneers of progress sitting well forward in their chairs, and debating the conversion of those women who clung sentimentally to the old traditions.

Their hostess was curious about Eve.

"A probationer, a novice, I suppose?"

"She is learning the discipline."

"I have very quick instincts. I don't think I quite trust that young woman."

Lizzie Straker, who was always ready to argue about anything, simply because she had a temperament that disagreed, rushed to defend Eve.

"Why, what's the matter with her? She came down to starving point, anyhow, for a principle. If that isn't being sincere, what is?"

Their hostess was not accustomed to being met and attacked with such impetuosity.

"She doesn't strike me as belonging to us."

"Why not?"

"As I explained, it was my impression. She doesn't strike me as being serious minded."

"Anyway, she didn't sit in a chair and theorise. She's been through the real thing."

Joan Gaunt had to interpose, for the gentlewoman of Horsham was showing signs of huffiness.

"Mrs. Falconer sent her with us."

"Mrs. Falconer? That noble woman. I am satisfied. She should know."

They left Horsham about five o'clock the following evening, their knapsacks well packed with food. The gentlewoman of Horsham dismissed them with the fervour of an early Christian, and held Joan Gaunt's hands for fully half a minute.

"It has been such an experience for me. It has been like seeing one's dearest ideals in the flesh. God bless you!"

Joan Gaunt went striding along the Guildford road like a veteran centurion, grim and purposeful. Lizzie Straker had a headache, and Eve offered to carry her knapsack and coat, but Lizzie Straker had a kind of soldier pride. She would carry her own kit till she dropped.

"Don't fuss me, old girl. I'm all right."

Eve enjoyed the long walk, perhaps because her companions were silent. A soft spring dusk was melting over the country. Birds were singing. There were yellow gates to the west. The hedgerows were clean and unsoiled by dust, and a delightful freshness distilled out of the blue-green grass.

It was pitch dark long before they reached the point where the road branched off to Godalming, though the sky was crowded with stars. Joan Gaunt had bought a little electric hand-lamp in Horsham, and it served to light up the sign-posts and the dial of her watch.

"Here we are."

She had flashed the light on a sign-post arm and read "Godalming."

"What's the time?"

"About half-past ten."

"Galahad won't be here till midnight."

"No. You have time for a rest."

Lizzie Straker was fagged out. Eve could tell that by the flatness of her voice. They went and sat in a dry ditch under the shadow of a hedge, and put on their jackets, for the double purpose of keeping warm and hiding their white blouses. Lizzie Straker lay down with her knapsack under her head, and in ten minutes she was asleep.

"We won't talk!"

"No. I'm quite ready for a rest."

A couple of farm labourers passed, one of them airing a grievance, the condemning of his pig by some sanitary official. "I be'unt a fool. A touch of de joint evil, dat's what it be. But he comes and he swears it be tu-ber-coo-lousis, and says I be to slaughter d'beast." The voice died away, bemoaning the fate of the pig, and Eve felt a drowsiness descending upon her eyelids. She remembered Joan Gaunt sitting erect and watchful beside her, and then dreams came.

She woke suddenly to find two huge glaring eyes lighting the road. They were the headlights of a stationary motor, and she heard the purr of the engine turning dead slow. Someone was speaking. A high pitched, jerky and excitable voice was giving orders.

"Turn out the headlights, Jones, and light the oil lamps. You had better shove in another can of petrol. Well, here we are; on the tick—what!"

Joan Gaunt's voice answered him.

"Last time you were an hour late."

"That's good. We had two punctures, you know. Where are the others?"

"Asleep in the ditch."

Eve woke Lizzie Straker. The headlights went out suddenly, and two figures approached, one of them carrying the tail lamp of the car.

"Hallo, it's Galahad!"

Lizzie Straker's short sleep had restored her vitality. She spluttered enthusiastically at the man.

"Hallo, old sport! here we are, ready for the limelight. Plenty of paraffin and shavings?"

"Rather!"

He turned the lamp on Eve so that she could see nothing but a round yellow eye.

"New comrade? Greetings!"

Joan Gaunt introduced them.

"Mr. Lawrence Kentucky—Miss Eve Carfax. We call him our Galahad."

The man laughed, and his laughter was falsetto. She could not see him, except when he swung the lamp away from her, and then but dimly, but she received the impression of something tall, fidgety, and excitable.

"Delightful! One more fair lady to champion. Great adventures, great adventures!"

Eve soon noticed that Lizzie Straker was particularly interested in Mr. Lawrence Kentucky. She hung close, talking in slangy superlatives, and trying to spread her personality all round him.

"How many miles an hour to-day?"

"Oh, we came easy! Respectable tourists, you know. All ready, Jones?"

"All ready, sir."

"Supposing we heave up the anchor? There's plenty of room for three at the back."

"But what about the house? Do you know it?"

"Rather! We're thorough, you know. Jones and I went over all the ground two days ago. We have it all mapped out to a T."

"I'm going to set light to this one. Joan had the last."

"All right, your honour, although Miss Gaunt's one up."

Joan Gaunt climbed in independently. Lizzie Straker waited to be helped. Mr. Kentucky helped Eve, because he had discovered something of the eternal feminine.

To Eve the adventure began by seeming utterly unreal. Even when the motor drew up in a dark lane, and the lights were turned out after the attacking party had loaded themselves with bags of shavings, tow, and a can of petrol, she was hardly convinced that she was off to help in burning down a house. She asked herself why she was doing it. The spirit of revolt failed to answer in a voice that was passionate enough to be convincing.

They went in single file, Lawrence Kentucky leading the way. He carried an electric torch which he used from time to time like a boy out for mischief. They climbed a gate, crossed a grass field, and came to a fence backed by straggling laurels and hollies. There was a place where two or three of the fence palings were rotten and had been kicked in by Mr. Kentucky when he had come to spy out the land. They squeezed through, one by one.

Someone whispered to Eve as she stooped to pass through.

"Mind the nails. I'll show you a light."

His torch glowed, and she had a momentary glimpse of his face, thin, neurotic, with restless eyes, and a mouth that had the voracious look that one sees in men who are always hungry for some new sensation. She could have imagined him swearing volubly, laughing hysterically, biting his pipe stems in two, a whimsical egoist who rushed hither and thither to escape from being bored.

"All right? Rather like playing oranges and lemons."

She knew at once that he wanted to flirt with her, but she had no desire to cut out Lizzie Straker.

They threaded through a big shrubbery, and came out against a black mass piled in the middle of a broad lawn. It was the house they had come to burn.

"The kitchen window, Jones—at it with the glass-cutter! Who'll stay outside and keep cave?"

Eve offered herself.

"Why, you'll miss half the fun."

"I don't mind."

The grass on the lawn promised a good hay crop. There was a wooden seat built round the trunk of an old lime, and Eve settled herself there after the others had disappeared. The night was absolutely soundless, stars scattered like dust above the solid parapet and low roof of the red brick Georgian house. It stood there, mute, deserted, with sightless eyes, and a sudden pity seized on Eve. It was as though the house were alive, and she was helping to do it to death. Houses were part of life. They held a spiritual and impalpable something that mattered. They had souls. She began to watch, as though she was to be present at a tragedy, with a feeling of tension at her heart.

Who had lived there? To whom did the house belong? Had children been born yonder, and had tired eyes closed in death? Had children played in the garden, and under this tree? It was illogical to pity bricks and mortar, and yet this sentimental mood of hers belonged to those more exquisite sensibilities that save life from being nothing better than a savage scramble.

A streak of light showed at one of the windows. Eve straightened herself, rested her head against the trunk of the tree, and held her breath. The streak of light spread into a wavering, fluctuating glow, just as if the heart of the old house were palpitating angrily. But Eve was allowed no leisure for the play of such phantasies. The incendiaries returned.

"Come along!"

Lizzie Straker was almost hysterical.

"It's going splendidly—splendidly! We found a big cupboard full of rubbish under the stairs. I lit it. Yes, it's my work!"

Eve became conscious of a growing indignation as they beat a retreat back through the shrubbery and across the field to the lane. They ran, and even the act of running seemed to her shameful. What a noble business was this sneaking about at one in the morning with petrol cans and bags of shavings!

She snubbed Lawrence Kentucky when he pointed back over the field gate and chuckled.

"She's going up in smoke all right. We did that pretty smartly!"

"It has been heroic, hasn't it?"

To her he was no better than a mean little boy.

They crowded into the car. The lamps were lit, and the engine started. The chauffeur drove dead slow along the lane.

"That's it, Jones; crawl for half a mile, and keep her as quiet as you can."

In another five minutes they were purring away into the darkness. Eve, when she glanced back, could see a faint glow above the tree tops.

Lizzie Straker exulted.

"There is something for them to talk about! That will be in the papers to-morrow."

Eve did not know how far they drove. The car kept running for the best part of two hours. Mr. Lawrence Kentucky was finessing, covering up their tracks, so to speak. He turned in his seat once or twice and spoke to Joan Gaunt. Day was just dawning when the car pulled up.

"This ought to do for you. You are three or four miles from Farnham, and this is Crooksbury Hill."

Eve threw aside her rug and climbed out. They had stopped on a flinty road among the towering trunks of a wood of Scots firs. The branches high overhead seemed a black tangle hanging in the vague grey light of the dawn. Not a bough moved. The great trees were asleep.

"I'll be getting on. Running to Oxford. Put 'em off the scent. Write and fix up the next. London address, you know."

He was saying good-bye, and receiving Lizzie Straker's more than friendly splutterings. The chauffeur, a swarthy young blackguard, was grinning behind his master's back. Mr. Lawrence Kentucky stared hard at Eve, for she was good to look at in the dawn light, with the smell of the dew everywhere, and the great trees dreaming overhead.

"Au revoir, Miss Carfax! Hope you've enjoyed it."

She gave him a casual nod, and went and sat down on the bank at the side of the road.

Joan Gaunt and Lizzie Straker, like the hardy veterans that they were, lay down under the trees to snatch an hour or two's sleep, but Eve felt wakeful and in a mood for thought. The night's adventure had left her with an impression of paltriness, and she kept picturing the black shell of the burnt house standing pathetically in the midst of its neglected garden. She remembered Lawrence Kentucky's chuckle, a peculiarly offensive and sneering chuckle. Was that the sort of man who could be called a pioneer of progress, or a knight of Arthur's Court? It struck her as pathetic that these women should have christened him Galahad. It just betrayed how little they knew about men.

She looked up at the tall trees and was instantly reminded of the fir woods at Fernhill. A quiver of emotion swept through her. It had been just such a dawn as this when she had fled from Orchards Corner. She realised that she was wiser, broader, less sentimental now, and that Canterton had not been the passionate visionary that she had thought him.

Lizzie Straker woke up and shouted "Breakfast!"

The gentlewoman of Horsham had fitted them out royally. They had a tea kettle to boil over a fire of dead wood, a big bottle of water, ham sandwiches, buttered scones, and a tin of Swiss milk. Even a tin opener had been included. That breakfast under Crooksbury Hill reminded Eve of Lynette's fairy picnics in the Wilderness. The larches would be all covered with green tassels. She wished she was with Lynette in the Wilderness.

Breakfast over, Joan Gaunt brought out her itinerary.

"Where do we go next? I've forgotten."

Lizzie Straker licked a finger that had managed to get itself smeared with Swiss milk.

"Let's see. Something beginning with B, wasn't it?"

"Yes—Basingford."

The pupils of Eve's eyes dilated. They were going to Basingford!

CHAPTER XXXIX

LYNETTE

They found themselves at the "Black Boar" at Basingford, sitting round a green table under a may tree in the garden. The "Black Boar" was an ancient hostelry, all white plaster, black beams, and brown tiles, its sign swinging on a great carved bracket, its parlour full of pewter and brass. It had the pleasant smell of a farmhouse rather than the sour odour of an inn. Everything was clean, the brick-floored passages, the chintz curtains at the windows, the oak stairs, the white coverlets on the solid mahogany beds. A big grandfather clock tick-tocked in the main passage. The garden at the back ended in a bowling-green that was remarkably well kept, its mown sward catching the yellow evening light through the branches of ancient elms.

They were having tea under the may tree, whose trusses of white blossom showered down an almost too sweet perfume. At the edge of the lawn was a border packed full of wallflowers, blood red and cloth of gold. It was sunny and windless. The tops of the tall elms were silhouetted against the blue.

"Are you going to preach here?"

It was Eve who asked the question, and Joan Gaunt who answered it.

"No. We are just private individuals on a walking tour."

"I see. And that means?"

"Someone on the Black List."

Eve smothered a sigh of relief. From the moment of entering Basingford she had felt the deep waters of life flowing under her soul. She was herself, and more than herself. A strange, premonitory exultation had descended on her. Her mood was the singing of a bird at dawn, full of the impulse of a mysterious delight, and of a vitality that hovered on quivering wings. The lure of the spring was in her blood, and she was ready to laugh at the crusading faces of her comrades.

She pushed back her chair.

"I shall go and have a wash."

"What, another wash!"

Her laughter was a girl's laughter.

"I like to see the water dimpling in the sunlight, and I like the old Willow Pattern basins. What are you going to do?"

Joan had letters to write. Lizzie was reading a book on "Sex and Heredity."

Eve left them under the may tree, washed her face and hands in the blue basin, tidied her hair, put on her hat with unusual discrimination, and went out to play the truant.

She simply could not help it. The impulse would brook no argument. She walked through Basingford in the direction of Fernhill. She wanted to see the familiar outlines of the hills, to walk along under the cypress hedges, to feel herself present in the place that she loved so well. For the moment she was conscious of no purpose that might bring her into human contact with Fernhill. She wanted memories. The woman in her desired to feel!

Her first glimpse of the pine woods made her heart go faster. Here were all the familiar lanes and paths. Some of the trees were her intimates, especially a queer dwarf who had gone all to tam-o'-shanter. Even the ditches ran in familiar shadow lines, carrying her memories along. From the lodge gate she could see the top of the great sequoia that grew on the lawn before the Fernhill house. It was absurd how it all affected her. She could have laughed, and she could have wept.

Then a voice, a subtle yet imperious voice, said, "Go down to the Wilderness!" She bridled at the suggestion, only to remind herself that she knew a path that would take her round over the hill and down into the valley where the larches grew. The impulse was stronger than anything that she could oppose to it. She went.

The green secrecy of the wood received her. She passed along the winding path between the straight, stiff poles of the larches, the gloom of the dead lower boughs making the living green above more vivid. It was like plunging from realism into romance, or opening some quaint old book after reading an article on the workings of the London County Council. Eve was back in the world of beauty, of mystery and strangeness. The eyes could not see too far, yet vision was stopped by crowded and miraculous life and not by bricks and mortar.

The trees thinned. She was on the edge of the fairy dell, and she paused instinctively with a feeling that was akin to awe. How the sunlight poured down between the green tree tops. Three weeks ago the bluebells must have been one spreading mist of lapis-lazuli under the gloom of the criss-cross branches. And the silence of it all. She knew herself to be in the midst of mystery, of a vital something that mattered more than all the gold in the world.

Supposing Lynette should be down yonder?

Eve went forward slowly, and looked over the lip of the dell.

Lynette was there, kneeling in front of the toy stove that Eve had sent her for Christmas.

An extraordinary uprush of tenderness carried Eve away. She stood on the edge of the dell and called:

"Lynette! Lynette!"

The child's hair flashed as she turned sharply. Her face looked up at Eve, wonderingly, mute with surprise. Then she was up and running, her red lips parted, her eyes alight.

"Miss Eve! Miss Eve!"

They met half way, Eve melting towards the running child like the eternal mother-spirit that opens its arms and catches life to its bosom. They hugged and kissed. Lynette's warm lips thrilled the woman in Eve through and through.

"Oh, my dear, you haven't forgotten me!"

"I knew—I knew you'd come back again!"

"How did you know?"

"Because I asked God. God must like to do nice things sometimes, and of course, when I kept asking Him———. And now you've come back for ever and ever!"

"Oh, no, no!"

"But you have. I asked God for that too, and I have been so good that I don't see, Miss Eve, dear, how He could have said no."

Eve laughed, soft, tender laughter that was on the edge of tears.

"So you are still making feasts for the fairies?"

"Yes, come and look. The water ought to be boiling. I've got your stove. It's a lovely stove. Daddy and I make tea in it, and it's splendid."

Every thing was in readiness, the water on the boil, the fairy teapot waiting to be filled, the sugar and milk standing at attention. Eve and Lynette knelt down side by side. They were back in the Golden Age, where no one knew or thought too much, and where no one was greedy.

"And they drink the tea up every night?"

"Nearly every night. And they're so fond of cheese biscuits."

"I don't see any biscuits!"

"No, daddy brings them in his pocket. He'll be here any minute. Won't it be a surprise!"

Eve awoke; the dream was broken; she started to her feet.

"Dear, I must be getting back."

"Oh, no, no!"

"Yes, really."

Lynette seized her hands.

"You shan't go. And, listen, there's daddy!"

Eve heard a deep voice singing in a soft monotone, the voice of one who hardly knew what he was singing.

She stood rigid, face averted, Lynette still holding her hands and looking up intently into her face.

"Miss Eve, aren't you glad to see daddy?"

"Why, yes."

A sudden silence fell. The man's footsteps had paused on the edge of the wood. It was as though the life in both of them held its breath.

Eve turned. She had to turn to face something that was inevitable. He was coming down the bank, his face in the sunlight, his eyes staring straight at her as though there were nothing else in the whole world for him to look at.

Lynette's voice broke the silence.

"Daddy, she wanted to run away!"

Eve bent over her.

"Oh, child, child!"

Her face hid itself for a moment in Lynette's hair.

She heard Canterton speaking, and something in his voice helped and steadied her.

"Lynette has caught a fairy. She was always a very confident mortal. How are you—how are you?"

He held out his hand, the big brown hand she remembered so well, and hers went into it.

"Oh, a little older!"

"But not too old for fairyland."

"May I never be too old for that."

CHAPTER XL

WHAT THEY SAID TO EACH OTHER

They walked back through the larchwood with Lynette between them, keeping them apart, and yet holding a hand of each.

"Miss Eve, where've you been all the winter? In London?"

"Yes, in London."

"Do you like London better than Fernhill?"

"No, not better. You see, there are no fairies in London."

"And did you paint pictures in London?"

"Sometimes. But people are in too much of a hurry to look at pictures."

Miss Vance, as much the time-table as ever, met them where the white gate opened on to the heath garden. It was Lynette's supper hour, an absurd hour, she called it, but she obeyed Miss Vance with great meekness, remembering that God still had to be kept without an excuse for being churlish.

Eve and Miss Vance smiled reminiscently at each other. It was Miss Vance's last term at Fernhill.

"Good night, Miss Eve, dear. You will come again to-morrow?"

"Yes; I will try to."

Canterton and Eve were left alone together, standing by the white gate that opened into the great gardens of Fernhill. Canterton had been silent, smilingly silent. Eve had dreaded being left alone with him, but now that she was alone with him, she found that the dread had passed.

"Will you come and see the gardens?"

"May I?"

He opened the gate and she passed through.

May was a month that Eve had missed at Fernhill, and it was one of the most opulent of months, the month of rhododendrons, azaleas, late tulips, anemones, and Alpines. Never since last year's roses had she seen such colour, such bushes of fire, such quiet splendour. It was a beauty that overwhelmed and silenced; Oriental in some of its magnificence, yet wholly pure.

The delicate colouring of the azaleas fascinated her.

"I never knew there were such subtle shades. What are they?"

"Ghents. They are early this year. Most people know only the old Mollis. There are such an infinite number of colours."

"These are just like fire—magic fire, burning pale, and burning red, the colour of amber, or the colour of rubies."

They wandered to and fro, Eve pointing out the flowers that pleased her.

"We think the same as we did last year—am I to know anything?"

She looked up at him quickly, with a quivering of the lashes.

"Oh, yes, if you wish it! But I am not a renegade."

"I never suggested it. How is London?"

Her face hardened a little, and her mouth lost its exquisite delight.

"Being here, I realise how I hate London to live and struggle in. What is the use of pretending? I tried my strength there, and I was beaten. So now——"

She paused, shrinking instinctively from telling him that she had become one of the marching, militant women. Fernhill, and this man's presence, seemed to have smothered the aggressive spirit—rendered it superfluous.

His eyes waited.

"Well?"

"I am on a walking tour with friends."

"Painting?"

"No, proselytising."

"As a Suffragette?"

"Yes, as a Militant Suffragette."

She detested the label with which she had to label herself, for she had a sure feeling that it would not impress him.

"I had wondered."

His voice was level and unprejudiced.

"Then it doesn't shock you?"

"No, because I know what life may have been for you, trying to sell art to pork-butchers. It is hard not to become bitter. Won't you let me hear the whole story?"

They were in the rosery, close to a seat set back in a recess cut in the yew hedge. Eve thought of that day when she had found him watching Guinevere.

"Would you listen?"

"I have been listening ever since the autumn, trying to catch any sounds that might come to me from where you were."

They sat down, about two feet apart, half turned towards each other. But Eve did not look at Canterton. She looked at the stone paths, the pruned rose bushes, the sky, the outlines of the distant firs. Words came slowly at first, but in a while she lost her self-consciousness. She felt that she could tell him everything, and she told him everything, even her adventure with Hugh Massinger.

And then, suddenly, she was conscious that a cloud had come. She glanced at his face, and saw that he was angry.

"Why didn't you write?"

"I couldn't. And you are angry with me?"

"With you! Good God, no! I am angry with society, with that particular cad, and that female, the Champion woman. I think I shall go and half kill that man."

She stretched out a hand.

"Don't! I should not have told you. Besides, it is all over."

He contradicted her.

"No, these things leave a mark—an impression."

"Need it be a bad one?"

"Perhaps not. It depends."

"On ourselves? Don't you think that I am broader, wiser, more the queen of my own soul? I am beginning to laugh again."

He stared at his clasped hands, and then raised his eyes suddenly to her face.

"Eve!"

His uttering of the name thrilled her.

"If you are wiser, why are you gadding about with these fools?"

She gave a little nervous laugh.

"Oh, because they were kind to me, because they are out to better things for women."

"Have they a monopoly of all the kindness?"

"I—I don't know."

"Yes, you do. I am an ordinary sort of man in many ways, and we, the average men, have a growing understanding of what are called the wrongs of women. Give me one."

She flushed slightly, and hesitated.

"They—they want us to bribe them when we want work—success."

"I know. It is the blackguard's game. But women can change that. The best men want to change it. But I ask you, are there no female cads who demand of men what some men demand of women?"

"You mean——"

"It is not all on one side. How are many male careers made? Isn't there favouritism there too? I know men who would never be where they are, but for the fact that they were sexually favoured by certain women. I could quote you some pretty extraordinary cases, high up, near the summit. Besides, a sex war is the maddest sort of war that could be imagined."

She felt driven to bay.

"But can we help fighting sometimes?"

"There is a difference between quarrelling and fighting."

"Oh, come!"

"There is, when you come to think about it. I want neither. Does quarrelling ever help us?"

"It may."

"When it drags us at once to a lower, baser, more prejudiced level? And do you think that these fanatics who burn houses are helping their cause?"

"Some of them have suffered very bitterly."

"Yes, and that is the very plea that damns them. They are egotists who must advertise their sufferings. Supposing we all behaved like lunatics when we had a grievance? Isn't there something finer and more convincing than that? The real women are winning the equality that they want, but these fools are only raising obstinate prejudices. Am I, a fairly reasonable man, to be bullied, threatened and nagged at? Instinctively the male fist comes up, the fist that balances the woman's sharper tongue. For God's sake, don't let us get to back-alley arguments. Sex is marriage, marriage at its best, reasonable and human. Let's talk things over by the fireside, try not to be little, try to understand each other, try to play the game together. What is the use of kicking the chessboard over? Perhaps other people, our children, have to pick up the pieces."

Because she had more than a suspicion that he was right, she began to quote Mrs. Falconer, and to give him all the extreme theories. He listened closely enough, but she knew intuitively that he was utterly unimpressed.

"Do you yourself believe all that?"

"No; not all of it."

"It comes to this, you are quoting abnormal people. You can't generalise for the million on the idiosyncrasies of the few. These women are abnormal."

"But the workers are normal."

"Many of them lead abnormal lives. But do you think that we men do not want to see all that bettered?"

"Then you would give us the vote?"

Her eyes glimmered with sudden mischief, and his answered them.

"Certainly, to the normal women. Why not?"

"Are all the male voters normal?"

"Don't make me say cynical things. If so many hundreds of thousands of fools have the vote at present, I do not see that it matters much if many more thousands of fools are given it."

"That isn't you!"

"It is a sensible, if a cynical conclusion. But I hope for something better. We are at school, we moderns, and we may be a little too clever. But if any parson tells me that we are not better than our forefathers, I can only call him a liar."

She laughed.

"Oh, that's healthy—that's sound. I'm tired of thinking—criticising. I want to do things. It may be that quiet work in a corner is better than all the talking that ever was."

"Of course. Read Pasteur's life. There's the utter damning of the merely political spirit."

He pulled out his watch and looked at it reflectively.

"Half-past six. Where are you staying?"

"At the 'Black Boar.'"

"I have something that I should like to show you. Have you time?"

She smiled at him shyly.

"Now and again time doesn't matter."

Canterton led her through the great plantations to the wild land on the edge of the fir woods where he had built the new cottage. It was finished, but empty. The garden had been turfed and planted, and beyond the young yew hedge the masses of sandstone were splashed with diverse colours.

"It's new!"

"Quite! I built it in the winter."

She stood at gaze, her lips quivering.

"How does it please you?"

"Oh, I like it! It is just the cottage one dreams about when one is in a London suburb. And that rock garden! The colours are as soft and as gorgeous as the colours on a Persian dish."

Canterton had the key with him. They walked up the path that was paved with irregular blocks of stone. Eve's eyes saw the date on the porch. She understood in a flash why he had not told her for whom he had built it.

Canterton unlocked the door. A silence fell upon her, and her eyes became more shadowy and serious as she went from room to room and saw all the exquisite but simple details, all the thought that had been put into this cottage. Everything was as she would have imagined it for herself. She touched the oak panelling with the tips of her fingers and smiled.

"It is just perfect!"

He took her to one of the windows.

"The vision is not cramped?"

"No."

She looked away over the evening landscape, and the broad valley was bathed in gold. It was very beautiful, very still. Eve could hear the sound of her own breathing. And for the moment she could not look at Canterton, could not speak to him. She guessed what was in his mind, and knew what was in her own.

"A place to dream in!"

"Yet it was built for a worker!"

She rested her hands on the window sill, steadying herself, and looking out over the valley. Canterton went on speaking.

"You can guess for whom this was built."

"I can guess."

"Man, as man, has shocked you. I offer no bribes. I ask for none. You trust me?"

He could hardly hear her "Yes."

"I know that chance brought us together to-day. May I make use of it? I am remembering my promise."

"Perhaps it was more than chance. It was rash of me to want to see Lynette. And I trust you."

He stood back a little, leaving her by the window.

"Eve, I do not ask for anything. I only say, here is a life for you—a working life. Live it and express yourself. Do things. You can do them. No one will be prouder of your work than I shall be. In creating a woman's career, you can help other women."

Her lips were quivering.

"Oh, I trust you! But it is such a prospect. You don't know. I can't face it all in a moment."

"I don't ask you to do that. Go away, if you wish it, think it over, and decide. Don't think of me, the man, the comrade. Think of the working life, of your art, the real life—just that."

He made a movement towards the door, and she understood the delicacy of his self-effacement, and the fine courtesy that forefelt her sensitive desire to escape to be alone. They passed out into the garden. Canterton spoke again as he opened the gate.

"I still believe all that I believed last summer!"

He had to wait for her answer, but it came.

"I am older than I was. I have suffered a little. That refines or hardens. One does not ask for everything when one has had nothing. And yet I do not know what to say to you—the man."

CHAPTER XLI

CAMPING IN THE FIR WOODS

Lizzie Straker and Joan Gaunt were at supper when Eve walked into their private sitting-room at the "Black Boar." Eight o'clock had struck, but the window of the room faced west, and the lamp on the table had not been lit.

"You're pretty late."

Eve sat down without taking off her hat. She had a feeling that these two had been discussing her just before she had come into the room, and that things which she was not expected to see had been, so to speak, pushed hurriedly under the sofa.

"I've had a long ramble, and I'm hungry."

She found a round of cold beef, and a dish of young lettuces on the table. Her companions had got as far as milk pudding and stewed rhubarb.

"You must have been walking about four solid hours. Did you get lost?"

"No. I used to live down here."

They stared.

"Oh, did you!"

"You've got pretty hot, anyhow."

"I walked fast. I went farther than I meant to."

"Meet any friends?"

"One or two."

She caught a pair of mistrustful eyes fixed on her. They belonged to Joan Gaunt, who sat at the end of the table.

"I think we'll have the lamp, Lizzie."

"Right oh! or Eve won't be able to hunt the slugs out of the lettuces."

"Don't be beastly."

"You might cut me a piece of bread."

The lamp was lit. The other two had finished their supper, but appeared inclined to sit there and watch Eve eat.

"You met some old friends?"

"Yes."

"I hope you were careful."

"Of course. I told them I was on a walking tour. I dare say I shan't see them again."

"No. I don't think you'd better."

Something in Joan Gaunt's voice annoyed her. It was quietly but harshly dictatorial, and Eve stiffened.

"I don't think you need worry. I can look after my own affairs."

"Did you live in Basingford?"

"No. Out in the country."

Lizzie Straker and Joan Gaunt exchanged glances. Something had happened to the woman in Eve, a something that was so patent and yet so mysterious that even these two fanatics noticed it and were puzzled. Had she looked into a mirror before entering the sitting-room, she would have been struck by a physical transfiguration of which she was for the moment unconscious. She had changed into a more spring-like and more sensitive study of herself. There was the indefinable suggestion of bloom upon fruit. Her face looked fuller, her skin more soft, her lips redder, her eyes brighter yet more elusive. She had been bathing in deep and magic waters and had emerged with a shy tenderness hovering about her mouth, and an air of sensuous radiance.

Supper was cleared away. The lamp was replaced on the table. Joan Gaunt brought out a note-book and her cypher-written itinerary. Lizzie Straker lit a cigarette.

"Business!"

They exchanged glances.

"Come along, Eve."

Somehow the name seemed to strike all three of them with symbolical suggestiveness. Her comrades looked at her mistrustfully.

They sat down at the table.

"As you happen to know people here, you had better be on your guard. There is work to be done here. I have just wired to Galahad."

Eve met Joan Gaunt's eyes.

"Are there black sheep in Basingford?"

"A particularly black one. An anti-suffrage lunatic. She has been on platforms against us. That makes one feel bitter."

"So it's a she!"

"She's a traitress—a fool."

"I wonder if I know her name."

"It's Canterton—Mrs. James Canterton."

Eve was leaning her elbows on the table, trying not to show how this news affected her. And suddenly she began to laugh.

Joan Gaunt's face stiffened.

"What are you laughing at?"

It was wholesome, helpless, exquisite laughter that escaped and bubbled over from a delicious sense of fun. What an ironical comedy. Eve did not realise the complete significance of what she said until she had said it.

"Why, I should have thought she was one of us!"

Her two comrades stared. They were becoming more and more puzzled, by this feminine thing that did not shape as they expected it to shape.

"I don't see anything to laugh at."

Eve did.

"But she ought to belong to us!"

"You seem to find it very funny. I don't see anything funny about a woman being a political pimp for the men, and a rotten sentimentalist."

"I should never have called Mrs. Canterton a sentimentalist."

"Of course, you know her!"

"A little."

"Well, she's marked down here with three asterisks. That means trouble for her. Of course, she's married."

"Yes."

"And dotes on her husband and children, and all that."

Eve grew serious.

"No, that's the strange part of it. She and her husband don't run in double harness. And she's a fool with her own child."

"But that's absurd. I suppose her husband has treated her badly, as most of them do."

"Oh, I don't think so."

"In nine cases out of ten it's the man's fault."

"Perhaps this is the tenth."

"Oh, rot! There's a man somewhere. There must be someone else besides her husband, or she wouldn't be talking for the men."

"I don't think so. If you knew Mrs. Canterton, you might understand."

Yet she doubted whether they would have understood, for busybodies and extremists generally detest each other, especially when they are arguing from opposite sides of the table.

Eve wanted to be alone, to think things out, to face this new crisis that had opened before her so suddenly. It was the more dangerous and problematical since the strong current of her impulses flowed steadily towards Fernhill. She went to bed early, leaving Joan Gaunt and Lizzie Straker writing letters.

When the door had closed on Eve, they put down their pens and looked at each other.

"Something funny."

"What's happened to her?"

Lizzie Straker giggled.

"She's met someone, a man, I suppose. That's how it struck me."

Joan looked grim.

"Don't giggle like that. She has been puzzling me for a long time. Once or twice I have almost suspected her of laughing at us."

This sobered Lizzie Straker.

"What! I should like to see her laugh at me! I've learnt jiu-jitsu. I'd suppress her!"

"The question is, is she to be trusted? I'm not so sure that our Horsham friend wasn't right."

"Well, don't tell her too much. And test her. Make her fire the next place. Then she'll be compromised."

"That's an idea!"

"She has always hung back and let us do the work."

They looked at each other across the table.

"All right. We had better go and scout by ourselves to-morrow."

"Galahad ought to be here by lunch time."

"We can make our arrangements. Leave after tea, hide in the woods, and do the job after dark."

Eve slept well, in spite of all her problems. She woke to the sound of a blackbird singing in the garden, and the bird's song suited her waking mood, being just the thing that Nature suggested. She slipped out of bed, drew back the chintz curtains, and looked out on a dewy lawn all dappled with yellow sunlight. The soul of the child and of the artist in her exulted. She wanted to play with colours, to express herself, to make pictures. Yes; but she wanted more than that, and she knelt down in her nightdress before the looking-glass, and leaning her elbows on the table, stared into her own eyes.

She questioned herself.

"Woman, can you trust yourself? It is a big thing, such a big thing, both for him, and for you."

It was a sulky breakfast table that morning. Lizzie Straker had the grumps, and appeared to be on the watch for something that could be pounced on. She was ready to provoke Eve into contradicting her, but the real Eve, the Eve that mattered, was elsewhere. She hardly heard what Lizzie Straker said.

"We move on this evening!"

"Oh!"

"Does that interest you?"

"Not more than usual."

A telegram lay half hidden under Joan Gaunt's plate.

"Lizzie and I are going off for a ramble."

The hint that Eve was not wanted was conveyed with frankness.

"You had better stay in."

"Dear comrade, why?"

"Well, you are known here."

"That doesn't sound very logical. Still, I don't mind."

The dictator in Joan Gaunt was speaking, but Eve was not irked by her tyranny on this particular morning. She was ready to laugh gently, to bear with these two women, whose ignorance was so pathetic. She would be content to spend the day alone, sitting under one of the elms at the end of the bowling green, and letting herself dream. The consciousness that she was on the edge of a crisis did not worry her, for somehow she believed that the problem was going to solve itself.

Joan Gaunt and Lizzie Straker started out from Basingford soon after nine, and chartered a small boy, who, for the sum of a penny, consented to act as guide to Fernhill. But all this was mere strategy, and when they had got rid of the boy, they turned aside into the fir woods instead of presenting themselves at the office where would-be visitors were supposed to interview one of the clerks. Joan Gaunt had a rough map drawn on a piece of note-paper, a map that had been sent down from headquarters. They explored the fir woods and the heath lands between Fernhill and Orchards Corner, and after an hour's hunt they discovered what they had come in search of—Canterton's new cottage standing with white plaster and black beams between the garden of rocks and the curtained gloom of the fir woods.

Joan Gaunt scribbled a few additional directions on the map. They struck a rough sandy road that was used for carting timber, and this woodland road joined the lane that ran past Orchards Corner. It was just the place for Galahad's car to be hidden in while they made their night attack on the empty cottage.

In the meanwhile Eve was sitting under one of the elms at the end of the bowling green with a letter-pad on her knees. She had concluded that her comrades had designs upon Canterton's property, that they meant to make a wreck of his glass-houses and rare plants, or to set fire to the sheds and offices, and she had not the slightest intention of suffering any such thing to happen. She was amused by the instant thoroughness of her own treachery. Her impulses had deserted without hesitation to the opposite camp.

She wrote:

> "I am writing in case I should not see you to-day. My good comrades are Militants, and your name is anathema. I more than suspect that some part of your property will be attacked to-night. I send you a warning. But I do not want these comrades of mine to suffer because I choose to play renegade. Balk them and let them go.

"I am thinking hard,

"EVE."

She wrote "Important " and "Private" on the envelope, and appealed to the proprietor of the "Black Boar" to provide her with a reliable messenger to carry her letter to Fernhill. An old gentleman was taking a glass of beer in the bar, and this same old gentleman lived as a pensioner in one of the Fernhill cottages. He was sent out to see Eve, who handed him a shilling and the letter.

"I want Mr. Canterton to get this before twelve o'clock, and I want you to make sure he has it."

"I'll make sure o' that, miss. I ain't likely to forget."

He toddled off, and before twelve o'clock Eve knew that her warning had carried, for a boy on a bicycle brought her a note from Canterton.

"Many thanks indeed. I understand. Let nothing prejudice you."

Joan Gaunt and Lizzie Straker returned about half-past twelve, and five minutes later a big grey motor pulled up outside the inn. Mr. Lawrence Kentucky climbed out, and went in to order lunch.

From her room Eve had a view of the bowling green and of the doorway of a little summer-house that stood under the row of elms. She saw Lizzie Straker walk out into the garden and arrive casually at the door of the summer-house. Two minutes later Lawrence Kentucky wandered out with equal casualness, appeared drawn by some invisible and circuitous thread to the summer-house, and vanished inside.

Eve smiled. It was a comedy within a comedy, but there was no cynical edge to her amusement. She felt more kindly towards Lizzie Straker, and perhaps Eve pitied her a little because she seemed so incapable of distinguishing between gold and brass.

Lawrence Kentucky did not stay more than five minutes in the summer-house. He had received his instructions, and Joan Gaunt's map, and a promise from Lizzie Straker that she would keep watch in the lane up by Orchards Corner, so that he should not lose himself in the Fernhill woods. Lawrence Kentucky went in to lunch, and drove away soon afterwards in his big grey car.

She found that Lizzie Straker was in a bad temper when they sat down to lunch. The *tête-à-tête* in the summer-house had been too impersonal to please her, and Lawrence Kentucky had shown great tactlessness in asking questions about Eve. "Is Miss Carfax here? Where did you pick her up? Oh, one of Pallas's kittens! Jolly good-looking girl."

Lizzie was feeling scratchy, and she sparred with Eve.

"You're a puzzler. I don't believe you're a bit keen, not what I call keen. I can't sleep sometimes before doing something big."

"I'm quite keen enough."

"I don't think you show it. You'll have to buck up a bit, won't she, Joan? We have to send in sealed reports, you know. Mrs. Falconer expects to know the inside of everybody."

"Perhaps she expects too much."

"Anyhow, it's her money we're spending."

Eve flushed.

"I shall pay her back some day before very long."

"You needn't think I called you a sponger—I didn't."

"Oh, well, would it have mattered?"

They spent the afternoon in the garden, and had tea under the may tree. Joan Gaunt had asked for the bill, and for three packets of sandwiches. They paid the one, and stowed the sandwiches away in their knapsacks, and about five o'clock they resumed their walking tour.

A march of two miles brought them into the thick of the fir woods, and they had entered them by the timber track without meeting a soul. Joan Gaunt chose a spot where a clump of young firs offered a secret camping ground, for the lower boughs of the young trees being still green and bushy, made a dense screen that hid them admirably.

Eve understood that a night attack was imminent, and realised that no individual rambles would be authorised by Joan Gaunt. She was to be penned in with these two fanatics for six long hours, an undenounced traitor who had betrayed them into the enemy's hands. Canterton would have men on guard, and for the moment she was tempted to tell them the truth and so save them from being fooled.

But some subtle instinct held her back. She felt herself to be part of the adventure, that she would allow circumstances to lead, circumstances that might prove of peculiar significance. She was curious to see what would happen, curious to see how the woman in her would react.

So Eve lay down among the young firs with her knapsack under her head, and watched the sunlight playing in the boughs of the veterans overhead. They made a net of sable and gold that stretched out over her, a net that some god might let fall to tangle the lives of women and of men. She felt the imminence of Nature, felt herself part of the mysterious movement that could be sensed even in this solemn brooding wood.

Her two comrades lay on their fronts, each with a chin thrust out over a book. But Lizzie Straker soon grew restless. She kept clicking her heels together, and picking up dry fir cones and pulling them to pieces. Eve watched her from behind half closed lids.

She felt sorry for Lizzie Straker, because she guessed instinctively that Nature was playing her deep game even with this rebel.

CHAPTER XLII

NATURE SMILES

About eleven o'clock Lizzie Straker's restlessness overflowed into action. She got up, whispered something to Joan Gaunt, and was about to push her way through the young fir trees when the elder woman called her back.

"We must keep together."

"I can't loaf about here any longer. I'm catching cold. And I promised to keep a look-out in the lane."

Joan Gaunt brought out her electric lamp and glanced at her watch.

"It is only just eleven."

"He said he might be here early."

Obviously Lizzie Straker meant to have her way, and her having it meant that Joan and Eve had to break camp and move into the timber track that joined the lane. The night was fairly dark, but Joan Gaunt had taken care to scatter torn scraps of white paper between the clump of firs and the woodland track. A light wind had risen, and the black boughs of the firs swayed vaguely against the sky. The sandy track was banked with furze, broom, and young birch trees, and here and there between the heather were little islands of short sweet turf that had been nibbled by rabbits. Joan Gaunt and Eve spread their coats on one of these patches of turf, while Lizzie Straker went on towards the lane to watch for Galahad.

Eve heard the turret clock at Fernhill strike twelve. The wind in the trees kept up a constant under-chant, so that the subdued humming of Kentucky's car as it crept up the lane was hardly distinguishable from the wind-song overhead. Two beams of light swung into the dark colonnade, thrusting yellow rays in among the firs, and splashing on the gorse and heather. The big car was crawling dead slow, with Lizzie Straker standing on the step and holding on to one of the hood-brackets. Jones, the chauffeur, was driving.

"Here we are."

Lizzie Straker jumped down excitedly.

"It was a good thing I went. He'd have missed the end of the lane. Wouldn't you, old sport?"

"I was looking for you, you know, and not for sign-posts."

"Get along, sir! You're not half serious enough."

"That's good. And me asking for penal servitude and playing the hero."

He climbed out.

"You had better turn her here, Jones, so that we shall have her nose pointing the right way if we have to get off in a hurry. Hallo, Miss Gaunt, you ought to be out in the Balkans doing the Florence Nightingale! What!"

Lizzie Straker was keeping close to him, with that air of ownership that certain women assume towards men who are faithful to no particular woman.

"Is Miss Carfax with you?"

Lizzie laughed.

"Rather! She's here all right. We are going to make her do the lighting up to-night."

"Plenty of inflammable stuff here, Miss Carfax. You can include me if you like."

But the joke did not carry.

The chauffeur had turned the car and put out the lamps. The war material was stored in a big locker under the back seat, and consisted of a couple of cans of petrol, half a sack of shavings, and a bundle of tow. The chauffeur passed them out to Kentucky, who had taken off his heavy coat and thrown it into the car.

"Now then, all ready, comrades?"

"Joan knows the way!"

Eve's mute acceptance of the adventure was not destined to survive the night-march through the fir woods. She was walking beside Joan Gaunt, who led the attacking party, Lizzie Straker shadowing Lawrence Kentucky, Jones, the chauffeur, carrying the petrol cans and bringing up the rear. The grey sandy track wound like a ribbon among the black boles of the firs, whose branches kept up a sibilant whispering as the night wind played through them.

It struck Eve that they were going in the wrong direction.

"We are walking away from Fernhill!"

Joan Gaunt snapped a retort out of the darkness.

"We are not going to Fernhill."

Eve was puzzled. She might have asked in the words of unregenerate man, "Then where the devil are you going?"

In another moment she had guessed at their objective, remembering Canterton's cottage that stood white and new and empty, under the black benisons of the tall firs. Her cottage! She thought of it instantly as something personal and precious, something that was symbolical, something that these *pétroleuses* should never harm.

"What are you going to burn this time?"

"A new house that belongs to the Cantertons of Fernhill."

Eve's sense of humour was able to snatch one instant's laughter from the unexpectedness of the adventure. What interplay life offered. What a jest circumstances were working off on her. She was being challenged to declare herself, subjected to a Solomon's judgment, posed by being asked to destroy something that had been created for the real woman in herself.

She was conscious of a tense feeling at the heart, and a quickening of her breathing. The physical part of her was to be embroiled. She heard Lizzie Straker giggling noiselessly, and the sound angered her, touched some red spot in her brain. She felt her muscles quivering.

"Would it be the cottage?"

Her doubts were soon set at rest, for Joan Gaunt turned aside along a broad path that led through a dense plantation. It was thick midnight here, but as the trees thinned Eve saw a whiteness shining through—the white walls of Canterton's cottage.

For the moment her brain felt fogged. She was trembling on the edge of action, yet still held back and waited.

The whole party hesitated on the edge of the wood, the women and Lawrence Kentucky speaking in whispers.

"Seems all right!"

"Silent as the proverbial tomb!"

"I'll go round and reconnoitre."

He stole off with jerky, striding vehemence, pushed through a young thuja hedge, and disappeared behind the house. In two minutes he was back again, spitting with satisfaction.

"Splendid! All dark and empty oh. Come forrard. We'll persuade one of the front windows."

They pushed through between the soft cypresses and reached the lawn in front of the cottage where the grey stone path went from the timber porch to the hedge of yews. Kentucky and the chauffeur piled their war-plant in the porch, and being rapid young gentlemen, lost no time in attacking one of the front windows.

"We are not going to burn this house!"

Eve hardly knew her own voice when she spoke. It sounded so thin, and quiet, and cold.

Lizzie Straker whisked round like a snappy terrier.

"What did you say?"

"This house is not going to be burnt."

"What rot are you talking?"

"I mean just what I say."

"Don't talk bosh!"

"I tell you, I am in earnest."

Lizzie Straker made a quick movement, and snatched at Eve's wrist. She thrust her face forward with a kind of back-street truculence.

"What d'you mean?"

"What I have said."

"Joan, d'you hear? She's trying to rat. What's the matter with you?"

"Nothing. Only I have ceased to believe in these methods."

"Oh, you have, have you!"

Even in the dim light Eve could see the expanded nostrils and threatening eyes.

"Let my wrist go!"

"Not a bit of it. What's this particular house to you? What have you turned soft for? Out with it. I suppose there's a man somewhere at the back of your mind."

There was a sound in Lizzie Straker's voice that reminded Eve of the ripping of calico.

"I am simply telling you that this cottage is not going to be burnt."

"Joan, d'you hear that? You—you can't stop it!"

Eve twisted free.

"I have only to shout rather strenuously. The Fernhill people are on the alert. Unless you tell Mr. Kentucky, or Galahad as you please to call him——"

Lizzie Straker sprang at her like a wild cat.

"Sneak, rat, moral prostitute!"

Eve had never had to face such a mad thing, a thing that was so tempestuously and hysterically vindictive. Lizzie Straker might have been bred in the slums and taught to bite and kick and scratch like a frenzied animal.

"You beast! You sneak! We shan't burn the place, shan't we? Leave her to me, Joan, I say. I'll teach her to play the traitor!"

Eve was a strong young woman, but she was attacked by a fanatic who was not too furious to forget the Japanese tricks she had learnt at a wrestling school.

"I've got you. I'll pin you down, you beastly sneak!"

She tripped Eve and threw her, and squirming over her, pinioned Eve's right arm in such a way that she had her at her mercy.

"You little brute, you're breaking my arm!"

"I will break it, if you don't lie still."

Joan Gaunt had been watching the tussle, ready to intervene if her comrade were in danger of being worsted. Lawrence Kentucky and the chauffeur had their heads inside the window that they had just succeeded in forcing, when the porch door opened suddenly, and a man rushed out. He swung round, pivoting by one hand round one of the corner posts of the porch, and was on the two men at the window before they could run. To Joan Gaunt, who had turned as the door opened, it was like watching three shadows moving against the white wall of the cottage. The big attacking shadow flung out long arms, and the lesser shadows toppled and melted into the obscurity of mother earth.

"Lizzie, look out!"

Joan Gaunt had plenty of pluck, but she was sent staggering by a hand-off that would have grassed most full-backs in the kingdom. Canterton bent over the two women. One hand gripped Lizzie Straker's back, crumpling up the clothes between the shoulder blades, the other went under her chin.

"Let go!"

"I shan't. I'll break her arm if——"

But the primitive and male part of Canterton had thrown off the little niceties of civilisation. Thumb and fingers came together mercilessly, and with the spasm of her crushed larynx, Lizzie Straker let go her hold.

"You damned cat!"

He lifted her bodily, and pitched her two yards away on to the grass.

"Come on, you chaps. Collar those two beggars over there!"

There were no men to back him, but the ruse answered. Joan Gaunt had clutched Lizzie Straker, dragged her up, dazed and coughing, and was hurrying her off towards the fir woods. Lawrence Kentucky and Jones, the chauffeur, had also taken to their heels, and had reached the thuja hedge behind the house. The party coalesced, broke through, melted away into the darkness.

Eve was on her feet, breathless, and white with a great anger. She knew that just at the moment that Canterton had used his strength, Lizzie Straker had tried to break her arm.

CHAPTER XLIII

EVE COMES TO HERSELF

Canterton went as far as the hedge, but did not follow the fugitives any farther. He stood there for two or three minutes, understanding that a sensitive woman who had been involved in a vulgar scrimmage would not be sorry to be left alone for a moment while she recovered her poise.

Then he heard Eve calling.

"Where are you?"

He turned instantly, and walked back round the cottage to find her standing close to the porch.

"Ah, I thought you might be following them. Let them go."

"I wanted nothing better than to be rid of them. Are you hurt?"

"That dear comrade of mine tried to break my arm. The elbow hurts rather badly."

"Let me feel."

He went close, and she stretched out her arm and let his big hands move gently over it.

"The landmarks seem all right. Can you bend it?"

"Oh, yes! It is only a bit of a wrench."

"Sit down. There is a seat here in the porch. I thought you would like it. There is something pleasant in the idea of sitting at the doorway of one's home."

"And growing old and watching the oak mellowing. They have left their petrol and shavings here."

"I'll dispose of them presently."

His hands touched hers by accident, but her fingers did not avoid his.

"I did not know that the cottage was to be the victim. I only found out just at the last. How did you happen to be here?"

"Sit down, dear, and I will tell you."

The quiet tenderness had come back into his voice. He was the comrade, the lover, the father of Lynette, the self-master, the teller of fairy stories, the maker of droll rhymes. Eve had no fear of him. His nearness gave her a mysterious sense of peace.

"What a comfortable seat!"

"Just free of the south-west wind. You could read and work here."

She sighed wistfully.

"Yes, I shall work here."

Neither of them spoke of surrender, or hinted at the obvious accomplishment of an ideal. Their subtle understanding of each other seemed part of the darkness, something that enveloped them, and did not need to be defined. Eve's hand lay against Canterton's on the oak seat. The lightest of touches was sufficient. She was learning that the light, delicate touches, the most sensitive vibrations, are the things that count in life.

"How did you happen to be here?"

"You had given me a warning, and I came to guard the most precious part of my property."

"And you were listening? You heard?"

"Oh, everything, especially that wild cat's tin-plate voice. What of the great movement?"

She gave a subtle little laugh.

"I had just found out how impossible they are. I had been realising it slowly. Directly I got back into the country my old self seemed to return."

"And you did not harmonise with the other—ladies?"

"No. They did not seem to have any senses, whereas I felt part of the green stuff of the earth, and not a bit of grit under Nature's big toe."

"That's good. You can laugh again."

"Yes, and more kindly, even at those two enthusiasts, one of whom tried to break my arm."

"I'm afraid I handled her rather roughly; but people who appeal to violence must be answered with violence."

"Lizzie Straker always came in for the rough treatment. She couldn't talk to a crowd without using the poison that was under her tongue. She always took to throwing vitriol."

"Yes, the business has got into the hands of the wrong people."

They sat in silence for a while, and it was the silence of two people who lean over a gate, shoulder to shoulder, and look down upon some fine stretch of country rolling to the horizon. It was the togetherness that mattered. Each presence seemed to absorb the other, and to obtain from it an exquisite tranquillity.

Eve withdrew her hand, and Canterton saw her touch her hair.

"Oh!"

"What is it? The arm?"

"No; but my hat and hair."

He laughed.

"How much more serious. And what admirable distress. I think I can help. Take this."

He brought out a pocket electric lamp.

"I always carry this at night. It is most useful in a garden. There is an old Venetian mirror hanging at the top of the stairs. While you are at work I will clear away all this stuff."

"What will you do with it?"

"Pitch the shavings into the coal cellar. The petrol we can use—quite ironically—in an hour's time."

"What do you mean?"

"I have been thinking. Go in and look into that Venetian mirror!"

She touched his arm with the tips of her fingers.

"Dear, I trust you. I do, utterly. I couldn't help it, even if you were not to be trusted."

"Is that Nature?"

"I think it must be!"

"Put all fear out of your heart."

She rose and drew apart, yet with a suggestion of lingering and of the gliding away of a dear presence that would quickly return. The light of the pocket lamp flashed a yellow circle on the oak door. She pushed it open and entered the cottage, and climbed the stairs with a new and delightful sense of possession. She was conscious no longer of problems, disharmonies, the suppression of all that was vital in her. A spacious life had opened, and she entered it as one enters a June garden.

Canterton had cleared away Lawrence Kentucky's war material, and Eve found him sitting in the porch when she returned.

"Very tired?"

"No."

"May I talk a little longer?"

"Why not!"

She sat down beside him.

"Our comradeship starts from now. May I assume that?"

"I dare to assume it, because one learns not to ask too much."

"Ah, that's it. Life, at its best, is a very delicate perfume. The gross satisfactions don't count in the long run. I want you to do big things. I want us to do them together. And Lynette shall keep us two healthy children."

She thought a moment, staring into the night.

"And when Lynette grows up?"

"I think she will love you the better. And we shall never tarnish her love. Are you content?"

He bent towards her, and took one of her hands.

"Dearest of women! think, consider, before you pledge yourself. Can you bear to surrender so much for the working life I can give you?"

She answered him under her breath.

"Yes. I want a man for a comrade—a man who doesn't want to be bribed. Oh, my dear, let me speak out. Sex—sex disgusted me in that London life. I revolted from it. It made me hate men. Yet it is not sex that is wrong, only our use of it. I think it is the child that counts in those matters with a woman."

His hand held hers firmly.

"Eve, will you grow hungry—ever?"

"For what?"

"Children!"

She bent her head.

"I will tell you. No. I think I can spend that part of the woman in me on Lynette and on you."

"On me."

"A woman's love—I mean the real love—has some of the mother spirit in it. Don't you know that?"

He lifted her hand and kissed it.

"And may I grumble to you sometimes, little mother, and come to you to be comforted when I am oppressed by fools? You can trust me. I shall never make you ashamed. And now, for practical things. You must be in London to-morrow morning. I have worked it all out."

"Remember, I am a very independent young woman."

"Oh, I know! Let me spend myself, sometimes. Have you any luggage at the 'Black Boar'?"

"No, only my knapsack, which I left in the car."

"Fancy a woman travelling with nothing more than a knapsack! Oh, Eve, my child!"

"I didn't like it. I'll own up. All my luggage is stored with some warehouse people in town. I have the receipts here in my purse."

"That's luck—that's excellent! We must walk round to the Basingford road to miss any of my scouts. You will wait there, say by the Camber cross-roads, while I get my car out."

He felt for his watch.

"Have you that lamp?"

"It is here on the seat."

"Just two o'clock. I shall tell my man I'm off in chase of a party who made off in a car. I shall bring you one of my greatcoats and pick you up at the cross-roads. We shall be in London by five. We will get some breakfast somehow, and then knock up the warehouse people and pile your luggage into the back. I shall drive you to a quiet hotel I know, and I shall leave you there. What could be simpler? An independent young woman staying at a quiet hotel, rather bored with London and inclined to resume a discarded career."

She laughed softly—happily.

"It is simple! Then I shall have to write you a formal letter."

"Just that."

CHAPTER XLIV

THE NIGHT DRIVE

Eve, waiting at the Camber cross-roads under the shadow of a yew that grew in the hedgerow, saw an arm of light sweep slowly down the open road before her, the glare of Canterton's headlights as his car rounded the wooded corner about a quarter of a mile from the Fernhill gates.

She remained in the shadow till she was sure that it was Canterton, and that he was alone.

Pulling up, he saw her coming as a shadow out of the shadows, a slim figure that detached itself from the trunk of the yew.

"All right! Here's a coat. Get into the back, and curl yourself up. It's as well that no Peeping Tom in Basingford should discover that I have a passenger."

Eve put on the coat, climbed in, and snuggled down into the deeply cushioned seat so that she was hidden by the coachwork. The car had not stopped for more than thirty seconds, Canterton holding the clutch out with the first speed engaged. They were on the move again, and, with deft gear-changing, gliding away with hardly a sound.

Eve lay and looked at the sky, and at the dim tops of the trees sliding by, trailing their branches across the stars. She could see the outline of Canterton's head and shoulders in front of her, but never once did she see his profile, for the car was travelling fast and he kept his eyes on the winding road that was lit brilliantly by the electric headlights. They swept through Basingford like a charge of horse. Eve saw the spire of the church walk by, a line of dark roofs undulating beneath it. The car turned sharply into the London road, and the quickening purr of the engine told of an open throttle.

They drove ten miles before Canterton slowed up and drew to the side of the road.

"You can join me now!"

He leant over and opened the door, and she took the seat beside him.

"Warm enough?"

"Yes."

He looked at her throat.

"Button up that flap across the collar. That's it. And here's a rug. I have had to keep myself glued to the wheel for the last twenty minutes. There is a lot of common land about here, and you never know when a cow or a pony may drop from the skies."

They were off again, with trees, hedgerows, gates, and cottages rushing into the glare of the headlights, and vanishing behind them.

"Would you like to sleep?"

"No; I feel utterly awake!"

"Not distressfully so?"

"No, not in that way. I have no regrets. And I think I am very happy."

He let the car race to her full speed along a straight stretch of road.

"I could drive over the Himalayas to-night—do anything. You have a way of making me feel most exultantly competent."

"Have I? How good. Shall I always be so stimulating?"

He looked down at her momentarily.

"Yes, because we shall not be crushing life to get all its perfume."

"Restraint keeps things vivid."

"That's it—that's what people don't realise about marriage."

She thrilled to the swift motion of the car, and to the knowledge that the imperturbable audacity of his driving was a man's tribute to her presence.

"I suppose most people would say that we are utterly wrong."

"It would be utterly wrong, for most people."

"But not for us."

"Not for us. We are just doing the sane and logical thing, because it is possible for us to live above the conventions. Ordinary people have to live on make-believe, and pretend they like it, and to shout 'shame,' when the really clean people insist on living like free and rational beings."

"You are not afraid of the old women!"

"Good God! aren't some of us capable of getting above the sexual fog—above all that dull and pious nastiness? That's why I like a man like Shaw, who lets off moral dynamite under the world's immoral morality. All the crusty, nonsensical notions come tumbling about mediocrity's ears. There are times when it is a man's duty to shock his neighbours!"

Eve sat in silence for some minutes, watching the pale road rushing towards them out of the darkness. Canterton was not driving the car so strenuously, but was letting her slide along lazily at fifteen miles an hour. Very soon the dawn would be coming up, and the white points of the stars would melt into invisibility.

"We don't want to be too early."

"No."

There was a pause, and then Eve uttered the thoughts of the last half hour.

"One thing troubles me."

"What is that?"

"Your wife."

He slackened speed still further, so that he need not watch the road so carefully.

"I feel that I am taking———"

"What is hers?"

"Yes."

His voice was steady and confident.

"That need not trouble you. Neither the physical nor the spiritual part of me owes anything to my wife. We are just two strangers who happen to be tied together by a convention. I am speaking neither ironically nor with cynicism. They are just simple facts. I don't know why we married. I often marvel at what I must have been then. Now I am nothing to her, nor she to me."

"Are you sure?"

"Quite sure. Her interests are all outside my life, mine outside hers. We happen to reside in the same house, and meet at table. We do not quarrel, because we are too indifferent to quarrel. You are taking nothing that she would miss."

"And yet!"

"Is it the secrecy?"

"In a way."

"Well, I am going to tell her. I had decided on that."

She turned to him in astonishment.

"Tell her!"

"Just the simple fact that I have an affection for you, and that we are going to be fellow-workers. I shall tell her that there is nothing for her to fear, that we shall behave like sensible beings, that it is all clean, and wholesome, and rational."

"But, my dear!"

She was overwhelmed for the moment by his audacious sincerity.

"But will she believe?"

"She will believe me. Gertrude knows that I have never shirked telling her the truth."

"And will she consent?"

"I don't doubt it."

"But surely, to a woman——"

"Eve, this sort of problem has always been so smirched and distorted that most people seem unable to see its outlines cleanly. I am going to make her see it cleanly. It may sound strange to you, but I believe she is one of the few women capable of taking a logical and restrained view of it. The thing is not to hurt a woman's self love publicly. Often she will condone other sorts of relationship if you save her that. In our case there is going to be no sexual, backstairs business. You are too sacred to me. You are part of the mystery of life, of the beauty and strangeness and wonder of things. I love the look in your eyes, the way your lips move, the way you speak to me, every little thing that is you. Do you think I want to take my flowers and crush them with rough physical hands? Should I love them so well, understand them so well? It is all clean, and good, and wholesome."

She lay back, thinking.

"I know that it looks to me reasonable and good."

"Of course it is. Not in every case, mind you. I'm not boasting. I only happen to know myself. I am a particular sort of man who has discovered that such a life is *the* life, and that I am capable of living it. I would not recommend it for the million. It is possible, because you are you."

She said, half in a whisper:

"You must tell her before I come!"

"I will!"

"And I shall not come unless she understands, and sympathises, which seems incredible."

Canterton stopped the car and turned in his seat, with one hand resting on the steering-wheel.

"If, by any chance, she persists in seeing ugly things, thinking ugly thoughts, then I shall break the social ropes. I don't want to. But I shall do it, if society, in her person, refuses to see things cleanly."

His voice and presence dominated her. She knew in her heart of hearts that he was in grim earnest, that nothing would shake him, that he would go through to the end. And the woman in her leapt to him with a new exultation, and with a tenderness that rose to match his strength.

"Dearest, I—I——"

He caught her hands.

"There, there, I know! It shan't be like that. I swear it. I want no wounds, and ugliness, and clamour."

"And Lynette?"

"Yes, there is Lynette. Don't doubt me. I am going to do the rational and best thing. I shall succeed."

CHAPTER XLV

GERTRUDE CANTERTON CAUSES AN ANTI-CLIMAX

"Run along, old lady. Daddy's going to write three hundred and seventy-nine letters."

"Oh, poor daddy! And are you going to write to Miss Eve?"

"Yes."

"Give her my love, and tell her God's been very nice. I heard Him promise inside me."

"That's very sensible of God."

Lynette vanished, and Canterton looked across the breakfast-table at his wife, who was submerged beneath the usual flood of letters. She had not been listening—had not heard what Lynette had said. A local anti-suffrage campaign was the passion of the moment.

It struck Canterton suddenly, perhaps for the first time in his life, that his wife was a happy woman, thoroughly contented with her discontent. All this fussy altruism, this tumult of affairs, gave her the opportunity of full self-expression. Even her grievances were harmonious, chiming in with her passion for restless activity. Her egoism was utterly lacking in self-criticism. If a kettle can be imagined as enjoying itself when it is boiling over, Gertrude Canterton's happiness can be understood.

"Gertrude, I want to have a talk with you."

"What, James?"

"I want to have a talk with you."

She dropped a type-written letter on to her plate, and looked at him with her pale eyes.

"What is it?"

"Something I want you to know. Shall we wait and turn into the library?"

"I'm rushed to death this morning. I have to be at Mrs. Brocklebank's at ten, and——"

"All right. I'll talk while you finish your breakfast. It won't take long."

She prepared to listen to him with the patient air of an over-worked official whose inward eye remains fixed upon insistent accumulations of business. It did not strike her that there was anything unusual about his manner, or that his voice was the voice of a man who touched the deeper notes of life.

"Eve Carfax is coming back as my secretary and art expert. She has given up her work in town."

"I am really very glad, James."

"Thanks. She got entangled in the militant campaign, but the extravagances disgusted her, and she broke away."

"Sensible young woman. She might help me down here, especially as she has some intimate knowledge of the methods of these fanatics."

"It is possible. But that is not quite all that I want to tell you. In the first place, I built the new cottage with the idea that she would come back."

His wife's face showed vague surprise.

"Did you? Don't you think it was a little unnecessary? After all——"

"We are coming to the point. I have a very great affection for Eve Carfax. She and I see things together as two humans very rarely see them. We were made for the same work. She understands the colour of life as I understand it."

Gertrude Canterton wrinkled up her forehead as though she were puzzled.

"That is very nice for you, James. It ought to be a help."

"I want you to understand the whole matter thoroughly. I am telling you the truth, because it seems to me the sane and honest thing to do. You and I are not exactly comrades, are we? We just happen to be married. We have our own interests, our own friends. As a man, I have wanted someone who sympathised and understood. I am not making this a personal question, for I know you do not get much sympathy from me. But I have found a comrade. That is all."

His wife sat back in her chair, staring.

"Do you mean to say that you are in love with this girl?"

"Exactly! I am in love with her."

"James, how ridiculous!"

Perhaps laughter was the last thing that he had expected, but laugh she did with a thin merriment that had no acid edge to it. It was the laughter of an egoist who had failed utterly to grasp the significance of what he had said. She was too sexless to be jealous, too great an egoist to imagine that she was being slighted. It appealed to her as a comedy, as something quite outside herself.

"How absurd! Why, you are over forty."

"Just so. That makes it more practical. I wanted you to realise how things stand, and to tell you that I am capable of a higher sort of affection than most people indulge in. You have nothing to fear."

She wriggled her shoulders.

"I don't feel alarmed, James, in the least. I know you would never do common, vulgar things. You always were eccentric. I suppose this is like discovering a new rose. It is really funny. I only ask you not to make a fool of yourself in public."

He looked at her steadily and with a kind of compassion.

"My dear Gertrude, that is the very point I want to impress upon you. I am grimly determined that no one shall be made a fool of, least of all you. Treat this as absolutely between ourselves."

She wriggled and poked her chin at him.

"Oh, you big, eccentric creature! Falling in love! Somehow, it is so quaint, that it doesn't make me jealous. I suppose I have so many real and absorbing interests that I am rather above such things. But I do hope you won't make yourself ridiculous."

"I can promise you that. We are to be good friends and fellow-workers. Only I wanted you to understand."

"Of course I understand. I'm such a busy woman, James, and my life is so full, that I really haven't time to be sentimental. I have heard that most middle-aged men get fond of school-girls in a fatherly kind of way."

He crushed his serviette and threw it on the table.

"In a way, you are one of the most sensible women, Gertrude, I have ever met."

"Am I?"

"Only you don't realise it. It's more temperament than virtue."

"I'm a woman of the world, James. And there are so many important things to do that I haven't time to worry myself about harmless little romances. I don't think I mind in the least."

He pushed back his chair and rose.

"I did not think you would. Only we are all egoists, more or less. One never quite knows how the 'self' in a person will jump."

He crossed the room and paused at the window, looking out. His thoughts were that this wife of his was a most amazing fool, without sufficient sexual sense to appreciate human nature. It was not serene wisdom that had made her take the matter so calmly, but sheer, egregious fatuity, the milk-and-water-mindedness that is incapable of great virtues or great sins.

"Have you thought of Lynette?"

"What has Lynette to do with it, James?"

"Oh, nothing!"

He gave her up. She was hopeless. And yet his contempt made him feel sorry.

Her hand had gone out to her papers, and was stirring them to crepitations that seemed to express the restless satisfactions of her life.

"Don't you over-work yourself, Gertrude?"

"I don't think so. But sometimes I do feel——"

"You ought to have a secretary, some capable young woman who could sit and write letters for eight hours a day. I can easily allow you another three hundred a year."

She flushed. He had touched the one vital part in her.

"Oh, James, I could do so much more. And there is so much to be done. My postage alone is quite an item!"

"Of course! Then it's settled. I'm glad I thought of it."

"James, it's most generous of you. I feel quite excited. There are all sorts of things I want to take up."

He went out into the garden, realising that he had made her perfectly happy.

CHAPTER XLVI

LYNETTE APPROVES

Eve came down to breakfast in the panelled dining-room at "Rock Cottage," and stood at one of the open windows, watching an Aberdeen puppy demolishing an old shoe in the middle of the lawn. The grass had been mown the day before, and the two big borders on the near side of the yew hedge were full of colour, chiefly the blues of delphiniums and the rose and white of giant stocks. Nearer still were two rose beds planted with the choicest hybrid teas, and mauve and yellow violas. The rock garden beyond the yew hedge had lost some of its May gorgeousness, but the soft tints of its rocks and the greys and greens of the foliage were very restful to the eyes. Above it hung the blue curtain of a rare June day.

"Billy, you bad boy, come here!"

The puppy growled vigorously, and worried the shoe up and down the lawn.

"Oh, you baby! You have got to grow up into a responsible dog, and look after my house."

She laughed, just because she was happy, and, kneeling on the window-seat, began a flirtation with Master Billy, who was showing off like any small boy.

"Now, I'm sure I'm more interesting than that shoe."

A bright eye twinkled at her.

"I suppose it is very wrong of me to let you gnaw slippers. I am sure Mrs. Baxter is harder hearted. But you are so young, little Billy, and too soon you will be old."

The door opened, and a large woman with a broad and comfortable face sailed in with a tray.

"Good morning, miss!"

"Good morning, Mrs. Baxter! Whose shoe has Billy got?"

"I'm thinking it's one of mine, miss."

"The wretch!"

"I gave it him, miss. It's only an old one."

Eve's eyes glimmered.

"Oh, Mrs. Baxter, how very immoral of you! I thought Billy's education would be safe with you."

"There, miss, he's only a puppy."

"But think of our responsibilities!"

"I wouldn't give tuppence for a boy or a puppy as had no mischief in him, miss!"

"But think of the whackings afterwards."

"I don't think it does no harm. I've no sympathy with the mollycoddles. I do hold with a boy getting a good tanning regular. If he deserves it, it's all right. If he's too goody to deserve it, he ought to get it for not deserving of it."

Eve laughed, and Mrs. Baxter put the tea-pot and a dish of sardines on toast on the table. She was a local product, and an excellent one at that, and being a widow, had been glad of a home.

"I've made you the China tea, miss. And the telephone man, he wants to know when he can come and fix the hinstrument."

"Any time this morning."

"Thank you, miss."

The panelled room was full of warm, yellow light, and Eve sat down at the gate-legged table with a sense of organic and spiritual well being. There were roses on the table, and her sensitive mouth smiled at them expressively. In one corner stood her easel, an old mahogany bureau held her painting kit, palettes, brushes, tubes, boards, canvases. It was delightful to think that she could put on her sun-hat, wander out into the great gardens, and express herself in all the colours that she loved. Lynette's glowing head would come dancing to her in the sunlight. The Wilderness was still a fairy world, where mortals dreamed dreams.

There were letters beside her plate. One was from Canterton, who had gone north to plan a rich manufacturer's new garden. She had not seen him since that drive to London, for he had been away when she had arrived at "Rock Cottage" to settle the furniture and begin her new life with Mrs. Baxter and the puppy.

She read Canterton's letter first.

"CARISSIMA,—I shall be back to-morrow, early, as I stayed in town for a night. Perhaps I shall find you at work. It would please me to discover you in the rosery. I am going to place

Guinevere among the saints, and each year I shall keep St. Guinevere's feast day.

"I hope everything pleases you at the cottage. I purposely left the garden in an unprejudiced state. It may amuse you to carry out your own ideas.—*A rivederci.*"

She smiled. Yes, she would go and set up her easel in the rosery, and be ready to enter with him upon their spiritual marriage.

Under a furniture-dealer's catalogue lay a pamphlet in a wrapper with the address typed. Eve slit the wrapper and found that she held in her hand an anti-suffrage pamphlet, written by Gertrude Canterton.

She was a little surprised, not having heard as yet a full account of that most quaint and original of interviews. But she read the pamphlet while she ate her toast, and there was a glimmer of light in her eyes that told of amusement.

"A woman's sphere is the home!" "A woman who is busy with her children is busy according to Nature! No sensible person can have any sympathy with those restless and impertinent gadabouts who thrust themselves into activities for which they are not suited. Sex forbids certain things to women. The eternal feminine is a force to be cherished!" "Woman is the sympathiser, the comforter. She is the other beam of the balance. She should strive to be opposite to man, not like him. A sweet influence in the home, something that is dear and sacred!"

Eve asked herself how Gertrude Canterton could write like this. It was so extraordinarily lacking in self-knowledge, and suggested the old tale of the preacher put up to preach, the preacher who omitted to do the things he advocated, because he was so busy telling other people what they should do. How was it that Gertrude Canterton never saw her real self? How did she contrive to live with theories, and to forget Lynette?

Yet in reading the pamphlet, Eve carried Gertrude Canterton's contentions to their logical conclusion.

"Motherhood, and all that it means, is the natural business of woman.

"Therefore motherhood should be cherished, as it has never yet been cherished.

"Therefore, every healthy woman should be permitted to have a child."

And here Eve folded up the pamphlet abruptly, and pushed it away across the table.

After breakfast she went into the garden, played with Billy for five minutes, and then wandered to and fro and up and down the stone paths of the rock garden. There were scores of rare plants, all labelled, but the labels were turned so that the names were hidden. Eve had been less than a week in the cottage, but from the very first evening she had put herself to school, to learn the names of all these rock plants. After three days' work she had been able to reverse the labels, and to go round tagging long names to various diminutive clumps of foliage and flowers, and only now and again had she to stretch out a hand and look at a label.

All that was feminine and expressive in her opened to the sun that morning. She went in about nine and changed her frock, putting on a simple white dress with a low-cut collar that showed her throat. Looking in her mirror with the tender carefulness of a woman who is beloved, it pleased her to think that she needed one fleck of colour, a red rosebud over the heart. She touched her dark hair with her fingers, and smiled mysteriously into her own eyes.

She knew that she was ambitious, that her pride in her comrade challenged the pride in herself. His homage should not be fooled. It was a splendid spur, this love of his, and the glow at her heart warmed all that was creative and compassionate in her. This very cottage betrayed how his thoughts had worked for her. A big cupboard recessed behind the oak panelling held several hundred books, the books she needed in her work, and the books that he knew would please her. There was a little studio built out at the back of the cottage, but he had left it bare, for her own self to do with it what she pleased. It was this restraint, this remembering of her individuality that delighted her. He had given her so much, but not everything, because he had realised that it is a rare pleasure to a working woman to spend her money in accumulating the things that she desires.

On her way through the plantations she met Lavender, and she and Lavender were good friends. The enthusiast in him approved of Eve. She had eyes to see, and she did not talk the woolly stuff that he associated with most women. Her glimpses of beauty were not adjectival, but sharp and clear-cut, proof positive that she saw the things that she pretended to see.

He offered to carry her easel, and she accepted the offer.

"Have you seen those Japanese irises in the water garden, Miss Carfax?"

"Yes, I am going to paint them this afternoon. Whose idea was it massing that golden alyssum and blue lithospermum on the rocks behind them? It's a touch of genius."

Lavender's nose curved when he smiled.

"That was one of my flashes. It looks good, doesn't it?"

"One of the things that make you catch your breath."

He swung along with his hawk's profile in the air.

"I fancy we're going to do some big things in the future. If I were a rich man and wanted the finest garden in England, I'd give Mr. Canterton a free hand. And, excuse me saying it, miss, but I'm glad you've joined us."

He gave her a friendly glare from a dark and apprizing eye.

"I'm keen, keen as blazes, and I wouldn't work with people who didn't care! Mr. Canterton showed me those pictures of yours. I should like to have them to look at in the winter, when everything's lying brown and dead. If you want to know anything, Miss Carfax, at any time, I'm at your service."

His manners were of the quaintest, but she understood him, that he was above jealousy, and that he looked on her as a fellow enthusiast.

"I shall bother you, Mr. Lavender, pretty often, I expect. I want to know everything that can be known."

"That's the cry! But isn't it a rum thing, Miss Carfax, how nine people out of ten knock along as though there were nothing fit to make them jump out of their skins with curiosity. Why I was always like a terrier after a rat. 'What's this?' 'What's that?' That's my leitmotiv. But most people don't ask Nature any questions. No wonder she despises them, the dullards, just as though they hadn't an eye to see that she's a good-looking woman!"

He erected her easel for her in the rosery, tilted his Panama hat, and marched off.

Eve sought out Guinevere and sat herself down before the prospective saint, only to find that she was in no mood for painting. Her glance flitted from rose to rose, and the music of their names ran like a poem through her head. Moreover, the June air was full of their perfume, a heavy, somnolent perfume that lures one into dreaming.

Suddenly she found that he was standing in one of the black arches cut in the yew hedge. She knew that the blood went to her face, and she remembered telling herself that she would have to overcome these too obvious reactions.

He came and stood beside her, looking down at her with steady and eloquent eyes.

"You have found out Guinevere?"

"Yes. We are old friends now."

"I am not going to market this rose. She is to be held sacred to Fernhill. How are you getting on at the cottage?"

Her eyes glimmered to his.

"Thank you for everything."

"And Billy pleases you?"

"He has a sense of humour."

"And Mrs. Baxter?"

"Has what they call a motherly way with her."

His eyes wandered round the rosery with a grave, musing look.

"I want to talk."

"Talk to me here. I want to know how———"

"How she accepted it?"

"Yes."

"She laughed. Thought it ridiculous. And I had been ready for a possible tragedy!"

"What an amusing world it is."

He moved a little restlessly.

"I want to get away from that. Let's walk through the plantations. I can't keep still to-day. I want to see you everywhere, to realise you everywhere."

They wandered off together, walking a little apart. All about them rose the young trees, cedars, cypresses, junipers, yews, pines, glimmering in the June sunlight and sending out faint, balsamic perfumes. Men were hoeing the alleys between the maples and limes, their hoes flashing when a beam of sunlight struck through the foliage of the young trees.

Canterton stopped and spoke to the men. Also he spoke to Eve as to a partner and a fellow-expert who understood.

"Do you think we make enough use of maples in England?"

"Isn't there a doubt about some of them colouring well over here?"

"They give us a very fair show. The spring tints are almost as good as the autumn ones in some cases. I want to see what you think of a new philadelphus I have over here."

They walked on, and when their eyes met again hers smiled into his.

"Thank you for that seriousness."

"It was genuine enough. I am going to expect a very great deal from you."

"I'm glad. I'll rise to it. It will make me very happy. Do you know I have learnt nearly all the names of the plants in my rock garden!"

"Have you, already!"

"Yes. And I am going to study every whim and trick and habit. I am going to be thorough!"

They came to a grove of black American spruces that were getting beyond the marketable age, having grown to a height of fifteen or twenty feet. The narrow path was in the shade, a little secret path that cut through the black glooms like a river through a mountainous land.

Canterton was walking behind her.

"Hold out your hand!"

Without turning her head she held her hand out palm upwards, and felt something small dropped into it.

"Wear it—under your dress."

It was a little gold ring, the token of their spiritual marriage.

They came out into the sunshine, and Eve's eyes were mistily bright. She had not spoken, but her lips were quivering sensitively. She had slipped the ring on to her finger.

"A king's ransom for your thoughts!"

She turned to him with an indescribable smile.

"I am Lynette's fairy mother. Oh, how good!"

"For her?"

"And for me."

"I have a formal invitation to deliver from Lynette. She hailed me out of the window. We are to have tea in the Wilderness, and Billy is asked."

"The Wilderness! That is where we forget to be clever."

They came round to the heath garden where it overhung the green spires of the larches.

"I am going on with my book. Your name will be added to it."

"May I sign the plates?"

"Oh, we'll have you on the title-page, 'Paintings by Eve Carfax.' And I shall ask you to go pilgrimaging again, as you went to Latimer."

She drew in her breath sharply.

"Ah, Latimer! I shall be dreaming dreams. But I want some of them to be real."

"Tell me them!"

"I want to help other women; help them over the rough places."

"You can do it. I mean you to have a name and a career."

"I don't want to live only for self."

"First make 'self' a strong castle, then think of helping the distressed. We are only just at the beginning of things, you and I. We'll have a rest home for tired workers. I know of a fine site in my pine woods. And you will become a woman of affairs."

"I shall never rush about and make speeches!"

"No, I don't think you will do that."

They turned towards the white gate, and heard the voice of Lynette—Lynette who had been giving chase.

"Daddy! Miss Eve!"

She came on them, running; glowing hair tossing in the sunlight, red mouth a little breathless.

"Oh, Miss Eve, the fairies have asked you to tea!"

"I know. I have heard!"

She caught Lynette, and kneeling, drew her into her arms with a great spasm of tenderness.

"I am going to be a fairy, one of your fairies, for ever and ever."

"Be the Queen Fairy!"

"Yes, yes."

"For ever and ever. I think God is very kind. I did ask Him so hard."

"Dear!"

Lynette had never been kissed as she was kissed at that moment.

Milton Keynes UK
Ingram Content Group UK Ltd.
UKHW050653260624
444769UK00004B/249

9 789362 098023